SINGLE
MOTHER

BOOKS BY SAMANTHA HAYES

The Reunion
Tell Me a Secret
The Liar's Wife
Date Night
The Happy Couple

SINGLE MOTHER

SAMANTHA HAYES

Bookouture

Published by Bookouture in 2021

An imprint of Storyfire Ltd.
Carmelite House
50 Victoria Embankment
London EC4Y 0DZ

www.bookouture.com

ISBN: 978-1-83888-839-8
eBook ISBN: 978-1-83888-838-1

For Ben, Polly and Lucy…
And for Grawar…
With love for ever xxx

PROLOGUE

Drizzle mists the air as she walks briskly through the deserted streets, the bag heavy in her hand. Her hood is up, her head down, watching her feet tread the wet pavement. It's early – barely past dawn and too early even for commuters. The station is only just opening as she arrives. She thinks she'll probably be the only person buying a ticket today and not actually going anywhere.

She'd been awake all night, and the decision was made. No looking back. A night filled with screams and blood-soaked sheets. Her man nowhere to be found – not that he'd be any use anyway. As ever, she'd coped with it all herself. Life was filled with one problem after another. Things to be dealt with. To be cleaned up and taken care of. Miserable, but it's how things were now, what she was used to – the weight bearing down, wearing her down, crushing her to death. She couldn't see a way out. Maybe she didn't want to.

She buys her ticket – one-way, of course – and heads towards the platform. Time to wait, time to think, grateful there's no one else around to hear should there be any noise.

The air smells of diesel as she sits on the wooden bench, waiting. But at least she's out of the rain. The bag is on her lap, both her hands resting gently on top. Some kind of comfort. She looks at her watch, noticing several other passengers gathering on the platform. She's far enough away from them not to be noticed.

Things used to be good once, she thinks with an inner smile. Fun and carefree, her big dreams unshattered, every day a breeze. She remembers the parties in London, the alcohol and cigarettes, the boys hungry for her, the wild outfits she wore – tiny suede skirts and long white boots, low-cut chiffon dresses with ruffles. She adored those boots. Wore them until they greyed with age.

Several blue and yellow trains pull up to various platforms and, eventually, one grinds up to platform six. She heads down to the furthest end of the train, opens a door on the last carriage and gets on, walking down the aisle past all the empty seats, trailing her hand along their velvety backs.

At the end of the carriage, she places the bag she's carrying in the overhead luggage rack, above seats forty-seven and forty-eight. She looks left and right. No one there. She wonders who, if anyone, will be sitting in these seats.

Not her, she thinks, making sure the bag is secure before she turns and heads for the nearest exit door. Once she's off the train, she walks briskly back to her car, the rain having stopped and the autumn morning sun now a slash of red hanging over the town.

She will drive home and get on with her day, get on with her life. And if she has to do it again, she will.

CHAPTER ONE

Mel stares at the recycling box. It's overflowing. She'd asked Kate several times last night to take it down to the bins at the back of their building but, as ever these days, her daughter had remained in her room. With everything that's happened recently, she hadn't wanted to get heavy with her.

'Kate, breakfast's ready. Hurry, or you'll be late for school,' Mel calls out, waiting for some kind of acknowledgment. No reply. 'It's eggs,' she adds, not needing to shout. Their flat is only small. The single bedroom belongs to Kate, while Mel sleeps on the sofa bed, hiding away the duvet and pillows every morning before Kate emerges. She keeps her clothes in a cupboard on the small landing. Space is tight, but they get by.

Egg, actually, Mel thinks, spooning the small amount of scramble onto a piece of toast. She hears Kate's bedroom door open and, a moment later, she comes into the kitchen wearing her school shirt, no tie, and her pyjama bottoms underneath. Her hair is unbrushed, the strawberry-blonde strands a frizzy halo around her pale, slim face.

'Where are your school trousers, love?' Mel says, pouring half a glass of orange juice for her. It's all that's left.

'In my room,' she replies without looking at Mel. Kate slides onto the chair, picking up her knife and fork. Mel notices the blush blooming on her cheeks, knows her daughter too well. 'Thanks for this, Mum.'

Mel sits down beside her, coffee mug between her palms. 'Kate—'

'Don't, Mum,' she replies, shovelling in her breakfast, still not looking up. 'Really, it's fine.'

Mel reaches out a hand to Kate's forearm. She's thin, Mel thinks. 'You know I'll listen and—'

'Mum!' Kate says – not a shout, exactly, more a choked hiccup. She snatches her arm away.

'OK, OK, love.' Mel gets up, scraping back the chair. She grabs the empty egg box and juice carton, cramming them into the recycling box, squashing everything down. Then, trying to appear busy, hoping that by backing off Kate will open up about what's been bothering her these last few days, she sorts through the pile of junk mail that has accumulated on the kitchen counter.

'Where does all this stuff come from, eh?' she says, trying to sound bright. She doesn't want the day to get off to a bad start. A *worse* start, she thinks, wondering how she's going to tell Tony, the landlord, that she can't quite make the rent this month. 'Pizza flyers, takeaway menus, and look…' She holds up a leaflet, waving it about. 'This one is offering to jet-wash our driveway.' She shakes her head. 'Didn't they notice we live in a first-floor flat?'

One by one, Mel stuffs the papers into the recycling box: local free newspapers, letters to 'The Occupier' – most likely trying to sell her insurance policies for appliances she doesn't own, or pre-pay her own funeral. She hesitates over a couple of envelopes, tentatively slicing open the flap with her finger. When she sees they're bills – red reminders – she tosses them into a separate pile on the counter. They'll have to wait.

Then a smart cream envelope catches her eye – better-quality than the usual junk mail. Plus it has her actual name and address printed on the front, and a local return address on the back. Glancing at the clock on the wall, she quickly tears it open, half pulling out the contents.

'Someone's certainly gone to town to get my attention with this,' she says, rolling her eyes at the wodge of wasted paper. When she sees it's nothing more than what appears to be a legal scam, she stuffs that into the recycling box too.

'How do they get away with it?' she says, shaking her head. She drains her coffee mug. 'No doubt they want cash upfront before I "claim what's mine".'

Kate stares up at her, dark circles under her eyes and the whites tinged pink. 'Claim what's yours?' she says, offering a little smile.

She's trying to appear normal, Mel thinks. For my sake. If Kate got her own way, she'd stay off school today. Stay off school *for ever*. Mel has to admit, she's tempted to allow her a day's respite – but then what about her work? She can't afford to take a day off, nor risk upsetting Dragon Boss. At twelve, Kate is too young to be left home alone. It kills her to know those girls at school are giving her daughter such a hard time. Kills her, too, that Kate won't allow her to speak to the head teacher to get the bullying dealt with.

'It'll make it *ten* times worse, Mum. I'm begging you, *please* don't say anything,' Kate had pleaded the first time she'd opened up about what had been going on, admitting why her belongings had gone missing, why one side of her hair had been hacked off, her blazer torn, why there were bruises on her shins. 'They'll probably move on to someone else soon, when they get bored of me.'

Since that day, Mel had been fighting every cell in her body not to go steaming into the head's office at Portman High. It was getting harder each day to keep the promise she'd made to Kate.

'Claim what's yours, as in?' Kate continues, scraping her plate. She knows as well as Mel that food is not to be wasted. Several times in the last month, Mel has gone without dinner so Kate can eat.

'Didn't look to find out,' Mel says, shrugging and bagging up the recycling into two bulging refuse sacks. She dumps them by the door ready to take out when they leave. 'Right, love, go and finish getting dressed and I'll drop you at school on the way to work.'

Kate clears away her plate and heads off to her bedroom. A few minutes later, she reappears, her hair neatly brushed and secured in a long ponytail down her back, her tie straight, her blazer buttoned up – admittedly now on the snug side, stretching across her shoulders. The sleeves are riding up past her wrists.

Mel stares at her daughter as she stands there, her school bag slung over her shoulder.

'Oh, *Kate…*' she says, wanting to hug her, scoop her up, do everything she can to make this better for her.

'Don't say a word, Mum, please.'

'But…'

Kate holds up a hand to silence her. 'It would have been worse if I *hadn't* done it, OK? There's a chance one of them might actually think it's… you know, *cool*.' She gives a little laugh then, makes a coy face at the thought of anything associated with her being construed as cool.

Mel closes her eyes for a beat before dropping her car keys and bag on the table. She gets down on her knees in front of her daughter. 'Wait,' she says, folding up an inch or two of the freshly hacked fabric of Kate's school trousers. 'Try them like this,' she adds, standing back to admire her work, while also heartbroken that her daughter has felt the need to do this. There was no way Mel could have afforded new school trousers this month. Kate dashes off to her bedroom to check the mirror, returning with a grateful smile.

'Thanks, Mum. They look much better,' she says quietly. 'Proper pedal-pusher chic. Who knows, I might start a new trend.'

Half an hour later, Mel pulls up at work, her heart sinking as she spots Josette's brand-new white BMW parked in a disabled bay outside the care home, even though her boss wasn't due in until lunchtime. It about sums her up, Mel thinks, squeezing her beat-up Fiesta into a spot under the trees where the pigeons always mess on the bonnet.

'Hi, Angie,' Mel says cheerily as she heads into the staff room. Her colleague, another carer, is just coming out, already in her uniform and ready for the handover. Angie smiles, returning the greeting.

Mel knows that, despite her worries, her anxiety and fears for what the future holds for her and Kate, it's a sum total of nothing if she doesn't keep her job. Josette seems to have eyes everywhere, and zero tolerance for her staff's personal lives. The only time Mel ever took a sick day, her boss docked her pay. While it was most likely outside of HR law, Mel wasn't about to argue and risk getting sacked. She needed every hour she could work while Kate was at school, and every penny that brought in.

'*Michael…*' Mel says, reminding herself to reply to him as she hangs up her coat in her locker. In the morning's rush, she'd forgotten to text him back. Just like she'd also forgotten to take down the recycling bags.

Oh yes, please do call round later! I need some Micky cheer. And I can work 10–5 in the shop on Sat again if you need xx

She hits send and puts her phone back in her bag, wondering what she'd do without him – her best friend, confidant and all-round go-to guy. She changes into the clean uniform hanging in the top of her locker, turning a blind eye to all the junk that's accumulated in the bottom over the months. She checks herself in the full-length mirror, tucking back a strand of dark hair that's escaped her ponytail, before heading off to get the handover reports.

*

It's as Mel's heading out of the staff room later that afternoon when her shift is over, having changed back into her own clothes, pleased as punch with her lucky find and keen to pick Kate up from school to give her the bag she's clutching, when she literally bumps into Josette, who's striding down the corridor, a large mug of coffee in her hand. The scalding liquid sloshes down Mel's front, making her jump back and let out a squeal as her hands sweep frantically at the mess, pulling her T-shirt away from her smarting skin.

'My office, if you would, please, Melanie,' Josette barks. '*Now,*' the taller woman adds, ignoring the look of pain on Mel's face.

CHAPTER TWO

Standing in Josette's office – all antique furniture, plush carpet and a huge potted palm in front of the tall window – Mel tries to ignore her throbbing skin, wanting nothing more than to douse it in cold water. But she knows it's more than her job is worth not to listen to Josette. She's got *that* look on her face.

'It's about Bob,' Josette says, not having even uttered an apology. Rather, in the corridor, she'd thrust her half-empty mug into a passing care assistant's hand and ordered her to bring her a refill immediately. 'Do you always have to wear such ridiculous tops?' she adds, scowling as she sits behind her desk.

'Bob?' Mel asks, suddenly panic-stricken, glancing down. KEEP CALM is printed across the front of her T-shirt, which Mel is now struggling to do. 'Is he OK?' She'd only been with him yesterday afternoon and, while he seemed fine, she can't deny that his respiratory issues have worsened over the last few months. She prays he hasn't been taken into hospital overnight.

'As fine as you can be at ninety-six with COPD,' Josette replies, sipping on the coffee that's just been handed to her. 'But there's been a complaint.'

'A complaint?' Mel says, wondering if she should also sit down. 'About what?' She sits down anyway, dumping her handbag and the carrier bag on the floor beside her. Her mind races, wondering what Bob – dear, kind, gentle, affable, funny, good-natured Bob – could ever have to complain about. He's her favourite resident. Yes, he's not been in the best of health lately, but he's all there mentally. Sharp as a button. And he loves life at The Cedars, getting involved with all the home has to offer. Not to mention his daily constitutional walk around the grounds, albeit with two sticks now and an accompanying carer.

'Yes, Melanie. A complaint. From his son.'

Josette sits sideways behind her mahogany desk, her long legs crossed, her tight skirt rising above her knees, tapping a pen on the edge of the desk with one hand. She flicks her glossy dark hair back over her shoulder with the other hand, still looking as fresh as she did at the start of the day. Mel only gave herself a cursory glance in the staff room mirror as she changed out of her uniform, preferring not to look too long at the tired face staring back, the dishevelled hair and smudged eyeliner.

'I… I don't understand. Is everything OK?'

'No, Melanie. No, it's not,' Josette says, suddenly standing and striding over to the huge window facing out over the lawns and the ancient cedar tree. She turns abruptly – a tall, slim silhouette against the sunlight streaming in. 'Bob's son says a large amount of cash has gone missing from his father's room.'

'*What?*' Mel says, twisting round. She grips the arms of the leather chair. 'That's terrible. But… but residents don't keep money in their rooms. Do they?' Mel knows that cash is discouraged, that any extras residents may wish to purchase are handled by an in-house card system and added to the bill. The Cedars has its own little shop, selling books, magazines, a few luxuries. Plus there's a hair salon on site.

Josette pulls a face, tightening the already tight skin on her forehead and cheekbones.

'Apparently, Bob's son had left him three hundred pounds in cash for emergencies. It was in a jacket pocket in his wardrobe. Not within our guidelines, of course, but we can't prevent such instances. But what we can prevent is theft. When Bob's son visited on Sunday, he went to check the cash and it was gone. He categorically states it was there two days before, on the Friday.'

'That's terrible,' Mel says. 'Maybe Bob hid it elsewhere and forgot.' She doubts that's true. Bob's mind is sound, even if his body isn't quite as robust these days.

'His son turned the room upside down. No cash.' Josette strides back over to her desk, towering above Mel in her patent black heels. She perches on the corner of the desk, arms folded across her white blouse. 'Do you know anything about this, Melanie?'

'Me?' she replies, instantly feeling her cheeks redden. She can't help it. '*No*, no, of course not.' She swallows. 'I'd never—'

'Money's tight as a single mother, am I correct?' Josette says, staring down at her. Her dark eyes bore out from beneath her straight-cut fringe.

'Well, yes, but I don't see—'

'So if you were, say, helping Bob to get dressed and the cash fell out of his pocket or, indeed, you discovered it in there, it's also correct to assume it would be very tempting for you to slip it into your own pocket. Yes?'

'No!' Mel says as firmly as she can without making matters worse. She absolutely won't be accused of something she didn't do. 'Of *course* I didn't take Bob's cash. I'm not a thief, Josette. Surely you know that? I'm a good employee, and—'

'Were you caring for Bob on Saturday, Melanie?'

'He was on my list, yes,' Mel replies, willing the burn in her cheeks to subside. She pushes back her shoulders and holds her head up. She won't be bullied into admitting to something she didn't do. She'd be fired for sure, and there's no way she can afford to lose her job. 'I was working alongside Clara. She'll vouch for me.'

'Were you ever alone with Bob in his room?'

'I really don't see why—'

'Just answer, please, then we can wrap this up so I can report to the family. Naturally, they're very distressed.'

Mel sits there, her mind melting into a mix of not understanding any of this to actually wondering if she may have somehow, inadvertently or accidentally, gathered up Bob's cash by mistake. And she's also conscious that she's going to be late picking Kate up from after-school club.

'I… I was alone with Bob for some of the time, I guess, yes,' she replies quietly, thinking back, her eyes narrowing as she tries to remember. 'But that's not unusual. Clara may have been called to help with someone else, or maybe went to fetch something. You know how busy it can get.'

Josette remains perfectly still, her arms clamped across her chest, her long legs stretched out in front of her as she sits on the edge of the desk.

'I took him for a walk. The weather was nice and he likes the fresh air.'

'Which meant putting a jacket on, I'm assuming? It's only April, after all.'

'Yes, yes, I helped him into a jacket. And he wore his tweed cap. But honestly, I don't recall seeing any cash. And if I had, I'd have mentioned to Bob about keeping it safe and reported it to the duty manager.'

'What colour was the coat?'

It's as if Josette isn't hearing her – hearing only what she wants to hear to dig herself and her care home out of an awkward situation. If she gets fired, Mel knows Josette will have her replaced within a matter of hours through the agency. She's expendable.

'Green?' Mel says.

'Are you asking me or telling me?'

Mel takes a breath, glancing away briefly, forcing herself to keep calm. 'It was green. A dark green corduroy coat with a brown collar. I remember commenting on how smart it was.'

Josette says nothing for a beat, just stares at her, as if she's waiting for more to come out. But Mel doesn't have anything else to say. She just wants to go and fetch Kate, imagining her standing alone outside the school gates. She can't help the brief glance at her watch.

'Do you have somewhere better to be, Melanie?'

'No, sorry. It's just my daughter… I have to fetch her and—'

'What's in there?' Josette says, lightly kicking the carrier bag on the floor with her court shoe.

'Just something I picked up for Kate. A pair of trainers,' Mel replies, looking down at the supermarket bag.

The tightening of Josette's jaw, the narrowing of her eyes, doesn't go unnoticed by Mel. And neither does the thumping in her own heart. She doesn't deserve this grilling.

Josette sits down behind her desk again, resting her elbows on the polished wood, her fingers steepled together in front of her face. 'You can go now,' she says, turning to answer her phone, ignoring Mel completely as she gathers her belongings, says goodbye and leaves.

CHAPTER THREE

'What a nightmare,' Mel mutters under her breath as she slams the car door, throwing her bags onto the passenger seat. How, after nearly three years of loyal service, could Josette possibly think that she would steal money from a resident? From *anyone*?

Quickly, she lifts up her T-shirt to examine her scalded skin. Sure enough, there's a red patch about the size of her palm just to the left of her navel. She blows on it, desperate to get home for some ice.

Mel shakes with anger as she drives away, trying to calm herself before picking up Kate. As soon as she'd left Josette's office, she'd messaged her daughter to say she was on her way. But Kate hadn't replied yet.

'Come on, come *on*,' she says impatiently at the lights. Every set seems to be changing to red as she approaches the junction. Finally, after taking a couple of shortcuts, she pulls up outside Portman High, scanning the street where Kate usually waits.

There's no sign of her.

It's only her second term – such a huge contrast to the primary school she loved – and she's not made any friends yet. In fact, she knows the opposite to be true. 'Kate, *Kate*, where are you?' she whispers, calling Kate's phone. It rings out, going to voicemail.

'Dammit,' she says, her heart rate rising. She dials again, just as she spots someone – a thin and stooped female figure – coming round the corner from the street just beyond the school. She squints, praying the figure resolves into Kate as she gets closer. At the same time, an old, rusty red van pulls slowly out of the turning, cruising alongside the person, and only when the figure flicks a quick wave at the van does it speed off. The light flares off the windscreen as it passes so Mel doesn't see the driver.

She gets out of the car, leaning against the open door, relief flooding through her. 'Oh, *Kate*, thank God. I was worried about you. You normally wait for me along here.'

'Hi, Mum,' she calls out more cheerily than expected, raising her arm. 'Sorry!' She picks up her pace into a run, her bag bouncing against her side as she approaches. She opens the car door, breathless. 'I… I just went to see if you'd parked round the corner,' she says, pre-empting Mel's next question.

'You know I always meet you here.' She pauses, watching as Kate does up her seat belt and dumps her school bag at her feet. 'Who was that?' Mel asks, glancing down the road in the direction the van had sped off.

'Who was what?' Kate replies, glancing at her phone, her shoulders drawn up to her ears. 'Sorry I missed your call, Mum. My… my phone was still on silent from classes.'

'Who was the person in the van you were waving at just now?'

'Van? I didn't see any van,' Kate says. 'What's for tea? I'm starving.'

After having to park the car several streets away – not unusual in their part of town – Mel unlocks the outside door of their flat, noticing that more of the faded blue paint has peeled off and flaked onto the pavement. She glances through the window of the fish and chip bar to the right, above which their tiny place is located. Tony is in there with a couple of his young staff, shaking the fryer baskets as they prepare for the evening shift. He looks up, giving Mel a wave before wiping his hands down his apron. She waves back, smiling, dreading having to ask him for a rent extension.

'Can we, Mum, *please*?' Kate says, noticing Tony has spotted them. Mel knows Kate will be salivating from the smell of fish and chips just as much as she is. It's an easy option and would make Kate's evening perfect, especially with what she's about to give her.

'We'll see. Let's get in first, OK?' Which really means 'let me see how much I can wring out of my overdraft'. Mel wants nothing more than for Kate to chill out in front of the TV, watching her favourite show with a hot, steaming parcel of fish and chips on her knees.

She lets Kate inside the narrow entrance hall first, locking the door behind them after they're inside. She stops still as her eyes grow accustomed to the darkness, with Kate running up the stairs two at a time.

'Odd,' she whispers to herself, shaking her head and picking up a couple of letters from the mat. She swears she just got a whiff of cigarette smoke – not fresh, but rather the stale smell of it on someone's clothes left lingering in the air. Maybe it followed us in from outside, someone in the street with a cigarette, she thinks, shrugging as she heads up, the carrier bag still in her hand and as yet unnoticed by Kate. She flicks the light on after she lets them both inside the inner flat door, putting Kate's shoes on the rack after she kicks them off, heading straight for her bedroom.

'Oh, great,' Mel says, rolling her eyes when she sees the two black bin bags of recycling. She could ask Kate to take them down, she supposes, bribe her with the promise of a fish supper, but she'll need to look in her purse first. The electricity will need topping up in a few days and she has to get more petrol before the end of the week. Until payday, every penny counts. Mel kicks one of the bin bags in frustration, wishing she could afford more things for Kate.

If it bloody well wasn't for… she thinks angrily, before stopping herself, determined not to fixate on him. I'm better than that, she tells herself, sighing as she sees that the bin bag now has a split down one side.

'Fancy a cuppa, Kate?' she calls out, taking her purse from her bag. 'Fifteen pounds twenty-seven,' she whispers, knowing that's easily enough for a portion of cod and chips – twice over if she were to treat herself too. But equally, she knows that there's some food in the cupboard that she was planning on using tonight – a tin of tuna, some canned tomatoes and some pasta. She should probably use that up.

Before she can call out to Kate again, Mel's phone pings an alert.

I'll be with you in five xx

Mel smiles, feeling a rush of warmth spread through her. Thank God for Michael. Her oldest friend and the person who gave her the strength to finally take a stand against Billy, the courage to leave. And Kate adores him, sees him as an uncle. A *father*, even. Her Saturdays wouldn't be the same if she wasn't able to hang out at For the Record, Michael's music shop, listening to her favourite bands, helping out with stock and dealing with customers. Mel knows he's been through hard times himself – right back from when they first met in the children's home – and together, somehow, they've always got through.

She goes to Kate's bedroom door, stopping outside. She hears her daughter talking in a low voice. Odd, she thinks. She rarely talks on the phone, preferring to message. She shrugs, hoping that she's finally made a friend at school. 'I'm just taking the recycling out, love. Then I've got a surprise for you.'

She waits, listens. Nothing. So she goes back to the kitchen and grabs the bin bags, struggling to hold them together as she heads down the stairs.

CHAPTER FOUR

'Micky!' Mel squeals in a silly voice as the stairwell is suddenly flooded with light. Michael is standing in the doorway, silhouetted, as though her guardian angel has arrived. 'You're certainly a sight for sore eyes,' she adds, struggling down the stairs with the bulging refuse sacks, treading carefully. It wouldn't be the first time she'd had an accident on them.

'I come bearing gifts,' he says, smiling up at her, his long, wiry arms holding up two plastic bags. Mel sees the flash of his insanely white teeth, the sparkle in his azure eyes. He cocks his head to one side and gives her a wink.

'Let me just get this lot outside to the bins,' she says, coming down. 'Oh… bloody hell…!' she calls out as her foot misses the step. She stumbles, grabbing the banister rail while, at the same time, dropping one of the bin bags – the one with the split in it. It tumbles down the remaining stairs, its contents spilling out along the way until the whole thing breaks open as it lands at Michael's feet. Bottles and cartons, cardboard packets and junk mail are strewn across the entrance hall floor.

'Christ, that was close,' Mel says, her heart racing from the near fall. Her legs like jelly, she carefully comes down the rest of the stairs and drops to her knees to gather up the mess. But Michael has beaten her to it.

'Stop,' he says, holding up his palms to her. 'You take these back up and leave this to me.' He puts a hand on her arm, somehow sensing she's not had the best day. He gives her the two bags he's brought.

'Is this what I think it is?' she says, peering into one of them, breathing in deeply and closing her eyes for a moment. 'It *is*, you bloody beautiful mind-reader,' she adds with a laugh. Then she takes a look in the other bag. 'Is it actually my birthday and I forgot?' she says, standing up as she spots the beers and wine.

Michael gives her another wink as he gathers up the mess. 'Go on, hop to it then. I'll be up before you know it.'

Mel leans down and gives him a peck on his cheek, catching the scent of his sweet perfume, smiling inwardly as she remembers him once telling her that he'd not worn a man's cologne in his entire life. And thankfully she can't smell the cigarette smoke any more. 'I'll get some glasses,' she says, knowing that Michael has keys to let himself back in. He insisted on a set just in case she ever needed help. If the *worst* ever happened.

She runs back up the stairs, wondering what she did to deserve a friend like Michael. 'Kate, get yourself out here, my love, and see what I've got. Uncle Micky has come a-calling.'

Mel hears Kate's bedroom door open. The mention of her favourite person in the whole world always gets her moving.

'What is it, Mum?' she says, appearing in the kitchen doorway, her eyes slightly bloodshot.

Mel hesitates, studying her daughter. 'Look what Micky brought us,' she says, pulling one of the wrapped-up fish and chip parcels from the bag, feeling the warmth through the paper.

'*Yay*,' Kate says with a brief punch to the air and the glimmer of a smile – as enthusiastic as she gets about anything these days. Then she turns on her heels and goes back to her room.

Sighing, Mel gets out a couple of glasses and the bottle opener, peeling the foil off the wine. She looks at the label, knowing Michael always chooses his wines carefully, even if it is just to accompany fish and chips. She cracks a smile as she recalls what he once said: *I choose my wines like I choose my men*, he'd told her. *Full-bodied and fruity. And always* very *expensive*.

Mel looks up. 'Just in time,' she says to Michael, pouring a glass of the white. 'And thanks for taking the rubbish out.'

'Most welcome,' he says, slipping off his denim jacket. He drapes it over the back of one of two chairs at Mel's small kitchen table. 'I found this among the rubbish. I think you must have thrown it out by mistake. It looks important.' He hands Mel an empty envelope along with some papers folded in half.

'Oh that... no,' she says, glancing up as she pours a second glass. 'I went through all my mail earlier and chucked out the junk. I'm just left with the bills now,' she says, ignoring the tight feeling in her chest as she eyes the stack of red reminders on the worktop. She's determined to enjoy this evening.

'But it's from a solicitor, Mel. I think you need to see it.'

Mel knows where Michael's concern is coming from – three years ago, when she'd appeared in court as a witness for the prosecution. He'd supported her all the way, dealing with much of the barrister's correspondence on her behalf. After everything that had gone on with Billy, she'd found it too overwhelming to sort out alone.

Mel swaps Michael a glass for the letter and gives it a quick glance, remembering it from earlier. 'No, it's just some silly scam. Trying to get me to sign up to their wills service, by the looks of it. Making out I've got an inheritance or something, to get my attention. It's the legal equivalent of "You're a guaranteed winner". Anyway, cheers!' she says, holding up her glass.

Michael chinks it with his, then holds his glass up to the light before swirling the liquid around several times. He takes a deep breath over the rim before taking a sip. 'Perfect accompaniment to cod and chips,' he says as Mel knocks back a much-needed large mouthful. Then his face, shadowed by the day's stubble, breaks into a full-blown grin. 'Katie-my-best-*matey*!' he sings out, standing up as Kate comes back into the kitchen. 'Get over here now!'

She trots over to him, suppressing her own grin, allowing her hair to shield her face from view. 'Hi, Uncle Micky. How are you?'

'All the better for seeing you, that's for sure, my darling,' he says, hugging her close. 'I brought the ultimate gourmet food. Get stuck in. There's Coke for you, too, my dearest little urchin.'

Kate laughs as he unleashes her from his arms.

'This one is yours,' he says, pulling out a marked packet. 'I got you a jumbo sausage as well as fish and mushy peas, plus extra chips with lashings of vinegar, just the way you like it.'

Mel watches on, the chill in her heart from Josette's grilling dissipating as she sees how happy Kate looks with Michael fussing over her. Apart from herself, he's the one solid rock in Kate's life. And even then, Mel sometimes has doubts, knowing she's made mistakes. *Terrible* mistakes. All she can do now is ensure that she never, *ever* repeats them. It's her and Kate against the world. They don't need anyone else.

'Can I have it in front of the telly, Mum?'

'Yes, yes, of course,' Mel replies as Kate turns to go. 'But wait, I've got something for you too.' She ducks out into the hall and returns with the carrier bag from work. 'Here,' she says, handing it to Kate, who's impatiently picking at her chips. 'A present for you. For being so amazing.'

'What?' Kate says, bemused, placing her food on the kitchen table before peeking into the bag. She gives a little gasp, one hand reaching in and pulling out a trainer. Her mouth opens wide. 'Adidas?' she says breathily, looking at Mel again before pulling out the other trainer and allowing the bag to drop to the floor. 'No *way*! Are these for me? They're exactly my size. They look brand new. But Mum…?' There's a flash of concern on her face, the glimmer of a frown.

'They most certainly are for you, my love,' Mel replies. 'And they're not quite brand new, but they hardly look as though they've been worn, right?'

'Oh, Mum,' Kate says, running up to give her a hug. 'I love them, *thank* you! You wait when I turn up at school in these.'

Mel smiles, knowing how much they mean to her daughter. 'Go and eat your food before it goes cold, then you can try them on.'

Beaming, Kate tucks the trainers under her arm and grabs her parcel of fish and chips. She high-fives her mum and Michael as she heads for the living room, a huge grin on her face.

'Best day *ever*,' she sings out.

*

'Someone's happy,' Michael says when he and Mel are sitting alone at the kitchen table, their chip papers spread out in front of them. He takes a sip of his Chablis, his eyes narrowing into appreciative slits.

'A welcome change,' Mel admits. 'And hopefully a self-esteem boost. I mean, I know it's not the way to solve—'

'Mel,' Michael says, reaching out and touching her wrist. 'It's OK. You don't need to justify how you make your daughter happy.'

Mel pauses, half-rolling her eyes. 'I know, but… but I just feel so *guilty* all the time. About all the dreadful stuff with her dad, all the moves we've had to make, the refuges, the uncertainty. I know for a fact she still adores him and hates that she doesn't get to see him. But worse is that she doesn't know *why* she can't see him. When it happened, she was far too young for the truth, although she'd witnessed enough. I guess I didn't think it through. Now she's twelve, she deserves some kind of honesty. But then she'll know I've been lying to her and—'

'Second warning issued, Melanie Douglas. Eat, drink and don't think about it. You made a little girl very happy just now. Oh, and while you're at it,' he adds, reaching for the solicitor's letter, 'for the love of God, read this. It looks important.'

CHAPTER FIVE

Mel stares at Michael, frowning, as she tries to process what she's just read, what it all means. She reaches out and drains her wine glass, knocking back the remains in one go. Nothing. It means nothing, she tells herself.

'Steady on,' Michael says through a mouthful of chips. 'That stuff's not water, you know.' He tops up her glass anyway, seeing the thoughtful look in her eyes.

'It's just well-written rubbish. A scam,' she says, grabbing a forkful of chips and stuffing them in her mouth. 'And cruel to prey on the vulnerable.' She drinks more wine. 'But I admit, they had me for a moment.' In my dreams, she thinks, carrying on with her meal.

'Call me nosy, but I had a skim read downstairs. It's about an inheritance, Mel. I really don't think it's a scam. Listen.' He swipes up the letter and begins reading. '"Dear Miss Douglas, reference the Moreton Inn estate".' He glances up. 'Does that mean anything to you?'

'Nope,' Mel replies indignantly, rolling her eyes. But then she takes a moment to think. 'No, no, it doesn't. But that's the whole point of the scam, surely? Something random and tantalising to make me believe I've got some distant relative leaving me their fortune. They picked the wrong person for that.' She eats some of her fish. 'This is delicious, by the way. Tony's on form tonight.'

Michael carries on reading. "'As agents for the executors of the will for the above referenced matter, I am writing to inform you that you are a beneficiary of the estate. Probate has been granted and associated affairs resolved, but since this is a complicated matter, with several attached conditions, I invite you to contact me by telephone or email at your earliest convenience, so we may discuss how to proceed with distribution.'" He glances up, waiting for a response from Mel. But all she does is shrug and shake her head. "'Please find details about our firm in the enclosed documents, plus an information form which you will need to fill out with your personal details, sign and return to our office"—'

'Yeah, right,' Mel says, rolling her eyes and laughing. 'Don't tell me, they want me to fill out my bank details, National Insurance number, mother's maiden name…?' She trails off then, making a scoffing sound when she realises what she's said.

Mother's maiden name… as if she's ever known it.

'And how much do they want from me upfront so I can claim my glorious fortune? Fifty quid? A hundred quid? Or are they chancing their luck with a juicy grand? I can't even buy my daughter new trainers, let alone give these piss artists anything.'

Michael sits back in his chair, the look on his face telling Mel that he knows she's mistrusting to the core – understandable, given everything that's happened in her life.

'Where did those trainers come from, by the way?' Michael asks. 'Charity shop?'

Mel thinks back to earlier in her boss's office, how Josette had been so nosy about the carrier bag. Her cheeks begin to colour with anger just at the thought of it.

'Close. There was a charity donations bag at work. Stuff left over from the spring fair to raise funds for the residents' recreation room. As if The Cedars bloody needs financial help,' she adds bitterly.

'Anyway, there was a second-hand clothes sale, a cake stall, a tombola. I was working, so didn't have a chance to look. Stuff that didn't sell was bagged up to take to a charity shop, except no one's got round to taking it yet. I spotted the Adidas logo through the top of a bag.'

'Surprised they didn't sell,' Michael commented.

'Me too, but given the average age of our residents is about eighty-three, and their families are generally in their fifties and sixties, it's hardly surprising.' Mel laughs. 'Anyway, I had to grab them for Kate. They were her size. And of course I donated the fiver on the price tag to the fund.'

'Lucky find,' Michael says, his eyes twinkling. 'Now, back to this.' He opens up the enclosed papers, scanning each of them briefly. 'Green, Lupton and Hedge… Family solicitors specialising in wills and probate.'

'They sound like a landscape gardening company,' Mel says as Michael pulls his phone from his pocket.

'Let's see what Google says about them.' He taps in a search and pulls up their website. 'They seem legit, look.' He gives Mel a glance at the screen. 'Their website certainly appears real and has a list of staff. About ten in all. This letter is from Robert Hedge. Look, here he is.'

'Anyone can pull up a generic image of a bloke in his late fifties in a suit to stick on a fake website, though,' Mel says, barely looking at it when Michael shows her again.

'What? Wait. So you think the website is fake as well as the letter?'

'Actually, no. I don't think the website is a scam. In fact, I'm pretty certain I've even heard of the firm. They're in Solihull, right? They're not far from my work.'

'Yes, you're right,' Michael says, clicking on the 'contact us' link. 'They're on High Street. So you think an established firm would risk their reputation by running a scam?'

'No-*oo* again,' Mel says in that way of hers – ending with a laugh to show she appreciates Michael's concern, but also that she's not stupid. 'I have a friend – *had* a friend,' Mel corrects, remembering how she had to cut off so many people after she finally escaped, fearing she'd be found. 'And she had this exact same thing happen. A letter from a legal firm, telling her she'd inherited half a million quid from a long-lost relative – only they'd had the foresight to use her actual surname in the scam, so it really did seem like a relative. And all she had to do to release the funds was fill out a form with all her personal info, including bank details, and send it back with an administration fee of fifty quid.'

'And?' Michael says.

'Hook line and sinker,' Mel says, shrugging. 'It wasn't the fifty quid they were after as such – though I imagine they're nice little bonuses if they hit several thousand gullible victims. No, they cleaned out my friend's bank account overnight. They had all the information they needed to steal her identity. Even though she only had a couple of hundred, it nearly finished her off. Her marriage was on the rocks anyway, but this took it over the edge. She just felt so... stupid. So *vulnerable*.'

'And you're not...' Michael says, eyeing her over the rim of his glass, knowing he's on thin ice. 'Vulnerable?'

'Oh do fuck off,' she says, play-kicking him under the table as the wine winds through her veins, helping her relax.

'Anyway,' Michael continues, 'this letter doesn't say anything about a relative. Just Moreton Inn, whatever and wherever that is.'

'It's still going in the bin,' Mel replies, leaning forward to grab the letter.

Michael swipes it out of the way.

'Not so fast. I really think you should follow up. There are no weird-looking phone numbers here. Only the office landline, which is the same as the one on the website.'

'Yeah, well, I don't really want to think about it right now. Like I said, I don't have money to part with for "admin fees" or whatever they're asking for.'

'They're not, Mel. And look,' he says, reaching out and taking her hand, 'as your best mate, I hate seeing you so... so defensive all the time. I don't just mean this letter. But whenever anyone tries to help, you put up your guard and shut them out. Even with me, these days.'

'And why the hell not?' she replies with a snort. 'I've finally got myself into a place where I can just about keep my head above water, financially and emotionally. Money's tight, but Kate and I are doing OK. I may not have got everything right in life, but I'm protective of how things are now. You know that better than anyone.'

Michael sighs. 'Protective of how things are until...' He purposefully trails off, doesn't need to say what goes through Mel's mind every single day. Until Billy gets out of prison...

'Hey, what do you guys think?' comes a chirpy voice, snapping Mel out of her thoughts. She and Michael turn to the kitchen doorway to see a beaming Kate standing there, new trainers on her feet.

'Cool or *what*?' she says, giving a twirl, holding her bunched-up chip papers.

'They look amazing, love,' Mel says, her heart warming.

Kate comes over, wrapping her arms around Mel. 'I think I might even sleep in them,' she says, laughing and kissing her mum's cheek.

As Mel hugs her daughter back, she glances at Michael over Kate's shoulder, unable to help the little sigh as they each exchange a knowing look.

CHAPTER SIX

'Ah, Melanie,' Josette says, her glossy dark bob and harsh fringe in sharp contrast against her pale skin. 'Finally,' she says, glancing at her watch.

'Morning, Josette,' Mel replies breathlessly. 'Sorry I'm a bit late. The traffic was awful. I'll work through my lunch hour, don't worry.'

Josette pauses, looking Mel up and down. 'Oh, I'm not worried.' She forces a smile. 'Come with me, please.'

'Er… sure,' Mel replies, hesitating before following Josette as she strides off down the corridor.

Finally, she stops outside the door to the staff room. Josette stares at it, then she stares at Mel, waiting for her to open it. Despite her hands being full with her packed lunch, clean uniform and her handbag, Mel pushes the door open and lets Josette pass through before following her in.

It's a bland room with pale green decor, divided up into a locker area and a relaxation zone with a few clinical armchairs for taking breaks. There's a kettle, a fridge for lunches, some magazines, a couple of plants that no one remembers to water. It's nothing like as luxurious as the residents' areas, but it does the job.

'Over here, please,' Josette says, striding towards the lockers. That's when Mel sees Stacy Fearn, the HR manager, and Amit Basu, general manager of The Cedars. Their faces are deadpan and serious, not returning Mel's smile, even though they're usually friendly. As a single parent too, Amit has always been sympathetic to childcare difficulties, allowing Mel to bring Kate in to work occasionally when Josette's away. Kate has even helped out with the residents a few times.

'She has a way about her, that girl of yours,' Amit had said just the other day as he spotted Mel watching Kate fondly, *proudly*. 'There's a holiday job waiting for her when she's older,' he'd continued.

Kate wasn't aware that Mel was in the doorway of Bob's room as she knelt down, helping him get his shoes on before their walk. Bob was recounting tales of his time in the Navy, how he'd been on submarines and aircraft carriers all over the world.

'I'll take over from here now, Kate,' Mel had finally said, not wanting to interrupt the tender moment. Josette was due back at the care home soon and she didn't want to get a dressing-down for allowing Kate to help. There was bound to be some health and safety or insurance reason why Kate shouldn't even be on the premises, let alone helping out. But Kate had gone off happily enough to wait in the staff room, giving Bob a glance and a smile over her shoulder as she left.

'Stacy, Amit, hi…' Mel says nervously now. The tension in the atmosphere is palpable.

'Morning, Mel,' Amit manages, but Stacy just offers a flicker of a smile, shifting awkwardly from one foot to the other.

'Which is your locker, Melanie?' Josette says, though each are clearly labelled. Mel's especially stands out, as Kate made a sign for hers, decorated with big, bright letters.

'This one,' Mel says, forcing herself not to add *obviously*. She glances between the three faces, only Josette's showing no emotion.

'Would you open it for us, please?' Josette says.

'What… why?' Mel asks, unable to hide her indignance.

'Just open it, Melanie.'

Mel shrugs, rummaging in her bag for the key to the padlock.

'There,' she says, opening the metal door. 'Can I ask what this is about?' She looks at Josette, who ignores her, and then to Amit and finally Stacy, whose expressions give nothing away.

'Remove your belongings,' Josette says, her tone flat.

'But… OK, sure,' Mel says, shrugging again. 'Excuse the junk in here. It's due a good clean-out, but I always have to dash off for Kate, and—'

'All of it,' Josette says, impatience creeping in.

Mel's eyes widen and she pauses, shaking her head briefly before pulling out a spare pair of work shoes – ugly, rubber-soled things she hates wearing, but which save her feet by the end of a shift. She drops them onto the floor. Then she takes out a carrier bag of old sports clothes from when she'd decided to get fit in her lunch break a couple of months ago. The daily runs lasted less than a week, and she'd forgotten to take her kit home to wash.

Josette takes the bag from her as she's about to drop it on the floor. She peers inside and makes a repulsed face, letting it fall.

'Oh, *this* is where it got to!' Mel says, rolling her eyes. 'I was looking for it everywh—' She stops when Josette snatches the denim jacket from her, checking inside the two top pockets before also dropping it on the floor.

Mel folds her arms across her chest, frowning. 'Josette, I don't mind showing you the contents of my locker…' She hesitates, eyeing the crisp packets and old tissues, wishing she'd had a bit of warning. 'But can you tell me what this is about? Are you checking everyone's lockers?'

'No, just yours,' Josette says, her eyes fixed on the inside of the locker. 'The rest, please.'

Mel sighs. 'Okaaay…' she says, perplexed as she pulls out a folded uniform tunic, a paperback she'd half read, a mandala colouring book that Kate was amusing herself with last time she was here and, finally, a small nylon zip-up bag that, if Mel was perfectly honest, could contain absolutely anything.

'What's in that?' Josette demands.

'I'm guessing my black sparkly top,' Mel replies, knowing it's the only smart thing she owns, even though it's a bit small now. 'I was going to go to Barb's drinks party but couldn't make it in the end. Shows how much I go out. I'd forgotten this was even—'

'Open the bag,' Josette says, the tiniest glint in her eyes as she flashes a look at Stacy.

'Sure,' Mel says, unzipping the bag and holding it open.

It takes a moment to work out what she sees – something unfamiliar and unexpected sitting on top of the sparkly top she correctly guessed was in there.

'What the…?' she hears herself saying, though it doesn't really sound like her voice as her eyes finally focus.

'Where did you get this from?' Josette says, reaching in and pulling out the bundle of £20 notes.

'I… I don't understand. I didn't, I mean, that's not mine. Not even *vaguely* mine. That's a whole load of money I simply don't have, and…' Mel drops the bag and covers her mouth with her hand, suddenly realising where this is heading. She looks up at Josette, who is flicking through the cash.

'Three hundred pounds,' she finally states. 'The exact amount that went missing from Bob's room.'

'What…? Wait. You don't seriously think that *I*… Tell me you don't think that I took it, Josette? It's simply untrue!' Mel forces her voice to hold steady, but she can feel the frustrated quiver in her throat, feel her body begin to tense from anger.

'Stacy?' Josette says to her colleague. 'Do you have the list?'

Stacy nods and shows her a piece of paper on her clipboard. She leans in to Josette and, between them, they compare the bundle of cash to the list of numbers on the paper.

'Same serial numbers,' Stacy confirms, looking up at Josette.

'How do you explain this?' Josette asks, her face slightly relaxed as if the thrill of the hunt has warmed her, made her almost human.

'I have no idea how that money came to be in my locker. If it's Bob's money, then I can assure you it wasn't me who took it. Either someone's set me up, or—'

'Who would set you up, Melanie? You're well liked here, aren't you?' Josette says. '*Were* well liked, perhaps I should say.'

'I have absolutely no idea, but I swear, hand on heart, that I did not steal Bob's money. He's my favourite resident. I would never do such a thing.'

'Then I'm afraid I'm going to have to suspend you with immediate effect. Stacy will deal with the procedure. We already have irrefutable evidence of gross misconduct here, so unless you can prove that Jesus Christ himself manifested this money in your locker, then I will be terminating your contract by the end of the week. A shame, as you're a good little worker.'

Mel feels her heart kick up, her mouth go dry and her cheeks colour. 'You're sacking me?' she says quietly.

'Smart as a fox, too,' Josette says.

'But I haven't done anything wrong. I *need* this job, Josette. Please…'

'Melanie, listen to me. You have form. This is not the first thing you've stolen.'

'What? What are you talking about?' Mel can't believe what she's hearing.

'You stole a pair of expensive trainers that were all set to go to *charity*.' Josette shakes her head.

'No… no, you've got that wrong. Yes, I took the trainers, but I gave Barb a five-pound note to put in the fundraising pot. That was the price on the shoes, I swear.'

'We've already checked with every staff member and none say that you gave them any cash. You are lying.'

'No, no, I'm *not*,' Mel says, feeling hot with anger. 'You have to believe me.' She hears her voice buckle and waver, hating that she's on the verge of tears.

'Stacy will sort out the paperwork and send it on to you,' Josette says, turning on her heel. 'Please take your... *stuff* with you when you leave,' she adds, nudging the sports bag on the floor with the tip of her court shoe before striding off.

'I'm sorry, Mel,' she hears someone saying. It's Amit. Then she feels a hand on her arm – Stacy's – and another offer of condolence.

'Yeah, me too,' Mel whispers, breathing in a huge gulp of air as she watches them leave the staff room. After a moment, after she's gathered herself – her mind racing, not understanding what on earth has just taken place, or how it could even have happened – she grabs her belongings and rushes out to her car, feeling the eyes of the other staff watching her as she leaves.

CHAPTER SEVEN

Mel can't face going home yet – a home that's not going to be hers for much longer now that she doesn't have a job. She drives away from The Cedars, glancing in her rear-view mirror as she heads off down the long, tree-lined drive, shaking her head in disbelief.

She *can't* have just lost her job. Can she?

She feels the anger building inside her – at the injustice of it all. A stark reflection of her past.

'I didn't even get a chance to say goodbye to Bob,' she says, driving slowly, mindful of several speed cameras along the route. The last thing she needs is a fine. 'I can't bear him thinking badly of me,' she whispers to herself, pulling onto a roundabout, not even sure where she's headed.

Ten minutes later, she finds herself swept along in the traffic to Solihull town centre. Seeing a parking spot, she takes it, pulls on the handbrake and cuts the engine.

'Christ,' she says, thumping the steering wheel. 'Christ and *bugger*!'

A woman with a pushchair stares at her as she passes, looking back over her shoulder with alarm as Mel lets out a half-roar and half-frustrated scream. She throws her head back against the headrest, closing her eyes.

Since Billy went to prison, since she finally extricated herself from his life three years ago, Mel has been content – happy, she could even say, if it weren't for Kate's troubles at school. After everything he'd done to her, it was a struggle, but she didn't grow up in foster homes and the council care system and not learn how to take care of herself. You either survived or you didn't. But now, it feels as if the reins are slipping from her fingers again. And that makes her scared. Panicked. *Angry.*

'Damn that bloody woman,' she says, leaning forward on the steering wheel, knowing that Josette has never liked her, never thought her good enough for a place like The Cedars.

'We offer a five-star end-of-life experience,' Josette had said at Mel's hour-long interview several years ago, which had felt more like a grilling.

But doesn't *everyone* deserve the best at the end of their life, regardless of how much money they have? Mel had thought, but kept quiet, especially when she was offered the job. With a regular income, she and Kate would soon be able to move out of the women's refuge, get a place of their own.

'But if you're going to be working at The Cedars, well… I need you to look *different.* Conform to our high standards.' Josette had touched the side of her nose then, indicating Mel would need to remove her nose stud. 'Plus you'll need sensible, plain footwear, a minimum of make-up and short, trimmed nails.'

Mel had curled up her fingers then, hiding her royal-blue nail polish.

'Basically,' Josette had continued, 'I need you to look… *normal.*'

Mel hesitated, knowing she'd never felt normal in her entire life. But, if it meant nearly sixteen hundred pounds a month in her bank account, plus she could still do a shift at Michael's shop each week, then she'd be able to afford a little place for her and Kate in no time. As well as start making a dent in the debts Billy had left her with.

Mel rests her head on the car window. Josette did this to me. She set me up. She *must* have, she thinks. She wanted me gone. I'm disposable to her. Not even worth recycling.

She screws up her eyes, refusing to let her past impact the present.

But thoughts of appeals, solicitors, court cases and some kind of revenge – *any* revenge – flash through Mel's mind. Getting through life alone, surviving, had been hardwired into her from the moment she was born – even though she'd not realised that as a baby. An *abandoned* baby.

She refused to be anyone's trash.

'It's unfair dismissal and I won't have it,' Mel tells herself, getting out of the car and locking up. She heads through the drizzle to her favourite coffee shop.

'A medium latte, please,' she says, pulling out her purse. Even a coffee is a luxury right now, but she doesn't care. She can't face being home alone with her thoughts. 'And one of those too, please,' she adds, pointing to a tray of chocolate brownies. She's got just enough cash on her.

In the window seat, Mel stirs her coffee and watches the drizzle turn into heavier rain. Shoppers and passers-by pop up umbrellas, some hurrying past with their coats pulled over their heads.

Mel closes her eyes as she takes a bite of her brownie, reminded of the first time she met Billy. It had been raining then, too, and Mel was soaking, standing at the shelter-less bus stop when Billy had joined the queue behind her, insisting she take his newspaper to shield her head. The bus was already fifteen minutes late.

'It's the best I can offer you,' were his first words to her, and little did she know then how true that would turn out to be.

He'd pulled a packet of cigarettes from his jacket pocket, flipping open the lid and holding it out to Mel. She'd given a quick shake of her head, her eyes flashing to the diagonal scar on his cheek. His sharp jawline – the smattering of stubble running from the top of his neck, up his cheeks and onto his shaved head, which she could just make out under the dark cap he wore – his piercing blue eyes and the scruffy army-style jacket he had on over a black

T-shirt, made him look more like a criminal than a *Times* reader. Someone she'd cross the street to avoid after dark.

If only she'd known.

He'd taken a long draw on his cigarette, his eyes fixed on Mel with… with a steely look in them. The look she'd later come to be excited by as well as terrified of. At that point, Billy was still an enigma.

And he still is, she thinks, taking a sip of her coffee, grateful he's got at least two more years behind bars.

Mel spots a newspaper on the vacant chair beside her, laying her hand on it, remembering how, at the bus stop, as the double-decker pulled into view, Billy had taken a pen from his top pocket and raised his right hand to her head, jotting down something on the edge of the newspaper – one of the few times he'd raised a hand at her and she'd not flinched.

As he'd got off the bus a couple of stops before her, he'd paused beside her, making a telephone gesture with his hand. It was only when the bus had pulled away, and she had mindlessly turned over the newspaper he'd given her, that she discovered Billy had written his name and phone number on the edge of it.

CHAPTER EIGHT

Mel drains her coffee mug and presses her forefinger into the brownie crumbs on her plate, licking them off. She wipes her hands and balls up the paper napkin, stuffing it in the empty mug.

'Are you leaving?' someone says – a bearded man with the small hand of a toddler clamped in his. Mel glances down at the little girl and smiles, briefly reminded of Kate, how Billy used to grip onto her hand when they were out and about. While he may have treated *her* badly, Kate had always been a daddy's girl.

'Oh, yes, I'm just going,' Mel says to the man, reaching for her bag and getting up. Before she heads outside into the rain, she feels around in her bag for her car keys, pulling out other items so she can see to the bottom.

That's odd, she thinks, staring at the envelope – the one containing the solicitor's letter. Michael must have put it in there last night without me knowing. She slides the letter out, revealing the firm's name: Green, Lupton and Hedge. Michael had insisted they sounded genuine. And their offices are only round the corner on High Street, she thinks, pulling open the door and heading out into the rain.

Five minutes later, having dashed along the pavement with no umbrella, Mel stands outside a red-brick building down a street occupied by various shops and estate agents, as well as solicitors' and accountants' premises. She's uncertain whether it's anger about her unfair dismissal or the growing curiosity about the letter that has drawn her here.

What if Michael is right? What if she *has* inherited something, and she ignores it? She could certainly do with a bit of extra cash right now, and it's not as if she's going to be so stupid as to part with any money upfront. Either way, if the letter is genuinely from these offices, they can confirm it. And if someone is using their firm as a front for a scam, Mel is sure they'll be grateful to know.

She rings the bell on the outside of the door and a moment later the latch buzzes and she heads inside.

'Hi,' Mel says to the smartly dressed receptionist. Her blonde hair is pulled back in a neat ponytail and her pale skin is lightly made up. She wears a plain grey skirt and a white blouse underneath her fitted jacket. Mel pushes her fingers through her soaking hair, praying the recent home root touch-up hasn't run onto her face as she stamps her feet several times on the doormat.

'How can I help you?' the receptionist says, eyeing Mel up and down.

Still holding the letter, Mel replies, 'I… I was wondering if you take on cases for people who can't immediately pay?'

The receptionist sits down behind the counter, half obscuring herself as if she's already lost interest. 'You mean no win, no fee?' She clears her throat slowly.

'Maybe. Yes, I guess so.'

'Which area of law are we talking about?' she asks idly, tapping something into her computer.

'Employment law. Unfair dismissal.' She takes the letter from its envelope and waves it about. 'It didn't say here if you deal with that kind of case, so I thought I'd call in and ask, seeing as I was nearby.'

The receptionist, who from her name badge Mel can now see is called Emma, glances at the letter. Mel leans on the counter, but immediately withdraws again, concerned she'll leave wet marks.

'That is an area of law we cover, yes,' Emma says, smiling politely. 'I see you've already had correspondence from us about it.'

'Oh… er, no,' Mel says, fluttering the letter again. 'This is about something else.' She feels the colour rising in her cheeks. 'An inheritance, apparently.' She pauses, watching the receptionist as her eyes flick from the letter and back to her. 'Though it's the employment case I'm really here about. I've, well… I've been fired. And it's really not right. They said I stole some money, but I was set up. It's complete rubbish.' Mel's stomach churns as she thinks of the scene in the staff room earlier.

'I'm sorry to hear that, Mrs…?'

'It's Miss. Miss Douglas. Melanie Douglas,' she adds, clearing her throat and wishing she'd not come in. She knows how solicitors work, that they'll want money upfront on account. Money she doesn't have. The plush grey carpet, the cream leather chairs set around a glass coffee table with neatly stacked magazines, the framed art prints on the wall – it reeks of at least three hundred pounds an hour. In fact, just being inside a solicitor's office makes Mel feel uncomfortable.

As if *I've* done something wrong, she thinks, her mind filled with memories of appearing in court as a witness for the prosecution against Billy. And, while he may have received a five-year sentence, Mel is all too aware that three of those years have already been spent.

Emma taps at her keyboard, her pink, manicured nails clicking lightly on the keys. 'Oh…' she says, glancing up at Mel, then back down at the screen. 'Miss *Douglas*,' she adds, almost as if she'd been expecting her. 'Welcome. Would I be able to take a copy of your ID, please?'

*

'Please, do sit down,' the man who introduced himself as Robert Hedge, senior partner, says once they're inside his office.

'Thank you,' Mel replies, perching on the edge of the upholstered chair. She hopes it doesn't stain from her wet clothes and, just in case, she slips off her quilted coat and drops it on the floor beside her.

'Here, allow me,' Robert Hedge says, coming round and retrieving the coat, hanging it on a stand behind his office door. 'Would you like tea or coffee?' he continues. His voice is somehow comforting, Mel thinks, already feeling a little more relaxed. On the surface, he doesn't look like the type of person who'd faze someone like Josette, but she knows how these lawyer types work. Beneath their often bland exterior lies a hidden Rottweiler. Hopefully, someone devious and tactical enough to outsmart Josette and her no doubt top legal team.

'I'm OK, thank you. I've just had a coffee.'

Robert nods and goes around the other side of the mahogany desk, sitting down. His office is quite different to the reception area – the cluttered bookshelves and dark antique furniture a stark contrast to the modern waiting room. He pulls in his chair, leaning forward on his desk with his hands clasped together in front of him. Mel notices a wedding band on his ring finger, and tasteful gold cufflinks protruding from the ends of his jacket sleeves. She guesses him to be about fifty-five, possibly a little older.

'Emma made a note on our system about an employment matter,' he says, turning to his computer monitor and moving the mouse with his right hand. 'I'm afraid to say we don't undertake no win, no fee type cases—'

'It's fine,' Mel says, suddenly feeling stupid. This firm clearly isn't anything like the adverts she's seen for lawyers touting such offers. 'I'm sorry to waste your time.'

'Not at all, Miss Douglas. I actually invited you in to discuss *another* matter.' He sits back in his chair. 'I'm assuming you also came to see us because of my letter?'

'I… well, it's where I got your address from, yes. I'm a bit upset, you see,' she says, taking a breath and glancing at the ceiling. 'I got fired this morning. For something I didn't do.'

'I'm very sorry to hear that,' Robert says. 'But like I said—'

'And I had your letter in my bag and thought… well, I thought you may be able to help with me with it. But I suppose I also wanted to see if you were real.'

Robert smiles, his dark brown eyes creasing at the edges – what Mel calls a 'well-worn' smile. He steeples his fingers under his chin, his expression an amused one.

'As you can see, I'm very real,' he says warmly.

'I mean, this… your firm.' Mel makes a sweeping gesture with her hand. 'If I'm honest, I originally threw your letter away. It just looked like some scam to me.'

'I shall make a note to review our firm's letterhead and branding, in that case,' he says with a wink and a kind smile. 'Make it less… scam-like,' he adds. 'But I'm very pleased you did call in to see us, Miss Douglas,' Robert says, glancing at his watch. 'Look, this may take a little while, so why don't I get my secretary to bring us in a pot of coffee and some biscuits, after all, and I can tell you all about this rather… *unusual* matter.'

CHAPTER NINE

Mel stares at the solicitor, a biscuit halfway to her mouth, her lips parted from shock rather than the bite she was about to take. Robert Hedge's words ring in her ears – alongside the thought that this *must* be a scam after all.

'A *hotel*?' she says when she's finally able to speak. She places the biscuit back on her plate.

Robert gives a pronounced nod, leaning back in his chair, watching Mel as the news sinks in.

'You're saying I've inherited an actual *hotel*? Like, a whole one?'

The solicitor smiles warmly again, as if he's thoroughly enjoying the moment. 'Indeed you have,' he replies. 'A whole one. Like I said, it's quite an unusual matter and, together with the hotel, there are significant funds due to be released, too. Plus several conditions that must be adhered to, as set out in the accompanying "Letter of Wishes".'

Letter of Wishes? Mel thinks, her mind racing.

'What's that? I mean…' She pauses, taking a sip of coffee. 'I mean, what is *any* of this? I simply don't understand. I don't have any relatives, for a start, and even if I did, I doubt very much that they know about me.'

Mel suddenly feels tearful, convinced there's been a mistake. It's as if the solitude of her entire existence, the sense of never belonging, is suddenly under a spotlight – as though the abandonment and shame that she's tried so hard to bury and forget have been dredged up and laid bare and raw in front of her. She doesn't like it.

'OK, let me explain further, Melanie. I know it's a lot to take in, but it's actually quite straightforward, if not a little unexpected. I understand that.' He smiles again, reaching for a biscuit and sipping his coffee.

Mel doesn't take her eyes off him.

'The estate in question is being handled by another firm of solicitors in Exeter. They are the executors of the original will. Probate took a while due to the unusual nature of the matter. The reason being, the sole beneficiary actually refused their inheritance. It's quite rare, but it does happen from time to time.'

Mel gives a small nod, a frown set firmly between her eyes. She still doesn't understand. 'Why would anyone refuse an inheritance?'

'There are many reasons – sometimes it's to do with tax implications, or jurisdictions and local laws, but most often it's due to ill feelings between the deceased and the beneficiary. A large number of people die intestate and next of kin naturally benefit by default, though a small number do refuse if there's been animosity or fallings-out and suchlike. Where there is a will in place, oftentimes it's outdated and doesn't always reflect feelings between the parties at the time of death.'

'I see,' Mel said, not seeing at all.

'There are several ways in which a beneficiary can deal with their right to refuse an inheritance. First, they can simply disclaim it. They have to disclaim the entire gift, though, and get no say in who benefits instead. The executors decide this. Secondly, the benefactor can accept the inheritance but immediately gift it on to someone else, say, a child or other relative, for instance. There are tax implications there, though, and the benefactor must survive at least seven years for tax not to apply to the new beneficiary.'

Mel puts her hand to her forehead, closes her eyes for a moment. The churning feeling in her stomach swells as she tries to absorb what she's being told. When she woke up this morning, dropped Kate at school, she had no idea that within a couple of hours she'd be suspended from work and sitting in a solicitor's office discussing an inheritance.

'Are you OK, Melanie? Would you like some water?'

'Oh… no, thanks. I'm fine. It's just been a strange morning, that's all. I'm trying to take in what you're saying.'

'I understand,' Robert says in a soothing voice. 'So, as I was saying, the other option for refusing an inheritance is to redirect it, if you like. This requires something called a Deed of Variation, which is a legal document that effectively alters the intended beneficiary, almost as if it was done before the deceased passed away. Are you still with me?'

'Yes, I think so,' Mel replies. 'Though I don't really see what any of this can possibly have to do with me. Like I said, apart from my daughter I don't have any family. I grew up in children's homes and with foster parents.'

'Right, so this last option is what has happened in this particular matter. The original and sole beneficiary of the entire estate refused to accept the inheritance, but also wanted to direct who should benefit from it instead. The Deed of Variation makes this possible.'

'OK,' Mel says quietly, all she can manage.

'And you have been named as a beneficiary, Melanie, with all taxes previously settled.'

'OK,' she repeats nervously. She looks past Robert and out of the window behind him, the view overlooking a small car park. A man gets into an expensive-looking white car while another vehicle pulls in and takes several attempts at parking. Normal people going about their normal lives. 'Why?' she asks, turning back to the solicitor.

'That is a question I can't answer, I'm afraid,' he says, clasping his hands under his chin. 'Not because of confidentiality or because I don't want to. Rather because I simply don't know. The original beneficiary who refused the inheritance has asked to remain anonymous, as well as keeping the benefactor's identity private too. Again, this sometimes happens when… well, when there have been ill feelings within families. I would suggest applying for a copy of the will, but without a name to search for, that makes it tricky.'

Mel gives a little nod as she tries to find the right words. 'But I've told you, Mr Hedges, I don't have a family. None at all. I don't have any friends or acquaintances who have died and certainly none who owns a… a *hotel*.'

'Perhaps it would help to imagine them as a long-lost relative. Someone who's got your back and wanted to give you a gift, shall we say?' Robert breathes in heavily, nodding his head a few times while holding Mel's gaze.

Kind eyes, she thinks.

'Maybe,' she says. But then adds, 'What if *I* don't want the inheritance or gift or whatever it is, either? I mean, what am I supposed to do with a hotel? And where is it…? Plus you mentioned conditions. It all sounds like a lot of trouble to me.'

'Before you make any big decisions, let me tell you a little more.' Robert puts his hand over his mouse and clicks several times, leaning towards the screen. Mel sees his eyes skimming over a document as if he's reading fast. Then he sits back again.

'The hotel is located on the South Coast. In a place called Halebury, close to Lyme Regis, I'm informed. It's currently trading but I can see from the latest accounts that business hasn't exactly been booming the last few years, and it's barely keeping afloat now. It's a smallish place with fifteen bedrooms, and has a skeleton staff currently.'

'Halebury?' Mel says, racking her brains. She's heard of Lyme Regis, of course, but has never been. But she's certainly never heard of Halebury. 'I don't know anyone down that way. It's in Devon, right?'

'No, West Dorset, actually. The hotel is called Moreton Inn. I don't have any photographs, I'm afraid, but you could google it,' Robert adds. 'If you decide you're interested.'

Am I interested? Mel wonders, confused. I could always sell it, buy another place, somewhere safe and easy to manage for Kate and me.

'You mentioned... funds, too?' Mel doesn't want to sound mercenary but it's cash she needs most now.

'Indeed.' Robert clicks a few more times. 'After taxes, the cash sum to be transferred along with ownership of the hotel is £378,542.'

Mel hears herself gasp involuntarily, feels her eyes widen to bursting point. For a moment, she doesn't feel real.

'*What?*'

'And twenty-eight pence, to be precise,' Robert adds with a smile.

'Three hundred and seventy-eight thousand pounds?'

Robert nods.

'For me. Like, mine to have?'

He nods again.

'There surely must be some mistake.'

'We will have to undertake further ID checks, of course, a bit of paperwork to complete, but nothing too complicated. And I can assure you, there is no mistake.'

'Fuck,' Mel says, standing up and going over to the window. She leans on the sill and stares out, her forehead against the glass. 'Sorry,' she adds, her breath misting the glass. 'I didn't mean to swear. It's just... I honestly can't believe this.'

'I mentioned a Letter of Wishes, Melanie,' Robert continues.

Mel returns to her seat, trying to compose herself. She doesn't know whether to jump for joy or freeze in disbelief.

'The first condition is that some of the money must be spent on improvements to the hotel. Moreton Inn must also continue to run as a hotel.'

'What if I want to sell it?'

'It's a bit of a grey area, to be honest. A condition of the will, which has been included in the Letter of Wishes from the original beneficiary, states…' Robert turns to his screen to read. '"Moreton Inn shall remain in the possession of the new beneficiary, Melanie Douglas, and not be sold or transferred at any time in the future. The property must continue to run as a trading hotel, restaurant and bar, and works carried out on the property as per the attached schedule as a minimum requirement."'

Robert slides his glasses onto the end of his nose, looking at Mel over the top of them. 'If conditions in wills are what we term *impossible*, then it's likely that a judge would allow them to be set aside. However, I'd say these conditions are more loosely *uncertain*, so it may prove trickier to get them removed.'

'But how on earth am I supposed to run a hotel? The nearest I've come to anything like that was serving cream teas when I had a Saturday job in a café aged sixteen.'

'There is one more condition,' Robert says.

Mel looks at him, raises her eyebrows slightly.

'There is a permanent resident at the hotel. A woman. The condition states that she be allowed to continue living there for as long as she requires, at no cost. Meals, laundry and cleaning to be provided.'

'A woman?' Mel says. 'Who?'

'I'm afraid I don't know further details at this point, Melanie.'

'So I'm expected to take over the running of a hotel that sounds as if it's on its last legs. Undertake renovation work and build the business back up. Never sell the place, likely spending the rest of my days there, and cook and clean for some woman who I've never met but I have to live with?'

'Yes,' says Robert, removing his glasses and pushing back in his chair.

CHAPTER TEN

'Come on, come *on…*' Mel says under her breath, cursing as the engine turns over but doesn't start. She waits a moment before trying again. On the fourth attempt, the engine of the old Fiesta finally goes, making her release the breath she's been holding.

She doesn't particularly remember the drive home – her mind all over the place as she attempts to take in the morning's events. And her suspension from work now doesn't feel quite so threatening – though it all boils down to whether she adheres to the conditions set out in the legal documents and accepts the inheritance. And if she does, she can tell Josette to go do one. Not that she won't miss The Cedars and the residents she's grown fond of, especially Bob.

'I just can't believe it,' Mel whispers to herself as she circles the block near home looking for a parking spot. There's Kate to consider for a start, she thinks, reversing into a tight space. She pulls on the handbrake, gathers up her belongings and heads over the road to the entrance of her flat, flicking a wave to Tony in the fish bar.

Three hundred and seventy-eight thousand pounds echoes inside her head.

It's as she's halfway up the stairs that Mel stops, sniffing the air. At first she thinks it's maybe burnt toast from earlier, but she and Kate scoffed down a bowl of cereal before they left. She goes up another couple of steps and takes another deep breath.

'No,' she says to herself, the back of her neck prickling. She knows it's not toast, and not quite the same as the cigarette smoke she thought she smelt the other day, either. It's more fragrant and earthy than that.

'*Weed*,' Mel says through a sigh, wondering where on earth it could have come from. Tony doesn't seem the type and, even though, as her landlord, he has a key, she knows he wouldn't come inside uninvited or without notice. She wonders if it's one of his staff popping out for a sly one, but her flat doesn't have windows facing the small courtyard out the back of the fish and chip shop where someone might have a quick smoke. But she's all too familiar with the unmistakable smell. God knows, she put up with it long enough when she was with Billy.

Assuming it must have seeped in under the less-than-draught-proof door out on to the street, Mel continues up to the flat. She dumps her bag and hangs up her coat before going to the kitchen and filling the kettle. She doesn't think she's ever needed a cup of tea more.

Mel drops down into the old sofa, careful not to spill her drink. As she puts her mug on the little table beside her, she spots her cards, reaching out for them. She's not looked at them in a few weeks, wonders if they would have predicted today's events if she had. Using both hands, she shuffles them deftly, closing her eyes as her mind buzzes with everything that's happened.

The tarot cards had been a gift from Sue, her last and favourite foster mother. Despite being in and out of children's homes, and living with various other foster parents, Mel is ever grateful for her time with Sue and her partner, Patrick. The three years she'd spent with them from age fifteen to eighteen were some of the happiest years of her life. Finally, she'd felt wanted. Accepted. *Needed*.

One of the cards drops from Mel's hands as she's shuffling, so she places it on the sofa beside her. *Never ignore the cards that escape*, Sue had said when she'd first explained the tarot to Mel. *They're the ones trying to speak to you most.*

What had struck Mel when she first arrived at Sue's home – a suitcase and holdall to hand, her entire worldly possessions – was that the *extra*ordinary was simply the ordinary. Whether it be family tarot readings around the dining table with the other kids Sue fostered, or open chats about sex or relationships for the older ones, listening to alternative music at full volume, no restrictions on how any of her charges dressed or expressed themselves – even that little tattoo on her shoulder Mel had proudly presented to Sue one day, aged seventeen – none of it had provoked a bad reaction. Sue was accepting of all her foster kids for who they *were*, not what society expected them to be.

When she's finished the shuffle, Mel draws two more cards from the pack, repeating the process twice more in order to form a basic spread of nine cards in three columns. 'Immediate past, present and near future,' she says, just about to draw the final couple of cards. It's at that moment she hears a phone ringing. And it's not hers.

'That's odd,' she says, standing and tracking the sound. It seems to be coming from Kate's bedroom, although she knows her daughter took her phone to school. She always checks that she has it with her.

As she goes inside Kate's room, the ringing stops. It's dark so she pulls the curtains open and, when she glances around, Mel can't see any sign of a phone. She picks up a school blouse and several bits of underwear off the floor before opening the bedside cabinet. But there's no phone inside. Then she has a quick look in the bedding – under Kate's black and purple duvet cover, under her pillows, too. She checks a couple of coat pockets, moves aside a few schoolbooks on her little desk that's mostly taken up by her precious gaming PC. No phone.

'Weird,' she says, using her own phone to dial Kate's number. If she's in lessons, she knows it'll be silenced. As suspected, it rings out to voicemail, so Mel hangs up. No phone rang in Kate's bedroom – not even a vibrating sound anywhere. She shakes her head, puzzled, and goes back to the living room, taking several large sips of tea. Then she turns over the final two cards of the reading – indicating the outcome, the future.

She's not sure if it's The Tower card immediately following Death that makes her shudder, her skin prickle with goosebumps as she tries to understand the huge implications the pair of cards represents – cataclysmic life changes, endings and unstoppable events – or the sight of Billy's name on *her* phone beside her as it lights up from his call.

CHAPTER ELEVEN

The old-fashioned bell on the shop door tinkles as Mel goes inside, holding it open as Kate follows.

'Hello, my lovelies,' Michael says, appearing from behind the counter – a reclaimed mirror-fronted bar he'd bought from an auction room years ago. Similar to its owner, Michael's shop is eclectic and curious in its decor, as well as being crammed full of unusual and collectable music – whether vinyl, CD, cassette, sheet music or even 8-track.

'You two are a sight for a pair of very sore eyes.' He briefly lifts the Lennon-style green-tinted shades perched on his hooked nose. The deep cuffs of his crisp white shirt cover half of his hands, while he wears a mauve bow tie at his neck.

'Hello, Uncle Micky,' Kate says, flashing him a brief smile before helping herself to a humbug in a jar next to the old-fashioned till. She goes over to the listening booth, clamping a pair of headphones to her ears, tucking her hair out of the way.

'Late night?' Mel says, putting her bag behind the counter. She takes off her jacket, hanging it up.

'Kevin came over.' He gives a flick of his hand, glancing down at Mel's T-shirt. '"Free Hugs",' he says, reading the slogan on it. 'Go on then, I'll take one of those.'

Mel hugs him back. 'Grindr Kevin?'

Michael raises one eyebrow.

'Which explains why I couldn't reach you.' Mel was still rattled from Billy's calls.

Michael pulls his phone from his pocket, rolling his eyes. 'I forgot to switch it back on this morning,' he says, waiting for it to power up. 'What if I've missed a message from Kev since he left this morn…'

He stops, noticing the concerned expression on Mel's face.

'What's wrong?' he asks. 'Do we need coffee?'

Mel nods, beckoning him out the back into the tiny kitchen.

Michael puts the machine on. 'Spill. You look like you've seen someone come back from the dead.'

'I… I might as well have done, Micky. I don't even know where to start.'

'The beginning?'

'I lost my job.'

'Wha-*at*?'

'Bitch boss finally fired me. Technically, I'm suspended, but as good as fired. She found "stolen cash" in my locker.' Mel makes quotation marks with her fingers.

'Fucksake,' Michael says.

'Oh, and I've inherited a hotel and a shit ton of money.'

'Wha-*aat*?' Michael says again. 'Was it that letter?'

Mel nods. Even summing up yesterday in bullet points is draining her.

'How… how much of a shit ton exactly?' Michael's tone is tentative, as if he hardly dare ask.

'Nearly three hundred and eighty grand,' Mel whispers. 'Plus a hotel. I mean… a bloody *hotel*, Micky.'

'*Christ*,' Michael says, pushing his hands through his hair, his eyes wide. He leans back against the counter. 'You look exhausted,' he says, seeing the bruise-coloured circles under her eyes where, one time too many, he's seen actual bruises.

'I didn't sleep a wink,' Mel says, dragging her hands down her face. 'But not for the reasons you think.'

'Oh, darling,' Michael says, gently taking her hands. He knows how sensitive she can be about touch. 'What else has happened? It's a truth universally acknowledged that a woman in possession of a large fortune doesn't have an expression like yours written all over her face.'

Mel sighs, taking a breath. 'Billy's out of prison.'

Michael hands Mel a mug of coffee. 'How do you know?' he asks, keeping his voice low.

'He called me.' Mel shudders, hugging one arm around herself. 'He must have got out early.' She takes a sip of coffee. 'I didn't answer, of course.'

'Did you block him?'

She shakes her head. 'If I do that, it'll make him angry. *More* angry. Plus he'll say I'm being obstructive when it comes to seeing Kate.'

'He can go do one when it comes to access. You were a murder statistic waiting to happen, Mel.'

Mel nods. A statistic who *grassed*.

'The other thing, Micky… and I know you'll think I'm crazy, but… but I think he's been in my flat.'

Wide-eyed, Michael listens as Mel explains about the weed smell.

'And just before Billy called my phone, another phone rang in the flat. It wasn't Kate's, but the sound was coming from her bedroom. What if it was Billy's phone? Maybe he came snooping and dropped it, and—'

'Mel, my love. Stop.' Michael places a hand on her shoulder. 'If it's true, that's what contact centres and non-molestation orders are for, right? Let's focus on the good stuff, for now, eh?' He gives her a gentle hug. 'Now, tell me everything the solicitor said and when you get to become Lady of the Manor?'

*

'*Dorset?*' Michael says after one of his regular customers leaves with an LP.

Mel nods, watching as he puts the cash in the till. It's been hard for him over the years, financially, and she knows he nearly lost the shop a few years back. But with hard work and determination, Michael took control of his gambling and cleared his debts. Like her, he's a fighter. She couldn't be more proud of him.

'I know, right? If Billy *is* sniffing about, then maybe moving away is for the best. But I can't stand the thought of not being near you. You're my rock.'

'Accept the hotel. Then sell it. Easy.' The shop doorbell tinkles as another customer comes in.

Kate glances up and takes off her headphones before going over to the customer to ask if he needs help.

'I can't,' Mel replies in a low voice. 'Apparently, there's a condition that says I'm not allowed to. Plus I have to live in it, renovate it, run it as a hotel *and* let some woman I don't know live there too.'

Michael looks thoughtful for a moment. 'What woman? And who is the inheritance from? You are certain it isn't a scam after all, aren't you?'

'Trust me, it's not a scam. I've got copies of the paperwork, various documents, checked out the place online, checked and double-checked the solicitor's credentials. It's all I did last night when I couldn't reach you.'

Mel feels a flutter in her stomach as she recalls the photos of Moreton Inn that she'd found online – the pretty stone building with its old paned windows, the slightly wonky chimneys and thatched roof overhanging the front façade like a too-long fringe. While the place looked a little run-down and unloved, it certainly oozed appeal and Mel couldn't deny that, while she'd felt a little overwhelmed seeing it, she also felt excited by the prospect of owning such a place, even if it was in need of updating.

But the online reviews had told another story – *Could be so good but old-fashioned decor with rude bartender let the place down... Has potential but not until the owners stop fighting... Nice breakfast and comfy beds but a strange woman scared my daughter. Won't stay again...* The list went on, with the mainly one- and two-star reviews largely focusing on the poor service, the jaded owner and her rude partner. Mel wondered who they were and if they'd since moved on and, of course, if they were anything to do with the mystery inheritance.

'And I have no idea who the woman living there is, or who this has all come from. I'm burning with curiosity but I was told they want to remain anonymous. The solicitor said that without the deceased's name, it'll be nigh on impossible to apply for a copy of the will.'

'Do you think Billy has something to do with it?' Michael exclaims, his eyebrows raised.

'Dad?' Kate is suddenly beside them, leaning on the counter as she takes another humbug. 'Is he coming home properly now?'

Mel scowls at Michael, wishing he'd kept his voice down. When Billy was sent to prison, Kate was too young to know the truth, so Mel had explained his absence by saying he'd gone away for work. She hated lying to her nearly nine-year-old daughter, the tales getting more and more tangled as time went on, but she'd had no choice. She didn't want Kate tainted by her criminal father, even though she knew she missed him dreadfully.

'But Dad told me he doesn't have to go to work like normal dads,' she'd once said. 'So how can he have gone away for it?'

Normal dads don't make money from selling drugs and robbing petrol stations, Mel had thought but didn't say.

'I... I've not heard anything, love,' Mel replies now to Kate, forcing a smile.

'How about you re-shelve this vinyl for me?' Michael asks, handing Kate a stack of records. 'They're from the jazz section.'

Kate's eyes narrow as she glances between Mel and Michael. 'Sure,' she says, taking them.

While Kate is busy, Mel beckons Michael into the kitchen again.

'Did you hear what she said?' Mel hisses urgently, grabbing Michael's arm. '"Is he coming home properly now?" What does she mean *properly*?'

Michael hesitates. 'I wouldn't read too much into it,' he says.

Mel chews on a fingernail, trying to stop her thoughts running away. 'But you know as well as I do he always finds me, worms his way back in.'

She shudders, still not able to understand how someone like her got caught up with someone like Billy. At the time, she'd been bored in life, drifting a bit, and Billy represented a change, the excitement she craved. But it wasn't many months until his mask slipped and the man beneath emerged.

'I feel like I'm going mad, Micky. I swear, Billy's been inside my flat. And now he's inside my *head*.'

Mel stops when she sees Kate in the doorway, less than three feet away.

'Mum?' she says, tears collecting in her eyes. 'There's… there's a man in the shop.'

For a split second, Mel's heart kicks up. *Billy?* But she knows that even after three years Kate would still recognise her own father.

Michael ruffles Kate's hair as he goes to help the customer. Mel knows business in the shop hasn't been great lately and feels bad about piling all her troubles on him.

Kate looks up at Mel, pulling her grey hoodie tightly around her. 'You were talking about Dad again, weren't you? What's going on?'

Mel feels as if ice is forming in her veins. 'I… no…'

'It's the second time you've mentioned him today. You never talk about him normally. And I know you've been lying to me all this time.'

Mel sees Kate's cheeks tinge pink, the look of betrayal on her face.

'Love…' Mel sighs. 'How about we get some of that frozen pizza you like for dinner tonight, and we can have a chat about it?'

Kate hesitates, her eyes narrowing and flickering. 'Frozen pizza? Is *that* what you think I like?' she says quietly, shaking her head. 'Well, I don't like it, Mum. In fact, I *hate* it. The box would probably taste nicer—'

'*Kate*—'

'I only say I like it so you don't feel bad because I know you can't afford anything else. But if Dad hadn't gone off, if you hadn't been horrid to him, then he'd still be here. I know the truth now.' Kate bows her head and covers her face. Her shoulders shake in time with her sobs.

'Oh, my darling…' Mel says, reaching out to her, drawing her in for a hug, breathing in the scent of her hair. 'But… what… what do you mean, "I know the truth now"?' she continues, her voice faltering.

Kate pulls a balled-up tissue from her jeans pocket. She blows and wipes her nose. 'Dad's told me everything, Mum. The truth.'

Mel can't move, as if her heart has finally frozen over, watching numbly as Kate turns on her heels and runs back out to the shop. A moment later, she hears a tinkle as Kate opens the street door, and then a crash as she slams it behind her. That's when Mel finally jolts herself into action and chases off after her daughter.

CHAPTER TWELVE

'Belt on?' Mel says, glancing across at Kate. Her daughter is staring out of the passenger window, her knees drawn up close to her chest because of all the belongings stuffed at her feet. 'Let's go then!' Mel adds, hoping for some kind of reaction, response, even a protest from her daughter. But a brief nod is all she gets.

Mel puts the car into gear and pulls away, concerned they won't make it to the end of the street, it's so heavily laden.

'Amazing what you can fit in a Fiesta when you try,' she says with a smile on her face. But inside, she's nervous. They've had to leave many of their belongings behind – Michael kindly stepping in with an offer of storage in his garage. Once they're settled, Mel will arrange for it to be collected. She still hasn't got used to the feeling of soon being able to pay people to do things for her.

Giving one last look up at the flat as she drives off – it has been their safe haven for several years now – she catches sight of Tony unlocking the fish bar. He gives them a wave, and Mel flicks one back. They've already said their proper goodbyes.

'Right, road trip music. What do you think? Heart FM?' Mel turns the radio on, glancing at the road ahead then back at the display as she tunes it. The CD player stopped working long ago.

'Really, Mum?' Kates says, glancing over at her, jabbing at the buttons and settling on Radio 1. Mel is simply relieved to have provoked a reaction, got her daughter to say something. She's been quiet all morning and barely said a word last night.

After a brief stop at the Shell garage on the edge of town – a full tank of petrol, a tyre check and drinks, chocolate and crisps bought for the journey – Mel drives off again, itching to get on the M5. It's at that point she'll feel as though they're finally on their way to a new life. The last two weeks have been fraught with worry, anxiety. Terror, if she's honest, though she's tried to hold it together for Kate's sake. With Billy sniffing about, the inheritance couldn't have come at a better time, though she's still mystified about where it's come from. Things like this don't happen to people like her.

After Kate had run out of Michael's record shop, Mel had chased after her, begging her to come back. Breathless, she had finally caught up with her and coaxed her back.

That evening, Mel had dipped into the utilities fund to order them a couple of proper takeout pizzas with all the extras, promising to be honest with her daughter. They'd sat talking about everything from school to homework to boys and friends – plus those who weren't friends – and finally the conversation turned to Billy.

'You mean he's been in prison *all* this time?' Kate had said, a huge piece of pepperoni pizza halfway to her mouth.

Mel had nodded, explained everything. It was still a skeleton truth, but not based on lies any more. She'd painted a much softer portrait of the man than he deserved – a smudged charcoal rather than angrily sprayed graffiti – but it was better than carrying on the deceit.

'Anyway, I already knew he'd been in prison,' Kate had said, stuffing a huge bite of pizza in her mouth. 'I just wanted you to admit it.'

Mel's eyes widened as she tried to hide her shock. She *knew*? She wasn't sure if she wanted to know exactly how, right at that moment. There were other things she wanted to talk about.

'How would you feel about getting away? Just me and you. A fresh start in a new place with no money worries.'

Kate had stopped chewing, running a finger underneath her pizza slice to break a string of cheese.

'In fact, the opposite of money worries,' Mel continued. 'Too much money to even know what to do with.'

Kate had reached for the remote control, lowering the volume on the TV.

'Like, getting the new PS5 for Christmas kind of no money worries?' She eyed her mum disbelievingly.

'Definitely the PS5 kind,' Mel replied, feeling her insides loosen a little. She'd do whatever it took. 'Look. This is where we'd be going.'

After retelling the story about the mystery inheritance in a way Kate would understand, Mel had opened up her phone's browser, flicking through a couple of pictures from the hotel's website. 'This is it. What do you think?'

Kate had taken Mel's phone then, zooming in on images of Moreton Inn – studying the cosy bar area, the large garden with its cluster of wooden tables and parasols, shots of the local beaches, the quaint village of Halebury with its pretty pastel houses and local bakery.

Kate raised her eyebrows. 'Oh my God, this looks *so* cool,' she'd said, her eyes wide. 'You mean, we get to live there? It's huge! But what about Dad? Can he come too?'

'How much longer?' Kate says, sighing impatiently. 'It's taking for ever,' she adds. Her legs squirm uncomfortably in the clutter around her feet – mostly items from her bedroom, hurriedly stuffed into carrier bags after Mel had made the snap decision to accept the inheritance, more out of urgency than considered choice. By that point, Mel didn't care who had left it to her or why. Just that she had to take it. She *needed* to take it. If what she suspected was true, that Billy was on her tail, then they had to get out fast.

'About an hour, maybe an hour and a half. Are there any crisps left?' Mel replies.

Kate twists round and grabs the food bag, opening two packets of cheese and onion and, for the next ten minutes or so, they sit in silence, crunching and listening to music that Kate knows all the words to and Mel hasn't even heard of. She sits at a steady sixty miles an hour in the slow lane, shielding herself from the crazy drivers in flash BMWs and white vans speeding past in the fast lane while she stays in the wake of a truck.

'"If you can't see my mirrors, I can't see you",' Mel reads from the sticker on the back as a black cloud of diesel exhaust bursts from the rear of the lorry.

Reminds me of Billy, she thinks, gripping the wheel tightly. All smoke and mirrors.

*

A flutter of excitement surges through Mel as finally, after three and a half hours behind the wheel, she spots the village sign – Halebury. She drops down into second gear as they enter, glancing across at Kate, who's fast asleep, her head resting on a bunched-up sweatshirt against the window. Mel leans forward, her neck and shoulders stiff from driving, and peers around, soaking up their new home. She allows herself a smile as she takes in the pretty cottages, the narrow lanes and the steep hills. She winds down her window and breathes in deeply.

'The sea,' she whispers, catching the fresh, briny scent. The sound of seagulls squawking overhead makes her feel as though she's on holiday, though she can't deny that her stomach churns every few minutes as she thinks of what they've escaped. *Please* don't let him find us, she silently prays. Please let this be a new start…

Following her satnav's directions, Mel indicates away from the village centre – complete with its memorial square, benches and pots of brightly coloured flowers – and heads up a hill. In her rear-view mirror, she catches sight of the sea – the deep-blue horizon beyond the rows of cottages – and can't wait to get down to the beach with Kate to explore. But for now, finding out what awaits them at their new home is her priority.

The lane narrows as Mel drives further up the hill and heads a little way out of the village, the hedgerows and trees above closing in and blocking out the daylight. As another car comes towards her, she's careful not to scrape the crumbling, ivy-choked wall to her left as they pass.

And then she spots it. Moreton Inn – unmistakable from the photos she's already seen online and just as pretty in real life. Her heart pounds, and she can barely take her eyes off the old, thatched building as she approaches, gazing up at the place. Some of the paintwork might be flaking, and there are weeds growing all around but, behind the slightly shabby façade, Mel sees the potential, sees nothing but the perfect home for her and Kate.

She parks on the verge opposite and pulls on the handbrake, looking for signs of life, if anyone is here to greet them.

'Are we here?' Kate says, waking and stretching the moment Mel cuts the engine.

'We are indeed,' Mel replies, feeling another flutter in her heart as she takes it all in – though she's not sure if it's from excitement or trepidation. 'What do you think?'

Kate stares out at the building. 'And that's all ours?' she says, rubbing her eyes. Mel nods proudly. 'Moreton Inn,' she reads from the faded painted sign hanging above the sloped-roof porch. 'Looks more like a country pub than a hotel.'

'You're right,' Mel replies, spotting the wooden tables and chairs set out in front, some broken and rotten. There's a stack of half a dozen or so beer barrels beside the entrance to the car park, along with a few brightly coloured plastic bottle crates. 'Come on, let's investigate.' And if we don't like it, we get back in the car and go, she thinks, though has no idea where to.

Tony was very reasonable about ending the lease on the flat with only two weeks' notice, rather than the required four, but only because his cousin from Ireland was coming over and needed a place to live. She knows Michael would put them up for a bit if necessary, but his place isn't huge and she wouldn't want to impose for long.

No, Mel thinks, shielding her eyes from the sun as she walks across the quiet lane, there's no other option but to make a go of it.

'It's, like, insane that you got given all this,' Kate says as they stretch their legs. 'And the air smells weird,' she adds, tipping her face to the sky, breathing in deeply.

'What you mean is it smells fresh,' Mel says with a smile. 'All this sea air and countryside,' she says, heading towards the front door of the hotel. 'We'll sleep well, if nothing else.'

And a decent night's sleep is what Mel craves most after two weeks of lying awake, startling at every sound. By the time they'd packed up and left, she was even more convinced that Billy had been sniffing around, and certain he'd been in the flat more than once. But that was Billy's style – to slowly toy with her, raise her anxiety, make her believe she was going mad. No, she thinks as she approaches the front door, I've done the right thing. He'll *never* find us here.

CHAPTER THIRTEEN

'Hello?' Mel calls out tentatively as she opens the oak front door. She glances up at the hand-painted licensing sign above the stone surround, but it's worn and faded and impossible to read. She thinks she makes out the name Joy but can't be sure. 'Anyone here?' When no one replies, Mel goes in, with Kate following behind.

What strikes her first is how dark it is inside, though that's because the curtains are closed. The faint smell of beer catches in the back of her throat as she sees they're in some kind of reception area. There's an old wooden counter to the right with a slightly wilting bunch of flowers and, to the left, a staircase with a worn carpet. The two windows either side of the door are draped in heavy velvet curtains, the burgundy fabric faded at the inner edges.

'Mum?' Kate whispers, taking hold of Mel's sweatshirt sleeve. 'Should we be in here, do you think? It doesn't look open.'

'It's OK, love. Probably everyone's busy out the back.'

Mel swallows, not even sure who 'everyone' is. She opens a door to the right of the desk and goes through, finding a much bigger room than the reception area, also with the curtains closed. It seems to be a lounge bar – an array of pub-style tables dotted around with velvet-topped stools and wooden chairs set next to them. A polished oak banquette lines one wall, again with a row of small circular tables. Down the other side of the room is a bar – Mel can just make out the glint of the glasses hanging upside down above the counter, as well as the many bottles along the back, stacked up in front of a mirrored wall. The usual beer pulls line the bar, mats and drip trays placed at intervals. The beery smell is stronger in here, but Mel can see it won't take much more than a good clean and a lick of paint to transform the entire space, and in winter the big open fire will make it so cosy.

'Hello?' she calls out again, beckoning to Kate to follow her. There's a door at the other end of the room, so they go through and find themselves in a light and spacious hallway with various doors off – one of which leads out to the car park.

'Yuck, it stinks,' Kate says, holding her nose.

'It's just disinfectant,' Mel says, thinking that's a good sign. Someone is cleaning the toilets, at least, which she can see are located just down the corridor. It's brighter out here, too, with a couple of skylights, lots of windows and a few houseplants balanced on the low sill that runs the length of the atrium. 'Guess that's the kitchen,' she says, hearing a clattering sound coming from behind the double swing doors. 'Come on. Let's see who's in there.'

Suddenly, one of the doors bursts open and a girl in her twenties is standing there with a pile of metal trays stacked in her arms.

'Oh!' she exclaims, grabbing onto the top few trays as they start to slide off. Mel lunges at them, placing them back.

'I'm so sorry,' Mel says. 'I didn't mean to startle you.'

'That's OK,' says the girl. She has bleached-blonde hair swept up into a tight knot on top of her head, the darker roots tugging at her temples. A floral hairband helps keep it in place. Her face is pale; her cat-like eyes, a piercing sea green, almost out of place on such a young face. 'Can I help you? If you're after food, we don't open for evening meals until five.'

'No, no... I was wondering if the manager was here? Or someone in charge? I'm Mel. Mel Douglas.' She pauses, waiting to see if the girl recognises her name, but her face remains blank.

'That'll be me, I suppose, then. No one else here, really. Apart from Rose, and she won't arrive for another hour. She does the cooking, you see. But there's a complaints box in reception. You can just fill that out if you like, and…' She trails off. 'And we'll see something is done about it.' A little shrug from behind the tower of trays. 'Maybe.'

'You're the manager?' Mel doesn't doubt the girl's capabilities, and she seems confident enough, but she's very young – probably only twenty-one or two – and can't have had much experience running hotels. Even places like this.

'Not really, but no one else is going do it, are they?' She giggles then, though chases it up with a sigh. 'Someone's got to keep the old place going.'

'Well, you can relax. I'm not here to complain. Is it you I should see about… about the hotel? About the transfer?'

'Transfer?' The girl makes a puzzled face, shifting her hold on the stack of trays.

'Do you want me to help you with those? They look heavy,' Mel offers, feeling awkward just standing there.

'Sure, thanks.' The girl eases the stack forward for Mel to take the top few. 'They're going out to the storage shed. There aren't many in for dinner these days, so we don't need half the cooking stuff in there. I was going to give the kitchen a good clean-out. Don't think it's been done in years, and it'll give me something to do. Make me look busy.' The girl laughs again. 'Keep me in a job.'

Mel follows her out of the back door and into the car park around the side of the building. It's a large space which opens up into a decent-sized garden and seating area too, though it's rather overgrown and the patio is uneven and broken.

Mel nudges Kate with her elbow, grinning as she sees her daughter sizing it all up. She's never really had a proper garden to play in before.

'Over here,' the girl says, leading them towards a stone lean-to store attached to the side of the hotel.

Mel follows, glancing up at the rear of the hotel. She doesn't know a lot about building works but is pleased to see that the thatch doesn't look in too much need of repair. The windows could do with a coat of paint though, she thinks and, just as she's looking away, she catches sight of a face at a top-floor window – a flash of something that could have just been a trick of the light. When she looks again, there's no one there.

'Key's in my pocket somewhere,' the girl says, balancing the trays with one hand as she rummages in her apron pocket. 'There we go,' she says once the padlock is off. 'Just dump them anywhere.'

Inside the store room, Mel sees that it's mainly filled with broken furniture, old linen bulging out of cardboard boxes and stacks of crockery. She puts the baking trays on a table as the girl directs, knowing that with a skip on site, she could have it all cleared out in a day.

'I'm Nikki, by the way,' the girl says, wiping her hands down her apron. 'Are you staying with us or just passing through?'

'We're the new owners. Well, my mum is. I'm Kate.' She puffs up proudly – something Mel hasn't seen in a long while.

Nikki pauses for a moment, the glimmer of a smile spreading across her feline-like features. 'Well, very pleased to meet you, Kate.' She reaches out a hand to shake and Kate reciprocates.

'I'm Mel. And it's true – by a strange turn of events, I've…' Mel hesitates, not sure how much she should reveal. 'I've become the new owner, yes. Has anyone informed you and the other staff?'

'No,' Nikki says brightly, accompanied by a little grin, as if such strange occurrences are completely normal.

She heads off back to the hotel then. Mel and Kate follow, glancing at each other and shrugging. They end up in the lounge bar area where Nikki pulls open all the heavy curtains before opening the wooden shutters behind. The afternoon sun streams in through the old glass panes, making the whole place seem much more homely.

'No one tells me anything,' she says, laughing. 'But I'm pleased you're here. Is it a buy-out or something? Are you from a brewery or one of those big hotel chains come to take us over?'

'Nothing quite so corporate,' Mel says, sensing the girl's disappointment. 'And I have no experience running hotels, just so you know.'

'Oh,' Nikki says. 'That's a shame. I was hoping the place was going to get a massive makeover, like on one of those TV shows. Then we all get new uniforms and secure jobs and customers actually start coming and give us something to do.'

'Sorry to disappoint,' Mel says. 'It's strange that no one has mentioned us arriving. The solicitor said it was all in hand.'

'Don't know anything about a solicitor, I'm afraid,' she says, going behind the bar and flicking some switches beneath the counter. Lights come on all around, making it almost seem as if one or two people might be tempted to stop by for a beer. Nikki crouches down, disappearing for a moment. Glass bottles rattle as she mumbles to herself, standing up again and jotting something down in a notebook.

'Got to bottle up,' she says, glancing at her watch. 'Not much in the fridge, and you never know…'

'Never know what?' Kate says, perching on one of the stools. She leans her elbow on the bar, eyeing all the upside-down bottles in the optics rack.

'If anyone might come in, of course.' Nikki blinks slowly at Kate. 'We have to be prepared. I mean, imagine if a coach party turns up. How silly would we look then?'

'Has a coach party ever turned up?' Mel asks.

'Well, no, but that's not the point. And in theory makes it more likely to happen.'

'No it doesn't,' Kate says, cupping her chin in her hands, watching intently as Nikki busies around slicing lemons, checking the ice buckets, testing the beer is flowing correctly.

'Joyce always used to say, "We should live our lives as though Christ was coming this afternoon". And to be fair,' Nikki continues, glancing up from picking out cocktail cherries and placing them in a bowl next to the lemon slices, 'she had a point.'

'That's stupid,' Kate says.

Mel nudges her in the ribs.

'Oww, Mum,' she says, shying away.

'How so?' Nikki replies, unfazed by Kate's directness. In fact, the two seem drawn to each other.

'Because Christ is dead, of course.'

'True,' Nikki says, placing her forearms flat on the bar and leaning forward. She gives a couple more slow blinks. 'But... He came back from the dead once, didn't He? And what if He does that again and ends up here? Where would we be then? That's what Joyce said. Anyway, I just do as I'm told.'

'Is Joyce here, Nikki?' Mel says. 'Is she the manager?' Perhaps this is the person Mel needs to speak to about the transfer. The solicitor had told her that she was expected. 'Can I speak with her?'

'That might prove hard,' Nikki replies, wringing out a cloth under the tap in the sink. She turns round, leaning on the bar again. 'Joyce is dead.'

CHAPTER FOURTEEN

'This is quite cute,' Kate says, standing in the doorway and peeking inside one of the bedrooms off the creaky landing. 'But it's small.'

'It's still twice the size of your bedroom back in Birmingham,' Mel says with a laugh, incredulous at all the space as they explore the hotel. 'Let's check out some of the other rooms. Apart from the final paperwork, the place is as good as mine, so we can take our pick. Have a different one each night if we choose.'

'That bed looks like an antique,' Kate says, running her hand along the carved wooden headboard.

'It's lovely, but it could do with some new linen,' Mel adds, eyeing the dated nylon bedspread. 'Come on, let's dump our bags in here for a bit and have a look around.'

Earlier, when Nikki had revealed that her old boss, Joyce, was dead, Mel had been reluctant to probe too much in case it was still raw. What if it was the stress of running Moreton Inn that had finished her off, or the terrible reviews made her take her own life? Or perhaps financial pressures and huge debts had given her no other option but to end things. But when Nikki had revealed that Joyce, in her mid-seventies, had died of a stroke, Mel had breathed out. Nothing sinister after all.

'I'm so sorry to hear that, Nikki. How upsetting for all the staff,' she'd said, relieved at least that the hotel wasn't to blame.

Nikki had shrugged then, her green eyes blinking slowly. 'Oh no,' she'd said before trotting off back to the kitchen, 'don't be sorry. Things are much better now.'

'How about this one?' Mel says, peering inside room number eight.

Kate walks up to her, having rattled the handle of the room next door. 'Number seven is locked,' she says.

'There's probably a key somewhere,' Mel replies as they go inside, making a mental note to find it.

'This one is OK, I guess,' Kate says, going through into the tiny en suite shower room. 'Wow, look at this funny thing. Why would you put a doll on a toilet?'

Mel laughs. 'Good grief, I've not seen one of these in a long time. My foster mum's aunt had one in her bathroom. Look.' Mel lifts up the plastic doll and reveals a toilet roll beneath its knitted skirt.

Kate bursts out laughing, her hands covering her mouth, her eyebrows raised. 'No *waaay...*' she squeals. 'That's so kitsch, it's unreal.' She pulls out her phone to take a photograph. 'This is going on Insta—'

'No,' Mel says suddenly, taking hold of Kate's wrist. 'No pics online, love.' Her heart speeds up. 'Not... not until we're settled, right?' She smiles, hoping Kate won't press for the real reason: that she doesn't want to give Billy a single clue as to their whereabouts. Even if he's not on Kate's list of followers, she wouldn't put it past him to have fake accounts.

'Sure,' Kate replies, tucking her phone away again. 'I'm not convinced about this room either. Let's look at the others.' She skips off ahead, going down a low-ceilinged, beamy corridor, up a short flight of steps and onto another landing area with four more bedroom doors.

'How about this room then?' Kate says, her hand on the knob of room twelve. 'Whatever it's like inside, I'm gonna have it, OK?'

she says with a cheeky grin. Mel is so relieved that her daughter's mood has lifted since they left Birmingham, that she seems excited at the prospect of a fresh start.

'It could be filled with spiders and snakes,' Mel jokes. 'But you've got to sleep in it whatever, though. That's the deal.' She gives Kate a little tickle.

'Oh, Mu-*um*,' she laughs. 'I'm going in and it's mine, all mine!' With her hand on the knob, she screws up her eyes, a big grin on her face, and pushes the door open but, a moment later, she opens her eyes and lets out a surprised squeak.

Mel comes in, taking her by the shoulders, staring at the floral armchair by the window. There's a woman sitting in it. A very pale and thin woman with mousy hair scooped up and neatly fastened on top of her head. Her skin is smooth and waxy, as if she's never been outside, making her difficult to age. She is reading a book and doesn't glance up.

'Oh, I'm *so* sorry,' Mel says. 'I had no idea anyone was staying here. Please, do forgive us.' She waits for the woman to say something, but she doesn't. She just continues to read, slowly turning a page. Mel wonders if she might be hard of hearing, so she goes up to her, waving her arm a little.

'Hello,' she says. 'I'm really sorry we've intruded. I didn't expect residents.'

After a moment, the woman slowly lifts her head and stares straight at Mel. She says nothing and doesn't even appear to be shocked by her presence. There's just nothing, as if she's empty inside. She blinks once, slowly, before turning her gaze to Kate, who has retreated to the door. Then she looks back at Mel again. No smile, no words, no flicker of shock, anger or surprise. Just nothing.

'We'll leave you in peace,' Mel mouths in an overstated way to make it easier to lip-read, in case she's deaf.

The woman just stares.

'OK, well, I'm sorry again,' she says, walking away backwards until she bumps into Kate. 'Come on, love, let's leave the lady alone. Sorry,' she repeats with a brief wave as they close the door behind them.

*

'That woman in room twelve was weird,' Kate says, dumping several holdalls from the car in room nine, the one she's finally chosen.

'Very,' Mel replies, lowering a box of stuff to the floor. 'And how on earth did we fit all this in the car?' she says, shaking her head at the things they've unloaded.

'She looked as though she'd been in there for ever,' Kate goes on. 'Maybe that's what happens to anyone who comes to stay here. They get trapped, like they're in some impossible computer game so they never leave.'

'I think *you've* been playing too many computer games,' Mel laughs, opening the holdall and taking out a stack of Kate's clothes. She goes over to the chest of drawers – an old brown thing with gold-coloured square knobs. When she opens the top drawer, it's lined with orange and green floral wallpaper. 'That's straight out of the Seventies,' she says, checking it looks reasonably clean before putting Kate's T-shirts and other tops in there.

'Sick,' Kate says, peering in. 'This place is like a museum. It's so cool. Even though she scared me a bit, that old lady is pretty cool too. Like a ghost or something.'

'I'd say less of the old, love,' Mel jokes, dumping a pile of Kate's underwear in another drawer. 'I don't think she can have been too much older than me.'

'She must have been at least eighty, I reckon. And that's super-old.'

'I reckon she's early fifties, fifty-five tops. And that's only fifteen years or so older than me. Your perception of old is very different to mine, young lady.' Mel goes in for a tickle then, making Kate squeal. That's when they spot Nikki in the doorway.

'Settling in OK?' she asks. 'I brought you these.' She holds out a pile of fresh towels – not the usual hotel-issue white bath sheets, but rather half a dozen patterned and striped towels in varying shades of turquoise, yellow and green.

'Thank you, that's kind,' Mel says, taking them and placing them on the bed. They smell fresh, at least, she thinks.

'We're opening up the bar shortly,' Nikki continues. 'We sometimes get a few in on a Saturday, so it'd be a good chance for you to meet one or two of the locals. Also, Tom said he'd come by for a pint. He's maintenance. Rose is in the kitchen making her famous lasagne. I told everyone you're here.' Nikki grins, the edges of her almond-shaped eyes almost reaching her tight hairline as she beams. She's changed into what looks like some kind of uniform – a stretchy black skirt and a white blouse with a name badge pinned crookedly above the top pocket.

'Great,' Mel says, wringing her hands together, knowing that somehow she has to make Moreton Inn profitable. And to achieve that, she needs a motivated team. Or a *new* team, she thinks, imagining Tom to be a pensioner who occasionally dabbles with a screwdriver if the mood takes him.

'See you downstairs then,' Nikki says, heading off and closing the door behind her.

'They're hoping you're going to save this place, Mum,' Kate says, lifting her beloved computer from its box and blowing dust from the top. Mel had saved and saved in the run-up to last Christmas, taken out a payday loan, done extra shifts at The Cedars, and still Michael had stepped in with the last couple of hundred pounds so she had enough to buy Kate the gaming machine she so longed for. He'd told Mel he'd had a spot of good fortune, that Kate deserved a decent gift. Mel didn't ask questions but accepted gratefully.

'That's what's worrying me,' Mel replies, laughing. 'But at least Nikki seems keen.'

'Too keen, if you ask me,' Kate says, putting her computer monitor on the dressing table in the window. 'She's trying too hard. Olivia at school does that. Comes across all goody-goody then stabs you in the back.'

'Well, I'm sure Nikki isn't like that. Let's give her a chance, eh?' Mel gathers up the towels and takes them into the bathroom, unfolding them to hang on the rail. But she freezes, stifling a squeal as the stiff body of a dead mouse falls out of one of them.

CHAPTER FIFTEEN

It was the delicious smell that drew Mel downstairs. After she'd disposed of the mouse, trying to convince herself that Nikki couldn't possibly have known it was there, all she wanted to do was lie on her bed and take stock of what had been a long and extraordinary day. Tiredness didn't come close to describing the deep ache in her bones. It hardly seemed possible that this morning she was emptying out the last dregs of their belongings from the little flat in Birmingham, loading up the car and then, as if by magic, she and Kate were in a hotel less than a mile from the sea in a village she'd never heard of two weeks ago.

Her hotel.

According to Robert Hedge, the other firm dealing with the matter had released documentation a few days earlier, allowing Mel to move to the premises as if it were her own. While the final paperwork hadn't quite yet been processed, Robert assured her that the legalities were in hand.

'Until the deed is transferred, you are still free to leave and disclaim the inheritance. But you can feel secure that it cannot work the other way round. The other party cannot withdraw. It all works in your favour, Melanie. Rest easy that someone has got your back.'

'But *who*?' Mel had asked, time and time again over the last couple of weeks. And she was always met with the same answer.

'I'm afraid it's not in my power to release that information, mainly because I don't know it myself. You may find, though,' he'd said, in that fatherly way of his, 'that in time, your benefactor reveals themselves.'

Various papers arrived to sign over the next few days, along with a couple of explanatory phone calls, and a quick visit back to the office to sign several documents and Mel was given the go-ahead to move to Moreton Inn. She'd had no idea what to expect and, having been here only a few hours, she was still none the wiser. Surely someone must know something. And she couldn't help wondering if Joyce had had something to do with it. She needed to find out how long ago the woman had died, plus her full name, then she'd be able to run a search on her will.

'That smells amazing,' Mel says, the swing door to the kitchen bouncing shut behind her as she goes in. 'Hi, you must be Rose. I'm Mel,' she adds, going up to the woman standing at the stove. The woman turns, revealing herself to be in her late fifties, greying hair piled up in a messy bun, with a sheen of perspiration on her ruddy round cheeks.

With a startled look, the woman hesitates before wiping her right hand down her apron front and extending it to Mel. 'I'm Rose, cook and chief bottle-washer,' she says, giving Mel a handshake that seems to go on for ever. 'Nikki told me all about you. Good luck to you, is all I'll say.' The woman's large chest heaves in time with her laugh as she exposes a rack of crooked teeth from behind her plump lips.

'Oh… thanks,' Mel says. 'Nikki said you're making lasagne.'

'Pretty much the only thing anyone comes in for,' she admits, clamping her arms around her large body. 'That said, fish-and-chip night draws a few out of the woodwork.'

Mel has a flash of homesickness, reminded of Tony's fresh battered cod, the smell winding its way up into their flat. She shakes her head briefly. After what's happened the last couple of weeks, there's no going back.

'I can't wait to try it,' Mel says, glancing around the old-fashioned kitchen.

Coughing loudly, Rose turns back to stirring the huge vat of bubbling sauce before dumping a pile of grated cheese into another pot simmering on a low heat. 'Things haven't been the same since… since Joyce passed away,' she says.

'How come?' Mel asks, hoping this is her chance to find out more.

'We've lost our way a bit, truth be told. Nikki's tried, but with no money to spend, it's been tough.' Rose turns away and lets out a second long, rasping cough. 'Joyce had her troubles. I'm no gossip and I didn't know her very well, but I do know that she loved this old place. It was her dream. But over the years, what with one thing and another, it turned into a nightmare for her.'

'Troubles?' Mel asks. 'I can see why she loved Moreton Inn. It certainly has charm.'

Rose stares at her, eyeing her up and down, one hand idly stirring the sauce. 'You mean you don't know?' She lets out a laugh.

'No, I don't know much at all, other than that I'm somehow meant to make the place profitable.' Mel feels her chest tighten at the thought. Nikki and Rose are clearly relying on her for keeping their jobs, and she has no experience of renovating property either.

'Best you don't ask, chuck,' Rose says. 'But we're… well, we're glad to have you here all the same.'

'I'm… I'm glad to be here too,' Mel replies, hoping that's still true. 'What can I do to help? If you're expecting customers, there must be something I can get on with?'

Rose pauses for a moment, looking confused. 'Help? Well… I mean, you could make sure the dining area is prepped and shipshape.' She pauses. 'While you're still here,' she mutters, turning back to the pan.

'Sure,' Mel replies, feeling somewhat adrift in her new home as she pushes through the swing doors.

*

'*Nah…*' Mel hears from across the room as she's filling up the glass salt and pepper shakers. The voice of a man. What she needs is a notebook, to write down everything that has to be changed – from big things, such as building works and renovations, right down to the smaller touches, like new salt and pepper mills rather than these old things.

She looks up.

'Nah…' comes the voice again. The man, early forties, is at the bar glancing over his shoulder at her. He turns back to Nikki, who hands him a pint. A *customer*, she thinks. Promising.

'Mel,' Nikki calls out, 'come and meet Tom.'

Mel lays down the ground pepper container, fighting back a sneeze as she gets up from the banquette. For some reason, she's not aware of crossing the heavily patterned carpet. Isn't aware of her hand reaching out and shaking that of the tall man as he extends his arm. And it's only when he says 'Nah' for a third time, with a glint in his unusually blue eyes, that she manages to speak.

'Nah?' Mel replies as if it's a perfectly normal thing to say around here, perhaps some strange local custom or greeting.

'Your T-shirt,' the man says in a deep voice as Mel struggles to unhook her eyes from his.

'Ohh,' she says, finally breaking the spell of whatever it is that has seemingly paralysed her. 'I couldn't resist buying it,' she adds. 'It kind of sums me up.' Mel laughs, wishing she hadn't when it comes out as a croak.

'Funny,' he says, turning back to the bar and taking a sip of his pint. Mel isn't sure that her Nah T-shirt is that funny – rather a bit old and faded now – but she humours him with a smile. Though before she can say anything, the man is unbuttoning his blue check shirt. Then he pulls it wide open.

Mel feels her eyes widening, a gasp creeping up her throat, not sure how much of himself he's about to reveal, but when he does, she can't hold back the spray of laughter.

'Now that's too funny,' she says, rocking back on her heels as she reads the 'Yess!' slogan on his T-shirt.

He gives an overstated shrug, each of his big hands up around his shoulders, a broad grin appearing within the smattering of blond stubble. 'Great minds,' he says. 'I'm Tom,' he adds. 'Seeing as Nikki's not going to intro…' He stops, spotting that she's not behind the bar any more, that it's just the two of them. 'Nice to meet you.'

'Nah,' Mel replies in a silly voice. 'I'm Mel, the new owner. I know I may look like some exhausted and overgrown teenage indie band groupie, but I'm ready to get stuck in.'

'*Yess*,' Tom replies, winking as he buttons up his shirt again. 'So what brought you to the area?' he asks, perching on one of the bar stools. 'And more precisely, why Moreton Inn?'

'Truth is,' Mel replies, taking the stool next to Tom's, 'I don't actually know.'

'Curious,' Tom says, having more of his pint. 'May I get you a drink?'

'Thanks. I'll have a Coke, please,' she says to Nikki who's just come back, deciding she needs to keep a clear head for now. A nightcap later won't hurt though, knowing her deep exhaustion will prevent her from sleeping. It's as if sleep is beyond her now – having kept vigil the last couple of weeks, only dozing lightly, waking up at the slightest sound. She'd needed to stay alert.

'So go on then. Give me three words to describe why you're here.' Tom grins at her, giving her a sideways look. For a moment, Mel can't speak, let alone think of three words that sum up her situation.

'Umm…' she says, biting her lip.

'Two words left,' Tom laughs.

'Christ,' Mel replies, laughing as he stares at her over the rim of his glass. She can't help her eyes wandering down his forearms – tanned and lightly covered in blond hair. *Strong* arms, she thinks.

Hands and arms used to doing manual labour. 'Nooo,' she says finally, laughing. 'It's too hard.'

'So your three words are "Umm", "Christ" and "nooo",' Tom says, making a puzzled face.

Mel covers hers, leaning her elbows on the bar. She laughs as she looks up, swishing her hair back over her shoulders. 'Actually, that's probably quite accurate,' she says. She's about to continue, but spots someone coming into the bar. The flutter of excitement in her stomach at the prospect of an actual customer makes her slide off her stool, as if she should be greeting them, welcoming them, ushering them to a table.

But when she sees who it is, she stops – freezes, one foot on the floor, the other still on the rung of the stool. It's the woman from room twelve.

'Must be six o'clock,' Tom says in a low voice, glancing at his watch.

Mel looks up at him, a quizzical look in her eye, before looking at the woman again, who is now seated at a table for one in the front window. It's as if she has teleported herself there without even moving. Mel watches as she lays her book on the table, simultaneously unfolding a paper napkin onto her lap.

'That's Miss Sarah,' Tom says quietly, leaning in close to Mel. 'She's been here for ever and never says a single word.'

CHAPTER SIXTEEN

'Never says a word?' Mel repeats, also whispering. 'Been here for ever?' Her mind whirs, putting two and two together, wondering if she's the woman Robert Hedge mentioned. She hasn't glanced up from her book since she sat down. It's as if she's part of the furniture, one of the fixtures and fittings, though Mel can't help thinking that her ghostlike presence, her pale face and frumpy plain clothing is actually drawing attention to her more than anything.

'Nope,' Tom says. 'Or rather, *nah.*'

'I'll be changing my T-shirt tomorrow,' Mel laughs, rolling her eyes. 'How come she never speaks?' she says quietly, sliding back onto her stool.

'No one really knows. Miss Sarah just *is.*'

'And she's been here a long time?' Mel's mind is racing, wondering why she has a right to stay at the hotel, have her meals provided. She takes a sip of her Coke.

'Yup. As long as I've had anything to do with the place. And that's a long while.' Tom laughs. 'My dad used to do odd jobs around here, look after the garden, and I'd come and hang out with him as a lad. I remember her from back then, though she was a lot younger, of course. In my late teens, I'd come in for a few pints with my mates and we'd sometimes see her.

'Then I moved away from the area, but Dad's health declined, so I came back a couple of months ago to look after him. That's when I took on a few maintenance jobs here and there. I don't need to as I've got my own construction company, but it gives me something else useful to do.'

'I see,' Mel replies, not seeing at all. 'I'm sorry to hear your dad's been poorly.' She studies the woman again, expecting to be caught staring. But she seems oblivious to anyone else in the room. 'Why is she called *Miss* Sarah?'

Tom shakes his head. 'Again, no idea. It's just what she was always known as,' he says in a low voice.

'How old is she?' Mel is mindful of keeping her voice low too.

'She's one of those people who never seems to age,' Tom says, emptying his glass to the halfway mark. 'When I was a kid, she can't have been that much more than a kid herself.'

'Has she *ever* spoken?' Mel asks, trying to understand the strange situation.

'Again, no one really knows. Joyce took care of her, and it was always just assumed they were mother and daughter. But after she died, nothing changed for Miss Sarah. Breakfast, lunch, dinner – always the same times, always eaten in here at that table. Occasionally she'll go for a walk, but aside from that all she does is read.'

Mel glances at her again, her mind bursting with possibilities. It's hard to tell if her hair is the palest grey or the lightest blonde. It's swept high on her head in a neat chignon, and the light blue cardigan she wears – or is it grey? – over a cream blouse seems to swamp her small frame. The colour of the A-line skirt she has on above sensible, flat black shoes is equally difficult to determine. It could be beige; it could be more of a greeny-grey. But however hard she is to gauge, there's no doubt in Mel's mind that this must be the woman the legal documents were referring to. The woman who has a right to remain. Remain *silent*, Mel thinks.

'What do you know about Joyce?' Mel asks. If she recently died, it makes perfect sense that she is the mysterious benefactor. But why? Mel doesn't know a single person called Joyce.

'My dad's the one to ask. He knew her well back then. Had a bit of a crush on her, if I'm honest. Joyce ran this place for donkey's years, though she never did anything much with it, as you can see,' he adds.

'So she actually owned Moreton Inn?' Mel asks.

'As far as I know,' Tom replies. 'She was… well, let's just say Joyce was one of those characters who didn't see much good in anything. If the sun was shining, she'd grumble that the weather was bad.' Tom laughs. 'I don't think she was always like that. Donald, her partner, had a lot to do with how she was, I suspect.'

'Donald?' Mel asks, trying to piece everything together. Maybe he was the one she should be focusing on. 'Is he still alive?'

Tom nods. 'And he's a nasty piece of work. He and Joyce weren't married but he was always hanging around here. Dad had a good few run-ins with him over the years. As did most people.'

'Does he ever come into the bar?'

'Not to my knowledge these days,' Tom says. 'And you wouldn't want him to. He didn't treat Joyce well. No one understood why she didn't just kick him out.'

'I guess… well… sometimes I guess it's not that easy,' Mel says quietly, glancing at the floor.

'Anyway, as you can see, Moreton Inn needs dragging into the present. I hope you've got deep pockets.'

Mel smiles, glad of the change of subject. 'Rose said there'd be a few customers in for food later.' The more she hears about the place's history, the more she's tempted to play her 'get out of jail' card and call Robert Hedge to reverse the process. But she knows she can't. Whatever secrets the place holds, she has to make a go of it.

'Ah, you've met Rose,' Tom adds, raising his eyebrows. 'She was very close to Joyce and was one of the few who got on with Donald, according to Dad.'

'She was?' Mel says, puzzled, remembering Rose's words. *I didn't know her very well.* Perhaps she'd misheard.

Tom nods as he sips his pint. 'So what made you buy the place?' he asks, ducking behind the bar and pulling a packet of nuts off the display rack. He waves them at Nikki and she nods, jotting something down in a notebook at the other end of the bar.

For some reason, Mel feels she can trust Tom, reckons he knows things that could help her. 'I… well, I didn't actually buy it. I was left it in a will. In a roundabout sort of way.'

'So are you Joyce's long-lost relative or something? Did you get tracked down by one of those heir hunter people?' Tom grins, pulling open the packet of nuts and putting it on the bar between them. 'Help yourself.'

'It'll sound weird, mainly because it *is* weird. But I have no idea if it was Joyce who left me the hotel. How long ago did she die?'

Tom thinks. 'Must be a bit over a year ago now, if Dad's correct. But his memory's not the best these days.'

'Nikki mentioned a stroke,' Mel says, finishing off her Coke.

Tom nods. 'Apparently, but…' He stares at her, as if he's about to say more but is gauging how much she already knows.

'But?'

'Probably just rumours, and I don't like speaking ill of the dead, especially as my old dad was as sweet as caramel on her.' Tom makes a fond face, as if the thought of his dad having a crush was amusing. 'But from what I've heard, it seemed like a bit more than a stroke to me.'

'Really?' Mel says, her heart kicking up. 'What happened?'

'I didn't see first-hand, of course, but put it this way: a stroke doesn't give you head injuries and a bloodied face, does it?'

Mel thinks. 'I suppose it could if the person having the stroke took a tumble afterwards.'

'Indeed,' Tom says. 'But not when you have the stroke in bed. In your sleep.' His voice is still low, cautious that no one overhears him. 'But as I said, I'm not one for tittle-tattle and can only go on what I've heard. Some of it's come from Dad, so may not be accurate. The old boy's not all there these days. His dementia's getting worse.'

'I'm really sorry to hear that,' Mel says, feeling unsettled. 'What was Joyce's last name?' She wants all the information she can get.

'Lawrence,' Tom says, draining the last of his pint and grabbing a few nuts before standing up to go. 'Joyce Lawrence. Dad once told me that when she took over Moreton Inn in her mid-twenties, she was a "fun, feisty blonde bombshell". His exact words. She had grand plans for the place, apparently, after her stage career didn't exactly take off in London. But when Bray came on the scene, she gradually turned into a downtrodden, miserable husk of a woman over the years. That's how I remember her as a lad – middle-aged and grumpy. We were all a bit scared of her.'

'Blonde bombshell isn't how I'd imagined her,' Mel comments.

'It's funny what Dad remembers,' Tom says, putting his coat on. 'He'll forget to wear shoes when he goes out, but ask him about things from forty years ago, and he's all over it.'

And it's as Tom is leaving, saying that he'll be back in a few days to go over any potential odd jobs that Mel may want doing, that Miss Sarah looks up from her book. As Mel walks past her table, she offers her a smile. But the woman just stares through her, as if she doesn't even exist.

CHAPTER SEVENTEEN

'I've brought you this, love,' Mel says, knocking gently on Kate's bedroom door before going in. The tray is balanced on one hand as she shuts the door behind her. 'You must be starving. Not sure I'll make a great waitress—' She stops, seeing Kate jump up from a lying to a sitting position on her bed, shoving something under the covers. Her cheeks burn scarlet.

'Everything OK?' Mel asks, sitting down beside her and handing her the tray.

'Thanks, Mum. This looks… delicious.' Kate ducks down to give it a sniff, then shrugs as if it might actually be, despite appearances.

'It tastes nice. I met Rose earlier, the chef, and she made huge quantities of lasagne. Then we had about two customers in, and each got free seconds just so it didn't go to waste. Rose and Nikki had some too, as well as… as well as that strange woman. She was in the restaurant.'

'The creepy, silent one?' Kate says, shovelling a forkful of food into her mouth. She makes an appreciative face.

Mel nods. 'She's called Miss Sarah, apparently. Bit weird, the "Miss" part. I reckon she's the woman who's allowed to live here. I still have no idea why. And it turns out the previous owner…' Mel trails off, deciding not to tell Kate the gory details.

'Maybe she's a ghost, really,' Kate says, wiping her chin with the paper napkin.

'A hungry ghost, in that case. She polished off a decent portion of lasagne. Rose carried it over to her and put it in front of her. Then Nikki brought over a lemon drink from the bar. They knew exactly what she wanted without her saying a word.'

Mel stops herself, not wanting to upset Kate. This is their new home and she doesn't want her unsettled. Moving here wasn't simply to escape Billy; it's also a chance for Kate to make friends, start a new school, shake off the past. 'Anyway, for such a skinny creature, Miss Sarah sank the entire lot within a few minutes. Then she scuttled off. Back to her room, I imagine.'

'Yeah, I saw her,' Kate says, glancing up.

'You did?'

'On the landing. I heard this weird weeping sound and went out to see what it was. She was just standing there, outside my room, crying but not actually crying. There were no tears or anything. Just this sound. Like a puppy whining for its mother.'

Mel's eyes widen. 'Oh God, that sounds strange. She didn't upset you, did she?'

'No. She just looked at me for a bit, and I looked at her and then she… well, then I just shut the door.' Kate's cheeks colour as she stares down at her plate, cutting up her lasagne.

Mel nods. 'Good. I'm going to introduce myself to her properly tomorrow. Guess I just have to accept her right to be here and treat her like any other guest.' Until I find out more, she thinks, looking around Kate's room. She ruffles her daughter's hair. 'You've done a good job in here, Katie. You've been busy.'

'It feels a bit more like home now.'

Mel sees that Kate has set up her beloved computer equipment on the table in the window and arranged a few framed photographs beside the monitor. She shudders when she spots a picture of Billy.

'Nice that you have a photo of… of your dad out, love. I don't recognise that one.'

Kate shrugs and eats more lasagne, not making eye contact with Mel, who knows that's a sign to back off.

Her eyes flick to her ex's photo again. There's no denying she still finds Billy attractive – the mischievous look in his eye bewitching. And while he wasn't the burliest man around, he never dodged a fight, never feared a six-foot-four man taking a swipe at him. Billy was agile and quick. Quick-witted, too. Sharp body, sharp mind.

'That looks pretty,' Mel says, eyeing the batik wall cloth Kate has pinned above the fireplace. She's draped a string of fairy lights over the mantelpiece and lit a few of her beloved scented candles. She's unpacked all her clothes, too, the empty bags stashed on top of the old wardrobe. Despite the worn carpet, the grubby paintwork, the room feels cosy with its sloping ceiling and exposed beams.

Kate glances up from her food and smiles.

'We'll get the rest of our stuff sent on soon,' Mel says, knowing she can't leave it with Michael for ever. 'If you want to stay on, that is.' Birmingham is no place for them now, not after what happened before they left.

Forty-seven – that's how many times Mel's phone had rung in quick succession, with Billy's name appearing on the screen over and over so fast that she didn't even have time to go into her settings to block him before the next call came.

Her hands were shaking as she lay on the sofa, wrapped up in her duvet with Kate sleeping only a room away. All she could do was put her phone on silent and watch her screen light up as if it were about to ignite in her hands. There were three voicemail messages left – each one silent, each one telling her nothing. Except the last one said everything – *I'm out here. I'm watching. I'm waiting.*

What she heard in the empty message made her get up off the sofa, her legs feeling weak as she checked all the windows were secure before barricading the front door with a chair wedged under the handle. The ambulance siren she'd heard moments before in the street below, the calls and jeers of a group of youths messing about and yelling out a girl's name – they were the exact same sounds she had heard in the background of Billy's voicemail. Her blood had run cold that night and she'd not slept a wink.

Kate looks up from her food, smiling. 'Yeah, I think I do want to stay here, actually,' she says with something of a sparkle in her eye. Something inside Mel relaxes.

'Agreed,' she replies. 'It's a funny old place, but there's something quirky about it that just feels…' Mel glances to the ceiling, trying to find the right words. 'That just feels… *homely*. Does that make sense?' She reaches out and touches Kate's hand as it rests on the bedcovers.

'Totally, Mum,' she replies, grinning. 'I can't wait to explore tomorrow. And I'll google the local schools, too. I could start next week after May half-term.'

Mel's heart swells. For Kate to be willingly discussing schools is a huge thing for her. She prays she'll fit in and not be picked on again. All she wants is for Kate to be happy. But the good feelings are short-lived as Mel senses something vibrating beneath the bedspread, directly underneath where her hand is touching Kate's.

A phone.

She glances at the bedside table where Kate has turned on the lamp and set out the book she's reading, along with her glasses, her headphones, a glass of water. And on top of the book is her regular phone – the Samsung Kate uses every day.

CHAPTER EIGHTEEN

Over the next few days, Mel spent her time finding out as much as she could about Moreton Inn and how it was run – or *not* run, as it soon became clear. Nikki and Rose, with the assistance of an occasional cleaner, had obviously been doing their best to carry things on since Joyce passed away, but without many customers or guests, without a clear vision and funds to build the business, even someone as inexperienced as Mel had no trouble seeing that they were on a downward spiral.

She'd delved through the record-keeping, poring over the books both before and after Joyce's passing, scanning down the itemised list of purchases. Everything from sacks of potatoes to kegs of beer, cleaning materials and bulk-bought crisps – the outgoings far exceeded the list of takings, especially with wages factored in.

Mel had also flipped through the payslips, going back several years, with one name particularly catching her eye – Donald Bray. As Joyce's partner, it made sense that he was on the payroll, although the amount he received each week was significantly higher than the others. And nowhere could she see evidence that Joyce was taking a wage herself.

Feeling overwhelmed, Mel had closed all the files and put them back on the shelf, deciding to focus on the renovations. The upshot was, she had no idea if she was up to the job of running Moreton Inn, and her resolve wavered hourly. The tasks ahead seemed mammoth and, four days after their arrival, she felt as though she'd been turning in circles. And there were still barely any customers.

'Why don't you come and help me pace out where the new extension will go?' she says to Kate, who has just emerged from her room at nearly midday. 'Get some fresh air instead of playing computer games all day.'

'Do I have to?' Kate grumbles, taking a bag of crisps from behind the bar.

'Healthy breakfast,' Mel says with a wink, giving an overstated look at her watch. 'And yes, you do. I need someone to hold the string tight while I peg it in.' Mel opens up another of the architect's plans she'd found in Joyce's office, spreading the large sheet of paper out on the bar.

'I found all these documents, look,' she says, beckoning Kate over. 'Seems as though planning permission was granted and is still current, the designs all drawn up and approved. But works were never actually started.' Mel wonders what prevented the build. 'It actually looks a pretty decent idea, and the quotes aren't astronomical.' She knew the funds soon to be released to her would easily cover the work as well as giving her a large buffer to live on until business picked up.

'Can't we go for a walk down to the sea instead?' Kate says, giving the plans a cursory glance as she stuffs her hand into the bag of ready salted. 'Yuck, these are stale,' she says after taking a bite. She drops the bag onto the bar.

'Hmm?' Mel says vaguely, distracted by several letters between the architect and Joyce. It was strange to see the deceased woman's handwriting, albeit in photocopies – a hard-to-read scrawl slanting diagonally down the page.

Dear Mr Taylor,

I must insist that you take my suggestion for the siting of the new extension seriously. Erecting it directly behind the restaurant is a mistake and will not enhance the character of the old building. I wish you to submit plans for the structure on the north elevation, as discussed at our meeting. There's simply no way I can condone the council's recommendation and refuse to proceed in that vein.

Sincerely, Joyce Lawrence.

The letter feels like a tiny insight into the woman's character, her determination about the extension clear. Mel wonders why she was so against the council's recommended location. And if Joyce Lawrence *is* her mysterious benefactor, then she wants to know everything about her. What if she's a relative? A long-lost aunt or distant second cousin?

The pang in Mel's heart doesn't go unnoticed – a tight tugging, familiar to her over the years. She made the decision a long time ago not to track down family members, and certainly not her mother, who had seen fit to discard her at birth. However tough the circumstances, however hard times were, Mel can't even begin to imagine abandoning Kate. As she'd once said to Michael, back when they were kids at the children's home, *If my mother saw fit to throw me out, then I* must *be trash...*

Unlike her, he'd done everything in his power to trace his birth parents, eventually reuniting with them, briefly, aged nineteen. But the pain that ensued for Michael was reason enough for Mel not to attempt something similar. While his mother had died two years before he traced his birth family, his father had immediately rejected him, stating that he couldn't possibly be related to a gay man. He'd got three other sons and told Michael that he didn't need another.

Unperturbed by his experience, hoping Mel's would be different, Michael had bought her a DNA testing kit last Christmas, thinking it would be fun and would help her feel more connected if she at least knew she had relatives, however distant, even if she chose not to get in touch or meet them. Mel had been tempted to do it, send off the sample of saliva that Michael had persuaded her to collect in the little tube, but she couldn't go through with it, and had thrown the sample in the bin. It felt symbolic – as though she were trashing her family just as they had trashed her.

'Seems like Joyce didn't like the architect's plans for some reason, nor the council's decision not to approve what she *actually* wanted,' Mel says to herself, biting on the end of her pen. 'Come on, Katie. Make yourself useful and follow me.'

Kate gets down off the stool, grumbling about being hungry, trailing Mel outside.

'This is where Joyce wanted the extension to be, on the north side,' Mel says, surveying the area. 'Which is silly, look, as it would have completely blocked the car park entrance, which clearly can't be moved.'

In the file, the architect, and indeed the council, had stated that the only viable place for an extension was directly off the back of the main building and, because the building wasn't listed, they'd given the go-ahead. Mel could see it would bring light flooding into the restaurant through the new orangery and open out on to what could be a lovely garden, if only it were tamed.

'You know what, love?' Mel says, ushering Kate over to the patio area. 'With the extension here, we could host wedding receptions.' She glances over at the overgrown area of lawn, spotting what looks like a raised stone pond and fountain among the brambles. 'Needs a bit of imagination, obviously,' she says, laughing. 'And weeding.'

Kate stands there, her hands shoved in her jeans pockets, her freckled nose slightly wrinkled, her eyes narrowing as she looks about.

'Right. You stand here and hold this while I measure ten metres.' Mel hands Kate the end of the builder's tape measure she'd found in a pile of tools left in the back hallway. She wants to get an idea of the size of the new extension, conscious of getting the garden into shape for the height of summer – only a month or so away. There's no point in landscaping areas that will be dug up.

'OK, don't move,' Mel says, banging a piece of wood into the ground. One by one, she marks out the four corners of the extension. 'We need a big terrace here, don't you think?' she says, glancing at Kate, who's texting with one thumb, the tape measure still in her other hand.

'Yeah…' Kate replies, staring at her phone.

'Oh, hello,' Mel says under her breath, distracted by a figure walking through the car park. 'Hi, Tom,' she calls out. She's not seen him since their first night here. Quickly, she smooths down her T-shirt and runs her fingers through her hair.

'Hi, Mel. Nice to see you're a "Badass" today, rather than a "Nah".' He stops, standing with his hands on his hips, spotting the pegs and string. 'Is this the new extension Joyce had in mind? Or *not* in mind, I should say.' He laughs. 'And who might this young lady be?' he adds, looking at Kate while sweeping an errant strand of blond hair off his forehead.

'This is Kate, my daughter. Tom does a few odd jobs around the hotel, Kate,' she explains, suddenly aware of how sweaty and dusty she feels, mainly from rummaging around in store cupboards earlier.

'Hi,' Kate says, still without looking up from her phone. Mel catches her breath as she spots what appears to be the outline of another phone in Kate's front jeans pocket. She knows she's going to have to ask her about it – where it came from, how she's afforded it. It was probably what she heard ringing in the flat that night. But Mel is wary of rocking the boat – especially as part of her isn't sure she wants to know the truth. And especially not in front of Tom.

'What do you mean, Joyce *didn't* have it in mind?' Mel asks Tom, catching the scent of his body wash or shampoo on the breeze. He's in work gear – torn jeans, heavy boots and a thick workman's top – and he's holding a pair of builder's gloves.

Tom smiles, dimples puckering his cheeks behind the smattering of stubble. 'Joyce wanted to extend the hotel, but only if it was done *her* way.' Tom points to the car park entrance. 'She insisted the architect put in for works here, and even though he knew it was futile, he told Joyce that she could maybe appeal. But she never did.'

'I see,' Mel says, shielding her face from the sun, wondering if Joyce was the stubborn type. 'The extension is the only major building work I'm going to tackle this year. I'll redecorate downstairs, and maybe revamp a few of the bedrooms so they're ready to let. But I want to focus on drawing in locals to the beer garden and get them eating our food first. I was awake most of the night concocting new menus, though I'm hardly a chef, plus I've got so many plans for how to promote the place, not to mention the things I've got in mind for the garden overhaul.' Mel takes a deep breath, feeling excited by all her plans.

Tom folds his arms, a small smile creeping across his face, an appreciative look in his eyes. 'Badass indeed,' he says, flicking a look at her T-shirt again.

CHAPTER NINETEEN

'That man fancies you,' Kate says as she and Mel walk arm in arm down the hill from the hotel a couple of days later. The lane is narrow, widening only when they reach the outskirts of the village. It's a pleasant fifteen-minute stroll to the sea but will be a harder walk on the way back. The afternoon sun hangs directly ahead of them and Mel is glad she brought her sunglasses.

'We could run a shuttle service several times a day for guests,' she says, thinking out loud. 'So they can get to the beach and explore the shops and sights easily. I could buy a six- or eight-seater, perhaps do outings to Lyme Regis, too.' Mel taps a reminder note into her phone, which is already bursting with new ideas she's had over the last few days.

'Don't ignore me, Mum,' Kate goes on, giving Mel a poke in the ribs. Mel turns suddenly, letting out a squeak and lunging at Kate for a tickle. They both laugh, stumbling and giggling. 'That guy, Tom. He definitely fancies you. I could tell the other day when we were measuring up the site. And he's come around a couple of times since, asking if you were about. I told him you were out.'

'He has?' Mel says quickly as their steps fall back into rhythm. Then she adds, 'Nonsense. It was just a joke we'd had about T-shirt slogans. He doesn't know yet that I'm queen of them.' She winks across at Kate.

'You want to put that sweary one on next time. That'll freak him out.'

The pair laugh, feeling the warm, late-spring breeze on their faces as they head down towards the sea. Kate had kept busy earlier, researching local schools and checking out doctors and dentists online, making a list of where they needed to register. But by the afternoon of their sixth day, they both decided they needed to escape the walls of Moreton Inn.

Mel had been woken early by the sound of gulls swooping low over the hotel, their cries reminding her how close to the sea they were. She was exhausted and felt overwhelmed by everything she'd taken on. Plus she still hadn't tackled the issue about Kate having what seemed to be a secret second phone.

Logic told her it was probably just an old one she was using to chat to her online gaming friends, to save giving out her real number. But at only twelve, Mel was uncomfortable with that too.

'And anyway, you're being ridiculous. Tom is definitely not interested in me. I'm sure I've already put him off,' Mel says, smiling and shaking her head as they arrive in the village centre. 'Wow, this is so pretty,' she adds, looking around the small square with its neatly cut grass and tubs of flowers.

'Which means you fancy him back, right? Ooh, Mum's in love,' Kate teases, chanting the last bit over and over.

'Stop it, young lady, or it's no dinner and bed by seven for you,' Mel jokes.

'But I've got a gaming session booked tonight,' Kate retorts, a concerned look on her face. It gives Mel a way to bring up what's on her mind as they head past a little row of shops – a baker, a butcher and a hardware store. Around the corner there's a greengrocer's.

'I'm waiting to spot the candlestick maker next,' Mel says, laughing, conscious she's still stalling mentioning the phone. 'How cute is this place?' she says, spotting the ice cream shop just as Kate does.

'Oh my God. *Want*,' Kate squeaks, dashing up to the window. A young couple sit outside with two waffle cones topped with pastel-coloured ices.

'Then you shall have,' Mel replies, coming up beside her daughter, who is ogling all the different flavours. 'But let me just dash into the newsagent next door to grab a paper first. Wait here a second.'

Mel leaves Kate to choose a flavour and goes into the small shop, looking around for the newspapers and magazines.

'Excuse me,' she says to a man, probably in his sixties or even seventies, judging by the gnarled and worn look on his face. He's tall with a gut hanging over his trousers, a stained shirt above, and it's not long before Mel catches a whiff of him. He stares at her, making no attempt to move out of her way as he blocks the small gap between the shelves. She notices his tattooed knuckles when he reaches out for something – LOVE and HATE written in faded, bruise-coloured ink.

'Can I get past, please?' she says, trying again.

He turns slowly, leering down at her with a grim expression that reminds Mel of a knotty old tree stump. Then he takes a step sideways, blocking her way even more.

'I just want to grab a newspaper,' she adds, not liking the look of him at all, nor the way he's sizing her up. His cheek twitches under one eye.

For a second, Mel wonders if she should forget the paper and leave, but she refuses to be intimidated by the rude man, so attempts to squeeze through the small gap, even if it means brushing against him. But when she tries, he shoves into her.

'Oww…' Mel cries as she stumbles, trying to keep her balance. But as he turns to leave, he pushes her again and Mel falls against the shelves, knocking some tins of food onto the floor.

The man glares back over his shoulder at her as he goes out of the door, with Mel rubbing her shoulder, stunned by what just happened.

'Are you OK?' someone says.

Mel turns and sees the shop assistant: a woman about her own age.

'Yeah, yeah, I'm fine thanks. Sorry about the mess.' She bends down to pick up the cans. The woman helps her then goes over to the shop door, staring out.

'He's a menace,' she says, glancing up and down the street. 'Comes in most days for his tobacco.'

'Who is he?' Mel asks, grabbing her newspaper and taking some coins from her purse.

'One of those local characters who's been around for ever,' she says, ringing up the amount on the till. 'His name is Don,' she says. 'Dirty Don, they call him,' she adds with a laugh. 'All the women try to avoid him.'

'I can see why,' Mel says, making a mental note to do the same. 'Thanks for the tip-off,' she adds, saying a quick goodbye before going back out to Kate, who's still drooling over the ice creams.

'Did you see a man just now?' Mel asks, hoping he didn't approach Kate.

'No,' she says vaguely, peering at all the flavours through the window.

'Good. Look, going back to what we were talking about, love. The gaming,' Mel adds, slipping her arm around Kate's shoulders.

'Mmm, definitely coconut and chocolate chip for me.'

'That other phone you have. Is that what you use to talk to your online friends with? I was wondering where it came from.'

Without answering, Kate slides away from under Mel's arm, heading into the shop and taking her little coin purse from her jacket pocket. Mel stands watching on, her mouth slowly dropping open as she pulls out a folded £20 note.

'Double coconut choc chip, please,' she hears her daughter say. Kate turns back to the door, calling out, 'Mum, what do you want?'

'Umm…' Mel says, stepping inside, feeling the cool air conditioning on her face. She quickly scans the flavours on offer. 'Passion fruit would be lovely, thanks, darling,' she says as if it's the most normal thing in the world for her daughter to have that much money in her purse. She racks her brain, trying to work out how much Michael paid for her last shift, how much Kate said she'd spent on that new game. It was only a few days before they'd left Birmingham that Kate was grumbling she'd used up all her pocket money.

Ice cream cones in hand, the pair wander down to the seafront, Mel aware that Kate still hasn't answered her question. They stand beside a small harbour nestled in the natural arc of the headland, various boats bobbing about at high tide. A man-made jetty forms the southernmost boundary, jutting out into the sea to protect the harbour from incoming waves. It's littered with fishermen casting long rods into the water, some standing high up on the white-painted breaker built on top of the quay.

'Oh my God, look!' Kate squeals, running up to the edge of the harbour, only a couple of painted bollards marking the drop into the water. One step forward and Kate would be on the deck of a small craft that looked as though it belonged to a weekend fisherman. 'Is that a seal, Mum?'

Mel strains her eyes, putting a flattened hand over her brow and tracking out to where Kate is pointing. Sure enough, Mel makes out the whiskery, shiny grey dome of a seal's head.

'Yes, it is!' she replies, delighted to hear her daughter so excited. A far cry from the sights of Birmingham and the horrors of her old school. She never thought she'd witness the day that Kate would be standing, ice cream in hand, her hair blowing in the sea breeze, spotting a seal.

'Quick, take a photo,' Mel says, offering to hold her cone. Kate plunges her hand into her pocket and retrieves her phone – not her *usual* phone. She waits until Kate has snapped a few photos before saying anything, until they're walking down onto the little beach a hundred metres further along the seafront. It's only when their shoes are kicked off and the cool, wet sand exposed by the tide is between their toes that Mel tries again.

'I couldn't help noticing you've got a new phone, love,' Mel says, knowing it's ridiculous to tiptoe around a twelve-year-old about such a thing. But this isn't any twelve-year-old. It's Kate. And Kate has been through too much to risk upsetting her. 'Do you want to tell me where it came from?'

Kate looks up at her, scuffing a groove in the pebble-littered sand with her toes. She uncovers a pretty scallop shell and bends down to pick it up, crunching the last of her cone.

'Think I'll start a shell collection,' she says, holding it up. 'And I read that there are loads of fossils in this area, too. Maybe I'll collect those as well. Perhaps I'll even become an archaeologist. How cool would that be? I could go to uni, and—'

'Kate, love,' Mel says, placing a hand on her daughter's arm. 'The phone – where did it come from?'

Kate avoids her mum's eyes, staring out to sea instead, raising her hand to point to a boat on the horizon. But Mel gently places a finger under her chin to turn her face towards her, tilting it up so she has no option but to look at her. Mel raises her eyebrows.

There's a moment's silence before Kate speaks, and later Mel almost imagines that she didn't hear the word, that her daughter's timid voice was carried away on the breeze and lost out at sea.

'Dad,' she says breathily, finally turning her head away.

CHAPTER TWENTY

Mel's heart is still thumping as they begin the walk back up the hill. With the hotel nestled near the top of a dead-end lane that seems to narrow down to a hair's breadth at the top, the route is tree- and hedge-lined, with the odd break in the foliage giving way to stunning views across the bay.

She'd had no idea what to say when Kate blurted out that single, shocking word: *Dad*. Instead, she'd chosen silence, perhaps giving an imperceptible nod in acknowledgment – she can't remember. But she knew if she showed her fear, her *anger*, then Kate would be upset. And she didn't want that, not now. Not in their new life. It was inevitable that Billy had come sniffing about after his release, and she prayed he wouldn't find them here.

'Weren't you going to get some fresh bread on the way back, Mum?' Kate says as they plod past a row of small terraced cottages staggered up the steep hillside – the last of the built-up part of the village, all but for a couple of larger, detached properties before they reach the hotel. The brightly coloured front doors of the terraced row, several of which have pots of geraniums and pansies outside, open directly on to the lane. An old woman sits outside one of the doors, perched on a fold-up stool, a cup of tea to hand. There is a telephone directory under two of the stool's legs to compensate for the steep incline.

''Ello, mi ducks,' the woman says with a nod and a smile as Kate and Mel walk past.

Mel returns the greeting with a quick wave. If she wasn't feeling unsettled, she'd stop for a quick chat, introduce herself. They're near neighbours, after all, and she wants nothing more than to fit in with the community. But that single word – *Dad* – is still reverberating around her head, making the inside of her skull buzz, feeling like a migraine brewing. Not to mention the run-in with that vile man in the shop.

After they've walked out of earshot, just as Mel is about to broach the subject of the phone again, she suddenly stops, grabbing hold of Kate's arm. She freezes in the middle of the lane, her body rigid and her nerves on fire. There's a man walking down the hill towards them, about a hundred yards up ahead. He's swaying and staggering, making him appear almost intoxicated.

Shit.

Mel's heart bangs in her chest, her eyes flicking left then right, searching for gateways or turnings between the houses – any kind of quick escape route. She can't yet make out who the man is – he's got his cap pulled low over his face – but she knows from experience that instinct doesn't work like that. Fight or flight is raw, it's immediate and doesn't bother with logic.

Billy.

'Mum?' Mel hears Kate say… then more words – asking if she's OK, does she need to sit down? 'Mum, you've gone white. Why have we stopped?'

'I… I…' Mel tries to speak but the words won't come. 'Quick,' she says. 'Down here.' Having spotted a narrow passageway to the side of the final terraced cottage – a tiny pale blue place with window boxes – Mel pulls Kate by the arm and heads towards it, her legs feeling like they're filled with jelly and lead at the same time.

'Why are we going into someone's garden, Mum? Are we allowed down here?'

Mel doesn't care. Yes, the passage appears to lead to the rear gardens of the terrace, a communal rat run, probably for dustbin access, but it gets them out of sight of whoever is coming down the lane. It was the cap that did it, Mel thinks, wishing she could have got a proper look at the man's face. And his gait – hard to tell if it was a swagger or a stagger. Both would fit Billy's manner. He was simply too far away, concealed within the shadows cast by the canopy of trees, to make out any defining features, let alone his age. But Mel wasn't taking any chances.

'That man,' she whispers to Kate, pulling her further down the passageway. 'He looked a bit… a bit odd. Like he might be drunk. So let's just wait down here until he passes, OK?'

Kate shrugs. 'Sure, whatever,' she says, kicking her heels against the wall of the cottage.

Mel keeps her eyes fixed on the lane at the end of the passage, straining her ears as the sound of something gets closer. The sound of crying.

'What's that weird noise?' Kate says, idly thumbing through her phone – her regular phone.

'Sshh,' Mel whispers. 'It's that man. He'll be gone soon.'

The footsteps get closer, and the choked sobs grow louder. Then suddenly the entrance to the passageway is blocked by the shape of a person – the man.

Mel can't help the squeal, dragging Kate further down the alley. To her dismay, around the corner at the end she's met with a locked wooden gate. There is no other way out. She stands there shaking, forcing Kate to stand behind her.

'It's just some old man, Mum. Why are you being so weird?'

Mel takes a deep breath as Kate's words sink in. She forces herself to focus on the shadowy figure blocking the exit. A sweat breaks out on her face, her limbs shaking in the aftermath of the adrenaline surge. She breathes out slowly as the panic subsides.

Kate is right. It's an old man. Not Billy. Not even that nasty person who shoved into her in the shop.

'Are… are you OK?' she says to him, daring to take a step closer.

'Is that you?' the old man replies, sniffing as he tips back his tweed cap to expose squinting eyes. He reaches out his arms and shuffles towards them, zombie-like.

'Who are you looking for?' Mel asks, getting a sense that the man, likely in his late seventies, isn't thinking clearly. For a start, he can't be looking for either her or Kate.

'Am I home?' he goes on, his voice a brittle croak with undertones of what would once have been, Mel suspects, something commanding and deep.

'I'm not sure,' Mel replies. 'Is this where you live?' She edges forward, hoping to usher him back out onto the lane. Even though he's not Billy, she doesn't like being trapped down the alley with no route out.

'I... I want to go home,' the man says, a slightly pathetic and resigned note to his words. Something inside Mel clicks, almost as if she's back at The Cedars rounding up an elderly resident who can't find their room, escorting them back.

'OK, don't worry. I can help you find your home. Let's go out onto the lane, shall we?'

The old man nods and turns, his sagging jaw wobbling a little, his gnarled hand reaching out for the side wall of the house as he steadies himself. Mel sees he's wearing tartan slippers on his shuffling feet – the wrong way round – and underneath his heavy overcoat, far too thick for such a warm day, the lower half of a towelling bathrobe pokes out.

'That's right,' Mel says, taking the man's elbow to steady him as he wobbles and staggers onto the lane. 'Do you know your address? Is this your house?' she asks, pointing at the cottage.

He looks at her through watery, pale blue eyes. She suspects that the wayward strands of grey hair protruding from beneath his cap were once blond, or a light brown. The skin on his face is wrinkled yet waxy and supple, with darker spots on his forehead and cheeks. Patchy grey stubble, barely there, frosts his chin.

He shakes his head.

'What about your name then? Can you tell me that?'

'That's Walter,' a nearby voice pipes up. 'He's always getting lost.'

Mel whips round and sees it's the old woman perched on her stool talking to them.

'Oh, thank you,' Mel replies. 'Do you know where he lives?'

The old woman lifts her thumb and beckons down the hill. 'Number thirty-four. It's the one with the green front door,' she adds, waving a hand before she hauls her wide hips up off the creaking stool. She heads inside, giving them a quick wave.

'OK, Walter,' Mel says, getting a firmer grip on the old man's arm, 'let's get you back home, shall we?'

But he stops, his bottom jaw quivering and his breath raspy and loud. He stares directly at Mel.

'Is that you, Joycie?' he says softly, his watery eyes lighting up. A smile spreads across his face as he takes both Mel's hands in his, cupping them between shaking, papery palms. 'You look so happy, Joycie. That's all I ever wanted for you, you know.' He chuckles, his expression telling Mel he's lost in a memory. 'You were always so sad.' He squeezes her hands, glancing over at Kate. 'And is this your little girl? I've been trying to find you for so long,' he adds, gripping her hands even tighter. 'I thought he'd finally killed you.'

CHAPTER TWENTY-ONE

'Freaky,' Kate says as they go in through the front door of the hotel, heading into the restaurant and bar.

'It was a bit, can't lie,' Mel says. For the rest of the walk home, they'd pondered why Walter had thought she was called Joyce, and if he was indeed referring to the Joyce who used to run Moreton Inn, or another person entirely. It was clear the old man was confused, but Mel couldn't deny the coincidence was strange. But what was stranger still was that he'd thought someone had killed her.

'Remind me to rip this carpet out,' Mel says. 'It's too dark and really worn,' she adds, deciding to put the odd encounter from her mind – *both* odd encounters. But she quickly silences herself when she sees two customers perched on stools at the bar. They've each got a pint of Guinness, and Nikki seems to know them as she leans with one hand on a beer tap, chatting and laughing.

'Can I go to the kitchen to get some food, Mum? I'm starving.'

'Sure, love. I'll join you in a moment.'

She watches Kate trot off to the kitchen where Rose will no doubt have something bubbling on the stove.

'Everything OK, Nikki?' she asks, nodding a greeting at the customers.

'All fine,' she replies. 'Though you look worn out.'

'You could say that,' Mel replies, rubbing her shoulder. When she lifts her T-shirt sleeve, there's a blue-grey bruise blooming.

'Ouch,' Nikki says. 'That looks painful.'

'Some horrid old man shoved into me in the newsagent.'

One of the customers at the bar, a man in his mid-fifties, salt-and-pepper hair, turns to Mel. 'What did he look like, love? Was he an ugly tall bloke that stank of pig shit?'

'About sums him up,' Mel says slowly. 'Do you know him?'

'Unfortunately, yes,' he replies, glancing at Nikki. Mel doesn't fail to notice the glare Nikki gives him, the slight shake of her head as if to shut him up.

'Who is he?' Mel asks, but the man is busy draining his pint.

'Right, best be off or the missus'll string me up.' He puts his glass on the bar and slides off his stool, giving a pitying look in Mel's direction as he says his goodbyes.

'Do you know who the old man is, Nikki?' Mel asks when the customer has left.

'Sorry,' Nikki says with a brisk shake of her head, tight-lipped as she turns to load the glass washer.

'The lady in the shop said he was known as Dirty Don. Was he Joyce's partner?'

'I said I don't know, right?' Nikki snaps back, her eyebrows raised.

'Sure, yes. Sorry,' Mel says quietly, retreating to the kitchen to find Kate.

*

'Love,' Mel says once Kate has finished eating, 'you said your dad gave you a phone…' She clasps her hands together, thinking of what to say next.

Kate shrugs. 'Yeah,' she says quietly, staring at the floor of the back hallway where Mel has ushered her.

'How…?' Mel asks. 'I mean, did he have it delivered to our old flat? Did he leave it with the secretary at school? What?' She shudders at the thought of Billy setting foot on school premises without her knowledge. He could so easily have snatched her. The authorities should have told her he'd been released.

'Not sure,' Kate says, her voice on the brink of something. Mel isn't sure if it's defiance or tears.

'Can you tell me *when* you got it then?' she says.

'I… I dunno,' Kate says, shrugging again. She's staring at the ceiling now, her arms folded across her chest.

'Why did your dad give you a phone, love? You've already got one.'

Kate suddenly glares at her. 'Why didn't you tell me he was out of prison, Mum?'

Mel feels herself go cold – the blood draining from her head, hands and feet. Her heart races and her stomach churns.

'I… I didn't know myself until recently. It… it was a bit of a shock, if I'm honest.'

'And you didn't think of how *I'd* feel?' Kate's eyes fill with tears. 'You know how much I've missed him. How much I love him.'

'Look, darling, your dad did some bad things, and he had to pay for that. You were young, and I've explained the reasons why I didn't tell you at the time.'

'He went to prison because of *you*, didn't he? You told them he'd done horrid things to you, that he was bad, and they locked him up!' Kate's voice is suddenly bitter. 'It's *your* fault!'

'No… no, love, *no*. It's not like that at all. I was a witness to some other crimes and had to tell the truth to the judge. I had no choice, and—'

'He said he wanted to make it up to me,' Kate says, sniffing back tears. 'Said he wanted to be able to do nice things for me, be a proper dad, and that's why he gave me the phone. So I could get in touch with him whenever I wanted.'

Tears stream down Kate's flushed cheeks. She wipes them with the back of her hand. 'He's… he's not a bad person, Mum. He told me it was all a mistake, him going to prison. That people had it in for him. That he didn't do anything wrong.'

Mel closes her eyes for a moment. 'Oh, *Katie*,' she says, pulling her daughter close and fighting every instinct to scream and rage. She's shaking inside. Filled with anger. The bastard has got to her. 'I understand, really I do, love. It's very hard for you. I know how much you love your dad.'

Kate presses her face against Mel's chest, sniffing back the tears. 'I miss him,' she says. 'When I saw him, he did that high five thing we used to do, do you remember? And just for a few minutes, it was as though he'd never been away.'

Mel stifles a gasp. 'You *saw* him?'

Kate gives a tentative nod. 'After school. That time you were late. I can't lie to you, Mum. You know I love you, too.'

Mel thinks back. It was the day Josette had hauled her into her office to give her a grilling about the money.

'Come outside and let's sit down,' Mel says, leading Kate out into the garden by the hand. They perch on a low brick wall, near where the end of the new extension will fall. 'Can you tell me what happened when you saw your dad?'

'Like what?' Kate asks, resting her chin in her hand, her elbow propped on her knee.

'How did he arrange to meet you? How did he get in contact? What did he say? How—'

'Mum, stop,' Kate says, scowling. 'It wasn't like that.'

'Well, what *was* it like then?' Mel replies, fighting her frustration.

'I was waiting outside school for you and you were late. Then Dad showed up. He said to get in his van, so I did and we just drove round the corner and talked a bit. I was so happy to see him. That's when he gave me the phone. He said it was a present and that I could use it to call him any time I wanted. He gave me some money too.'

'You got into his *van*? That's... that's nice,' she manages to get out. 'How did he know which school you were at?'

Kate shrugs. 'I dunno. Dads know things, I guess. And I only sat in his van for a few minutes, and then you texted and I thought I'd better go. It was nice to see him, Mum.'

Mel remembers how Kate had sauntered round the corner, waving at a van. Yes, that was it… an old red van. Mel wishes she'd taken more notice of it now, got the registration number at least. But never for one minute did she think it would be Billy. She'd not been able to get a look at the driver.

'OK,' Mel says, trying to stay calm. 'Have you spoken to him since? Have you called him? Have you told him where we are?'

Kate hangs her head, giving it a little shake, her shoulders slouching forward. 'No, he doesn't know where we are. But that's the thing. Apart from a call I missed before we left Birmingham, he's not been in touch at all since. He promised I could call him any time and he even put his number into my new phone. But when I dial it, it doesn't connect.'

Some small mercy, Mel thinks, glancing up at the back of the old, thatched building, her line of sight falling on a top-floor window. She takes a deep breath, feeling light-headed all of a sudden, and she's not sure if it's because of Billy finding Kate, or because Miss Sarah's face suddenly ducks away behind the curtains.

CHAPTER TWENTY-TWO

The mini digger judders up the slope of the car park, its caterpillar tracks making light work of the crumbling tarmac as Tom guides it around to the site where the footings will go. It hadn't taken much for Mel to be convinced over the last couple of weeks that building works should start sooner rather than later.

'Breaking ground is what you need to do,' Tom had told her when he'd stopped off for a pint in the bar one evening. There were two other customers passing through who'd come in for something to eat, making the place seem busy for a change. Though Mel knew it was far from that. 'By making a start on the foundations, getting the drainage in place, it'll mean you won't need to renew planning with the council.'

'I see,' Mel had replied. It had only come to light several days before that the approved plans would soon expire – something Mel had missed in her many hours of poring over the works she had planned for the hotel. Plus, for the last twenty-four hours, she'd been blindsided by the news that the full funds had just been released from the solicitor and the title of the property secured in her name. Everything was finally official. There was no going back now. Melanie Douglas was the new owner of Moreton Inn and all the problems that came with it.

'Kate,' Mel had said yesterday when she'd arrived home from her new school, a big grin on her face. So far, she'd loved every minute of it and had already made several friends. 'Come here, love.'

They were standing in the kitchen, Mel clutching her phone in her shaking hands, her cheeks flushed and her eyes wide.

'What is it, Mum?' Kate said, dumping her school bag on the floor. 'Is everything OK?'

Mel had given a little nod. She'd just got off the phone to Robert Hedge, who had told her the good news.

'I've got something to show you. Ready?'

'Er, yeah...' Kate replied, grabbing a banana from the fruit bowl and peeling it before coming up to her mum. She peered at the screen when Mel held it out. 'What's that?' she said, barely batting an eyelid.

'That, my darling girl, is my banking app. Click on this link.'

Kate bit into her banana and tapped the screen, staring at what she saw. She'd stopped chewing then, her mouth dropping open as she took it all in.

'Oh. My. *God*,' she said slowly in a whisper. She glanced up at Mel, who was wide-eyed and grinning. 'Is that...?'

'Ours? Yes, love. All £378,542.'

'And twenty-eight pence,' Kate added, checking the savings account balance again.

They were silent for a moment, both staring at the screen in disbelief, before grabbing each other, squealing and jumping up and down. They only stopped when Rose arrived for her shift.

Later, lying in bed, Mel had checked her banking app at least another dozen times, just to make sure the money was still there, that there hadn't been some terrible mistake. And when she woke in the morning, she logged in again, and there was the same huge sum in her account.

'Thank you, whoever you are,' she whispered to her phone. 'Or *were*. I'll use it wisely,' she added, knowing that rushing out to buy a flash car or a whole new wardrobe simply wasn't her style. This was a chance to make her and Kate's future secure.

Mel watches as Tom gets the mini digger into position. Since she'd made the decision to go ahead with the build, he'd been very helpful. *Too* helpful, at times, she wondered, but then she remembered what Kate had teased her about.

'I can organise equipment hire, get a team of lads together,' Tom had said. 'Manage the whole build, if you like.'

Over the last couple of weeks, they'd chatted about lots of things, including his line of work – how he'd started off as a builder's mate, gradually learning the trade, eventually taking on clients of his own, taking on staff, buying land, developing it. He'd explained to Mel how he missed getting his hands dirty these days, especially since he'd come back to Halebury to take care of his father.

'In fact, it'd do me good to get down and dirty,' he'd said. 'I'm going a bit stir-crazy looking after Dad all the time. He has a carer come in now, so it gives me a chance to get out. All he does is watch TV these days. It's sad. He was once such a powerhouse of a man. So much a part of the community.' Then he'd explained how he'd lost his mum when he was eight, how his dad had never really got over her death. 'The only other woman Dad ever had eyes for was Joyce. But she was besotted with that monster, Donald Bray.'

'Camera at the ready?' Tom shouts above the noise of the digger, his hands on the levers in the cab. The yellow machine sits at an angle on the slope, the clawed bucket pulled back and ready to eat into the weedy paving.

'Ready as I'll ever be!' Mel calls back, holding her phone out in front of her. She plans on documenting the hotel's journey back to life, making an album to look back on.

An almighty clang makes her jump, the ground tremoring as Tom brings the digger's bucket down over and over to lever up the first of the paving slabs. It takes several goes to grab and lift one, but as soon as that is loosened, the others come away like rotten teeth, cracking and crumbling, exposing soft, dark earth beneath.

Tom heaps the waste into a skip, deftly working the controls in the cab as he manoeuvres the machine back and forth. As yet, there's been no mention of payment, which she knows will have to be discussed. The important part, he'd told her, was just to get the works commenced.

Mel watches on, one hand on her hip and the other at her brow as she takes in the scene in front of her, every so often aiming her camera and taking a photo. *Her* hotel. *Her* extension. *Her* business. *Her* money paying for all this. *Her* daughter crossing the car park with the new friend she'd met on the beach the other day. *Their* happiness.

But more importantly, no Billy.

She gives a quick wave to Kate and her friend, Chloe, as they walk past, deep in conversation, hardly able to believe that only a few weeks ago, she'd been struggling to make ends meet in a tiny flat in Birmingham, with Kate desperately unhappy at school and her job on the line.

'Oi, oi, Tommo,' she hears someone shouting above the noise of the digger as it growls through the earth.

The engine noise slows and dies as Tom cuts the power, leaping out of the cab as another man, a bit older than Tom, swaggers up the drive. He's also dressed in workwear and heavy boots, a pack slung over one shoulder. After they've exchanged greetings, Tom tugs off his outer shirt to expose a grey vest, his broad shoulders lightly tanned from the decent weather.

Mel goes inside to make some tea and returns ten minutes later with a tray of mugs, setting it down on a pile of bricks.

'Never say no to a cuppa,' Tom says, striding up to Mel. 'Or never say *Nah*, should I say?'

'I took a day off,' Mel replies, laughing and looking down at her plain white T-shirt. She glances up again, catching Tom's eye for a moment – a look shared.

'Aye up, me stomach thinks me throat's been cut,' says the other man. He's shorter and stockier than Tom, and his head is mostly bald with a monk-style haircut sitting on top of a chunky neck and shoulders. His pale and slightly hairy belly protrudes from beneath his luminous work vest, hanging over his khaki knee-length shorts. He reaches for a mug.

Tom's eyes narrow, faint creases of smile lines appearing either side as he grins. 'Mel, this is Nige. We've worked together for donkey's years. Nige, this is Mel. Also known as the person brave enough to take on Moreton Inn.'

Nige holds out a thick, stubby arm towards Mel, the fingers of his hand spread like a chunky starfish. Mel returns the gesture, catching sight of tattooed letters written across his knuckles. She can't quite make out what they spell.

'Nice to meet you too, Nige,' she says. 'Are you local?'

'Born and bred,' he replies, giving Mel's arm a good shake, making her shoulder socket twinge. 'Did a bit of work for Joyce over the years, so I know the old place well.' He slurps from his mug of tea.

'You knew Joyce?' Mel asks. 'Do you know much about her? If she had a big family, many relatives?'

'If she did, she never spoke of them. She had enough on her plate as it was, with that bloody girl.'

'Bloody girl?'

'She still here, is she, Tommo?' Nige continues. 'The crazy one?' He nudges Tom, sloshing his tea.

Tom clears his throat. 'She is, mate, so keep your voice down.' He rolls his eyes, turning to Mel. 'He means Miss Sarah.'

'If she were my gal, I'd have given her a clip round the ear and told her to sort her attitude out,' Nige continues. He takes a packet of cigarettes from his pocket, lighting one up. 'Don were far too lenient with her.'

'Don… as in Donald?' Mel's heart misses a couple of beats as she wonders if it's the man from the newsagent.

'Yeah, Joyce's bloke. Don Bray.'

'Anyway, Mel, Nige is my wingman and he's good at what he does,' Tom continues, seeming keen to change the subject. 'He'll help get this place whipped into shape in no time.'

'Excellent,' Mel replies with a nervous laugh, offering round the biscuits. 'You'd better let me know how much this is all going to cost, too.' Mel laughs again, placing a hand on her phone in her pocket. She's already checked her banking app another three times today, just to make sure.

Tom shifts from one foot to the other, sipping his tea. 'I can have a quote with you by the end of the week, if you want us to tackle the work going forward,' he says.

Mel glances over at the girls and sees Kate holding up a jam jar to the sun. It's stuffed full of leaves and twigs and, no doubt, bugs and insects and various fossils she and Chloe have been collecting. They're laughing and chatting together, with Chloe tucking back a strand of red hair as she grins.

'Thank you,' she says. 'I'll look forward to the figures. But remember – I'm not made of money, you know.' She smiles, her heart skipping as Tom does that thing with his eyes again, almost as if they're smiling too.

'Oi, Tommo, that's not what we've heard, is it, eh?' Nige says, nudging him again. And that's when Mel sees the word HATE tattooed across his knuckles as he brings his cigarette to his mouth.

CHAPTER TWENTY-THREE

Over the next few days, Mel barely stops grafting. With Kate happily in her second week at school, it's a load off her mind, leaving her to focus on the work she can tackle herself at the hotel. The first job is giving the bar and restaurant a makeover. It's got so much potential.

'What do you think?' Mel had asked Kate after the head teacher had shown them around the school.

'It looks *awesome*,' she admitted. 'And the girl I met on the beach, Chloe, goes there and says everyone is really nice. She does computer club on a Wednesday and said I should join too. She's into programming and stuff.'

Mel had let out a contented sigh as she'd started up the Fiesta and driven back to the hotel. But she knew that, at some point, she'd have to have a quiet word with the head teacher about Billy, informing her that Kate was allowed to take the bus home, but wasn't to be taken out of school by anyone except herself.

'Do you think we'll manage it between us?' Nikki asks now, a velour-topped stool in each hand as they clear the last of the furniture out of the bar, piling it up in the reception area.

Mel flexes a bicep and grins, pointing to her T-shirt. 'Unstoppable' is printed across the front, making Nikki laugh.

'I didn't put this on for nothing,' Mel says, heading back into the bar and using a claw hammer to prise up the edge of the carpet. 'I don't care if I have to cut it up into tiny pieces with a Stanley knife, this is coming out,' she adds with a grimace as she pulls hard at the corner, staggering backwards as it gives. The satisfying sound of the gripper rod losing its hold on the disintegrating hessian backing spurs Mel on. 'You get the other corner, Nikki, and let's see if we can't roll the whole thing up into just a couple of large pieces. Tom will be around somewhere with Nige. The two of them will have it in the skip in no time.'

Once the underlay is pulled up and chucked out the back, along with the levered-up gripper, Mel stands back, taking stock of what they've discovered underneath. 'This was a lucky find,' she says, admiring the polished wooden floorboards. 'The carpet has actually protected them over the years.'

Leaving Nikki to vacuum, Mel lugs the bar tables outside to the corrugated shelter where she's set up the paint sprayer Tom hired for her.

It's as she's about to pick up yet another table from reception that she freezes, spotting Miss Sarah standing on the bottom stair, staring directly at her. Then her eyes dart between the out-of-place furniture and the empty restaurant area beyond. Mel sees a tiny flicker beneath one eye, a barely perceptible tightening of her jaw.

'Hi, Miss Sarah,' Mel says cheerily. It's not the first time she's attempted to make conversation with the woman since they've been at Moreton Inn, but each time she's been met with the same silence. 'I'm having a revamp of the restaurant and bar,' Mel continues now, pointing to the now carpet-less area. 'It's going to be so much brighter and cleaner,' she adds. 'I'm going to paint all the furniture and give it a new lease of life. Cheer it all up a bit. What do you think?'

Miss Sarah says nothing. She carefully comes down the last step, her bony fingers gripping the banister rail until the last moment, and then she picks her way through the muddle of furniture, curtains and boxes to get through to the restaurant. She heads directly to the spot where her table used to be. When she sees the entire room is empty, she simply stands and waits where her chair once was.

'Oh, you want your lunch, don't you?' Mel says, coming up behind her and glancing at her watch. She hadn't realised the time. 'Rose has some soup on the go in the kitchen. It smells delicious. Why don't you head through and ask her for some? There's enough to feed an army, and I can smell bread heating up too.'

Surely that will elicit something from her, Mel thinks. But Miss Sarah just stands there, her thin arms hanging down by her sides, her chest rising and falling slowly beneath her pale pink cardigan. She stares at the wall ahead.

'Or I can bring some soup up to your room, if you prefer?' Mel asks, positioning herself in front of her so she has no choice but to look at her. 'Is that a good idea?' She catches a faint smell of lavender, as if her clothes have been stored with a little bag of it. 'OK,' Mel adds awkwardly, clearing her throat and heading off to the kitchen.

'Think I've upset Miss Sarah's apple cart a bit,' she says to Rose, who's bent over a large stainless-steel pot of soup. She explains what's just happened, with Rose glancing up occasionally as she stirs. 'Can I get a tray of food for her?'

Ten minutes later, Mel carries the tray upstairs, balancing it with one hand as she knocks on the door of room twelve. There's no reply, so she goes inside and finds Miss Sarah sitting in her chair with a book on her lap. Except she's not reading it. She's got her eyes screwed up tightly closed, as if she's about to scream – her face puckered up and contorted as though in great pain. And even though Mel stands there for a few moments, watching, waiting, absolutely nothing comes out of her.

'It was *so* weird,' Mel tells Tom as they each slurp some of Rose's creamy chicken soup from mugs. The sun is warm on their backs as they perch on the low brick wall that is soon to be torn down by Tom's mini digger. He's made good progress with the footings over the last few days, though he met with more complicated drainage issues than anticipated, which had delayed the works for a day or two.

'I mean, she literally said nothing,' Mel goes on. 'She was just sitting there with her eyes shut tight. I mean really screwed up, like a kid would do.' Mel sighs, drinking more soup. 'To be honest, Tom,' she continues, 'I'm getting a bit creeped out. I'm going to ask the solicitor to look into it for me. See if he can find out what's going on.' Mel takes a deep breath, dunking some of the crusty bread into her mug. 'Mmm, Rose isn't actually a bad cook, you know,' she adds, eating hungrily. 'There's hope for this old place yet.'

Tom sits there, deep in thought, with that look in his eyes again – the look Mel now calls his 'faraway' look, though she also knows he's still focused on her. He's barely taken his eyes off her since she came out with the soup.

'You really are, aren't you?' he says, flicking his eyes to her T-shirt. '"Unstoppable". I admire that. Your feet have barely touched the ground since you arrived. You deserve some downtime, too, you know, Miss Douglas. Some good, old-fashioned fun.'

Mel is about to bite into the bread, having wiped a large chunk of it around the inside of her mug, scooping up the chunks in the soup, but stops. *Fun?* she thinks. Is that… some kind of veiled invite? Is he testing the waters to see if I'll… go on a *date*? She's not had a date since… She thinks back, but she honestly can't remember. It was way before she met Billy, and that was fourteen years ago now.

'Fun, eh?' she says, grinning. 'Fun is cracking on with spraying these tables and stools.' She laughs, biting into the bread and chewing, but suddenly stops, spitting it out onto the ground. 'Christ,' she says, wiping her mouth and frowning. 'What was *that*?' She peers into the dregs at the bottom of her mug, putting her finger in and fishing something out. When she holds it up to the light, she sees quite clearly that it's a shard of broken glass.

CHAPTER TWENTY-FOUR

For the next few days, Mel forced her aching and exhausted body out of bed each morning, donning her old, ripped jeans, an old T-shirt and fastening her hair up messily on top of her head. After Kate had left for school and she'd sunk several coffees, she'd wasted no time ploughing on with the seemingly endless list of tasks to get Moreton Inn ready for a new launch.

'I think this shade, definitely,' Mel says to Andy, the man in charge of the decorating team. Tom had called in a favour last week, managing to secure the firm at short notice, and an army of white-overalled decorators had arrived at 8 a.m. sharp and were now swarming throughout the downstairs rooms of the hotel as they sheeted up and brought in their prepping equipment and priming paint.

Mel taps her finger over a pale shade of grey, almost bordering on sage, as the main colour to transform the chunky wooden bar. 'And I'd like the overhead part painted in this slightly darker grey. I think with the good lighting up there, it'll look really on-trend but still traditional.'

Andy nods, making a note in his phone of the colours so he can order in what's needed.

'On-trend isn't something I've ever heard said about this old place,' Tom says, appearing beside them.

Mel feels his hand brush against her back.

'And just to let you know,' Tom continues as Andy walks off, 'some guy just pulled up out the back asking if you had any rooms vacant. I said you're renovating and not open for guests yet. Is that right? Plus he looked a bit unsavoury,' Tom says. 'Wasn't sure you'd want him here,' he adds, looking around the chaotic scene. The entire floor of the restaurant and bar is sheeted off, with the far end of the room clouding in dust as two decorators sand down the front shutters, ready for a new coat of white paint.

'Unsavoury?' Mel says, catching her breath. 'How do you mean?'

'I shouldn't judge, I suppose, but sometimes you get a… a feeling about people, if you know what I mean. He looked like trouble, is all I can say.'

Mel frowns. 'What was he driving?' It's only when Tom looks down at her hand that she realises she's gripping onto his forearm tightly.

'Good question,' Tom says, thinking. 'A beat-up old Transporter, I reckon.'

'What's a Transporter?' Mel asks in a panicked voice. 'And what… what colour was it?'

'Are you OK?' he asks. 'You've gone as white as a sheet. Do you want to sit down?'

Mel nods, staring blankly across the room. Surely not… *surely* she's allowed more than a few weeks of peace before he tracks her down?

'I'm… I'm fine,' she says.

'It's a type of van, the kind a tradesman might use,' Tom says. 'And it was red. A battered old thing.'

Seeing Mel is distraught, Tom goes off to make her a coffee, returning with a couple of biscuits for her too.

'Look, I have the observational skills of a bat and a memory like a sieve, so please do take with a pinch of salt what I said about that man,' he says, handing Mel a coffee. 'I might have got the van details wrong, but he looked unsavoury. Take a break for ten minutes. You look done in,' he adds.

Mel smiles briefly. 'Thanks,' she says, biting into a biscuit, hoping it will perk her up. Tom wasn't to know why what he'd said had bothered her so much. After she finishes her drink and Tom has gone back out on site, she busies herself with taking down the many pairs of old and dusty curtains in the bedrooms.

'I can't believe it,' she mutters under her breath, lugging yet another load of faded fabric out to the yard to fill what seems like a never-ending supply of skips. 'I swear, if he's found me, I swear... I'll... I'll *kill* him...'

'Remind me not to cross you any time,' Nige calls out, looking her way with a large shovel to hand as he stands knee-deep in the footings. The mini digger was unable to reach the last part that needed excavating. Tom had said the only way forward was to dig manually, which meant him and Nige putting in some back-breaking graft for several days.

Mel hurls the pile of old curtains into the skip, turning her head away as a cloud of dust billows up. She catches sight of Tom glancing over at her, shovel in hand. She can't be sure, but she thinks he gives her a wink, a little smile. She hurries back inside.

'How are you both getting on?' she says to Rose and Nikki, who are stripping the kitchen for a deep-clean. 'Is all this to be thrown out?' she asks, examining ancient-looking packets of food.

'Yup,' Nikki says cheerfully from the top of a stepladder as she sloshes a cloth out of a precariously balanced bucket of water. 'It's all long out of date. And it's disgusting up here,' she says, referring to the tops of the wall cupboards. 'Decades of grease and grime.'

Rose is on her knees, pulling old cookware from deep under the worktops. She makes a grunting sound, before emerging with some old saucepans and hauling herself up. She peers into them, pulling a face. 'Three dead spiders and...' She makes a noise in her throat. 'Mouse droppings,' she adds, dumping the lot in a pile by the door. 'There'll be a dead mouse or two in there somewhere, mark my words, bloody things.'

'Really?' Mel says, making a mental note to call the pest control man. 'What about other cupboards around the hotel?' Mel asks. 'Do you think we've got an infestation?'

Rose turns to face her, hands on her wide hips. 'Oh no, definitely not. They're after the food, not a kip in the towels.' She laughs then – a deep, throaty sound, almost like a growl – giving Mel a lingering look.

'OK... well, good,' Mel says quietly, frowning, knowing she didn't tell anyone about the dead mouse she'd found in her towels. 'I'll call someone out anyway to set some humane traps. Oh, and the decorators are painting in here tomorrow, so if you could get it cleared out by the end of today, that would be great. I'm happy to bribe with cake or alcohol!'

'My kind of bribe,' Nikki says, her face beaming.

'We need this kitchen gleaming and functional. I've got lots of online things planned to promote our new menu before the launch. Rose, you're a great chef, and Nikki, you're excellent in the bar and serving. We're going to rock this opening and bring Moreton Inn back to life,' she says, with a sharp nod of her head. 'We'll have customers flooding in, you'll see.'

'Aye aye, captain,' Nikki says, giving a salute from the ladder, grabbing on with her other hand as she wobbles. Rose doesn't say anything, rather stares at Mel for a moment, her expression giving nothing away, before she lowers herself back under the worktop, making a groaning sound as she drops to her knees.

Mel goes back to taking down the curtains and, with another armful of ancient and mildewed curtain fabric, she heads out to the skip again, feeling grimy and hot. She's lost count of how many times she's been up and down the stairs today and wants nothing more than a cool shower. It must be one of the hottest days of the year so far.

'Nooo… ohh… *stop!*' she suddenly cries, jumping back as the freezing water hits her face and neck. The curtains fall from her arms as she gasps for breath, shielding her face. Instead of moving away from the source of whatever's spraying her, all she can do is stand there, frozen, trying to work out what's happening. Water runs down the neck of her T-shirt on her bare skin and she feels her wet hair dripping down her back.

'Christ, careful, Nige,' Tom calls out sternly from the trench. He leaps out, running over to turn the tap off. Then he pulls off his check shirt, offering it up to Mel.

'You OK?' he asks her.

Mel nods, wiping her face. 'Yeah, thanks.' Her heart skitters when, beneath the scent of laundry detergent on his shirt, she catches a vague hint of fresh sweat.

'Sorry,' Nige replies slowly, flicking the trigger on the nozzle gun several times, while staring at Mel. 'Accidents happen. The catch must have got stuck.'

'Oh dear, I look a right state,' Mel says, laughing, catching her bedraggled reflection in a window. She gives Tom back his shirt. 'But wait,' she says, going up to Nige and taking the hose from him. She inspects it, pulling a puzzled face. 'It was working fine earlier.' She trails the hose over to the tap and turns it on. 'Let's test it, shall we?' Mel points the nozzle directly at Nige, who's now only a couple of feet away and, before he can react, she presses the trigger and a jet of water shoots out all over him.

His hands come up to bat away the water, coughing and spluttering as he lunges to grab the hose off her. But Mel is too quick and darts backwards, laughing and waving the jet all over him, making certain most of him is drenched.

'Oops, sorry,' Mel says, finally releasing the trigger. 'I don't think there's anything wrong with the hose gun at all,' she says, laughing. Though she falls silent when she sees Nige's red face, his angry expression, the glare he's giving her.

'You got me good,' Nige says, his voice flat as he folds his arms tightly across his body. 'Women aren't to be trusted. I'll be sure to get you back.'

For a second, Mel freezes – hearing Billy's voice instead of Nige's, recognising the same pent-up look on his face, the twitch in his jaw.

Can't you take a joke? she wants to say but decides to keep quiet. She's learnt the hard way that answering back only ever made things worse.

'I… I'm sorry,' she says, dropping the hose.

Nige makes a grunting sound, wiping his face on the bottom of his T-shirt. He goes back over to the trench, grabbing his shovel and slamming it into the earth over and over, all the while his angry stare fixed on Mel.

CHAPTER TWENTY-FIVE

'Micky… oh, *Micky*, how I've missed your face…' Mel says in a silly voice, flopping back onto her pillow, her wet hair wrapped up in a soft white towel – one of three dozen she'd ordered for the hotel that had arrived that morning. The rest of her is clad in a soft waffle bathrobe – again from a batch she bought for the guest rooms. 'I can't believe how long it's been since we spoke.' She draws up her knees, resting her arm on her leg to keep the phone steady as she FaceTimes Michael, feeling exhausted but satisfied. 'I want to know all your news. Like, *now*.'

'Correction,' Michael says, also dressed in his favourite robe – a tatty burgundy thing Mel knows he's had since for ever. He's at home, sprawled on his saggy dark green sofa, a gin and tonic to hand in what looks more like a bowl than a glass. '*I* want to know all *your* news. Like *now*.'

Mel laughs, soothed by his voice. He's always felt like a brother to her, right from the moment they'd met in the children's home. His calm but assertive manner, his positive attitude, even aged only eight, had taught her how to have her own inner strength, unaware way back then how much she'd one day need to draw upon it.

'Oh, Micky, Micky, Micky… you wouldn't believe this place,' Mel says at the screen with a laugh and a sigh. 'It's absolutely lovely, but I'm working so hard. It'll be worth it, though. I've got the decorators in at the moment, and the extension footings are under way. But…' Mel lowers her voice, 'there's a woman in room twelve. She's very strange.'

'Whoa, slow down there, my lovely,' Michael says, taking a long sip of gin before lighting a cigar. For a moment, the screen is filled with grey-blue smoke as he draws and blows out. 'Who's very strange, apart from yours truly, of course?'

'Miss *Sarah*,' Mel replies quietly. 'The woman who has the right to live here. Seems she also has the right not to speak to anyone. Not a word. And no one seems to know why. Not Nikki or Rose, or Tom… or anyone. Well, I mean, they're the only three I've asked, to be fair, but—'

'Wait, you mean the person mentioned in the Letter of Wishes doesn't say anything?' Michael's face pinches with concern as he lays his cigar in an ashtray, suddenly sitting upright, looking tense. 'That's not right, Mel. I… I really didn't expect that. Have you tried talking to her?'

'Yes, I've tried several times but I get nothing back. It's freaking me out. Kate is absolutely loving life here and I don't want anything to upset that. God, and what's worse, Tom said he saw a man earlier. In a red van, and it's made me think that Billy's found us. You know how paranoid I get. But then I also thought that old man in the village, Walter, was Billy from a distance, so I admit my mind is working overtime. I'm just exhausted, Micky. Oh, and we've got mice.'

'Oh, darling,' Micky says. 'What a lot to deal with. Anything else?'

'There was glass in my soup,' she says, laughing. 'I hadn't got the heart to tell Rose, as I'm sure she'd have been mortified if she'd known. She'd spent the entire morning making it from scratch. At least there weren't any customers in.'

'That could have been really dangerous, Mel.'

'I know,' she says, raising her eyebrows. 'There must have been a breakage in the kitchen and she hadn't realised where the pieces had ended up.'

Mel takes a sip of the wine she's poured for herself. The hotel is all locked up and she needed something to help her relax and sleep. Wine and a chat with Michael seemed the obvious medication. But Tom's words have been playing on her mind all day. *He looked a bit unsavoury…*

'I'm so pleased to hear Katie is getting on well,' Michael says after Mel fills him in on her new school, telling him how she's already made a friend – Chloe – and how she's getting involved with after-school clubs.

'It's as though she's found this new confidence, like a new Kate – or perhaps the *real* Kate – who was there all the time, but just hiding.' *Cowering*, Mel thinks. 'She and Chloe hit it off right away. They're into the same things and have even started a fossil collection together. They love nothing more than digging about in the garden and… well, and just being *kids*. Anyway, once I'm a bit more sorted with the bedrooms, you *must* come down and stay. Will you be bringing Grindr Kev, or have we moved on now? The few guest rooms I'm tackling are shaping up beautifully. Wait, I'll send a pic, hang on…'

And Mel quickly switches screens, firing off a couple of work-in-progress shots to Michael.

'Alas, Grindr Kev is no more,' he replies. 'But you know me, my little black book is stuffed with contacts all over the country. I've taken your advice and looked up one or two blasts from the past.' He laughs, then checks out the pictures Mel sent. 'You've done an amazing job, Mel. Where *did* this interior design goddess come from?'

Mel smiles, pleased he approves. 'I've been doing loads of online promotion, too. I've set up a Facebook page and plugged it on loads of holiday sites. I've got some enquiries already. And the restaurant and bar area is already looking like a new place. The locals are positively salivating from the flyers I've distributed. It's all kind of snowballing, Micky, and I'm so bloody excited, I can't tell you. But…' She trails off, having another sip of wine, flopping back onto her pillow as she feels something dangerous bite deep inside her.

'But you're hardwired to self-sabotage anything good that may actually happen to you for no other reason than… it might actually be good?'

Mel gives a silent nod. Stares directly into Michael's bright blue eyes. If nothing else, she's adept at fighting back the tears now. Has been for as long as she can remember.

'Only *weak* people cry like babies…' Billy had once said, his hand around her throat, his knee pressed hard between her legs. She can't even recall why he'd got her pinned up against the kitchen wall of the little terrace in Birmingham they'd rented together just a few months earlier. A home for them and the baby growing inside her. They'd been together a year by that time, and she hoped things would get better.

He'd slammed her head back against the wall then, making her see stars as she tried to work out what she'd done wrong.

Billy had adored Kate from the moment he'd set eyes on her. But soon after the birth, Mel became disposable again. A piece of trash. It was what she'd grown up learning, after all. And the familiarity was some kind of comfort.

'He's got more red flags than a communist rally,' Michael had once told her when Mel described her new boyfriend to him, a few weeks after meeting Billy at the bus stop. He'd begged her not to go out with him, but she'd not listened.

'I never saw them myself,' Mel whispers to herself as she lies on the bed now, having finished her call with Michael. 'I never saw Billy's red flags.' She sips her wine, wondering how she'd been so completely colour-blind.

CHAPTER TWENTY-SIX

When she wakes, Mel feels refreshed – as though she's been asleep for a hundred years. She breathes in deeply, her eyes adjusting to the sunlight streaming in through her curtainless bedroom window. The new ones still haven't arrived.

She stretches out, remembering the call with Michael last night before she fell asleep. It was good to talk, she thinks, sitting up and glancing at her phone to check the time. The window is open a few inches and she feels the fresh sea air wafting gently over her skin.

Shit!

'Kate!' she calls out. 'Katie, it's twenty to eight!' She leaps out of bed and grabs her robe, wrapping it round her, fumbling with the belt. She knows how long it takes her daughter to get going in the morning, plus there's the ten-minute walk to the school bus stop. If she misses it, Mel will have to drive her, and she's got builders to see to first thing.

'Kate, you've got exactly fifteen minutes to be up, washed, dressed, fed and your sports kit gathered,' Mel calls as she flings open her bedroom door. She's about to call out Kate's name again when she stops.

She hears voices around the corner on the landing.

Two female voices, whispering.

Mel halts, straining her ears, catching the odd word or two.

One voice certainly sounds like Kate's – there's no doubting that. But the other voice she doesn't recognise at all. It could be

Nikki, she thinks. The girl's so keen, she wouldn't be surprised if she'd arrived at work early. But no, it's too old-sounding for Nikki.

Pulling her robe around her, Mel heads down the corridor and around the corner. She suddenly stops, her bare toes curling into the carpet, her hand reaching out to the wall.

'Kate, love?' she says, her eyes flicking between her daughter and Miss Sarah, who is standing about three feet away from Kate. The woman's arms are folded across her small chest, her shoulders bony and protruding beneath the cream blouse she's wearing. It's the first time Mel has seen her in short sleeves, and she's surprised by how muscular her forearms seem, despite their thinness. And her skin is smooth and pale – making her appear much younger than Mel had originally thought.

'Love, you're going to be late for—' But Mel stops, seeing that Kate is fully dressed in her uniform, her hair brushed and neatly tied back, and she has her school bag in one hand and her sports kit in the other.

'I'm all ready to go,' Kate replies breezily. 'And I've had breakfast.'

Mel touches her head. 'I overslept. I'm so sorry, love. I should have woken you.'

'That's OK, Mum. I set my alarm.' She flashes a little smile at Miss Sarah, whose blank expression doesn't change.

'Well… well done, love. Why don't you go downstairs and unlock the front door so Rose and Nikki can get in?'

Kate nods and heads off, giving a last glance to Miss Sarah as she goes.

Mel crosses her arms, mirroring the frail-looking woman standing in front of her.

'Good morning, Miss Sarah,' she says, once Kate is out of earshot. She takes a step closer, offering a smile in the hope it will elicit something. It doesn't. 'I can't help wondering,' Mel continues, 'if… if I just heard you and Kate having a little chat. I

mean, that would be wonderful if you were. Kate's a lovely girl…
but it would seem…' She pauses, making a pained expression.
However she says it, it's not going to come out right. 'It would
seem a little… perhaps a little strange that you don't speak to
anyone else. I'd love to have a chat with you, too. Get to know
you. Perhaps we could have breakfast together?'

Mel waits, studying the soft, powdery skin on Miss Sarah's
face. Hardly a line or wrinkle – which figures for someone who's
most likely never made a facial expression in goodness knows how
long. But unless her ears just deceived her, then Mel knows she
is capable of speaking.

Nothing. Miss Sarah remains silent.

It's just as Mel is turning to go, letting out a barely audible
sigh of frustration, when she catches sight of a tiny glimmer of a
smile – barely a twitch – on the older woman's lips.

*

'Bushed. Done in. Knackered. Beat. Fried. Pooped and worn out.'

Just home from school, Kate giggles, dumping her school bag
on the bar before giving Mel a big hug. 'Poor old Mum,' she says,
giving her a squeeze. 'Shall I make you a cuppa?'

Mel pulls back, looking at her daughter for a moment. 'Are
you feeling OK?' she asks, giving her a quick tickle. 'That'd be
lovely. Thank you. Then… then I was wondering if we could have
a quick chat.'

'Sure, Mum. Why don't we sit outside? It's a lovely day.'

As Kate heads off to the kitchen, Mel unwraps a few more of the
new glasses that arrived earlier in the day, ready to be washed and
put away in the freshly painted bar. She can't help the occasional
glance around the restaurant area, seeing everything taking shape.

'Coming,' Mel calls out in response to Kate a few minutes later as
she squashes down another empty cardboard box. She grabs several
others and heads outside, chucking the cardboard into the recycling

skip as she passes. 'Just what I need, thanks, love,' she says, taking the tea and perching on the wall next to her. 'Good day at school?'

Kate nods eagerly. 'It was ace. I got picked for the relay team and we did dissection in biology. And I had chicken, chips and salad for lunch.'

'Sounds like a good day indeed, then,' Mel says, building up to what she has to say. 'You know this morning, on the landing, when I overslept? I… well, I couldn't help overhearing you talking to Miss Sarah. At least, that's what it sounded like.'

Kate bows her head, picking at her fingernails.

'What was she saying, love? She never says a word to me.'

Kate shrugs and sips her tea.

'I think you'll agree it's weird that she lives with us but doesn't speak. I mean, she literally could be anyone – from someone really vulnerable to a serial killer.'

'She's not a killer,' Kate snaps back.

'Oh? How so?' Mel says in a coaxing voice. But she knows Kate, knows how she clams up when pressed. 'Did she tell you that?'

Kate shrugs again, then gives a little nod. 'I guess.'

'It's important you tell me what she said, love. After you'd gone downstairs, I tried to talk to her but she didn't reply. Can you remember what she said to you?'

Kate stares up at the sky for a moment, tracking an aircraft, watching its disintegrating vapour trail. 'She… she said something about being just like me once. Or liking me. I can't remember. Her voice was very quiet. But…'

'Go on, love, it's fine.'

'But it's not the first time she's spoken to me, Mum. She once said that this place has secrets,' Kate whispers, clearing her throat. 'Bad, *bad* secrets.'

After Kate goes back inside to get on with her homework, Mel stays sitting on the wall, surveying the building site, but mainly thinking about what her daughter just told her.

Bad secrets… She shudders, wondering if they're linked to her inheriting Moreton Inn. Nothing about the situation is normal, yet she would hate to think her presence here was tied to anything bad, let alone secretive.

Trying to put it from her mind, she checks the building progress on the extension. The footings are dug out now, all the new drains laid and connected, and the bulk of the soil and rubble removed for where the new terrace will go. Countless skips of rubbish, both from inside the hotel and out, have been filled and collected, with empty ones arriving every day. Tom has been managing all the building works according to the council's plans and, once the concrete is poured ready for the first bricks to be laid, he told her he'll be getting the planning officer out to sign off on the commenced works. Mel finishes her tea, knowing she couldn't have done any of this without him.

'Catching the last rays?'

She swings round, caught off guard. She thought everyone had gone home.

'Oh… hi.' She smiles, chucking the dregs of her tea onto the mud behind her. She sits down on the wall again. 'I was just admiring your handiwork.'

Tom comes up and sits down beside her, leaning forward with his forearms on his grimy jeans. 'Excuse the state of me,' he says. 'Hard day at the office.'

'It shows,' Mel says, staring straight ahead, tapping a fingernail on her empty mug.

'Go on then,' Tom says, giving her a friendly nudge.

Mel turns briefly, her eyebrows raised, head tilted.

'What's up? I might not know you very well yet, but I can see something's troubling you.'

A couple of wood pigeons coo-coo in the trees at the end of the garden, making Mel want to cry for some reason. Sounds of her childhood, of days lying on her back in children's home gardens, making wishes with dandelion heads.

'It's so peaceful here,' she says, avoiding answering. 'So perfect.' She laughs then, closing her eyes briefly as the warmth of the sun catches her cheeks. 'But... but I just *know*...' she adds, staring at the footings again. Then she checks herself, shakes her head as she remembers Michael's words. *You're hardwired to self-sabotage...*

'What do you know, Miss Douglas?' Tom says, twisting round to face her.

Mel senses his eyes on her. 'I guess it's hard to believe I'm actually here and this is all mine. I just want the best for Kate and...' She stares at the sky, willing herself not to spew everything out to Tom. She so easily could.

'And you're worried you're going to wake up and it was all a dream?'

Mel laughs. 'Something like that,' she says, flashing him a look. 'Kate told me something concerning just now,' she adds.

'I saw you two deep in conversation as I was loading up my van.'

'Apparently, she spoke to Miss Sarah this morning. As in Miss Sarah actually *spoke*. I don't think it was much more than a few words, but...' Mel pauses, taking a couple of breaths. She doesn't want to betray her daughter, but then Tom may be able to throw some light on it. 'Kate said Miss Sarah told her that the hotel has... that it has bad secrets.' She looks at him, hoping to read something reassuring in his expression, but his face remains blank.

'I see,' he says. 'And that's all she said?' He clears his throat nervously.

'She said something about her being just like Kate once – though I find it hard to believe she was ever remotely like Kate.' Mel laughs. 'But what a sinister thing to say to a kid, right? I tried to talk to Miss Sarah afterwards but she didn't say a word, of course. I'm rattled having her here. It's weird, as—'

'What you need,' Tom says suddenly, clapping his hands on his thighs, 'is dinner cooking for you. You've done nothing but work since you arrived. I prescribe a Tom surf 'n' turf special with a couple of bottles of wine and a bloody good laugh.'

Mel pauses, not expecting that. She was hoping to hear his opinion about what Miss Sarah said.

'Oh… I… Well…'

'Tomorrow is Friday. After work, I'll go home, shower, and then return early evening with the best prawns you've ever had and a couple of fillet steaks. As for the wine, I've been waiting for a special occasion to open something I've had stashed away. You won't need to do a thing, Miss Douglas. And I won't take no for an answer.'

CHAPTER TWENTY-SEVEN

It had been necessity rather than vanity. That's what Mel told herself, anyway, as she arrived back at the hotel from Lyme Regis, the next town along the coast. A scout around the shops was both a novelty and a much-needed break, as the last couple of weeks had been spent doing a lot of heavy lifting, deep-cleaning, rearranging, placing large orders for supplies, not to mention overseeing the extension build and making sure Nikki and Rose were on track with plans for opening the new restaurant.

She was both buzzing and drained.

And terrified that Tom had asked her on what sounded like a date.

First thing that morning, the new bedroom curtains had arrived and Mel had wanted to get them up in at least two of the guest rooms so they were completely finished. Before she'd left, she'd stood back and admired her handiwork, snapping photos to send to Michael.

He'd texted back immediately:

I approve. Book me in!

And he was right, Mel had thought. The two guest rooms were unrecognisable and it turned out that, with the outdated furniture painted a fashionable French grey, the sturdy pieces actually looked attractive. The beds, while comfortable, had had a good airing and were made up with crisp new white linen, each with plenty of plump pillows and a soft cream throw at the end. The en suite bathrooms, though small, had been scrubbed and bleached to within an inch of their lives, and the limescale dissolved to reveal gleaming taps and tiles. Plush white towels and scented toiletries completed the simple but clean look. Mel couldn't wait to get started on the other bedrooms but was resigned to having to break the lock on room seven. She'd not been able to find the key anywhere and it was the only room the master key didn't fit.

Satisfied, Mel had left for the shops at lunchtime, determined not to have to wear one of her old T-shirts for tonight's dinner with Tom.

'Don't see it as a date,' she'd told herself a hundred times on the way there, and while looking in the changing room mirror as she'd tried on at least ten different outfits. Finally settling on a pretty summer dress – nothing like she'd owned in a long time – Mel impulsively bought a pair of sandals and a silver necklace to go with it.

'Not, not, *not* a date. Remember your vow,' she muttered to herself as she wandered around, choosing a few new items for Kate too. It hardly seemed real that there was so much money in her bank account now, yet her instinct was still to head for the budget shops and scout about for bargains. For a while she'd had an internal battle with herself about spending fifty pounds on a dress, and twice that on things for Kate, but when the changing room assistant had gasped, told her how lovely she looked, Mel had got out her card without hesitation.

'We *deserve* it,' she tells herself, beeping her car locked with one hand, the other loaded up with shopping bags.

'Someone's treated themselves,' Rose comments as Mel passes her outside the kitchen. 'Lucky you, being able to afford it,' she adds, peering into the bags. She sighs. 'I think I've perfected them tartlets,' she goes on. 'There's one left for you to taste and approve, but the lads are enjoying the others for lunch. Especially Nige.'

Mel glances out of the window at the group of builders, including Tom and Nige. There are five of them in total today, each with a mug of tea and a delicate tart to hand.

'Someone poke me,' Mel says, laughing, watching as Tom puts down his mug and pulls off his T-shirt to reveal a tanned and muscular body. She feels her cheeks flush. 'I'm splashing out on new clothes and feeding a team of builders goat's cheese and cranberry tartlets for lunch. Life has certainly taken an unusual turn.'

She's about to head off when Rose sharply jabs her upper arm. Mel stops, rubbing the spot. It hurts, but Rose's sour expression prevents her from saying anything. Old instincts kicking in.

'You said poke you,' Rose says, her face blank and her arms folded over her large chest. 'By the way, Nikki wanted to see you. She's in the bar, stocking up with the new drinks.' Rose taps the side of her nose with a chubby finger, the stern expression suddenly gone.

'Oh… OK, thanks,' Mel replies, bemused, but unable to help another quick glance outside as she pushes the restaurant door open. 'Hey, Nikki,' Mel says as she goes in, admiring how much progress the young girl has made. 'This actually looks like a bar people might want to drink in.'

'I'm going to have to watch some YouTube videos to learn what to do with all this stuff,' Nikki says, holding a bottle of orange liquid out in front of her. 'Never heard of it,' she says, shrugging and putting it on the mirrored display behind the bar along with a row of other brand-new spirits.

'I think you'll find it goes quite nicely with prosecco and soda,' Mel says. 'With ice and a slice of orange.' She only knows this because it's what Michael used to make her on a Saturday night when she and Kate went back to his place after a day working at the shop. In summer, it was a tradition. They'd sit on the balcony chatting, while Kate binged on his Netflix account, with the smell of something gently bubbling in the slow cooker eventually driving them inside to eat.

'Oh. Right,' Nikki says with a puzzled expression. 'Anyway, great news. We have…' She pauses, drumming her hands excitedly on the bar. '…a guest! A whole entire paying guest. Can you believe it?'

'What?' Mel says, not expecting that at all. She remembers what Tom had said – someone asking about a room. She glances nervously at the door, half expecting Billy to walk in wearing one of the new bathrobes, a smug look on his face – the one that told her to brace herself, to prepare for the worst.

'I should be on commission,' Nikki adds. 'Don't tell anyone, but I hiked the price a tiny bit,' she adds in a whisper, putting her thumb and forefinger an inch or so apart in front of her squinted eyes, making them appear even more cat-like. 'He looked as though he could afford it in his swanky suit and posh accent. He sounded a bit… up himself though, can't lie.'

'Nikki—'

'It was only by twenty quid. Just to test the water, you know. Didn't want you to sell yourself short.'

Mel shakes her head, admiring Nikki's gusto. 'But… I mean, we're not actually open for business yet. We don't even have…' She trails off as she sees Nikki's expression change. 'Actually, that's brilliant news, Nikki. Well done you. We should toast that, for sure! Which room is he in?'

'I put him in number five,' Nikki said. 'He looked well pleased when he saw it.'

'How long is he here for? And what about dinner, breakfast? Oh, God…' Suddenly, everything seems very real. She'd not expected this at all. And what about Miss Sarah? She's sure to put off any guests and she doesn't want her mentioned in any TripAdvisor reviews.

'Don't panic. Rose had a food order arrive today. He's booked in for dinner, and she's going to test out her new menu on him.

And breakfast is all taken care of. I'll be here at seven. And we've got plenty of drinks, at least.' She sweeps a hand around the newly stocked bar.

'Wow, ok*aay*,' Mel says, one hand gripping the shopping bags tightly, the other touching her forehead. She'll have to cancel dinner with Tom, let him know that the kitchen will be in use and she'll need to work. She can't not be around for their first guest. She ignores the pang of disappointment in her stomach, wondering if it's actually relief. 'How long is he staying?'

'That's the great thing,' Nikki says, leaning forward on the bar. 'He didn't say. He left it open-ended but said it would be for a few nights at least.'

Mel absorbs the news then gives a definitive nod. 'We've got this, Nikki,' she says, holding up her right hand, palm out. 'Haven't we?' She pulls a silly but excited face.

'Damn right, boss,' Nikki chimes, giving her a high five back.

Lying on her bed, with Kate happily pulling her gifts from the bags, tearing off price tags and trying them on, Mel composes a text to Tom.

So sorry. I have my first guest tonight. Can we take a rain check on dinner?

She presses send and flops back down on her pillow.

'Mum, these are just amazing! I've never, *ever* had so much new stuff. Not even at Christmas. Thank you so much.' Kate ducks down to the bed and gives Mel a tight hug, momentarily warming her heart. 'Is it OK if Chloe comes for a sleepover tonight? I can't wait to show her all my new stuff. Her mum's dropping her off soon. I said you wouldn't mind.' Kate stares down at Mel. 'Mum? What's up? You look really sad.'

Mel sits up. 'Oh, it's nothing, love. Honestly. I'm fine.' She forces a smile. 'And of course Chloe can stay over tonight.'

'Thanks, Mum.' Kate pulls the dress Mel had bought for herself from its bag. 'This is lovely,' she says. 'Special occasion?'

Mel sighs. 'Not really. It was silly even buying it. I'll take it back in a few days. It's not my thing at all.'

'Nonsense, Mum. It's so pretty. Reckon you'll look amazing in it when Tom takes you out on a date.'

'Stop it, young lady,' Mel says, mustering a laugh. She whips the dress from Kate's hand and shoves it back in the bag. She won't be needing that tonight. Stupid of her to think she would. She and Kate are just fine, the two of them together.

Mel's phone pings.

OK, I understand x

Mel sighs. He didn't even put up a fight.

'Who's that?' Kate says, peering over Mel's shoulder. 'Tom? Ooh, look, he put a kiss.'

Mel shoves her phone down on the bed.

'I know he likes you, Mum. I can tell. Is that why you bought the dress? Are you trying to impress him? Do you like him too? Is he your boyfriend now?' Kate chants, dancing around. 'Oooh, Mum's in lurrrve…'

Mel rolls her eyes. She was in love once, yes. Stupidly, with Billy. But at least that love, albeit toxic, produced such a little firecracker, she thinks, getting up off the bed and chasing Kate for a tickle.

'Enough of that, young lady. We've got a hotel guest staying, don't you know. So best behaviour from you, please, and no running around the corridors.'

Kate gives a sharp salute. 'Yes, ma'am,' she says, giggling, standing to attention. Then she whispers, 'But I know you like him, Mum.'

CHAPTER TWENTY-EIGHT

'Good evening, Mr…' Mel glances down at the laptop on the reception desk, wishing she'd had time to change into something a little smarter. She didn't want to put on the new dress since she's planning on returning it anyway, but apart from jeans, T-shirts and baggy sweaters, she owns little else. Before the move, she was either wearing her work uniform or simply just at home. She scans the booking system for their only guest's name as he comes down the stairs.

'Good evening, Mr Spencer, and welcome to Moreton Inn,' she says cheerily, smoothing down her T-shirt and running her fingers through her hair.

The man stops on the bottom step, staring at Mel for what seems far too long.

'Good evening,' he replies in a deep, commanding voice. He offers a small smile.

'How's your room?' Mel asks, feeling nervous. 'Everything to your satisfaction?' She might not look the part right now, but she can at least try to sound it.

'Very nice indeed, thank you. Is it possible to get a drink before dinner?'

Mel glances at her watch. 'Of course. The bar has just opened. Please excuse all the ongoing renovations. You're actually… well, you're our first customer since I took over the place.'

'Excellent. On both counts,' he says through a mouth so pursed, Mel wonders if his lips have a drawstring.

As he comes down the last step, she sees that he's several inches taller than her. As Nikki reported, he's dressed in a smart suit – though his tie is loosened at the collar, his top button undone. She wonders if he's in the area on business – perhaps for a company conference and he'd not wanted to stay with his colleagues, maybe preferring somewhere more personal. For some reason, she gets the impression he's a bit of a loner. There's a serene look about him, as though he's comfortable in his own skin. A confident man with an agenda.

'Follow me. The bar is just through here, and… well, it's not going to be jumping with people tonight. Though we do have a couple of locals in occasionally. And you never know, it's Friday night, so…' Mel halts herself, prone to over-talking. He probably just wants a quiet beer, a meal and then to retire to his room with a good book. She opens the door to the bar, signalling for Nikki to take over. 'Enjoy your drink, Mr Spencer,' Mel says, wanting nothing more than to get up to her room to make herself more presentable.

Upstairs on the landing, she finds Miss Sarah standing between her and Kate's bedroom doors, arms dangling down by her sides and her head slowly turning between one room and the other.

'Hello,' Mel says, resigned to getting no reply. 'Are you going down for your dinner?' she asks. 'Just to let you know, we have a guest staying tonight.' When, of course, Miss Sarah doesn't say anything, Mel moves past her and opens her bedroom door, closing it behind her. She leans back against it, wishing she'd not mentioned the guest. The less interaction Miss Sarah has with people staying, the better. She makes a mental note to chase up Robert Hedges, the solicitor, in the morning. Find out where she stands legally. It's beyond unsettling now.

Mel quickly changes into a fresh white T-shirt, deciding that will have to do for tonight, hoping the slogan isn't too flippant. Her jeans are clean and, as she's applying mascara and a slick of lip gloss, she's reminded of how Billy would grill her if she ever tried to make herself look nice, questioning where she was going, who she was seeing.

She gives her hair a quick brush, deciding to wear the pretty new necklace she bought for herself. In defiance, she spritzes herself with some body spray – something she was never allowed to wear – and heads downstairs again to help.

*

Mel halts in the doorway to the restaurant, her heart sinking. Miss Sarah is standing beside her usual table in the window, her arms hanging limply beside her, her shoulders slightly hunched. She's positioned herself about four inches from their only resident, who has unwittingly sat himself down in Miss Sarah's place with a pint of Guinness and the newspaper. He either seems oblivious to her presence or is putting on a good show of ignoring her off-putting behaviour.

Mel glances at Nikki, who's behind the bar. She shrugs, a concerned expression on her face as she slowly polishes a glass. Several locals – two older couples and an older man that Mel has seen in a few times before – sit at the bar, joking and placing bets on what's going to happen next.

'Death by butter knife, I reckon,' one says too loudly.

'Drink over his head?' another says, laughing.

'Or maybe they'll get a room,' the first man says, glancing in Miss Sarah's direction.

One of the women tells them to pipe down, for which Mel is grateful.

She grabs a menu off the bar, takes a breath and heads over to the table. 'Mr Spencer, I'm so sorry but this table is reserved. Could I ask you to move to another one?'

The man looks up at her, giving a quick glance at Miss Sarah, who remains standing perfectly still right next to the table.

'Oh,' he says. 'Of course. Sorry, I didn't see a sign.' He stands and hesitates, waiting for Miss Sarah to step aside, but she doesn't. So he pulls his chair back even further, gathers up his pint and newspaper and follows Mel to one of the tables against the banquette.

'You'll have a bit more space here, anyway, Mr Spencer,' Mel says, smiling. 'Sorry about that,' she mouths in a whisper. 'She's a… well, she's a long-term guest and has her routine. Same table every meal.'

The man glances over at Miss Sarah, who's now sitting down reading her book. 'Interesting,' he says, dragging his eyes away from her. 'And please, call me Angus.' He beams a smile and holds out his hand. 'And I'm *very* pleased to meet you.'

Mel gives his hand a brief shake in return and is about to give him the menu, when she feels another hand on her arm.

'You're needed out the back. *Urgently,*' Nikki says, removing the menu from Mel. 'I'll take it from here. Really, Mel, you need to go outside. *Now.*' She whispers the last word, making a tense face, her eyes flicking towards the kitchen. 'There's… there's a big problem down in the spinney. You know, right at the end of the garden?' Nikki's face is flushed and her words breathy, as though she doesn't want to say whatever has happened in front of their guest.

'Right…' Mel says slowly, wondering what could possibly have happened that's so urgent. It's just a patch of untouched land, possibly once an orchard. 'I'll leave you in Nikki's capable hands then, Angus. Enjoy your meal.' And she heads off outside.

Smoke. She can smell *smoke*.

Christ, she thinks. Something's on fire.

'Girls, hi…' Mel says as she rushes past Kate and Chloe. They're sitting on the low wall near the footings, huddled over their phones, looking at something and giggling. They've each got an assortment of tools beside them – trowels, little gardening forks, teaspoons and a couple of old paintbrushes, as well as some containers.

'We're going on an archaeological dig,' Kate says. 'Chloe says there are loads of fossils around here.'

'Great,' Mel calls back, distracted. She stops a moment. 'Can you smell smoke, girls? Burning?' She sniffs the air. 'Stay here while I investigate, OK?'

Mel hurries on, the sound of the girls giggling and spraying out laughter behind her as she runs off. Definitely smoke, she thinks, rushing up to the end of the large garden, tripping a couple of times as the long grass and weeds get caught around her ankles. She's hardly been up here yet but, as she approaches the spinney, she sees that it looks as though part of it has been cleared – almost from the inside out. And from the tops of the trees, which form a kind of canopy over an opening, she sees smoke winding its way out.

'Heavens,' she thinks, wondering if the builders started a bonfire earlier to burn waste and it's got out of hand. 'They really should have asked me,' she mutters, hoping the trees haven't caught fire.

But as she heads into the spinney, she thinks she hears music. The slow, soulful beat of something she vaguely recognises. And there's no doubt that some kind of machinery has recently cleared a path through the undergrowth, cutting away all the brambles and nettles. Her eyes grow wide as she enters what almost feels like a room or the inside of a yurt.

'Oh my *God*,' she says, gazing around at the candles and fairy lights draped in the branches. In the centre of the little clearing sits a firepit with gentle flames licking up out of the coals. And the music is coming from a portable speaker with a phone attached to it. When her eyes finally adjust, she sees several camping chairs with blankets draped on them and Tom sitting in one of them, a folding table beside him piled with food and drink.

'Welcome to your very own grotto,' he says, standing up and raising his glass – his white smile outshining all the lights. 'Drink?' he offers, pulling a bottle of prosecco from a cool box.

Mel's hands come up over her mouth as she takes it all in, letting out an incredulous laugh. 'Yes, yes, I would like a drink *very* much,' she splutters from behind her hands, quite unable to believe what she's seeing – that someone has done all this for *her*.

CHAPTER TWENTY-NINE

'Seriously, I can't believe you've gone to all this trouble,' Mel says, taking the plastic flute. She laughs, looking around. 'It's absolutely magical. Perfect, in fact. But you know I've got a guest staying in the hotel and—'

'Melanie Douglas, you have *one* guest staying at the hotel, not an entire coach party. And a few locals at the bar who, if needed, can serve their own beer and write it on their tab. Nikki is very capable and can handle things by herself for a few hours. And she's very good at secrets, you know.'

'Secrets?' Mel asks, suddenly reminded of what Kate said about Miss Sarah. She sits down beside the fire. 'You mean, she was in on this?'

'Of course,' he says, tapping the side of his nose. 'I said I was cooking you dinner tonight, and that's what I'm going to do. It's hardly…' Tom hesitates, clearing his throat and pushing up his shirtsleeves. 'Well, it's hardly romantic sitting in a catering kitchen with a hot and sweaty Rose fussing about, is it?'

Mel raises her eyebrows – unsure if it's from appreciation or fear at his use of the word 'romantic'. No one has ever done anything like this for her in her entire life. She shudders.

'Are you cold?' Tom says. 'I brought blankets in case it gets chilly later. But with the fire, it should be toasty for a while yet.'

'No, no, I'm fine. And thank you,' she says, taking an olive from the pot Tom offers her. 'This is all lovely and *very* unexpected.' She glances around the canopy of trees. 'Nice touch with the candles and lights,' she says, admiring the strings twinkling in the greenery. 'If I had known, I would have dressed up a bit,' she adds, grateful at least for the bit of make-up she bothered with.

'I think you look perfect,' Tom replies in a voice that does something to Mel's insides. 'Your T-shirt is…' Tom pulls a face then, his eyes flicking down to her front.

Mel peers down at it too, remembering when Billy gave it to her. She should really have thrown it away, but she'd got so few clothes to wear, and it was something to put on, at least, so it had just stayed in her drawer.

'"Hands off",' Tom reads as he leans forward to add more charcoal to the fire. 'Understood, Miss Douglas,' he says, raising his eyebrows above a wry smile.

'Are you *sure* you don't want a job as a chef?' Mel says, peeling the shell off her fourth huge prawn. 'Whatever you've marinated these in, they're delicious.'

'Surf and turf barbecue nights for the guests, do you think?' Tom says, turning over a steak on the grill. 'Do help yourself to more salad.'

Mel nods, licking her fingers. She uses the tongs to grab more leaves from the Tupperware tub. Tom has thought of everything – right down to the condiments and napkins.

'One medium-rare steak, madam,' he says, putting the fillet on her plate. 'It's from the local butcher and will melt in your mouth.'

'Thank you,' Mel says, tucking in.

Tom tops up her drink and settles back in his chair with his plate balanced on his knee. He picks up a prawn and deftly pulls off its shell, tossing the remains in the fire.

'I'm sorry about Nige and the hose,' he says. 'He was out of order with what he did. I had a word with him afterwards.'

'It was just an accident,' Mel says, glancing up from her plate. 'Wasn't it?'

Tom gives her a look but doesn't say anything.

'I don't think he liked me getting my own back, though. I thought he'd be able to take a joke.'

'Nige is great with jokes as long as he's not the butt of them,' Tom replies. 'Must run in the family.'

'Family?' Mel asks, sipping her wine.

'Nige is Donald Bray's nephew. His mum, Jean is… rather *was*… Bray's sister. She passed away a couple of years ago. Cancer.'

'Sorry to hear that,' Mel says, trying to get the connection straight. 'So… Nige is Joyce's partner's nephew?'

'Correct.'

'I think I had a run-in with Donald in the newsagent the other day.'

'Did he smell of pig muck?' Tom asks, laughing. 'And have "Love" and "Hate" tattooed on his knuckles? All the Bray men have it.'

'Yes, he certainly smelt of something,' Mel replies. 'He was very rude. Virtually knocked me over. The shop lady said they call him Dirty Don. With good reason, it seems.'

'That's him,' Tom says, peeling another prawn. 'And believe me, the name fits.'

'The more I know about him, the more unpleasant he sounds. Best avoided, I think. Does Nige get on with him?'

'There was a bit of a falling-out between them when Joyce passed away. Nige hasn't said much but the upshot is, both men were… or *are*, I should say… bitter.'

'Bitter?'

'I'm not one for gossip, Mel, but from what I've heard from Dad, Bray thought he had his feet well under the table here. Reckoned he'd get the lot when Joyce died. But he didn't. He couldn't get her to marry him, and she didn't change her will.'

'I see,' Mel says, suddenly stopping chewing. 'So Bray's going to have a grudge against the person who *has* inherited Moreton Inn,' she says, thinking out loud more than anything. She reminds herself to look online, to see if she can find a record of Joyce's death and perhaps even get a copy of her will. It might be a lead.

'I guess,' Tom says, giving her a look, raising his eyebrows.

'And that would be me,' she whispers, remembering the angry look in Bray's eyes. She wonders if Nige soaking her with the hose was such an accident after all.

'So,' Tom asks, 'what did you do before you moved here?'

As she eats, Mel tells him about her tiny flat above the fish and chip shop, Kate's troubles at school and her job at The Cedars – as well as regaling him with tales of Josette.

'She sounds like a nightmare on legs,' Tom says. 'You're well out of there.'

Mel nods as she cuts into her steak. But Donald Bray is still on her mind.

'And what about Kate's dad? Is he on the scene?'

Mel stops chewing, knowing that if she swallows it, it won't go down easily. But she can hardly spit out a mouthful of delicious food. So instead, she takes a large sip of prosecco to help it along.

'Oh, I *see*,' Tom says with a laugh.

'No. No, you don't see at all,' Mel replies sternly, dabbing her mouth and giving him a look. 'Sorry, I didn't mean to sound harsh. It's a long story.'

Tom glances at his watch and shrugs. 'I'm going nowhere.'

'The short version is, he was in prison. And… and now he's not.' Mel knocks back half of her drink. 'He adores Kate, so he'll want to see her. Actually, more than that. He'll want to *take* her. I know my ex. Thankfully, he doesn't know where we are.' *Yet*, Mel thinks.

'I'm sorry to hear that,' Tom says. 'So that's why you came here? To escape?'

'Not on purpose,' Mel says, eating more steak. 'Inheriting this place was a happy accident. Almost as if... as if someone has my back. Yet I don't know who. It's driving me crazy not knowing, if I'm honest.'

'Your mystery benefactor.' Tom looks at her in that way again.

Mel nods, her smile falling away as she remembers Michael's words. *It's a truth universally acknowledged that a woman in possession of a large fortune...* He may have been joking about her sour expression at the time, and she knows he changed the words, but just add *...is easy prey* at the end and it could easily apply right now with Tom.

Tom has flirted with her since he found out she was the new owner. And now this lavish spread – all the trouble he's gone to, despite her saying she couldn't have dinner with him tonight. On top of all that, she's basically just told him how vulnerable she is. How could she be so gullible, so *stupid?*

'Anyway, I'm determined to find out who's behind it,' Mel continues, trying to rein in her thoughts. 'I don't have any family, you see. No one to inherit from.' She just wants to finish her food and leave as soon as seems polite.

'I'm absolutely stuffed,' she says ten minutes later. 'That was delicious, thank you so much, Tom.' Mel clears up the empty plates and other utensils and stacks them back in the crate Tom's brought everything in. 'Would you like a hand taking these to your car?'

'But we've not finished this yet,' he says, holding up the bottle. 'Besides, I didn't bring the car,' he adds with a wink and a smile.

The way he says it, the look he gives her, has Mel's heart thumping. But the prosecco winding through her veins, relaxing her, has her sitting down again. Sharing one more drink surely can't hurt? It's not as though he's just proposed.

'Sure, go on then,' she says, holding out her glass as he pours.

'So how come you don't have any extended family?' Tom says, adding a few twigs to the firepit. 'You seem like this really strong, together woman, yet…' He sips his wine, the flickering light of the flames reflecting in his eyes. 'Yet I sense another side to you, too.'

Mel half snorts, half laughs, smiling as she looks at him – his strong jaw accented in the candlelight, his kind eyes watching her – and, against her better judgement and everything she's been so vehement about these last few years, Mel feels something loosen inside. As if it might just be safe to open the door a little, to let Tom inside. Or, she wonders, allow a part of herself out.

'A *train*?' Tom says, shaking his head fifteen minutes later when Mel has recounted the story – or at least what she knows of it.

'Arriving Birmingham New Street station at 10.24 a.m., apparently.'

'That's crazy. I'm so sorry that happened to you, Mel.'

Mel shrugs. 'One of the cleaners found me, swaddled in a blanket and packed in a zip-up holdall like left luggage on the rack. She was called Melanie – hence my name. They let her choose my last name, too. No idea why she picked Douglas. Someone at the hospital wrote a letter explaining it all. It got passed around with me as a kid. Foster parents, children's homes – me and my few belongings got shifted around so often, I thought it was normal.'

'What kind of person would abandon a newborn baby on a train, for God's sake?' Tom says, opening another bottle of prosecco. 'Think this calls for it.'

'My mother?' she says with a wry laugh. 'She must have had her reasons, but I just can't fathom a good enough one, especially since I've had Kate.' Mel takes a sip of her topped-up drink, raising her glass at Tom. She feels more relaxed than she has in a long time, despite her earlier reservations. *He's not Billy*, she keeps reminding herself.

'Everything's gone through my mind over the years – that maybe she was very young, had no money, was addicted to drugs or alcohol, she was raped or abused, or I was an accident and she simply didn't want me. You hear of women getting pregnant who don't realise it until they give birth, and I wondered if that was the case. That the shock drove her to do something out of character. Or perhaps she already had a hundred children and couldn't cope. Or maybe she was ill, and—'

'Mel,' Tom says, reaching across the small gap between their two chairs and touching her wrist. 'Maybe you don't have to find a reason. Have you thought what it would change if you had answers? Do you want to find her?'

'Hell, no!' Mel says. 'Not a chance.' She looks down at her hand. Somehow, his fingers have wound between hers. It feels good and terrifying at the same time.

'Then maybe it's time to let go of the questions. Because perhaps there simply aren't any answers.'

As she looks into Tom's eyes, Mel thinks about this – never, ever again having to wonder about her heritage, her background, or the mother who didn't want her. It would feel like a weight lifted.

But before she can make sense of how she feels, she sees Tom's face drawing closer in the firelight. His eyes are locked on hers as his mouth gently connects with her lips. And suddenly, it's as though all her worries and fears and feelings of not belonging dissolve in the kiss, as if they never even existed.

Just for that briefest of sweet moments, she feels as if she's home.

Until she hears a scream.

Kate.

CHAPTER THIRTY

Mel freezes, opening her eyes that she didn't realise she'd closed as she'd fallen into the kiss. Her entire body is covered in goosebumps from the scream – unmistakably Kate's.

'God,' Mel says, gripping the arms of the fold-up camping chair as another piercing yell cuts through the twilight. 'That's Kate.'

She leaps up, stumbling over the rough ground of the spinney as she charges back towards the hotel, hearing Tom following her. A second later, he is running beside her, holding her hand as they weave through the tall grass, bushes and brambles.

'Kate?' Mel calls out. 'What's happened? Where are you?'

But as she draws close to the building, she doesn't need to search far to find her daughter. She and Chloe are close to where she left them earlier as they giggled together over their phones. Now, both girls are waist-deep, standing on the hardened concrete in the footings of the extension. Kate's hands are clutching the sides of her pink face as she lets out scream after scream, staring down into the earth.

Beside her, Chloe looks ashen and is shaking as she points down at something, imploring Mel and Tom to hurry.

'What is it?' Mel calls out as they draw up at the crumbling edge of the trench. 'What's going on?'

Before either of them can answer, Tom has his arms around Kate's waist and hoists her out, and then does the same with Chloe – getting them away from whatever danger it is they appear to have found. All sorts of things race through Mel's mind – a gas leak, an unexploded Second World War bomb, a nest of poisonous insects… she can't possibly think what would cause Kate to be in such a state.

'Kate, *talk* to me,' Mel says, taking her by the shoulders and looking her in the eye. But Kate remains silent, completely in shock.

'Down there, Mrs Douglas,' Chloe says in a shaky voice. 'We were pretending to be archaeologists on a dig. We didn't mean it. We're so sorry, please don't tell us off.'

'What? What on *earth*—?'

Mel halts when she sees Tom's face. He's jumped into the trench himself and is bending down, staring back up at Mel, his brow drawn tight in a frown.

'Go inside, girls,' Mel says, patting each of their backs. 'Ask Rose for some hot chocolate. I'll be in shortly.'

Kate just stands there, only moving when Chloe takes her hand. 'Come on, Katie. Let's get in. It's horrid. Think I'm gonna puke.'

Mel watches Kate, who glances up at the rear windows of the hotel for a moment before silently following her friend back inside. Then Mel turns to Tom, crouching down by the trench to see what it is he's looking at. She feels her heart hammering in her chest, as if it's pumping its way up her throat.

'Oh *Christ*,' Mel says, covering her mouth when she sees it. Her stomach churns. 'Is that…?' She can't bring herself to say the words.

Tom wipes his big hands down his face, exhaling loudly behind them. He tips back his head and takes a breath before crouching down again. He pulls his phone from his back pocket, swiping on the torch to get a better look. 'I think… yes, I'm afraid I think it is.' He takes a moment, shining the torch beam over the crumbling earth lining the side of the trench as Mel watches on.

'You can see where the girls have been digging around here, look.' Tom points at an area of dry mud chiselled out in the side of the footings. There's a plastic pot on the side of the trench filled with interesting-looking stones and a few fossils. The results of their 'dig' so far.

'It doesn't look as though they've disturbed it, thankfully,' Tom says, his voice subdued. 'The digger bucket must have come just inches away from it. It would have smashed it up.'

'It's… it's…' Mel stutters, getting down on her knees, leaning forward on her hands to get a closer look. The light is fading and she prays it's just a trick of the shadows, perhaps just some old tree roots highlighted by the bright light of Tom's phone. But the longer they stare at it, the more obvious it becomes.

Kate and Chloe have unearthed the skeleton of a baby.

'There's no doubt,' Tom says, standing up and hauling himself out of the three-foot deep trench. 'Those bones are… well, they're tiny. And the skull looks undeniably… human.' Tom turns his back on it, bending forward and taking a breath.

Mel also retreats, unable to look at it any more. She knows she'll never be able to unsee the foetal position of the leg bones, the way the skull was twisted sideways, the eye sockets glaring out at them – the dark holes filled with mud, making it appear almost sad. Mel shudders.

'We need to call the police,' Tom says, pacing about.

Mel nods, unable to think straight. 'Yes, yes, I guess that's what we have to do,' she says, feeling nauseous again.

'Unless…'

'Unless what?' Mel says, covering her mouth with her hand. 'Surely you don't mean…?'

Tom glances at the mini digger parked at one end of the site. 'There's fuel in it,' he says. 'It would save you an awful lot of hassle, delays and bad publicity.'

Mel stares at him before turning and going back to the trench, forcing herself to look at the bones again. She can even make out tiny fingers amid the chalky soil. She sighs, tipping her head back and staring up at the rear of the hotel, most of the windows stripped of their curtains – apart from room twelve. Miss Sarah's room.

For a moment, Mel thinks she sees the net drapes twitch, as if they're being watched.

She turns back to Tom. 'No,' she says vehemently. 'I couldn't possibly even consider it. For a start, the girls know it's there. Word would get out. And besides, I couldn't live with myself. However it came to be there, it's a matter for the police.'

Tom nods solemnly. 'For what it's worth, I agree totally,' he says, coming up to Mel and gently putting an arm around her back. She drops her head onto his shoulder as they both stand at the edge of the trench, taking a moment to absorb what's happened.

Mel sniffs, nodding. 'Good,' she says. 'I need to make sure the girls are—' But she stops abruptly, one hand gripping onto Tom's shirt as she presses against him. 'Look,' she whispers, staring back up at the hotel again. 'Miss Sarah… at her window.'

'Where?' Tom replies, tracking Mel's gaze.

'There. Up there, watching us, look,' Mel says, staring directly back at the woman's gaunt and ghostlike face. They lock eyes for a moment – Mel trying to read something in the woman's blank expression. But it's impossible and, before she can even blink again, Miss Sarah has let the net curtain fall back into place and retreated into the darkness.

*

'Thank you, Rose,' Mel says as she sees the two girls are each drinking a mug of hot chocolate. 'Is everything OK in the restaurant?' While she may have felt a little giddy from the prosecco up in the spinney with Tom, she feels completely sober now.

'All grand,' Rose replies, clattering plates into the dishwasher. 'There are quite a few locals in tonight,' she adds. 'Reckon old Moreton Inn has life in it yet, eh?' She tips her head sideways, wiping her sweaty face on her sleeve. 'Or death…' Mel swears she hears her whisper when her back is turned. 'We sold four cod and chips tonight to them lot at the bar, plus a lasagne and salad for the chap who's staying. Though Nikki says he's—'

'Yes, yes, Rose, thank you,' Mel says, her mind whirring. She wishes no one had come in tonight, let alone a guest arriving. 'I think you should go home now. We won't get any more in tonight.' Mel glances at her watch.

'Nonsense,' Rose says. 'We've got forty minutes until we stop serving food at nine. You never know, we might get a couple of dessert orders. Nikki's told them about the cheesecake I—'

'I'm closing early tonight, Rose. So if you don't mind, I'd appreciate you finishing up in here and heading home. I'll pay you up to the end of your shift.'

Rose stops for a moment, a tea towel between her hands. She glances between Mel and Tom, standing side by side, a hurt look on her face. 'Ohh, right, I see,' she says, tapping the side of her nose. 'A bit of alone time, is it? I'll be out of here then. And you girls, come on, drink up. Or why not take a slice of cheesecake up to your room with—'

'Rose, no. The girls are staying here. And please, as quickly as you can.'

Rose's expression changes again, a deep frown forming between her eyes. 'Understood,' she says with a solemn nod. She turns and puts the last few plates in the dishwasher, flicking the machine on. A quick wipe down of the draining board and stainless-steel surfaces and she dries her hands. 'I'll see you tomorrow then,' she says, removing her apron and heading off.

When she's gone, and when Tom has gone off to tell Nikki to not serve any more drinks, that everyone should finish up and go home, Mel steps outside the back door, keeping an eye on the girls through the window as they huddle together on stools at one end of the kitchen. Chloe has her arm around Kate and is talking to her, gently rubbing her back.

'Hello, yes, put me through to my local police station, please,' Mel says when the operator asks how she can help.

CHAPTER THIRTY-ONE

'They're on their way,' Mel says quietly, filling the kettle. 'Coffee?' she asks, wanting to be completely in control of her thoughts when the police arrive. Tom nods.

'Not the ending I'd had planned to the evening,' he says, touching her hand briefly.

Mel looks up at him. 'Me neither,' she says, glancing across at the girls, who are still huddled together in the kitchen.

'It's not your fault,' she hears Chloe telling Kate. 'You didn't know it was there. You're not in trouble.'

Kate sits on the stool, her shoulders slightly hunched and her head drooping forward. She hasn't spoken a word since they came inside, and she's staring straight ahead, gazing at nothing.

'More hot chocolate, you two? Or something to eat?' Mel says, trying to sound normal. 'And Kate, darling,' she adds, going up to her daughter and giving her a squeeze, 'I know what you found in the trench is upsetting, but Chloe's right. You weren't to know and it's not your fault. OK?'

Kate doesn't move. Just the occasional blink of her eyes.

'Chloe, do you still want to stay over, or should I call your mum?' Mel flashes a look at Tom, who's spooning coffee into two mugs.

'Can I stay over, please, Mrs Douglas? I'm worried about Kate. I can look after her, if that's OK?'

Mel winces briefly at the *Mrs*, though casts it aside.

'Of course, love,' Mel says, wondering if she should inform the girl's mum. But she decides to wait and see what the police say, knowing that it will do Kate good to have her friend here. She's more likely to talk to her than anyone else. 'Why don't you girls go up to Kate's room and watch some telly or play some games?'

'But what's going to happen, Mrs Douglas? Are you going to dig the… the body up?'

Again, Mel winces inwardly, but not at the misuse of her name this time. 'Well, firstly, it's bones, Chloe. And we're not sure what kind of bones yet. But no, I'm not going to disturb it. I've alerted the authorities so they can decide what to do.'

Chloe's big eyes circle around in their sockets. 'You mean the police?' She pulls a packet of mints from her pocket and offers one to Kate. Kate doesn't move, so Chloe pops one in her own mouth before holding the little plastic tub out to Mel. 'In case it's human?'

Mel shakes her head. 'No thanks, love. And we're not sure what it is out there, but best to be on the safe side, eh?'

'What if there's more, like it's a whole spooky graveyard or something? They could do, like, a TV documentary on it and we might get to be in it, Katie. Like one of those crime watch things you see.' Chloe jiggles up and down with excitement, clearly over the shock of what they discovered. But for some reason, Kate remains silent.

'C'mon, Katie, let's go and play *Fortnite*. No point us being archaeologists any more tonight.' When Kate doesn't make a move, Chloe takes her hand and gives it a tug, giving Kate no option but to put her feet on the ground when she's off-balance. When Chloe gives her arm another gentle tug, Kate reluctantly follows her.

'I'm here if you want to talk, love,' Mel calls out to Kate, watching the girls leave the kitchen. 'She's very upset,' she says to Tom, taking the coffee he's made for her. 'Understandably so. What do you think happened?'

'My best guess,' Tom says, perching on the stool Kate has just vacated, 'is that they've disturbed a very old grave. I'm not sure what the process is, but it'll probably need to be resited. Much paperwork, I imagine. It looked pretty ancient to me, but then I'm no expert.'

Mel sips her coffee thoughtfully. One minute she's drinking prosecco by candlelight, eating delicious food, and the next she's calling the police because of what looks like the skeleton of a baby in the footings of the extension. 'Surreal,' she says. 'I know it's the last thing I should be thinking, but it's going to cause massive delays to the building works. If you need to go to other jobs, Tom, I understand—'

'Hell-*ooo*…?' comes a voice from behind the swing doors as they open an inch or two.

Mel goes over and pulls one wide open. 'Oh, Mr Spencer. How can I help you?' She has no idea how much he just overheard.

'Any chance of some of that cheesecake I was promised?' he says. His gaze darts behind her, flicking about the kitchen.

'Oh…' Mel says. 'Yes, of course,' she adds, trying to suppress the sigh. There's no point annoying her first paying customer over a dessert. After tonight's discovery, she's going to need all the good reviews she can muster. 'Take a seat and I'll bring some out to you.'

'Good, good,' the man says. 'And… well, don't forget to call me Angus. I'm going to be around for a while, after all.' He laughs then – a kind of throaty, grunting sound that makes Mel feel nauseous all over again.

'You are?' Mel says, her voice croaking.

'I've important matters to take care of, you see,' he replies with a stare that sends a shudder through Mel. She doesn't like the way he looks at her.

'Great,' she says, forcing a smile. 'I'll bring your dessert in a minute.' And she makes a point of shutting the kitchen door to end the conversation.

*

'Nikki, can you close up here, please?' Mel says quietly behind the bar. 'Did Tom give you the message?' She grabs some empty glasses and puts them in the washer ready for a cycle. Over on the banquette, she's aware of Angus Spencer watching her, lifting small mouthfuls of cheesecake into his mouth and slowly licking them off the spoon, as if he's trying to make it last longer and delay having to retire to his room.

'Yes, he did, but… but what about *them*?' Nikki says, flicking her eyes to the couple of locals propped against the bar. Mel hears them discussing the football. 'They'll have at least another three rounds before the night's out. Don't you want the business?'

'Not tonight, Nikki,' Mel replies quietly.

'Oh, how come? Is there a prob—?'

But Nikki stops and Mel catches her breath as two uniformed police officers walk through the door, each of them glancing around and getting their bearings.

'Good evening,' the female officer says to both Mel and Nikki as she approaches the bar. 'Is Miss Douglas here, please?'

'Yes, yes, that's me,' Mel says, suddenly aware of a clattering sound as well as her cheeks burning scarlet as the locals stare at her. When she glances behind the officers, she sees that Angus has dropped his spoon on the floor and, in the process of picking it up, has knocked over his pint. 'Nikki, would you clean up for our guest while I see to this, please?'

'Of course,' Nikki says slowly, reaching for several cloths from the small sink behind the bar without taking her eyes off the officers.

'Follow me,' Mel says. 'We'll go somewhere more private.' As she heads out of the back of the restaurant, towards the kitchen, she catches sight of Angus, his eyes tracking her as she leaves.

*

Ten minutes later, after the constables have introduced themselves as PCs Angie Gordon and Stuart Latch from the local constabulary,

Mel leads the way out through the back hallway and onto the building site.

'As you can see,' she adds quickly, having unlocked the door with several keys. 'The area is cordoned off securely from staff and hotel guests. All the health and safety measures are in place for the build.'

'I don't doubt that,' the male officer says.

'The girls were digging around here,' Mel adds, noticing that Tom has followed them out. She feels strangely comforted to have him beside her, as if he is in this with her, too. For a fleeting second, she almost feels their kiss still tingling on her lips. 'They're into fossil hunting, you see. They figured it was a good time to root around in the deep trench before the blocks and bricks go in and it gets backfilled.'

'And they found more than they were bargaining for?' PC Latch says, his uniform cap under his arm. PC Gordon follows suit and removes her hat too as they approach the trench.

'Indeed,' Tom says. 'The screams were… well, they were loud. The girls are very upset.'

'Down there, look,' Mel says, pointing to the section of trench that's approaching the ninety-degree turn where the extension wall will cut across parallel to the rear of the hotel. 'If you look, about a foot up from the concrete, you can see the bones lying facing out. It's as if… as if…' She can't bring herself to say, *It's as if the baby had been buried in its sleep…*

There's silence for a moment as the officers retrieve their torches and shine two cones of light into the ground. They mumble a couple of things between them, and PC Gordon turns down her radio volume as it crackles at her shoulder.

'Am I looking at the right thing?' PC Latch says. Then he draws in a sharp breath. 'Oh right, OK, yes… I see.' He steps back, straightening himself up for a moment. But PC Gordon is still peering into the trench, shining her torch all around.

'Are you sure it's not a cat or a dog, or some other pet? It's quite hard to tell.' She stares down intently, squinting and tilting her head from side to side.

'To my mind, I don't think there's any mistaking it's human remains,' Tom says. 'A very tiny human. I googled examples of pet skeletons, and I'm afraid this is very different.'

Mel takes a step or two closer to the trench, steeling herself to take another look, in case she can convince herself that the skull is indeed that of a small dog or cat. Or maybe even a rabbit. Her eyes scan over the dry soil, carved away cleanly by the bucket of the mini digger, apart from the area where the girls were scratching around with their trowels. It takes a moment for her brain to spot what she's seeing, but when she focuses again, her heart sinks.

There's no mistaking it's human.

As Tom talks to the other officer, PC Gordon straightens up and flicks off her torch, walking away from the footings to make a call on her radio. Mel hears something about suspected human remains, about CID, about building works being halted and photographs being sent to experts. She cups her face in her hands, exhaling hard. Nothing in her life makes sense any more.

CHAPTER THIRTY-TWO

'So,' PC Latch says, leaning forward in an attempt to seem less intimidating. At least that's what Mel supposes he's trying to do as she studies his expression – him sitting opposite Kate and Chloe, the pair of them nestled together on the banquette in the now-empty bar area. Nikki had finally coaxed the few customers home, Mel noticed thankfully when they'd come back inside. And, after as much of an inspection as the officers could do visually outside, given that the light was fading fast, they'd asked to have a few words with the girls. Or the *budding archaeologists*, as PC Gordon had put it.

'You were both looking for fossils?' PC Latch continues.

Chloe nods earnestly, sweeping back her fiery hair. Then she scratches her nose, wrinkling it up. 'Yes, we found loads. Perfect conditions,' she adds in an authoritative voice.

Kate sits perfectly still, slightly hunched.

'Perfect conditions for?' PC Gordon asks, a notebook on her lap as the officers perch on the newly painted stools.

'Digging, of course,' Chloe says, shrugging. 'Not too much rainfall recently, but just enough so that the ground wasn't like stone. And that bulldozer thing had done half the job for us. It was like… like…' She swishes back her hair again, sticking out her chin. 'Like finding buried treasure.'

Mel watches Chloe, wondering why she seems about five years older than Kate, who's sitting there, limp and mute. Perhaps if

Chloe kept quiet for a moment, she thinks, Kate could get a word in. Mel presses her palms together in her lap.

'Kate, love?' Mel says as the officers make notes. 'What do you remember happened?'

Kate stares at the carpet. Her eyes appear vacant – almost non-human, like the soil-filled sockets of the tiny skull. Mel shudders.

'Darling?' She reaches forward and strokes her daughter's knee. 'Talk to me, sweetheart.' She touches Kate under the chin, gently trying to tilt her head up. But she's rigid.

'Did you find any other bones in your… dig?' PC Gordon asks in a voice more suited to talking to five-year-olds. 'And did you put them in your little bucket?'

'What?' Chloe says, whipping out her phone from her pocket when it pings with a message. 'We have an artefacts container. Not a little bucket. We photograph, measure and label everything we find.' She taps out a reply on her phone then looks the officer straight in the eye. 'And no. We didn't find any other bones. As soon as we spotted the skeleton, we stopped digging. Well, actually, Kate started screaming.'

'I see, and—'

'Will we get a reward? Like, if we've discovered a murder or a Viking burial or something? What if there's a hoard there too? Like a load of gold coins and ancient jewellery. Do we get to keep it? What if—?'

'Let's take it one step at a time, shall we?' PC Gordon says, her eyes narrowing with her smile. 'Do you have any pictures of the… of the skel… of the bones on your phone?'

'Yeah, loads,' Chloe says, whipping her device back out of her pocket again just as it pings. She laughs as she reads whatever's on the screen. 'Can a couple of my other friends come over to look at the skeleton, Mrs Douglas? They said it's super-cool.'

'What?' Mel says, horrified. 'You've told your *friends*?'

Chloe shrugs. 'No. They saw my Insta post.' Then she holds the screen in front of the officers. 'Look, this is Katie just as we're about to start digging.' Chloe swipes left a couple of times. 'Ha ha, look. She's being silly here.'

Mel leans forward, something warm stirring inside her as she sees her daughter mid-star jump over the trench. Chloe must have been standing down on the concrete footings, looking upwards as she took the photo.

'Posing as ever,' Chloe says, nudging Kate, who looks as though she might topple off her seat if she's pushed any harder. Chloe swipes forward through a couple more pictures.

'Stop, wait,' Mel says, leaning in closer. 'Go back a photo or two.'

'But I've got some of the bones and—'

'Go back,' Mel insists.

Chloe does as she's told.

'There, that one. Can you enlarge it?' It's the picture of Kate doing the star jump. Mel takes Chloe's phone off her and zooms in so she can see a close-up of Kate's side, but also the windows at the back of the hotel.

'It's a photo burst,' Chloe says. 'Cool, eh?'

'What do you mean?' Mel asks.

'Look,' Chloe says, taking back her phone. She presses and holds the screen and suddenly a stream of consecutive pictures flashes up, reminding Mel of the cartoon flipbooks she made as a kid.

'There!' Mel says as she watches Chloe speed through the burst for a second time. 'Did you see her?' Mel glances up at Tom, who's standing over them, also watching. 'Miss Sarah was at the window. And she had her arm up, as if she was tapping on the glass.'

'Tapping?' Tom says, leaning in and taking hold of Chloe's phone. 'May I?' he asks as the girl relinquishes it. 'I'd say it looks more like she's banging on it.'

*

'Mrs Douglas?'

Mel whips her head up, not realising that she'd fallen asleep until she's woken by the voice. As she sits up, she feels a sore patch on her forehead where she'd rested it on the table in the bar, half cradling it on her arms as she'd leant down and drifted off. Combined with the shock of earlier, the shot of brandy she'd had after the police left had contributed to her dozing off.

'Hi, Chloe. Is everything OK?'

The girl's expression is a mix of caution and concern. Her copper hair is in two thick plaits and she's wearing pale pyjamas with penguins printed all over. Suddenly, she doesn't seem like the overconfident twelve-year-old going on eighteen any more.

'Katie's asleep,' she says, coming a little closer to the banquette where Mel had dropped down, exhausted, after Tom had left.

Did I even thank him properly for the meal? Mel tries to remember. She thinks she must have, but with all the talk of CID investigators coming tomorrow, about experts from the university and exhumation paperwork, she can't be sure. Her mind is all over the place.

'That's good,' Mel says, stretching. 'But you can't sleep?'

Chloe shakes her head, clasping her hands in front of her and shifting from one foot to the other.

'Hot milk?' Mel suggests. The girl nods and follows Mel into the kitchen.

'Mrs Douglas,' Chloe says in a questioning voice, chewing on a nail, 'how bad is it if… if I tell you stuff that Kate told me.'

Mel turns to face her, one hand on the pan of warming milk. 'Ok-*ay*…' she says slowly. 'That depends on what it is, I guess.'

'I mean, it's not like she told me not to tell anyone. But… well…' For a moment, Chloe focuses only on her finger, then she stares at the ceiling as she gnaws.

'What kind of stuff?' Mel asks, coming over to where she's perched on the stool. 'I know she's very upset about earlier. I'm glad she's been able to talk to you about it.'

'No, no, it's not about that. She still hasn't said a word. It was the other day. Something about… about a man.' Chloe removes her finger from her mouth, inspecting it before folding her arms.

Billy…? Mel thinks, her heart beating fast. Has Kate been confiding in Chloe about her dad? Has he contacted her again or, worse, maybe even found them?

When it became clear that Kate wasn't using the phone that Billy had given her any more, Mel had quietly taken care of it, hoping Kate wouldn't notice it had gone. If Billy wanted to contact Kate, then he would have to get past her first. Or go through the courts. She knew court was the last place Billy wanted to be, so she'd kept the phone charged up in her bedside cupboard, checking it from time to time for texts or missed calls. So far there had been nothing.

'A man? What man?' Mel asks, sounding more abrupt than she'd intended. 'It's fine to tell me about it, Chloe,' she says in a more encouraging tone.

'A bad man,' Chloe replies, shaking her head. 'He did bad things to… to someone. A relative, she said. It really upset her.'

It certainly sounds like Billy, Mel thinks, wondering if Kate is confiding in Chloe without *actually* confiding. Talking to a friend about a previous trauma is natural, but knowing Kate, she wouldn't want to be specific, would be ashamed of the details. The poor kid is torn between loving her dad and despising him.

'Do you know the man's name, Chloe?' Mel asks.

Chloe shakes her head. 'She wouldn't say. But she said she spotted him down in the village.'

In the village? Mel thinks, wondering when this was. Perhaps after the school bus dropped her off one afternoon, when she was walking home. Kate's not allowed out alone otherwise.

'Do you know if he spoke to Kate? If he saw her?'

Chloe shakes her head. 'Kate said she was spying on him. That she followed him.' She bites at her nail again for a moment. 'Thing is, Mrs Douglas, well… I really like Kate. She's my bestie now and I don't want to be a snitch.' She lets out a little whimper. 'But my mum's always going on at me to keep away from strangers and stuff.'

Mel strokes Chloe's shoulder. 'No one's going to think you're a snitch, Chloe. You've done the right thing by telling me.'

Chloe nods, letting out a little hiccup. 'Kate said she wants to get revenge for what he did. I'm scared for her.'

'What he *did*? Who to?' Mel says, her eyes widening. So many questions, but she doesn't want to make her clam up either. 'And what does she mean by revenge, Chloe?'

'She said he'd hurt people for too long.' Chloe shrugs, making a pained expression. 'She said he shouldn't be allowed to get away with it any more. She, like, got really upset about it.'

'I see,' Mel says, her mind joining the dots. 'I'm really pleased you told me this.'

Chloe nods, a troubled look on her face. 'And… and the other thing…' she continues, sniffing and rubbing her eyes from tiredness. 'That weird woman upstairs, Kate says she knows about it, too. That they've been talking.'

And before Mel can ask anything else, she hears hissing and spitting on the stove behind her as the milk pan boils over.

CHAPTER THIRTY-THREE

Mel takes a breath and knocks sharply on the door. She's barely slept a wink – her mind racing all night long. After she'd settled Chloe back into bed and checked that Kate was comfortable and sleeping, she'd had a bath, tried to unwind, but she couldn't. She'd maybe managed forty-five minutes, perhaps an hour of dozing, then watched it get light before giving in and getting up.

When there's no answer, she knocks again and turns the door handle. But, unlike before, room twelve is now locked. Already armed with the master key, Mel takes it from her pocket and unlocks it. She wants answers, and she wants them now.

'Miss Sarah,' she says, going right in – not caring if the woman is still asleep, sitting in her chair reading or even doing aerobics. Enough is enough. 'I'm sorry for the intrusion, but we need to speak about—'

Mel stops in her tracks, her eyes adjusting to the dim light. The curtains are still drawn and Miss Sarah is sitting perfectly straight and still on the edge of her bed. Apart from her underwear, she is completely naked – her body pale and sinewy. Mel's eyes are drawn to her stomach and thighs, both of which are covered in a map of thin, silvery scars.

'Oh… I… I'm so sorry – I didn't realise that…' Mel knows there's no viable excuse for barging in, but after what Chloe had told her last night, she couldn't contain herself. 'Perhaps we can talk later. It's about Kate. I'm worried about her, and I think you…' Mel trails off. 'Oh, Miss *Sarah*,' she says, spotting the tear slowly rolling down her cheek. 'Look, I can see I've caught you at a really bad moment…'

Mel looks around the room, spotting a dressing gown at the end of the bed. She reaches for it, doing a double take as she picks it up. Concealed beneath the robe is a laptop computer, it's screen semi-open and glowing beneath. She hesitates for a moment, noticing that it looks like an older model, but is more concerned with Miss Sarah's privacy. She drapes the cream-coloured gown around the woman's shoulders, coaxing her to put her arms in, which she does. Mel loosely fastens it up with the belt.

Then she surprises herself by sitting down on the bed next to her and gently rubbing her back. She can't get the image of all those scars out of her mind, sensing that each of the faded lines criss-crossing her skin has a story to tell. She just can't imagine what.

'Miss Sarah, I know you don't like talking, or perhaps find it difficult… but I do know that you and Kate have been chatting. I think that's really nice, of course, and Kate is a lovely girl. But she's been through a lot in her life, and I…' Mel trails off, not knowing how to word it without betraying Chloe. 'And I wouldn't want her to be upset about things that are maybe best confided in me. Does that make sense?'

Nothing. Silence. Miss Sarah stares straight ahead. The tear that was on her cheek has rolled down past her chin and dried in a salty streak.

'Kate and I are close, and she tells me everything.' Mel pauses, wondering how true that actually is. 'And… well, I understand that she told you about someone she saw in the village. A man.' Mel swallows. Waiting.

Nothing.

'This man, Kate's dad, well, the thing is, she thinks that he deserves…' Mel hesitates, unsure how much Kate has revealed to Miss Sarah. 'Well, let's put it this way. She's really angry at him – for lots of reasons. That's understandable, of course, but…'

Mel trails off as an image of Kate standing in her and Billy's bedroom doorway flashes through her mind. Billy, fuelled by rage, had Mel pinned down on the bed.

'So I'd really appreciate…' Mel continues, '…that if Kate has been confiding anything worrying to you, you could please let me know.'

Nothing.

Mel sighs, frustration brewing. 'Look, I understand that you find it difficult to speak, Miss Sarah, but I think you're going to have to. You're living in my property now, yet I know nothing about you.' Mel leans closer to the woman, putting her face in front of hers, in the hope it might elicit a reaction. But it doesn't.

'Fine,' Mel says after a few moments waiting. 'Then I'll have to sort this mess out my way. You'll be getting a letter from my solicitor. I'll be looking into…' Mel hesitates. She doesn't want to use the word eviction, knowing how terrifying and disempowering it is. But then she's also had enough of this woman. 'Well, I'll be looking into alternative housing arrangements for you.'

She gets up and heads to the door, stopping and turning to face Miss Sarah. 'If it helps, then write it down for me or something. Christ, draw a picture if you have to, but just communicate with me!' She shakes her head, sighs and leaves the room just as Nikki is coming along the landing, a concerned expression on her face.

'A man? What kind of man?' Mel says, striding down the corridor with Nikki trotting beside her. 'And what the hell does he want?' The weekend hasn't got off to a good start.

If it's Billy finally showing his hand, Mel thinks, then I'm in no mood for his games. He can go do one and I'll take out a non-molestation order faster than he can say 'prison'.

'A man from the papers,' Nikki says breathlessly. 'He's heard about… well, he asked me about a body.'

'Oh, for heaven's sake,' Mel mutters under her breath as she goes down the stairs, dreading to think what hashtags Chloe put on her Instagram post. When she gets down to reception, a young man is standing there, likely the local hack on his first assignment with the scent of blood in his nostrils by the looks of him.

'Thanks, Nikki,' Mel says. 'I'll take it from here.' Nikki scuttles off into the bar with a grateful expression for being excused.

'How can I help you?' Mel says, folding her arms behind the reception desk. You've caught me on the wrong bloody day, she thinks, saying a silent prayer for him yet managing a small smile, knowing that riling a journalist wouldn't be the cleverest of moves.

'Jacob Ingram, *Evening Post*,' he says, holding out a hand. Mel offers him a brief handshake in return. 'I'm here about the human remains,' he says, as if it's the most normal thing in the world. 'Can you comment, Mrs…?'

'It's Miss. Miss Douglas. And no, I can't.'

For a second, Mel thinks she's fazed him enough to send him on his way. But then she realises the opposite is true. His insipid grey eyes briefly flash wider, as if he's actually got the taste of blood in his mouth now and quite likes it. He squares up, mirroring her posture – folding his arms and planting his feet wide apart.

'Am I correct in saying that the police have cordoned off an area at the rear of Moreton Inn pending further investigations after the discovery of a body, Miss Douglas?'

Shit, Mel thinks, curling up her toes inside her trainers.

'I can't comment on that, I'm afraid.'

'Can you tell me if your plans to reopen Moreton Inn have been delayed because the remains of an infant were found in the footings of your new extension?'

'I've nothing to say to you about anything. You're wasting your time here.'

Jacob Ingram stares at her for a moment, with one hand kneading his chin. 'In that case, perhaps you'd like to tell me about what you have in mind for... for the old place?' he says with a smile. 'My uncle used to come in here, back in the day.' He gives a sweeping gaze around the revamped reception area. 'It was a right old dive, according to many,' he continues. 'But Joyce had her regulars. Plus the occasional guest, usually never to return.' He lets out a laugh – far too high-pitched for a man. He sweeps his mousy fringe off his forehead. 'Have you seen the TripAdvisor reviews, Miss Douglas? What changes are you making?'

Mel pauses for a moment. If she doesn't give anything away about human remains, then this could work in her favour. Free publicity if he runs a piece about the reopening of the hotel and restaurant. She forces a smile and relaxes her posture, leaning forward on the desk.

'Well, as you can see, I'm really bringing Moreton Inn up to date – a dash of modern while still retaining the old charm,' she says. 'We'll be serving traditional pub food with a gourmet twist, as well as catering for functions, weddings and parties in our new extension. All our bedrooms are being refurbished to create a country-meets-seaside theme, with luxurious bedding and complimentary toiletries. If you like, I can show you around or let you sample our menu later?'

'It all sounds delightful,' he says with a wry smile. 'Remind me to book in. And I'll send my fiancée along to discuss weddings.' The smile turns into a grin, exposing slightly yellow and crooked teeth. 'But about the remains found on the property. Can you confirm if they were human? What did they look like? Do you have any photographs? Are they still in situ? Would you show me the site? Do you believe there was foul play? How are the police dealing with the incident? How is your daughter now, having made the discovery? Would it be possible to speak with her, and—'

'Get out,' Mel says sharply, realising a promotional piece isn't on his radar in the least. '*Now.*' She jabs a finger towards the front door. 'And if you don't, I'll be calling the police again to have *your* bones removed this time.'

'So you're not denying that you called the police, that human bones have been found buried at Moreton Inn, Miss Douglas?'

'Now!' Mel shouts, startling Kate as she comes down the stairs.

'Is this your daughter, Miss Douglas? Would you mind if I had a quick word?' Jacob approaches Kate as she stands on the bottom step, pressed up against the wall. Her eyes are wide and terrified, her face pale with a deep frown.

'Can you tell me about the bones you found?' Jacob says, tapping a few buttons on his phone. Mel sees him press the red record button before he holds it out under Kate's chin. 'How did you feel about the discovery? Was there any clothing, or hair, or even flesh on the bones? Was it male or female? How big would you say the—'

It only takes one swipe for Mel to knock his phone from his hand and stamp on it the second it hits the floor. She hears the screen crack beneath her heel in a satisfying crunch.

'I said get out of my hotel *now*! And don't bloody well come back, you scum journalist piece of shit! How dare you—'

'Hey…' a voice says from behind her. 'Everything OK, Mel?' She feels the warmth of Tom's hand on her back as she turns to look up at him.

'I was just saying goodbye to Mr Ingram here,' she says through gritted teeth, adrenaline churning up her stomach. 'He's from the *Evening Post*. Clearly the area is *very* light for news at the moment.' She glares at the man as he picks up his smashed phone.

Tom advances towards the journalist, who's nearly a foot shorter than him. 'I think you need to do what Miss Douglas says and leave immediately.'

Without a word, Jacob Ingram retreats, giving a sharp-eyed look back over his shoulder before the door closes behind him.

'Kate, are you OK, my love?' Mel says, hugging her close. 'Thanks, Tom,' she says – grateful to him, yet disliking the fact that it took another man to finally get rid of the journalist. 'Kate?' Mel says, focusing on her daughter. She gently holds her at arm's length, looking her in the eye. 'Did you sleep OK, love? Just ignore that idiot man before. He doesn't know what he's talking about. Come on, let's get some breakfast. What do you fancy?'

Kate doesn't say a word but follows her mother into the kitchen.

'Darling, what's wrong? I know last night was upsetting, but don't worry, sweetheart. Everything's in hand. It'll all be fine.'

Kate shuffles over to the stool she sat on last night when Chloe was comforting her. She stares at the floor, balling up her fists in her lap.

'Where's Chloe? Is she coming down for breakfast too?'

'Ah, yes, a message for you,' Tom says, having followed them into the kitchen. 'I bumped into Chloe's mum in the car park just now. She'd come to pick her up and asked me to thank you for having her.'

'Already?' Mel says, glancing at her watch. 'I thought she was staying until lunch, Kate? Wasn't she enjoying herself?'

Of course she wasn't enjoying herself, Mel thinks. She and Kate found the bones of a baby in the garden and she's been interviewed by the police.

'Mel?' Tom says, beckoning her with a quick flick of his head.

Mel follows him out into the back hallway. Standing there, she can't help glancing out through the large windows, to where the blue and white police tape has cordoned off the building site. PC Gordon said someone would be in touch today and, meantime, no one was to set foot in the area.

'Chloe's mum asked me what was going on. She said Chloe had phoned her not long before in floods of tears. She said she wanted picking up immediately.'

'Oh, great,' Mel says, pushing her fingers through her hair. 'That's all I need. I've managed to alienate Kate's friend as well as her mum. No doubt word will spread around her other mates and she'll end up being ostracised at school again. Why does history keep repeating itself?' Mel shakes her head, pushing back her hair as she sighs. 'And I swear, if that little shit journo prints a word about that…' Mel points outside. 'Then I'll… I'll… bury *his* bloody body under the patio!'

'Hey… hey… it's OK.'

Tom reaches out to Mel, wrapping his hands firmly around her forearms, drawing her closer. For a moment, their eyes lock but, at the feel of his strong hands gripping her, *restraining* her, Mel suddenly yanks her arms away and, without thinking, she lashes out and hits him on the shoulder.

'*No!*' she screams, jumping back several paces. She glares up at him, her breathing hard and fast, her pupils dilated and her heart thrashing inside her chest. Instead of seeing Tom standing there, his expression bemused, for the briefest of moments Mel sees the pointed and angry features of Billy's face leering back at her as he comes in for the attack.

CHAPTER THIRTY-FOUR

'Miss Douglas?'

Mel freezes.

She glances behind the man – behind *Tom* – to see a woman standing there. A woman in uniform – PC Gordon. Mel's breaths are short and sharp, her chest tight, her forearms still burning from Billy's grip.

From *Tom's* grip.

'Mel, I'm so sorry… I didn't mean… I wasn't going to hurt you. The opposite, in fact,' Tom says, keeping his voice low.

Mel hears Tom's words, sees the concerned and apologetic expression on his face, but is preoccupied with her racing heart and the police officer standing behind him in the doorway. There are two men alongside her – neither in uniform. They've come round the back entrance.

'Hello again,' Mel manages to say. She gives Tom a quick look, tries to apologise to him with her eyes, but judging by his bewildered expression, he's not picked up on it.

'I'd like to introduce Dave Clements, a biological anthropologist from Bournemouth University, and DI Steve Armitage from CID,' the officer says. 'They'd like to do an evaluation of the site now it's daylight. Is it OK with you if they crack on?'

'Oh, yes, of course,' Mel says, clamping her arms around her. The two men nod and head back outside.

'Meantime, I'd like to have another word with your daughter, if that's possible,' PC Gordon says.

Mel stares at her.

Kate. She's just behind the kitchen doors. Dear God, don't let her have heard me explode at Tom just now, she thinks. Mel wants to dissolve from the inside out for how she just reacted. She *hit* him. How will she ever make him understand that it was an automatic reaction, that him touching her in that way triggered a protective reflex she never thought she'd have to use again?

'Yes… yes, of course. Or rather, you can try,' Mel replies quietly to the officer. 'She's through here in the kitchen. But she's not said a word since she made the… the discovery.' Mel lowers her voice to a whisper. 'I know it was upsetting for her, but it's not like Kate to be… well, to be mute.'

Miss Sarah is suddenly on her mind. What is it with this place and people not talking?

'Perhaps she'll speak to you,' Mel adds. 'Being the police.' She beckons the woman through to the kitchen, leaving Tom standing alone.

'Love?' Mel says, pleased to see that Kate has made herself some breakfast. She's sitting at the stainless-steel worktop, shovelling Cheerios into her mouth. Milk dribbles down her chin, which she wipes away with the back of her hand. 'Katie, PC Gordon is here again. She'd like to have a word with you, if that's OK?'

Kate lifts her head slowly, looking first at her mother and then across at the officer. Her expression remains blank as she slowly chews.

'I can leave you two alone, if you like,' Mel says, but the officer shakes her head.

'Please stay. Kate, I just wanted to ask if you found anything else yesterday on your dig. It must have been fun playing archaeologists. You're certainly a good one, finding those bones and knowing not to disturb them.'

Mel cringes inwardly at the officer's tone. Kate will not like being talked to like a little kid.

Kate says nothing. She spoons more cereal into her mouth.

'I understand you're upset about it though, and I'm sure there'll be a very rational explanation. But it's our job to make sure everything's done properly.' She clears her throat.

Kate stares out of the window. When Mel follows her gaze, she sees the two men standing on the edge of the footings trench, one of them bending forward, his wispy hair flopping forward. He pushes it back out of the way, while the other man – the detective – stands with his hands on his hips and a concerned look on his face.

'Did you find items of clothing, for instance? Or anything else that you might not expect to find buried?' The officer waits in case Kate decides to speak and, when she doesn't, she clears her throat again and continues. 'Maybe you found something really unusual – or something you didn't even think was important. I'd really like to have a look at what else you discovered yesterday.'

'I think it was mainly just fossils,' Mel chips in when Kate remains silent. 'It's all still outside where they left it.'

Both women stand beside Kate as she scrapes her cereal bowl. Mel reaches out and strokes her back.

'Katie, please will you speak to the officer? You can't ignore the police, love. I understand you're upset, but I don't understand why you've gone totally silent. It's not like you.'

Kate refuses to meet Mel's eye. When it becomes clear that she's not going to say a word, the officer suggests she and Mel go outside.

'I'm really sorry,' Mel says, squinting in the bright sun as they join the two men. 'She's a lovely, obliging, helpful girl normally. I just don't understand it.'

'People cope with trauma in all kinds of ways,' the officer says.

Mel looks up at the clear blue sky, something resonating within her.

'She'll likely open up before long. I wouldn't push her, if I were you. The main objective is to ascertain if the bones are human and roughly how long they've been there. And that's down to the anthropologist for now.' She smiles.

'Detective?' Mel hears Dave Clements, the university expert, call out from the trench. DI Armitage is wearing latex gloves and rooting around in the bucket of stones and fossils that the girls collected. By the looks of it, there are bits of broken glass and china, a few old nails and some copper pipe in there as well.

The DI heads over to his colleague, careful as he treads across the uneven building site. 'What is it, Dave?'

The slightly older man stands up from the trench, putting one hand in the small of his back and covering his brow with the other. His salt-and-pepper hair blows out from the long ponytail hanging down his back. He flashes Mel a quick look before turning to the detective.

'The bones are definitely human.' He gives a nod, seemingly unfazed. 'And they belonged to a very young infant indeed. A newborn baby, I'd say, judging by the position of the skull bones relative to each other. I've carefully removed some of the earth, as you can see, and if you look here...' He points to a more exposed area around the top of the head. 'The cranium is still elongated from the birth canal. This child died very young indeed. Possibly only hours old, or maybe even stillborn.'

Mel covers her mouth, her eyes screwing up at the thought of what she's just heard. 'How awful,' she says, though no one hears her behind her hands.

'At first glance, I'd say they're not particularly historic, either. It's hard to tell without proper dating in the lab, but going on colour, texture and several other factors, my best guess is that death occurred anything up to fifty, maybe sixty years ago. I very much doubt it was less than ten years ago.'

Mel gasps.

'So... so is there a possibility that we've simply unearthed a grave? Can you tell if there was or is a coffin surrounding the bones? I mean...' Mel trails off, not wanting to state what everyone is thinking: that this infant never had a proper burial.

'Very unlikely it's an official grave,' the detective chips in. 'I ran a quick search on past consecrated ground in the area and this land wasn't mentioned. There are no records of authorised burial sites in the vicinity either.'

'I see,' Mel says. 'So what will happen now?'

'I'll get my colleague up here with me to remove the bones. There'll be a lot of careful extraction, photographing, documenting and the like. Then they'll be taken back to our lab for testing.'

'Meantime, we'll be looking into all registered births and deaths, checking our cold case files and opening an investigation,' the detective says. 'Tell me, Miss Douglas, who owned the property before you took it over? Is there anyone we could speak to about its history?'

Mel sighs, wishing she knew the exact answer to that herself. She tips back her head, knowing this will mean stalling building works for quite some time. She closes her eyes, drawing a deep breath to calm her nerves. It's only when she opens them again, catches sight of a familiar figure looking down on them from an upstairs window, that she wonders.

'There is one person who may be able to help you,' she says, thinking that if she can't get Miss Sarah to speak, then perhaps the police can.

CHAPTER THIRTY-FIVE

Mel leans on the worktop as she waits for the kettle to boil. The officers and the anthropologist haven't long gone, Kate has disappeared up to her room and when Mel came back inside, she discovered Tom was nowhere to be found. She sighs as she imagines him confused and bemused by her outburst earlier, wondering what kind of woman she is to react so violently just because he touched her on the arms when, the evening before, she'd allowed him to kiss her.

He's probably gone home, relieved that the building works have been halted so he doesn't have to see me again, Mel thinks.

'Idiot, idiot, *idiot*,' she mutters, tossing a teabag into a mug, determined to put it out of her mind. There are more important matters to deal with now.

Earlier, she suggested that Nikki may as well go home, take the day off, because she wasn't sure if they'd be allowed to have customers, and she'd texted Rose a similar message. As it turned out, before she left PC Gordon said she would check with her boss, but she saw no reason for the pub and restaurant not to trade, as long as the site at the back was cordoned off sufficiently from the car park and not interfered with. The anthropologist had left the area sheeted off with a large tarpaulin.

As she carries her tea through to the small office behind the reception area, she thinks back to her little flat in Birmingham, her job at The Cedars, Josette, Saturdays working in Michael's shop, Kate zoning out with her headphones on, the evenings spent back at his flat with a few drinks and delicious food while Kate binged on Netflix.

'God, I miss you, Micky,' she whispers, wanting nothing more than a hug from him. She knows he'd rationalise everything that's happened in the last twenty-four hours – convince her that Tom would understand her strange reaction if she explained, that the bones would turn out to be a thousand years old or more, that business wouldn't be affected at all, and she'd get a great write-up in the local paper because there simply wasn't any other story to tell.

'Oh!' Mel stops suddenly, tea sloshing over the side of her mug. 'Can I help you?'

Angus is bent over her desk in the small room, riffling through a folder – an *accounts* folder. Mel had recently brought all the paperwork up to date, poring over old ledgers and files, entering figures into a spreadsheet before printing it all out to reconcile with the bank. It was a mess, but she'd made good progress doing a couple of hours each evening after Kate had gone to bed.

Angus freezes, his hands mid-turn of a page.

He looks sideways at Mel, licking his lips nervously. He clears his throat. 'Ah… I realise this doesn't look good,' he says, his voice wavering, giving a nervous smile.

'No, you're right. It doesn't look good at all. What are you doing snooping through my paperwork?'

Mel sees that Angus is trying to think up an excuse, the way his eyes flick about the office, his jaw lightly twitching.

'I thought you were outside talking to the police,' he says.

'I think *you* should be talking to the police,' Mel retorts, coming closer and putting her tea on the desk. She grabs the file off him and snaps it closed. 'Why are you in here? This is confidential.'

'It was the girl who works here. She told me I could look.'

'Nikki?' Mel says, frowning. 'When?'

'Literally just now. I wanted information on room rates, and she said I could help myself.'

'Nikki told you to come into my office just now?'

'Absolutely.' Angus shoves his hands in his jeans pockets. 'This very second. You must have just passed her in reception.'

'Then Nikki must have a twin sister,' Mel says. 'Or you're lying.'

'I swear—'

'I sent Nikki home at least an hour ago.'

'That other girl who works here, then… I'm not good with names.'

'There is no other *girl* who works here,' Mel replies. 'Unless you mean Rose, who wouldn't appreciate being called a girl. And she's not here either. You're not doing a good job of convincing me, Mr Spencer. Now, why don't you tell me why you're really looking at my private documents?'

'All I can do is apologise,' Angus says earnestly. 'I… I was… um… I was checking to see what room rates you usually charge. I felt the price was a little high, that's all. And… and it turns out I was right. I'm being overcharged by twenty pounds.' He points at the closed file.

Mel stares at him, narrowing her eyes, her head filled with memories of Billy's lies.

'I don't believe you,' she says, calling his bluff.

For a moment, Mel thinks she catches the flicker of something behind his eyes – remorse even, perhaps regret. It's what Billy would do – make her feel sorry for him.

But that was then, and this is now.

'Room rates are printed on the leaflet in all the rooms and on our new website and Facebook page,' Mel says defiantly. 'If you thought you were being overcharged, you should have spoken to me. You didn't need to snoop in here. What are you *really* doing in my office, Mr Spencer? You'd better tell me the truth. I have

PC Gordon's mobile number and I'm happy to call her to have a word with you, if you'd prefer.'

Angus stares at her blankly. Then he closes his eyes briefly, sighs and covers his face. When he drops his hands, his expression has changed completely. His eyes are heavy, pleading, earnest and… and almost *kind*-looking, Mel thinks, refusing to be taken in.

'OK, I confess. I… I was trying to find out about *you*. Anything I could.'

'About *me*?' Mel says, her tone changing too. 'Why?'

'Because I'm your brother.'

CHAPTER THIRTY-SIX

Mel drops down into her office chair, not taking her eyes off Angus. Her mind can't assimilate and process what he's just told her. She's far from a daytime drinker, but right now she'd give anything for a stiff Scotch.

'My… my *brother*?' she asks, not even recognising the sound of her own voice.

Angus nods, slowly lowering himself into the chair on the other side of the desk.

'But…' Mel has no idea what to say. She can't deny that she doesn't have any brothers, or even sisters, because she simply doesn't know.

'It's crazy, I know. And I understand you're in shock,' Angus says, a tinge of excitement to his voice. 'I've been searching for you… well, for a while now.'

'A while?' Mel says, thinking she's never going to be able to form a coherent sentence again.

Angus nods.

'Before I broke the news to you, I was trying to find out for certain that you were who I thought you were. I didn't want to deliver a bombshell like that if I was wrong. And now I'm in no doubt. Melanie Isobel Douglas, you are my long-lost sister.' Angus leans forward, forearms resting on his knees, his hands clasped together and his face eager. 'And I'm so *very* pleased to meet you.'

'Wow,' Mel says, pushing back in her chair, staring at him. If she'd ever imagined what her brother might look like, which she hadn't, Angus is about as far from anything she would have dreamt up for a sibling. 'I… I'm finding this a bit difficult to take in.' She studies his face, wondering if she can see similarities between them.

For a start, is he older or younger than her? It's hard to tell, she thinks. It could be either. His ears aren't dissimilar to hers, she supposes – rather too small and one set slightly higher than the other. His hair – well, it's a different shade to hers entirely, but she supposes it could have been less mousy as a child. But his jaw and chin are different to hers – more masculine, of course, though his jowls already seem to be sagging and he doesn't have her dimple.

'How… I mean where… why…?' Mel starts again. 'What I'm trying to say is, how did you find me? And why did you want to? And are you… well, are you completely certain?'

'It's a long story,' Angus admits. 'But in short, I was adopted soon after I was born. I never knew my real family. Didn't even know my mother's name or anything about her. She… she abandoned me as a baby.' He looks at the floor.

Mel stares at him, dumbfounded. *Abandoned by his mother…* Something stirs inside her – a thread of familiarity. The vaguest hint of a warmth that she's never felt before. It makes her want to hurl herself at him, hug him close, breathe him in – the scent and feel of someone made of the same genetic material as her. She nods, desperate to say *Me too, me too!* but decides against it. Giving too much away wouldn't be wise. And besides, she's always sworn she didn't want anything to do with her biological family. *Trash…*

'I'm really sorry to hear that,' Mel says. But at least you had an adopted family, she wants to add. Unlike me, who was passed from one children's home to another, foster parent after foster parent, being rejected, handed round like a piece of left luggage. Literally.

'It's OK,' Angus says. 'I had a good childhood. My adopted parents were always very honest with me and told me about my background when I was in my early teens. When I turned eighteen, they encouraged me to find out about my biological parents if I wanted. But at the time, I didn't. It's only more recently, since my adopted parents passed away, that the urge has taken me. It wasn't an easy task, I can assure you.' A globule of spit forms in one corner of Angus's mouth, frothing as his excitement grows. 'I'm just so very glad to have found you, Melanie. I think...' He grins, one bushy eyebrow rising above his glasses. 'I think we kind of look similar, don't you?'

Mel stares at him. 'Maybe,' she says. 'Where did your – or *our* – mother abandon you? Where did your adopted parents live, and where did you grow up?' She narrows her eyes, trying to size him up, not trusting him an inch – yet she doesn't know why. Something about him is just... *off*.

'I was left outside a police station in Taunton. Such a cliché,' he says, rolling his eyes. 'I know absolutely nothing about my mother, though. Well, not *yet*,' he says with a twinkle in his eye. 'I'm still searching for her.'

'Taunton? That's not too far from here, right?' Mel's heart begins to pound. If he's close to finding *his* mother, then perhaps he's close to finding her mother too. And if what he's saying about where he was abandoned is true, and she's inherited a hotel not far away from there... Mel shakes her head as her mind floods with possibilities. She wonders if they have the same father, too.

'It's in Somerset, but only the next county and less than an hour's drive from here. How strange that you've been living here all this time. I wonder if we've passed each other before? Do you ever go to Taunton? That's where I still live. The crazy thing is, I often come down to the beach here at Halebury or Lyme Regis. I bet we've been within spitting distance of each other at the very least.'

'Stop!' Mel says, suddenly feeling overwhelmed. 'You're jumping the gun here. I'm not from this area at all. Far from it. I've only been living here a few weeks. I'm... I'm from Birmingham. I've lived there all my life.'

The excited expression on Angus's face falls away. 'Oh,' he says. 'I see. That changes things a bit then. Though when you were adopted, perhaps you were moved from the area where you were born?'

'I was never adopted,' Mel says flatly. Apart from Michael, she's never spoken to anyone about this in detail. She can't decide if it's cathartic telling a stranger, if he even *is* her brother, or foolish and reckless. He could be a con man, for all she knows, and has made all this up on the spot to avoid being caught snooping and stealing from her office. But then... he was abandoned too, she thinks, feeling confused. This detail alone is too similar to her own story. 'I was in and out of children's homes all my life, with stints at foster homes.' Mel folds her arms.

'If you were born in the south-west, like me, then how come you ended up in Birmingham? Or perhaps our mother moved up there after she gave me up. How old are you, and—'

'No, stop,' Mel says again. She pushes her fingers through her hair. 'I don't want this,' she says. 'I don't want to hear any of it. It's too much to take in, especially on top of everything else that's happened in the last twenty-four hours.'

Mel drops forward, cradling her head in her hands. She screws up her eyes, wishing she could rewind time to when she was sitting under the trees with Tom, the firepit blazing, sipping a glass of prosecco.

She feels a warm hand on her shoulder and whips up her head.

'I understand,' Angus says kindly. 'And I'm sorry to have upset you.'

Mel looks at him, seeing something in his eyes – something familiar, almost. And if she wasn't always so mistrusting and suspicious, she'd say it looked a lot like honesty.

'It's OK,' she says, standing up. 'You didn't know.'

Angus stands in front of her, slipping his hands into hers, clasping them together as he brings them up to his face.

'I… I was…' Mel begins, staring into his eyes. 'I was abandoned on a train,' she whispers, shuddering from the inside out. 'It nearly kills me to admit it,' she confesses. 'I was found by the cleaner at the end of the line, which just happened to be Birmingham.'

She sees Angus's eyes grow wide, his mind whirring behind them, joining the dots that she already has. He holds her hands tightly under his chin, their faces only inches apart.

'That's terrible,' he says to her, his dark eyes boring into hers. 'Even worse than being dumped at the police station. At least it was pretty much guaranteed I'd get found quickly. Who knows what could have happened to you? What if they hadn't seen there was a baby inside the bag and—'

'Please… don't,' Mel says and, for some reason, she finds herself reaching out and putting her forefinger over Angus's lips. Over her *brother's* lips. He pulls her closer – the embrace powerful, and it's as they stare into each other's eyes that Mel realises she never mentioned she was abandoned in a bag.

'Hi, Mel—' comes a cheery voice from the doorway. 'Oh… I'm sorry… Guess I'll come back later then,' Tom says, clearing his throat awkwardly as he stares at the pair of them. 'Or maybe not,' he adds, raising his eyebrows. He gives Mel a brief glance, a confused look, before turning on his heels to leave.

CHAPTER THIRTY-SEVEN

It had taken an awful lot of coaxing to get Kate into the car later that afternoon. Mel had sat on her bed for a good half hour, trying to get her to say something. She'd talked to her about what had happened the night before, encouraging her to say how she felt. And she'd chatted breezily about what to have for supper later, the weather, school – and then she'd suggested they go and get an ice cream together in the village.

But Kate had remained silent. She'd lain on her bed staring at the ceiling, not even reaching for her phone when it pinged several times. Mel could see that it was Chloe's name on the screen, probably concerned for her friend.

'Wow,' Mel says, changing down to second gear as they approach the sea, staring out across the bay as it comes into sight. 'I'll never get tired of this view. We're so lucky to have it right on our doorstep.'

On the way, she'd pulled up outside the ice cream shop in the village and nipped in for a cone each for them. She'd glanced around the little square of shops, wary of an encounter with Donald Bray as she walked past the newsagent back to the car, but thankfully there was no sign of him.

They'd sat in the car, staring out across the bay, Kate licking her cone in silence and, when they'd finished, Mel had driven west to the next town along the coast to explore. After everything that had happened – the bones, Kate not speaking, Angus claiming to be her brother, Tom walking in on them and clearly getting the wrong end of the stick, especially after she'd *hit* him – she'd needed to get out to clear her head.

'Nothing like a bit of sea air, eh?' Mel says, unclipping her seat belt. 'Come on then, let's get some of it into our lungs,' she adds, patting Kate on the leg. Kate gets out of the car and follows Mel along the esplanade and down the ramp onto the shingle beach. The tide is at the midway mark and Mel leads the way down to the shore, her still-silent daughter following as they crunch along the pebbles.

'What do you think about getting a dog, Kate?' she asks, hoping that will elicit a response. 'You can choose the breed. I reckon you'd go for…' She makes a pondering noise, hoping Kate will engage, excited by the idea of a puppy. 'I think you'd go for a springer spaniel or perhaps a cockapoo. Am I right?'

Kate stares out to sea, scuffing her feet through the stones. She doesn't reply.

'Wow, there are some amazing fossils, look. Did you know that this stretch of coastline is known for them? It's not called the Jurassic Coast for nothing.'

Mel bends down and picks up a couple of shells and what looks like a fossil of some kind – a perfect spiral of ridges. She inspects them and holds them out to Kate. 'They're perfectly intact, look. For your collection, perhaps?'

Kate gives an idle look before taking them and shoving them in her pocket without saying a word. Mel sighs.

'Love, why won't you talk to me? I'm so worried about you.' She gently takes her daughter by the shoulders, standing in front of her. 'I know what happened is upsetting, but you can tell me absolutely anything, you know.' I'm pretty unshockable, she wants to add but doesn't.

Kate remains silent. Just breathes slowly, her eyes watery from tears as she stares out to sea, her pale hair billowing around her face in the onshore breeze.

'OK. I understand you don't want to,' Mel says, hoping that taking the pressure off will help. 'Let's just walk instead.' She takes hold of Kate's hand and leads her off along the beach, the waves to their left gently licking up the shingle.

An hour later, after a bracing yet silent walk, they head back to the car, Mel's pockets filled with more fossils for Kate to add to her collection. It's after she's driven across the bridge over the River Axe – the muddy estuary filling up with the incoming tide beneath them – that she spots the red van in her rear-view mirror, her heart thundering to catch up as it misses a few beats.

Keeping her cool, she heads a little further north, turning right onto the main road towards home. Mel glances behind her again. The red van is still there, though she can't remember seeing it when they left Seaton. She tries to focus on the road ahead, but the sight of it looming behind her makes her swerve, clipping the verge with the left wheel. Kate whips up her head, looking across at her mum.

'Sorry, love,' she says, reassuring her as her eyes flick from the rear-view mirror to the road ahead and back again. She grips the wheel tightly. 'Just me misjudging the bend,' she adds, biting her lip as she gives another glance behind. The van is still there, at just enough distance so that she can't see the face of the driver. She can't even read the number plate properly, especially since it's back to front, and she's concerned about putting the car right into the hedge if she doesn't concentrate.

A couple of miles later, Mel purposefully slows right down on a long stretch of straight road, where it would be easy for the van to overtake. But it doesn't. Instead, it also slows, dropping back further. And when she speeds up, the van speeds up too.

By the time they enter Halebury, Mel's heart is thumping and her palms are sweating. She can't possibly go straight back to the hotel. If it *is* Billy, there's no way she's about to lead him to where they live. So instead, she weaves a confusing path through the narrow streets of the village – some of which are one-way. The van follows her to a point, but at a distance, and it's only when she turns down a particularly narrow lane, with bollards at the entrance so only the smallest of cars can fit down, that she loses sight of whoever was following her.

Supposedly following me, she thinks, breathing out through a relieved sigh, trying to be rational about it. On top of everything else, she's not sure if she can cope with Billy closing in on her. She prays it was just her overwrought mind playing tricks.

'How many red vans do you think there are in the country, darling?' Michael says, after Mel explains what had happened.

'How on earth do I know?' she says, affronted. 'I'm only bothered about one. And this one was old and beat-up and had that same faded red paintwork I saw on the van outside Kate's old school. I don't think it's coincidence, Micky.'

'Well, I do,' he says. But Mel knows by the tone of his voice that he's only trying to placate her, knowing how anxious she gets. 'How on earth would he know where you are?' he adds. 'It's not as if you've moved just down the road from your old flat and he might have spotted you by chance. You've moved a three-hour drive to the South Coast, for heaven's sake. It's not going to be high on Billy's list of likely guesses as to where you've gone now, is it?'

'No,' Mel says quietly, sipping the large gin and tonic she poured for herself when they got back. She was pleased to see half a dozen or more people in the bar, some of them having a meal. But she didn't stop to chat to Nikki, who was serving. She retreated to her room with her drink for some privacy while she called Michael.

'Anyway,' she continues, 'while it's a worry, it's only one of a few things that have been going on. You couldn't bloody make it up, Micky,' Mel says, relaxing back onto her pillow, feeling soothed by his voice.

'Good things or bad?'

'Depends if you think finding human remains in the footings of my new extension and some guy tipping up here claiming to be my brother are good things or not. Oh, and Tom – who, for the record, I was actually starting to like and felt as though, you know, there might be a little spark with – well, I thoroughly put him off when he saw me and my supposed brother, that he didn't *know* was my brother, in a tight embrace. Not to mention that I had a meltdown and hit him.' Mel takes a large sip of her G&T. 'Like I said, you couldn't make it up.'

'I bloomin' well leave you alone for ten minutes…' Michael says with a laugh.

'Not funny.'

'Let's backtrack a second, darling,' Michael says. 'Human remains? I mean… are you sure? Whose, how and why?'

Mel recounts the story of how the bones were discovered, the police investigation, the building works being on hold, and finishes up by telling him that Kate hasn't spoken a word since.

'That's certainly not like Katie,' Michael says, concerned. 'The poor kid must be traumatised. Give her time.'

'I agree to a point, but it smacks a little too much of the woman in room twelve for my liking. Almost as if she's learnt it from her.'

'Possibly,' Michael says. 'But what's confusing me more than *anything* is that you just told me you have a *brother*. Explain yourself, woman.'

'Trust me, weird is the new normal around here, Micky. If aliens landed in the back yard this evening it wouldn't surprise me. But yes, some guy booked into one of my rooms a couple of days ago. Then I caught him snooping in my office, and now he's confessed to being my brother. I have no reason to disbelieve him, and none to believe him either, yet his story is remarkably similar to mine. And there's... well, I suppose there is a passing resemblance between us. But then we got interrupted by Tom, and I don't know much more.'

'A *brother*,' Michael says again. Mel hears him blow a breath through the gap between his top teeth. 'As in, a real DNA-in-common type of brother...?'

'Apparently,' Mel replies, sounding as bemused as Michael.

'Well, I certainly never saw *that* one coming,' he adds. 'Not in a million years.' He makes a thoughtful sound, leaving Mel hanging, expecting more. But then there's just silence.

'What do you mean, you never saw that one coming? Were you expecting something then?'

'No, no, of course not. And if Tom saw you in an embrace with your... with this supposed brother of yours, then just explain to him what happened.'

'It's a mess,' Mel says. 'It looked way more than an innocent hug if you didn't know the context.'

'So you like him then, Tom? Tom who will have to pass muster with me, I might add.'

From some deep reserves, Mel lets out a dry laugh.

'Yeah, stupidly, I do. He made this really romantic meal in the garden with candles and fairy lights and wine, and he cooked—'

'Then go and tell him,' Michael says matter-of-factly. 'Make him a nice meal, a cake – whatever – and surprise him. Explain everything, just like you have to me, and go get the man, Melanie Isobel Douglas.'

Mel laughs again, wondering how a few minutes of Michael always manages to bring her back down to earth. 'Maybe,' she says.

'But don't—'

And then there's silence on the line as they're cut off. Mel tries to call back but it goes straight to voicemail. Ten minutes later, she gets a text from Michael telling her his battery died, and that he'll call her tomorrow as his new date is about to arrive. A few moments later, Mel receives another text.

And be wary of this person. Brother, really? Let's talk soon xx

CHAPTER THIRTY-EIGHT

The next day, with the building work outside stalled, Mel decides to put up some more of the curtains in the newly painted bedrooms. She wants to keep busy, knowing that if she stops, she'll overthink and worry about everything.

As she carries the new curtains upstairs, she runs over all the outstanding jobs in her head – the finishing touches she needs to make to get the next two bedrooms ready for business. A couple of soft sheepskin rugs, she thinks, and fresh white cotton linen on the bed will really stand out against the striking fern-green accent wall around the old fireplace in room ten. She painted that one herself and is particularly pleased with the effect.

But she's still puzzled by what she saw on her laptop earlier, mulling over what it could mean. The government wills and probate website was easy enough to navigate – enter the deceased's name and year of death to apply for a copy of the will – but what confused Mel was that there was simply no record of a Joyce Lawrence on the database in this or any of the surrounding areas. Almost as if she hadn't even died. Mel had snapped her laptop lid shut in frustration. It didn't make sense, and certainly didn't tally with Joyce being the original benefactor. She was no further forward.

Grappling with the heavy curtains, Mel opens the door and goes in, dumping them on the bed. The room is bright and airy now – with sparkling windows, stripped floorboards and lovely views over the fields opposite.

Mel turns – then stops. Her hands come up over her mouth in shock, not able to take in what she's seeing right away. She closes her eyes for a moment, hoping it will be gone when she opens them. But it's not.

Someone has daubed HATE in huge, blood-red letters above the fireplace – the wall she recently painted herself.

'Oh my *God*,' she whispers, unable to take her eyes off the dripping letters. 'Who would *do* that?' she says, slowly walking up to it. She touches the H, rubbing her thumb and forefinger together. The paint feels as if it's still slightly damp, as if it was done in the last few hours, and the E looks as though someone has been rubbing at it. Then she notices the floor – the splotches of red paint spilled on the sanded boards, the trail leading to the door.

Mel covers her face and lets out a frustrated growl and scream, only stopping when her throat begins to hurt. Angry as hell, she turns on her heels to find out who has been in today and, more importantly, *why* someone would do such an evil thing.

It's as she's striding along the corridor that she sees the detective who was here on Saturday morning coming up the stairs. She clears her throat, trying to compose herself quickly.

'Oh… hello, Detective,' Mel says, wondering if she should mention what she's just discovered, or if someone has already reported it and that's why he's here.

'The young lass downstairs let me in and said you were up here,' he says. 'Hope you don't mind.'

'No, no, of course not,' Mel says.

'The place is looking very different already,' he says with a small smile – one that doesn't alter the plain landscape of his face. 'I used to drink in here, back in the day when I lived in Halebury.' A scant smattering of stubble, partly grey, partly a nondescript colour, sits beneath doughy cheeks and grey eyes. His hair, again of no discernible colour, is swept to one side over the crown of his head. Not quite a comb-over, but on the way.

'Oh, really?' Mel says, wondering if he knows anything about Joyce and her partner. 'And thanks,' Mel says. 'It's coming along. Shall we go downstairs?'

He nods and follows Mel into her office.

'If it's about the graffiti,' she says, offering him a seat, 'I don't think it happened very long ago. Or if it's Kate you want to speak to, then you're out of luck. She's not said a word since Friday night. She's really upset by what happened.'

'Graffiti?' the detective says, frowning and shaking his head. 'I don't know anything about that, I'm afraid. And I'm sorry to hear about your daughter,' he adds, sitting down and adjusting his dark brown trousers. 'But it's not her I've come to see. I'm here to oversee the two experts from the university while they remove the remains. Apologies for the weekend intrusion, but they're off on a field trip tomorrow and this investigation can't wait. They'll be done today.'

Relieved that he doesn't want to speak to Kate, who's in her bedroom on her computer, she opens her mouth, about to ask when building works can resume. But she catches sight of Miss Sarah through the open door, coming down the stairs and passing through reception. Like some kind of Brontë-esque ghost, Mel can't help thinking.

She leans forward across the desk. 'It might be worth having a word with... well, with my rather unusual lodger,' she says instead, in a low voice. 'Though you'll be doing better than me if you get a word out of her. She's been part of the furniture for years and never speaks. But... well, the weird thing is, I swear I overheard her talking to my daughter the other day. And Chloe, Kate's friend, has since confirmed this.'

'She has indeed been here for as long as anyone can remember,' the detective says with an amused expression. 'A bit of an oddity. I don't think anyone's ever heard her speak, so don't take it person-ally. It was kind of a joke back then. When Joyce had the pool table and dart board, me and the lads used to come up here after college for a few pints. I'm ashamed to say, we used to wind her up something rotten. Misspent youth and all that.' He grins. 'But while I'm here, it can't hurt to have a word with her,' he continues, easing himself up out of the wooden chair. 'Or at least try.'

Mel leads the way, finding Miss Sarah in the restaurant area, at her usual table as expected, with a book set out in front of her.

'Miss Sarah,' Mel says, as she stands next to her, the plain-clothes officer at her side, 'this is DI Armitage. He'd like a word with you.' Mel doesn't feel good about making Miss Sarah think she's followed through with her threat of legal action. But if it gets her to speak, then it's worth it. 'Good luck,' she mouths at the detective, making an exasperated face.

'Hello, *Miss* Sarah,' he says, sitting down. 'It's been a while.' He clears his throat. 'Maybe you don't remember me, but I have a couple of questions, if you wouldn't mind, regarding a matter I'm investigating.'

Silence. Miss Sarah stares at her book, though from behind the bar, Mel can tell her eyes aren't directly focused on it.

'How long have you lived at Moreton Inn now?' she hears the DI ask.

Miss Sarah says nothing. Just the shallow rise and fall of her chest beneath her cream cardigan as she sits perfectly still.

'I remember you from when I was about seventeen or eighteen. Thirty-one years ago, can you believe?' DI Armitage pauses, in case she replies. But she doesn't. 'I'm up for retirement next year. The big five-oh.'

Another pause.

'Joyce's lass, aren't you? I was sorry to hear about your mother's passing last year.'

Mel grips the bar, tea towel in hand. So Miss Sarah *is* Joyce's daughter as Tom had assumed. It makes perfect sense, she supposes. But it could also suggest that Joyce didn't own Moreton

Inn, she ponders, pretending to be busy behind the bar. If she owned it, then surely she'd have left it to Miss Sarah, who seems determined never to leave.

'As you may know,' the detective continues, 'some human bones were uncovered during the building works here.' He clears his throat again when there's no reaction from her. 'Naturally, we're keen for any information on how they came to be there. A first assessment likely dates them within living memory.'

Miss Sarah sits quite still, although Mel notices that she briefly scratches her head – a bony finger playing with her scalp for a moment, adjusting some hair. Then her hand returns to her lap.

'When did Joyce take over Moreton Inn, Sarah, can you recall? You must have been early twenties when me and my mates used to come in, right?' The detective gives a warm smile. 'Self-declared pool champion of 1989.' He laughs. 'Billy Joel on the jukebox and a pint or three of Strongbow, and I was a happy lad.'

Mel admires the detective's attempt at drawing something out of Miss Sarah through nostalgia – but it seems she has none of her own to share. She remains perfectly still and perfectly silent.

'Kate?' Mel says, tapping on her daughter's bedroom door. 'Are you OK, love?' She goes in to find Kate sitting at her computer, headphones on, with her right hand on her mouse and her left hand furiously tapping the keyboard. Some kind of chase is taking place on her screen.

Kate visibly startles when Mel appears at her side.

'There's some food for you downstairs, love,' Mel says when Kate removes her headphones. 'You must be starving. You didn't eat lunch.'

Kate sips from a glass of water on her desk, and Mel thinks she gives the briefest of nods, acknowledging what she said.

'I'll see you in the kitchen then. Rose made lamb curry.' She decides to leave her to it, hoping that hunger will drive her downstairs.

On the way through reception, Mel spots several copies of the local weekly paper that had been delivered yesterday evening. She grabs them, knowing a couple of the regulars like to read them over a pint, and is about to put them out on the end of the bar when one slides from her grasp, falling open on the floor.

And that's when she sees the headline of a story on page two.

SKELETONS IN THE CLOSET AT MORETON INN

Mel freezes, hardly daring to pick it up. 'The *scoundrel*,' she whispers, knowing even without reading it that the journalist's piece isn't going to be about a fresh start for the hotel, the renovated bedrooms or the delicious new menu. He had it in for her from the start, intent on getting the story in print the same day.

Dropping the other newspapers onto the bar, she heads out to the back hallway to read it, chewing on a nail as her eyes scan the piece.

At first glance, an Instagram post by local school girl, Chloe Wright, looks like any other young girl having fun: a harmless fossil hunt in the garden. But closer examination reveals a much grislier discovery. Adding hashtags #bones #body #shallowgrave and #Halebury to her post, Chloe reveals that she and her best friend, Kate Douglas of Moreton Inn, found more than they bargained for.

Human remains, allegedly those of an infant, were discovered by the pair of schoolgirls in the grounds of the hotel as it undergoes extensive renovation. Experts have been called to the scene and the police, who refused to comment, have cordoned off the area pending an investigation. One source believes that the remains were possibly buried within the last fifty years, which could lead to a murder enquiry being opened.

The new owner of Moreton Inn, thirty-nine-year-old Melanie Douglas, also refused to comment, being more concerned with the delay to the hotel's building works than a potential crime. 'A dash of modern while still retaining the old charm,' Miss Douglas stated gleefully when asked about her vision.

But even with a new menu, refurbished bedrooms and plans to host weddings, Miss Douglas has an even greater task ahead of her than simply countering the many one-star TripAdvisor reviews – namely, winning over the locals, generations of whom have enjoyed a pint at Moreton Inn when it was under the care of long-time local, the late Joyce Lawrence.

And with my own wedding set for next year, I for one will not be celebrating on the site of a potential murder scene and will be giving Moreton Inn, and its skeletons, a wide berth.

Jacob Ingram, Evening Post

'Fuck, fuck, *fuck*,' Mel says, louder than she'd intended. She hurls the newspaper across the hallway, hitting a plant on the windowsill and sending it tumbling to the tiled floor. The pot smashes, spraying shards of china and soil everywhere. Mel growls in frustration and kicks at the mess, swearing to herself as she clutches her head.

'How *could* he?' she yells. 'What a complete bastard!' She paces about, raging and cussing to herself, completely unaware that Rose has come through the double doors of the kitchen, hearing the commotion.

'I give up! I swear to God, I damn well give up. I may as well go back to Birmingham and get back with Billy. At least Kate would be happy to see her dad and… and…' She trails off, realising that hot, fat tears are streaming down her cheeks. She covers her face with her hands, letting out sobs that have been stored up for a long time.

She takes a deep breath, forcing herself to calm down, knowing that Kate will be coming down for her supper at any moment. She slides her hands down her face, sucking in more air, only to see Tom standing in the back doorway, his mouth half hanging open and his eyes wide as he witnesses the scene.

'Mel, are you OK? I called by a couple of hours ago, but…' He trails off, noticing the look on her face. He reaches out a hand to her, trying to calm her down, and that's when Mel sees several of his fingers are smeared with red paint.

She opens her mouth to speak, but nothing comes out.

'Are you OK?' Tom says, looking concerned.

Mel frowns, her eyes scanning him up and down, noticing red paint on his jeans too.

Tom looks down, rolling his eyes. 'I know I'm a mess,' he says, laughing. 'Nige and I just came up to collect a few things from the site. There's another small job we're going to squeeze in…'

Mel stares at him like a wild animal, slowly backing away.

'OK,' he finally continues. 'I can see it's not a good time. I'll come round another day.' He returns her stare for a moment, his expression confused, then without saying another word, he turns on his heel and walks briskly away.

'*Fuck*,' Mel whispers to herself when he's gone, slumping back against the wall. Then she catches sight of Rose, who flinches slightly in the doorway. 'Don't say a *word*,' Mel says through gritted teeth.

Rose makes a pained face, giving a little nod, disappearing back into the kitchen, leaving Mel to slide down the wall and bury her head against her knees.

CHAPTER THIRTY-NINE

Mel got up early the next day, determined to put Jacob Ingram's stupid piece out of her mind – not to mention the sight of the forensic experts removing the remains piece by careful piece yesterday. A man and a woman from the university had spent many hours in the trench, hunched over the burial site as they carefully exhumed the bones, meticulously photographing, labelling and packing away everything they unearthed.

When she came downstairs, she was relieved to see Kate in the kitchen wearing her school uniform, her hair neatly plaited, shovelling cereal into her mouth while watching something on YouTube, one leg swinging idly under the counter.

'I'm glad you feel like going to school today,' Mel had said as she made a coffee. 'It'll do you good to see your friends.'

Kate had simply glanced up and given her mother a look for a couple of moments before dumping her empty bowl by the sink, grabbing her school bag and heading off. She hadn't spoken a word since Friday evening.

It's just not like her.

Mel texted to Michael later that morning, in reply to him asking how they both were.

Hopefully, school will get her to open up. Do you think I should call the GP?

She'd put a shrugging emoji then, followed by several kisses. Michael had replied soon after, advising Mel to give her time, another day or two, and meantime to keep talking to her.

'Maybe she saw me having my meltdown,' Mel whispers to herself as she stands at the top of the ladder that afternoon, hanging more curtains. She'd tried to scrub off the vile word daubed in room ten, but the red paint wasn't budging. There was no option but to paint over it, so she'd ordered another can of the fern green.

'Frankly, I wouldn't blame anyone for not speaking to me after my little outburst yesterday,' she mutters, ashamed that Tom had seen her in that state. And she should have just asked him about the paint on his hands, given him a chance to explain. It could have been from another job… anything. She found it hard to believe that Tom was responsible for the graffiti.

Her cheeks colour as she remembers how he'd walked in on her and Angus embracing. Angus had since made himself scarce, with Nikki mentioning that he'd been down early for breakfast and then gone out for the day. He'd taken dinner in his room both nights, too. Mel knows she can't put off having a conversation with him for ever.

'Oh, *Tom*,' she whispers, securing yet another curtain hook on the track as the stepladder wobbles beneath her. The surprise dinner he'd made for her seems a lifetime ago now, not just three days. And that kiss… the feel of his warm, soft lips.

As she fastens up the final few hooks, she remembers what Michael had said. *Make him a nice meal, a cake – whatever – and surprise him.* There'll be a bit more explaining to do now, Mel thinks, knowing she'll have to confess everything about Billy for him to understand. And she'll tell him about the newspaper piece too, how it had sent her into a tailspin. Her mind is made up – she's going to take Michael's advice and apologise for it all.

*

'Rose, you're a gem,' Mel says an hour later in the kitchen. 'I couldn't have made this without you. My baking skills aren't exactly top-notch.' She smiles, glancing up from frosting the cake. 'And I owe you an apology for getting my knickers in a twist yesterday. I've worked so hard these last few weeks, and I just saw red at what that upstart journo had written.'

'No need,' Rose says, placing a flour-covered hand on Mel's arm. 'Besides, you should see me cussing and blinding at home,' she adds. 'Scares Eddie half to death when I get one on me.' Her ruddy cheeks swell as she grins.

'Eddie? Is he your husband?' Mel asks, arranging the edible lilac and orange flowers on the cream-coloured topping.

'No, he's my Jack Russell,' she says with a pensive look. 'Married to my kitchen and my dog, maybe, but not to a man.' She clears her throat, and Mel swears she hears her mutter something about Nige never asking her as she clatters dirty dishes into the dishwasher.

'Here, try this,' Mel says, offering a clean spoon for Rose to taste the frosting. 'It's not too sweet, is it?'

'Perfect,' she says, licking her lips. 'I bet your sponge will taste delicious, too,' she adds, raising her eyebrows. 'And don't forget to pack the champagne.'

'Thanks, Rose,' Mel says. 'Would you mind checking in on Kate later? She'll just be in her room doing homework or on her computer. I won't be back late, but given how she is… well, I'd rather there was someone looking out for her.'

'No problem at all,' Rose says, a grin creeping across her face. 'It'll be my pleasure. I'll take her up some hot chocolate, see if I can't get her to have a natter.'

*

Mel sighs, staring into the full-length mirror. She twists round one way, then the other, feeling guilty for checking out her appearance when there's so much else on her mind – mainly Kate. But if she doesn't do this, she's told herself a hundred times already, then she knows she'll regret it.

'You deserve to be happy too,' she says to her reflection. 'Even if you do always self-sabotage anything good in your life.'

After a shower and a blow-dry, and some light make-up, she'd slipped on her new dress, having given it a quick iron. Now, she fastens up the necklace she bought last week and puts on her flat cream sandals. Turning up in paint-covered dungarees and a headscarf to hide her dusty hair wasn't going to cut it, but she's wondering if the little white flowers on the coffee-coloured fabric make her look too…

'Too *feminine*,' she says to herself, scowling as she adjusts the short, ruched sleeves. But she has nothing else decent, so she heads down to the kitchen to grab the cake tin and the basket. On the way, she stops in on Kate, explaining she's going out for a couple of hours. Or maybe more if it goes well, she thinks, knowing that Rose will look after her daughter and call her if anything happens.

'I'll check in on you later then, love,' Mel says, crossing her fingers behind her back in the hope of a response. Kate is sitting at her desk, hunched over her schoolbooks. She thinks she sees a tiny nod of her head – which, after everything, is a breakthrough.

As she walks past the colourful terraced cottages on the way into the village, Mel gives a cheery hello to the old lady who's sitting out on her phone-book-propped stool again, a cup of tea to hand as she watches the world go by. With the basket over her arm and a shawl draped round her shoulders, Mel tries to put everything out of her mind – at least for this evening.

'Just be heartfelt and honest,' she whispers in time with her footsteps as she trots down the steep hill. 'Hi, Brian,' she says to a familiar face, one of her regulars, as he comes out of his front door. For a moment, he doesn't say a word and Mel wonders if it's because he's read the newspaper piece, but then he gives her a wave and greets her with a smile, giving her directions to Tom's street.

'Oh, this is charming,' she says five minutes later as she turns down a cobbled passageway. It's on an incline, heading down towards the sea, with half a dozen or so painted cottages tucked away. She tries not to be nosy but can't help a little peek through several of the windows that face directly on to the alley.

Picking her way carefully along the uneven cobbles, she catches sight of the setting sun glinting off the waves as it dips behind the hill to the west of Halebury, and she hears the seagulls crying and circling over the shore. As she approaches Tom's cottage, number seven, she pauses, taking a breath to gather herself.

Here goes, she thinks, tapping the top of the cake tin, hoping Tom doesn't mind her calling by unannounced. Surely he won't turn down cake and champagne? She's just about to knock on the front door when she spots movement inside his front window. She can't help a quick glance.

Tom... yes, it's Tom standing there, the lamp on the dresser beside him lighting up his face as... as...

Mel goes giddy, trying to work out what she's seeing. She knows she shouldn't be looking in, that she should now be walking briskly on by, but she's transfixed, frozen, wanting to make certain that what her eyes are telling her is actually true.

Tom has his arms wrapped around a woman – a beautiful woman with long, dark hair trailing down her back as she tips up her face towards him – and he's pulling her close, her back arched, each of them smiling and gazing into the other's eyes.

'Oh my... *God*,' Mel whispers to herself, thinking that they look like the happiest couple alive. Tears well up in her eyes.

Later, alone, Mel will recall the flash of the woman's straight white teeth, the look of adoration in Tom's eyes as he gazes down at her, the way his big hands slowly move up her slim and shapely body, along her tanned arms and onto her face, cupping it, gazing at her as if they've missed each other for a hundred years.

Finally, she prises her eyes away from the window, forcing herself to put one foot in front of the other. A moment later, and she's running. Running down the cobbled passageway, stumbling, her ankle twisting sideways as she careers towards the sea.

A loud car horn makes her jump, causing her to dart back as she tries to cross the esplanade. She turns, panting, her heart thumping at the near miss. The car made no attempt to stop, and Mel swears she caught sight of the vile man from the newsagent – Donald Bray – driving.

She lets out a self-indulgent whimper as she crosses the narrow esplanade, not having a clue where she's going. All she knows is that she can't go back to the hotel just yet. Not without having to explain and lose face even more.

Stupid, *stupid* woman! she cusses in her head. Why would you think he was interested in *you*? Did you see her? She was stunning.

'Please don't let them have seen me,' Mel pleads, sniffing back the tears and trying not to show she's upset. '*Please…*'

She walks westward along the esplanade, dragging her feet and staring at the pavement, the basket of cake and champagne still hooked over her arm. Eventually, the houses peter out, indicating the edge of the village. Up ahead on the beach are some flat rocks, so she veers down onto the shingle so she can lie low and watch the waves for a while. She doesn't know what else to do.

CHAPTER FORTY

The first few swigs of champagne do nothing to calm Mel's nerves. As soon as she'd sat down on the rocks, she'd wasted no time ripping the foil and wire off the bottle and popping the cork. She's angry – angry with herself for thinking Tom would be interested in her in the first place.

'You're broken,' she says out loud, knowing no one apart from the gulls can hear her. The tide is creeping up the beach, the water getting closer with each set of waves as she sits, knees drawn up, on the shelf of smooth rocks. 'If your mother abandoning you didn't completely break you, Billy finished the job off,' she mutters, coughing and spluttering on the bubbles as she takes a large swig directly from the bottle. 'And ain't karma a bitch,' she says, wishing she could get the image of Tom and that woman out of her mind.

She puts the bottle down on a flat bit of rock and takes the cake tin from the basket, removing the lid. Inside, the thick frosting still looks as perfect as it did when she applied it.

'I'm ridiculous,' she says to the cake. 'Thinking you'd make everything OK. You're just a stupid sponge made by a stupid woman.' Then she digs the fingers of her right hand into the centre of the cake, paddle-like, and scoops out a fistful of sponge and cream, pushing it into her mouth greedily.

'Mmm, deli…' she says, then stops. Licking her cream-covered lips, she frowns, thinking it's not that delicious after all. There's a strange taste to it – as though some other ingredient has been added. She can't quite place it, so she plunges her fingers into the cake again, enjoying the sticky feeling between her fingers. Not caring about the odd flavour, or the strange colour of the sponge, she shovels in more and more, washing it down with a couple of swigs of champagne, coughing as the bubbles fizz up her nose.

'It's disgusting, but somehow makes everything feel a bit better,' she says in a bitter voice, stuffing her mouth again. Crumbs spray out and she knows she has cream and jam all over her chin, but she doesn't care. Doesn't care who sees her necking from the bottle either. Anything to take away the pain, the humiliation. How the hell, she wonders, holding up the bottle fifteen minutes later, seeing that only half of it is left, can so much bad luck come out of so much good?

'*Curry*,' she says suddenly, turning up her nose as she sniffs her fingers. 'It tastes like it's got bloody curry powder in it.' She wonders if she mistakenly used that instead of baking powder, though doesn't think that even she, with her limited cooking skills, would have made that error.

Shrugging, she stuffs in more cake, swigs more champagne. Then she hiccups.

'Jinxed, that's what you are.' She belches, her entire body jumping with another hiccup. 'Oh, God,' she says, holding her stomach, feeling sick. She cups a sticky hand over her mouth, closing her eyes and breathing in slowly, listening to the sound of the waves lapping at the pebbles as she wills herself not to throw up. When the nausea doesn't subside, she dumps the tin and the bottle in her basket and lies back on the rocks, ignoring the pain as a jut of shale digs into her spine.

For a while, she stares up at the sky, watching the clouds scudding across the blue, trying to see shapes and faces in them like she did as a kid with Michael. But she can't see anything – not even the vaguest hint of an animal shape or anything else she recognises. With the sea breeze wafting over her body, she pulls her shawl tightly around her and closes her eyes, willing the nausea to subside.

And it's only when she feels something cold and wet lapping at her feet that she jumps, sitting up quickly, realising she'd fallen asleep and the tide has crept up her legs, soaking the bottom half of her dress.

A few people in tonight, Mel sees, as she walks past the bar window, trying not to stagger. She creeps through reception, holding onto the wall, and heads straight upstairs, the basket hooked over her arm. She doesn't want to see anyone, knows that Nikki and Rose can easily handle whoever is in. She just needs to sleep and forget tonight ever happened.

Kate, she thinks, wanting nothing more than to hold her daughter. Mel glances at her watch, hiccupping again. She covers her mouth: 8.25. She must have fallen asleep on the rocks for at least an hour. The nausea has all but subsided, but she won't be eating anything else tonight, she knows that.

Tomorrow's a new day, Michael would always say when things got her down. Simple, but true, she ponders, tapping lightly on Kate's bedroom door before going in. In the morning, everything will seem different.

At first, she thinks Kate isn't in there, that perhaps she's downstairs with Rose, but the curtains are drawn and the room is dark. It's only when her eyes adjust that Mel sees the outline of the lump in the bed, that Kate has buried herself under the duvet, obviously wanting an early night. There's a glass of water on the bedside table and her phone is plugged in, charging beside it.

It'll probably do her good to get some extra sleep, Mel thinks, deciding not to disturb her. She blows her a silent kiss and closes the door, turning to go to her own room. But she stops, placing a hand on the wall to steady herself, feeling a thrumming headache brewing behind her forehead.

Having no idea if it's the alcohol driving her on, or just plain bad judgement, Mel heads to Miss Sarah's room, knocking sharply on the door. She's about to go straight in when the door opens. Miss Sarah is standing there in a cream nightdress and an expression on her face that makes Mel wonder if she somehow knew she would be paying her a visit.

'Since you don't speak,' Mel says rather too loudly as she steadies herself on the door frame, 'you can listen to me instead.' Uninvited, she squeezes past Miss Sarah and goes into the room, dropping down into the armchair by the window, putting the basket at her feet. She pulls the tin out, takes off the lid and holds it out to her. 'Cake?' she says, offering the broken-up and messy remains. Cream, jam and orange-coloured sponge are smeared around the inside of the tin, making it look anything but edible.

'I said, do you want cake? It's curry flavour.'

Miss Sarah doesn't reply. She sits down on the edge of the bed nearest to Mel and stares at her, her hands clasped neatly in her lap.

'I'd offer you a swig of champagne, but can't lie – I sank the whole lot myself down on the beach.' She laughs then, grabbing the bottle and tipping it upside down over the tin, just to make sure. 'Shame,' she adds. 'We could have had a party.'

Then, to Mel's surprise, Miss Sarah gets up and goes over to a dark wooden cupboard. She opens one of the doors, giving Mel a glimpse of the contents – books, piles of papers, photograph albums, her old laptop, plus other bits and pieces she can't make out. Miss Sarah closes the cupboard door and returns to the bed with a bottle of Scotch and two glasses. Mel watches on, shocked, but takes one of the two shots that Miss Sarah pours.

'*Cin cin*,' Mel says, raising her glass at the absurdity of the evening. With common sense already blurred from the champagne, she takes a hefty sip and closes her eyes, making an appreciative sound.

'You know what?' Mel says after a moment, opening them again to see Miss Sarah nursing her own glass. 'I've had a really shit day. A really shit *few* days, actually. The weird thing is,' she lets out a sardonic laugh, stifling a hiccup, 'is that I feel I can tell you all about it. You're hardly going to spill the beans to anyone, are you?' Mel shrugs, sipping more whisky, enjoying the feeling of it searing the back of her throat.

'I'm trying my bloody best, but to be honest, it's all getting a bit much. Thing is, Miss S, I never asked for any of this.' She flashes her a look. 'Now, before you think I'm an ungrateful cow who doesn't deserve a massive inheritance handed to her on a plate, I'm really not. If you knew some of the stuff I've been through…' She tips back her head then, allowing another painful laugh. 'Well, you'd realise that I'm the opposite.'

Mel hiccups again, her shoulders jumping as she covers her mouth. 'Bit tipsy though, aren't I?' she says with a giggle. 'And who'd have thought you'd turn out to be my bestie? I mean, I do have a best mate, Michael, but he's back in Birmingham. I miss him, you know. He's my partner without being my partner, if you see what I mean. He's gay, so…' Mel gives an overstated shrug. 'So that ain't ever gonna happen. We've known each other since we were eight. Same children's home. Bet you never thought that about me, eh? That I grew up without a family.' Mel sips more drink, leaning forward towards Miss Sarah. 'I was abandoned as a baby, you see. Dumped on a train by my mother. Can you believe someone would do that?'

As she leans closer still, Mel's eyes connect with Miss Sarah's, searching for even a glimmer of understanding. As she focuses, which is hard in her drunken state, Mel is sure she sees a flicker of something. No, she *feels* it, as if whatever Miss Sarah wants to say is stuck in there and there's no way she's letting it out.

'So the last thing I expected was to inherit a hotel and a load of money…' Mel pauses, trying to swallow down yet another hiccup, but it doesn't work, and she ends up belching and hiccupping at the same time. 'Christ, 'scuse me,' she says, covering her mouth. 'And then there's this Angus bloke. He's meant to be my brother, can you believe?' Mel pauses, hearing nothing more than a drunk woman rambling and feeling sorry for herself. 'And those bones in the garden. And Kate not speaking. Was that your idea, was it? That she clam up?' Mel shakes her head, sighing. 'Tell you what, Miss Sarah, it's more than I can deal with right now.'

As she's sipping the last of her whisky, she stops, thinking she heard something. Was it Miss Sarah making a noise – some kind of sound coming from the back of her throat? Or was she mistaken, and it was coming from the landing? Mel shrugs, unsure. Doesn't even care.

'Anyway, tell me, why are you called *Miss* Sarah? It's a bit weird. Is there a story behind it and—'

Mel stops. Definitely a noise. Not Miss Sarah. She holds her breath.

Then, slowly, she stands up and creeps over to the bedroom door, trying not to stagger. When she yanks the door open, it takes her a moment to realise that it's Angus disappearing down the corridor.

CHAPTER FORTY-ONE

Bleary-eyed from a poor night's sleep filled with bad dreams, headaches and regret, Mel screams. A guttural, blood-curdling scream sent up from deep inside her as she pulls back Kate's duvet.

Pillows. Four pillows are laid out in a row, the duvet having been shaped over them to look like her daughter. How could she have been so *stupid* not to notice last night?

Because you were drunk! she screams in her head.

Mel steadies herself, her breathing fast and panicked as she forces her brain to work, denying what she can't bear to admit.

Kate has run away – or worse.

It was the headache that had woken her half an hour earlier, with the morning sunlight streaming across her face. Not that she'd really slept properly. From pouring sweat to being freezing cold, to tossing and turning and drifting off only to be woken by nightmares, which included Billy forcing her to eat cake while Tom watched on as he barbecued tiny bones, Mel had peeled her eyes open and groaned, remembering what had happened and pulling a pillow over her head to block everything out. She just wanted the world to go away.

'Why… why, oh *why*?' she'd whispered, remembering the entire bottle of champagne she'd drunk plus the whisky Miss Sarah had given her. Then she pulled the pillow off her head and sat up, clutching her temples when she remembered seeing Angus walking briskly away from Miss Sarah's door as she'd opened it. There was no reason for him to be on that part of the landing – his room was at the other end of the corridor. He'd been eavesdropping on their conversation. Or rather, my self-indulgent monologue, Mel had thought.

And then her thoughts had turned to Kate, how today was the day she was going to do anything in her power to get her to talk, to open up, to confide in her. Nothing else mattered – not Angus, not the bones, not seeing Tom in his living room with another woman. As far as Mel was concerned, hangover or not, today she was going to devote herself to Kate. She'd give her a sick day off school, and they'd have a picnic on the beach, she'd thought, dragging herself into the bathroom and turning on the shower. She'd focus only on her daughter.

Fifteen minutes later, she was carrying the breakfast tray she'd made for Kate through the restaurant area when she spotted Angus tucking into his full English, a cup of coffee to one side, a newspaper to the other. He was leaning over it, chewing idly, sipping his coffee, looking completely relaxed in the casual blue shirt he was wearing over jeans.

'Good morning,' Mel had said, standing directly in front of his table. Miss Sarah wasn't at her usual spot by the window, presumably having already eaten.

Angus had looked up, slowly. 'Morning,' he replied, confidently yet with a hint of caution.

'Any particular reason you were outside Miss Sarah's door last night?' she'd continued.

'Oh, was I?' he'd replied, cutting up some bacon. He'd given an innocent smile then, making Mel wonder if the alcohol had made her unnecessarily suspicious.

'Maybe I was mistaken,' she'd said, not wanting to argue. 'I think we need to talk, though. About this brother and sister thing.'

Angus had laid down his knife and fork then and given her his attention.

'About how you found out,' Mel had continued. 'And proof. And what it is you want, exactly, by coming here out of the blue.'

'That's fair enough,' he'd replied, leaning forward, elbows on the table. 'And very sensible of you. It'd be my pleasure to explain everything over a cup of tea. I'd like us to get to know each other more.'

'Fine. Good,' Mel had said, nodding her head perfunctorily, feeling bad for being short with him. 'Better take this up to Kate then, wake the sleeping beauty.'

Angus had smiled and Mel had felt his stare burning into her back as she left the restaurant and headed up to Kate's bedroom.

Except when she went in, Kate wasn't in bed, and that's when she screamed, dropping the tray on the floor when she discovered the pile of pillows.

'She's *nowhere*,' Mel says frantically down the line. 'I mean, like, she's completely disappeared. And she's not taken her phone or her purse. At first I thought she'd run away, but there's no stuff missing.' *Except the phone that Billy gave her*, she wants to say but can't bring herself to. She went cold when she saw it had gone from her bedside cupboard. 'What the hell do I do, Micky?' Mel can hardly breathe her chest is so tight. 'She's turned into a pile of bloody pillows overnight, and it's all my fault.' Mel lets out the sob she's been holding in, trying to keep herself level-headed while she'd been searching. But now, having stopped to think, not knowing what else to do but call Michael, Mel is on the verge of exploding with worry.

'Where are you, Mel?' Michael says calmly.

'In the garden. I've just got back from driving around the village. I went to check at school in case she'd gone early, then down at the beach, Chloe's house, all over the place. No sign of her.'

'Right, well, sit down and take a few slow, deep breaths. You're going to pass out from hyperventilation if you're not careful.'

'Sorry, yes, yes, OK,' Mel says, still breathing rapidly. She drops
down onto the low wall, tipping her head back as she forces her
brain to think where Kate may have gone. But lurking at the back
of her mind is a thought too terrifying to consider.

'Listen to me, Mel. Kate is a sensible girl. She won't have gone
far, and she'll come back all apologetic that she worried you. That's
the most likely outcome, OK?'

'Mmm,' Mel replies weakly, cradling her head, not knowing
what to do with herself. Nikki and Rose hadn't seen Kate that
morning when she asked them, and Angus hadn't either as Mel
tore around the hotel calling out her name.

'Obviously, I'll let you know if she turns up at my place. She
may have hopped on a train. Meantime, I think it's worth calling
the police. I don't want to worry you, Mel, but…'

'It's OK. You can say it. Don't think the thought hasn't already
occurred to me,' Mel says in a voice that's barely holding up. '*Billy*,'
she whispers. 'I know he's behind this.'

'That's what you need to be careful about. If he's snatched her,
then it's most definitely a police matter. Given the history, they'll
take you seriously. It's time to call them.'

'I agree,' Mel says, barely feeling real. As she stands up, her legs
feel as if they'll give way at any moment. 'I'll do it now,' she adds,
spotting someone walking up the driveway. 'Oh Christ, that's all
I need,' she mutters down the phone. 'Got to go, Micky. I'll keep
you posted.' And she hangs up, unable to even force a smile as
Tom walks towards her.

'Late night?' Tom says, laughing as he draws up beside her.
Briefly, he rests a hand on her shoulder, giving it a little squeeze.
But then he retracts it quickly, a concerned look spreading across
his face, obviously remembering what happened last time he
touched her.

'Sorry… what?' Mel says, preoccupied.

Tom clears his throat. 'Lovely day, isn't it?'

'Not really,' Mel replies. 'Kate's gone missing.'

'What? When… I mean where, how? Christ, Mel, I'm so sorry to hear that.'

Mel shakes her head in the hope it will prevent the brewing tears. 'She's not been right since she found… you know.' Mel glances over at the cordoned-off trench. 'I only went out for a few hours last night, and—'

'So I was right about the late night at least then, eh?' Tom says with a wink.

If only you knew… Mel wants to say.

'Tom, listen, this is serious. She wasn't in her room when I came home. Well, I *thought* she was. I checked in on her as usual but she, or someone, had made a body shape out of pillows, so I'd think she was asleep in bed. Wherever she's gone, it was all planned.'

'Oldest trick in the book,' he says, smiling. 'Did it countless times as a teen,' he adds.

'That's not helping, Tom,' Mel says, her voice on the verge of tears. 'How I wish it *was* just her and Chloe playing a teenage prank. But it's not. I've checked with school and all her friends, searched high and low, done everything I can. She's nowhere. I need to call the police now, because…' Mel looks away, unsure if she wants to tell him. 'I think she's been kidnapped,' she blurts out.

'*What?*' Tom's voice is deep, serious. 'Who by?'

'Her father,' she replies, getting straight to the point. 'He's recently been released from prison. And I know he'll stop at nothing to see Kate and… and get her back. He knows he has no legal leg to stand on, as I have full residency rights and there's no contact order currently, but Billy won't accept that. He does things *his* way. I don't want to talk about it, but just so you know, he… he used to knock me around. All kinds of abusive stuff.' She clamps her arms around her body, hugging herself.

'Christ, Mel. I'm *so* sorry.' Tom blows breath between his teeth. 'I think calling the police is absolutely the right thing to do. How can I help?'

Mel touches her head. 'I… I don't know. Perhaps help search for her. Let me call the police first and I'll see what they say.' And with that, Mel pulls her phone from her pocket and dials 999.

CHAPTER FORTY-TWO

Having been transferred to the local constabulary and made a report, Mel heads back inside the hotel to double-check all the rooms yet again. Perhaps Kate decided to sleep in another bedroom and is lying low in a cupboard. She prays she finds her daughter snuggled in a duvet, curled up at the bottom of a wardrobe, needing the security of a hiding place. They'll talk everything through, have a nice picnic on the beach, play some games... But as Mel flings open bedroom door after bedroom door, she knows that's not the reality of the situation.

Kate has gone.

'You definitely think she's been kidnapped, Mel? It does seem pre-planned to me, with Kate making it look as though she was in bed,' Tom had said before he'd left to drive around the village as well as search the beach, especially up near the rocky part. There were caves nearby, apparently.

If only I'd stayed home, watched TV with Kate...

'You don't know Billy,' was Mel's reply. 'He's either cooked this up with her, telling her to keep it a secret, dressing it up as a fun game. Or, knowing I was out, he'd have come into the hotel and simply taken her against her will. To give himself a head start, he would have planted the pillows under the duvet himself. He knows I check in on her every night before I go to sleep.'

'Hey, hey there...' comes a voice now, then a hand on her back.

Mel forces her head up off her desk and sees Angus standing beside her. She wipes her face, hating that he's found her crying. She has to be strong, for Kate.

'Everything's going to be OK,' he says in a soothing voice as he sits down. Mel notices his eyes flick over her desk and her computer screen.

'You don't know that,' she says, pulling a tissue from a box. 'I wish the police would hurry up.'

'I'll stay with you until they arrive,' Angus says.

'You don't have to,' Mel says, looking directly into his eyes. Kind, genuine eyes, she thinks.

'Nonsense. That's what family is for, right?'

Mel gives a little nod, sniffing again. 'Thanks,' she says. 'I can't believe we're actually blood relatives. That Kate has an uncle.' Mel gives a tiny smile, wondering what Kate will make of that. Anyone claiming that title has a hard act to follow. Michael will always be Kate's number one 'uncle'.

'It's fate that I found you, I swear,' Angus says, taking hold of Mel's hand. 'And fate that you came to live here, so close to me. What made you move to Halebury?'

Mel looks at him, too distracted to know where to begin. 'Long story, but in short, I inherited this place.'

Angus arcs his head slowly in acknowledgment as he takes in what she's saying. 'Ahh,' he says. 'Let me guess, that would have been in the last couple of months, right?'

'Yes,' Mel says, frowning.

'Me too,' Angus continues, giving a couple of thoughtful nods. 'As in, I also recently received an inheritance. Though not a hotel, exactly. Just a bit of cash. A useful little sum, but...' He trails off, shakes his head. 'Anyway, that doesn't matter. What matters is finding Kate.'

'Hang on,' Mel says. 'You had an inheritance at the same time as me?'

Angus nods.

'Who from?' Mel sits forward on the edge of her seat.

'The strange thing is,' Angus says, 'I have no idea. And no way of finding out, either. It was all very cloak-and-dagger. It was completely anonymous.'

Mel's shoulders slump as she recognises the story. 'Same here,' she says. 'I was told the benefactor wanted to remain unidentified. Frankly, I wasn't in a position to argue. I'd just lost my job and my abusive ex was…' She trails off. 'Anyway, I had no idea how many other beneficiaries there were, least of all one who would turn out to be my brother. Do you think it was from a relative?'

'Possibly,' Angus says. 'But I'm as in the dark as you about it.'

Mel watches him, seeing a grey, sad look sweep over his face. 'What's wrong?' she asks, reaching out to him.

Angus shakes his head, his floppy fringe falling over his brow, making Mel catch her breath. She swears she sees a likeness with Kate – that faraway look in his eyes, the way his mouth quivers before he speaks. 'It's nothing.'

'No, tell me,' she insists. 'As you said, we're family.' Her heart thumps as she suddenly remembers that half of hers is missing. 'It'll keep me occupied until the police come.'

'I've just not had a great run of luck, that's all,' he says with a resigned laugh. 'There's no way I'm going to trouble you with it now, and especially not the reasons behind it. You've got enough on your plate. But suffice to say that my little inheritance was short-lived. Debts, through no fault of my own, swallowed up the cash. But I've still got my job, which I'm grateful for, though it doesn't pay well.'

'I'm really sorry to hear that,' Mel says, feeling bad for him. 'What is it you do?'

'I'm a carer,' Angus says with a fond smile. 'I know, I know… not exactly a glamorous career, but I love it. I used to be based in the community, but now I only have one client. He was my favourite out of all the people I looked after, and he needed someone for full-time care, so that's what I do. He's only my age but relies on me completely. We're almost like brothers. It makes me nervous being away from him now, but a trusted colleague has taken over his care for a few days.'

'You're *kidding* me?' Mel says, shaking her head. 'A carer?'

Angus looks up.

'Before I moved here, I worked in a care home.'

'Get out of here,' Angus replies. 'Really?'

Mel nods, straining her ears for the police.

Angus reaches out for her hands. 'More than a coincidence, I'd say,' he says. 'Caring is obviously in our DNA.'

Mel manages a smile, wondering if he's right. 'And I understand about favourite clients,' she says. 'I miss Bob terribly. He was ninety-six and always had such a positive outlook. I loved him to bits. But then I got fired and…' She trails off, not wanting to go into it now.

Mel glances at her watch. If the police don't arrive soon, she's going to call again.

'Anyway, like I said,' Angus continues, 'my windfall money is gone now. Not that it was much in the first place. Looks like you did OK out of your share, though,' he adds with a laugh.

Mel frowns. 'You don't think our inheritances were equal?'

Angus blows breath between his teeth. 'Honestly? No way,' he says without a shred of bitterness, still smiling. 'But that's OK. Even if there were other beneficiaries aside from us, my couple of thousand pounds quickly got used up. Someone wrote off my car, so I had to use it to buy another in order to get to work.'

'That's…' Mel says, not knowing what to say, 'terrible,' she adds. She knows it's no time to feel guilty, but she can't help it. 'It doesn't sound right at all to me. And really not fair.' She wishes the police would hurry.

Angus closes his eyes for a moment. 'Thanks, Mel. And I'm sorry for even mentioning it. I shouldn't have while you're worrying about Kate.'

Mel nods in agreement, her heart suddenly thumping at the sound of the hotel front door opening. 'Look, Angus,' Mel says, one ear cocked, 'we'll sort something out, OK? I... I wouldn't be able to live with the inequality of all this. You're... you're my brother, after all.' She touches her forehead, unable to think straight. 'I'll make sure you're—'

But Mel stops as her office door opens wider and she sees two police officers standing there, Nikki nervously bobbing about behind them – the same two officers who were here just a few days ago. Suddenly, everything seems very real.

CHAPTER FORTY-THREE

'I'll leave you in private,' Angus says, rising and giving Mel a gentle pat. Something shifts inside her as she feels his warm hand on her shoulder. She doesn't feel quite so alone in the world any more.

'Thanks, Angus,' Mel says, their eyes meeting. She gives him a brief smile, all she can manage, as he leaves.

'It's just not like Kate,' Mel tells the two PCs, feeling even more anxious after she's explained how she found Kate's bed stuffed with pillows. 'I'm just so worried that her father has snatched her. He's... well, he's not long out of prison and has a vendetta against me. He absolutely adores Kate and knows it would kill me if he took her.'

'If this is correct, do you think she's at risk with him?'

'He wouldn't lay a finger on her,' Mel says confidently. 'He'd kill anyone else who did, though,' she adds. If there was one thing she'd always respected Billy for, it was his protectiveness and love for his daughter. 'But Billy is...' Mel hesitates, 'well, he's not exactly a good role model. I was a key witness that led to his conviction. I have sole residency and there's no arrangements order in place for contact. If he's got her, he'll never bring her back, I'm certain of that.'

'Two motives to take Kate, then. He adores her and he wants to get back at you.'

Mel nods. 'Yes, and he also wants to punish me for daring to leave him.'

'It seems premeditated with the pillows in the bed,' PC Gordon says as they follow Mel up to Kate's room. 'Almost as if Kate was part of the plan herself, or was willing to go.'

'That's what worries me,' Mel says, watching as the police snap on gloves and carefully pick through her things – opening her bedside table, inspecting her phone, looking in a couple of drawers. 'Because I know she wouldn't have been willing to go. She just wouldn't, not without telling me first.'

'Has she been upset about anything recently? Did you two have any kind of falling-out?' PC Gordon asks kindly.

'She was very upset about what she unearthed outside – the bones. You know the situation there. But we hadn't fallen out over it. I was doing everything I could to get her to open up, to talk to me.'

Like leaving her alone last night when she was *clearly* still so troubled… Mel thinks, inwardly chastising herself.

'Billy was in touch with her before we left Birmingham a few weeks ago,' Mel continues. 'He gave her a mobile phone with his number on. I'm not proud of this, but I ended up taking it so he couldn't use it to contact her but… but when I checked earlier, it had gone from my room. Kate must have taken it with her. The stupid thing is, I don't have its number. I didn't think I'd need it. I've tried calling Billy from my phone, but it goes straight to voicemail. Christ, I'm so worried about her. Can't you get officers out there looking for her right away?'

'Absolutely, Miss Douglas, don't you worry about that. We're already on it. Now, it's best you calm down and let us get on with our job.'

Mel doesn't know what else to do. After the officers left, taking a few of Kate's things, including her regular phone, she went out searching again, spotting Tom several times as she drove around the area. She pulled over, winding down her window as he came up off the beach, shaking his head.

'No sign so far,' he said. 'But if she's still in the area, someone will find her. I've spread the word far and wide.'

'Thank you,' was all Mel could bring herself to say, shaking as she gripped the steering wheel. Tom promised he'd come back up to the hotel soon.

Torn between wanting to be out searching and waiting at home in case Kate returned, Mel eventually went back to Moreton Inn and sat in her study, the door wide open so she could see out into reception.

'Here,' Rose says, placing a cup of tea on her desk, 'drink this.'

Mel glances up and nods gratefully.

'She was fine when I checked in on her last night,' Rose adds, a worried look on her face. 'All tucked up in bed. Then I spotted you coming back early, so figured I didn't need to look in on her any more.'

'It's OK, Rose,' Mel says, 'it's not your fault. I don't think she was in bed when you looked. She'd faked it. Or someone had.'

After Rose leaves, Mel reaches into her desk drawer and pulls out her tarot cards. Simply holding them brings some kind of comfort. She closes her eyes as she shuffles, remembering her favourite foster mother doing the same if Mel had ever had a problem as a teenager.

Let's see what the cards have to say, shall we? Sue would say, with tea and Battenberg cake all part of the ritual, before spreading them out on the small dining table. Whether what the cards told them was true or not didn't matter to Mel – it wasn't about that.

What will be will be, Sue always said at the start of the reading. Consulting the cards was more about taking back some kind of control or, Mel thinks now as she deals out a spread, a way of searching deep inside herself.

She stares at the colourful and detailed pictures, her mouth slowly opening, her heart sinking. The cards couldn't be more indicative of her situation – loss, grief, desperation, anxiety, worry and devastation are all shown clearly.

'Five of Cups, Nine of Swords, Three of Swords, Ten of Swords…' Mel hangs her head, her hair falling over her face. Then she deals several more cards to elaborate on the previous ones, to see if there is any comfort at all to be had in the outcome.

She stops, hearing a noise – the front door of the hotel opening. And then voices.

It's just as she sees she's dealt the Six of Cups – the card of childhood, innocence and friendship – alongside The Lovers, that Michael and Tom are suddenly standing in her office doorway.

'Oh my *God*,' Mel says, leaping up. 'Micky!' She launches herself at him, burying her face in his shoulder and hugging him tightly. 'I can't believe you're here. You must have driven like a loon after we spoke.'

'I did indeed,' Michael says as best he can with Mel hanging round his neck. 'Has Katie come back yet?' he asks, holding her at arm's length.

'No… no sign still. I'm going out of my mind with worry.'

Michael glances at her desk. 'I can see,' he says, knowing she always turned to the tarot in times of stress.

'I've virtually ransacked the village looking for her,' Tom says, shaking his head.

Mel nods, a frown set between her eyes. 'Thank you,' she says, introducing the two men as they shake hands. She's just about to suggest they sit in the bar, to form a new search plan between them, when her phone vibrates in her pocket. She whips it out, answering with shaking hands when she sees PC Gordon's number on her screen.

'Yes, yes, OK,' she says, listening. 'When was that?' she asks, glancing at Michael and Tom in turn. 'Last night?' Mel puts a hand to her forehead, a frown crumpling her face. 'Oh God,' she says, almost in tears. 'But no description of the man? I understand, yes.

OK, thank you, please do.' And she hangs up, steadying herself by sitting down on the edge of her desk.

'News?' Tom says, gently touching her arm.

'Someone thinks they saw her in the village last night,' Mel says, her voice wavering. 'They... they thought she may have been with someone but couldn't be certain if they were together or not. They described Kate quite clearly, but whoever she was possibly with was wearing a hat and had his back to them as they passed.'

'Anything else?' Tom asks.

'Apparently, there was another sighting of her a bit later. Somewhere sounding like Camborough Lane, I think?' Mel says, wishing she'd paid more attention to the name. 'It...' She takes a deep breath. 'It sounds like Billy definitely took her, Micky.'

'A small comfort, but at least she's not out there alone,' Michael replies.

Mel nods, but she also knows that, if it's true, Billy won't give her up easily. She might never see her daughter again. 'The police are going to do a thorough search and house-to-house enquiries. They're also getting details of his van and are out looking for it.'

'Was it Combrook Lane?' Tom says, thinking.

'Yes, that's it,' Mel replies.

'It's up the other side of the village,' Tom says. 'It doesn't lead anywhere except to a couple of farms and an old, half-ruined cottage. Walter wouldn't let me go up that way as a lad, because...' Tom trails off, clearing his throat.

'Wait, your dad is called Walter?' Mel says, putting two and two together. 'Does he live in the little terrace of cottages just down from here on the hill?'

'That's him,' Tom says. 'Have you met him?'

'He was lost,' Mel says. 'Kate and I took him home.'

Tom looks at her for a moment, hesitating. 'That's kind, thank you. His memory certainly isn't what it used to be. Everyone looks out for him, but I'm going to need more care for him soon.'

'But that doesn't answer why Kate was walking down that lane last night,' Mel says, shuddering and choking back a sob. 'Even if it was with Billy. You'd think he'd want to get her out of the area immediately.'

'Come on,' Michael says, taking Mel by the arm, 'let's get you a fresh cup of tea while we wait for news.'

Mel nods reluctantly and, as she's sliding off the desk, she knocks one of the tarot cards onto the floor from the pack. She bends down to pick it up and, turning it over, sees the face of the Devil staring back at her.

CHAPTER FORTY-FOUR

Nikki brings the hot drinks over to the table in the corner where Mel sits with Michael and Tom.

'I don't feel real,' Mel says weakly to Michael, who's sitting on the banquette beside her. 'Tell me this isn't happening, Micky. If only I hadn't gone out last night, Kate would still be here.'

'Katie's not daft,' Michael says. 'I can't see her getting on a train on her own, or trusting a stranger. She's probably just spending time with her dad. Not ideal, but she knows you wouldn't approve and has gone about it the wrong way. But at least you know Billy won't lay a finger on her.'

'But he also won't bring her back either. What if he takes her overseas? He has contacts in Spain, you know.'

'Look, this is where Combrook Lane is,' Tom says, showing Mel a map on his phone. He switches it to satellite mode and zooms in. Mel winces at the patches of woodland and open fields around the area with just one or two farm buildings dotted around.

'It looks so remote,' she says, turning away. She checks her own phone, making sure the volume is switched up. Then she dials Billy's number again, but it goes directly to his message service as before. 'I don't see why Billy would be taking her somewhere like that.'

'Any news?' comes a voice nearby. When Mel looks up, Angus is standing there, concern written on his face. His eyes flick to Tom, then linger on Michael for a moment.

'Not much,' Mel says, updating him briefly about the sighting.

'If there's anything I can do, please let me know. We're family, after all.'

'Thank you,' Mel says and watches Angus walk off, heading towards the toilets.

'Is that the guy who says he's your brother?' Michael asks quietly, scowling at the man's back.

Mel nods, barely registering what he's saying.

'Your brother?' Tom says. 'Him?' He glances at the space where Angus has been.

'Yes,' Mel says vaguely. 'He turned up as a guest a few days ago and then dropped it on me that we're siblings. Apparently.' She shrugs.

'I saw him in the village,' Tom continues, sipping slowly on his tea.

Mel nods, barely listening as she tries Billy's number again. Nothing.

'He was talking to someone. I swear it was that same guy in the van who'd come looking for a room the other day, remember? I came to tell you about it a couple of days ago but... but you seemed pretty upset about something at the time, so I left.'

Mel looks up, tensing. '*What?* Can you describe him? And I'm sorry. I'd just read a pretty damning piece by that journalist in the local paper and was upset.'

'He was rough-looking, though not a big bloke. Guess he had a mean face, but not unattractive either. He had a scar on his cheek, I remember that much.'

'A scar?' Mel says, closing her eyes briefly before reaching for her phone. 'Is this him?' she says, pulling up a photograph.

'That's him,' Tom says, leaning across to look.

'It's Billy,' she tells him. 'My ex.' She'd already sent the picture to PC Gordon when they were here earlier.

'He was sitting in his van with the window down, parked near the seafront. Angus was standing beside the van. The pair of them seemed deep in conversation. It's not hard to spot who's local and who's not around here, and they both stood out a mile, especially as I'd seen the guy in the van up here before. He must have hung around the area.'

'Christ…' Mel says, dropping her shaking head into her hands. 'I've been so stupid. Angus is obviously on Billy's payroll,' she whispers, conscious of him being within earshot. 'Billy must have sent him here. It's his style, especially as you'd already turned him away in the car park. He figured he'd call on someone less dodgy-looking to get inside. To get to Kate.'

'But I don't understand why Billy would show his face here in the first place and risk you seeing him,' Tom says. 'And why would Angus claim to be your brother?'

Mel stares out of the window for a moment. 'You don't know Billy,' she says. 'It's how he works. He had no intention of staying here. He picked his moment to speak to you, hoping I'd find out he'd been here. It was his way of rattling me, of unnerving me, letting me know he's still on my tail. Classic Billy.'

Mel sips her tea, her hand shaking as she brings the mug to her mouth.

'And as for getting Angus to pretend to be my brother…' Mel blows out, shakes her head as she thinks. 'I don't know. Guess he knows my weak spots and he's playing on them. This is bloody war as far as I'm concerned,' she says, standing up then sitting down again, not knowing what to do with herself. 'I swear to God, I won't rest until I've got my Katie back.' She slaps a hand down on the table. 'He's pushed me too bloody far this time.'

'Hey, hey, steady there,' Michael says. 'Getting worked up isn't going to find Kate, and that's our main priority now. Let the police deal with Billy once they've got him.'

But Mel's attention is turned to the restaurant door again as Angus comes back in from the toilets.

'Can I get anyone a drink?' he says, approaching the table.

'Drink?' Mel spits, standing up again and pushing past Michael. 'You're offering me a bloody drink, as if nothing's wrong?' She gets up close to him. 'Don't think I don't know who you are and what you're up to. In fact, I bet it was you who put the pillows under Kate's duvet, wasn't it? After you'd manhandled her out to Billy, knowing I'd gone out.' Mel feels a rage building inside her, making her want to lash out. She clenches her fists down by her sides.

'Mel, don't,' someone says... then she feels a hand on her arm. She looks round. It's Michael. 'Come and sit, Mel. Let the police handle this.' He glances at Angus, giving him a warning look.

She shrugs out of his way, aware that someone else has just come into the bar area. She doesn't care if it's a customer. Doesn't care if she scares them away, making them think the place is run by a madwoman. *It is!*

'I'm sorry, Mel, I don't know what you're talking about,' Angus says calmly, flashing a concerned look at Michael and Tom.

'You're not my fucking brother!' she yells.

'Mel, there's a customer. Keep your voice down,' Michael says, trying to guide Mel back to the table. Again, she yanks her arm away.

'You helped Billy kidnap Kate, didn't you? You're nothing but a crook, worming your way in here and snooping through my stuff. How pathetic, claiming to be my brother. Is that the best you could come up with?'

Mel paces about, pushing her fingers through her hair in frustration, bumping into a stool and knocking it over.

'Mel, you're upset,' another voice says beside her. This time it's Tom. He catches her in his arms as she circles round, her hands flapping limply by her sides. 'Come and sit down. Do you want me to phone the officer for an update?'

Mel stares at Tom, looking up at him as he holds her as if she's a wild animal, trapped. For a second, she imagines she's the woman she saw through his window last night, that this is how she felt being embraced by him. Only there are no warm smiles and glints in his eyes now. No romantic gestures. Mel's heart thunders inside her chest.

'Yes. No... I don't know!' she sobs. 'All I know is that *he's* a fake. There's no way I've got a brother, let alone one who's just happened to conveniently find me.' She turns to Angus again, who's frozen to the spot beside the bar. 'Tom saw you talking to my ex,' she shouts at him, jabbing a finger in his direction. 'I know you're working for Billy. How did he pay you? Cash, or drugs, or a combination? Or maybe you owed him one from way back. Billy never forgets to call in a favour.'

'Mel, I really don't know what you're talking about. I came here in good faith, but I can see this isn't a good time for you. I understand the news about having a brother must have come as a shock, but...' He trails off, looking at Michael for support. 'But I think it's best if I leave now.'

Tom slides a comforting hand around Mel's waist. 'Sit down, Mel,' he says. 'You're shaking.'

'No,' she whispers, her voice trembling. 'Don't believe anything this man says. He's a fake and a liar. Billy sent him to get Kate, I know he did!' She raises her voice again, catching sight of Miss Sarah at her usual table – the customer she'd thought had come in. As ever, she has a book in front of her, though this time she's not reading it. Her head is half turned towards them, her eyes blinking slowly.

'If you're my brother, then prove it,' Mel continues, edging back onto the banquette. 'Otherwise I'm calling PC Gordon to tell her you were seen talking to Billy recently. I know you've got something to do with Kate's disappearance.'

'I'm happy to chat with the police,' Angus says calmly. 'It's true I spoke to a man in the village. He was asking for directions. He was a little… rough around the edges, perhaps, but I thought he was a friend of yours, Melanie. He seemed to know all about you and had come a long way to visit. He told me his phone couldn't pinpoint your exact location or something, so I gave him directions here. He asked me where he could get a pint and a decent meal.' Angus shakes his head and raises his eyebrows, folding his arms across his chest. 'I'm sorry you don't believe me, and I know you've been through a tough time. But I'm telling you the truth.'

'That doesn't make sense,' Mel replies, looking at Tom for reassurance. 'Billy came sniffing about here before you even came to stay, Angus. Why would he need directions when he already knew?'

Angus shakes his head, looking confused. 'I have no idea. But look, I understand why you'd doubt me. I probably would too.' He fishes his phone out of his pocket and taps it several times, scrolling down. 'I don't know if this helps at all, but here's a scan of the original letter I got from a solicitor in Exeter. It's about the inheritance I received.'

Mel takes his phone and zooms in on the letter, dated several months ago, just like hers. She sees it's addressed to him, Angus Spencer, in Taunton, and sent from a solicitor in Exeter, reminding her of something Robert Hedge had said.

Michael peers over her shoulder, reading it too.

'It looks the same as the letter you got, Mel,' he says quietly in her ear. 'The one you nearly threw away, insisting it was fake, remember?'

Mel nods. 'Yes,' she says quietly. 'It is the same. But that doesn't mean he's my brother, though. Does it?' she adds, doubting herself now. She puts Angus's phone on the table, not knowing where to look.

'I know it's a lot to take in, Melanie,' Angus goes on, his hands clasped in front of his navy V-neck sweater, 'but I swear I don't know your ex, and neither do I have anything to do with Kate going missing.' He pulls out a little stool at the table and sits down opposite her, a concerned look on his face. 'You have to believe me.'

Mel opens her mouth to speak, but something stops her in her tracks, silencing her.

A sound. Some kind of noise.

Unintelligible at first.

Everyone is quiet, no one moving, as if for a moment time has stood still.

'No,' a voice says from across the room.

Just a single word. So weak and barely audible that Mel wonders if she even heard it. Slowly, she turns to see where it came from.

And in the window, with the evening sunlight streaming in around her, Miss Sarah is standing up beside her table, her book on the floor at her feet and her hands clasped in small, white fists by her sides. Her entire body is shaking and her mouth is open, her jaw quivering. Her eyes bulge within their sockets.

'No…' she says again, as if it's taken everything she has inside her to utter the single, brittle word.

All eyes are on her and everyone is silent. No one able to say a thing.

CHAPTER FORTY-FIVE

'*No. No. No.*'

Mel stares wide-eyed at Miss Sarah, hardly able to breathe as the word echoes around the room. No one dares to move.

She stands there, shaking as if she might shatter into a hundred pieces from the effort that one syllable took to utter, the halo of light around her dissipating as the sun vanishes behind a cloud.

Mel finally brings herself to slide off the banquette and go over, treading so carefully and slowly, as if she's creeping up on a timid wild creature, trying not to scare it away.

'Miss Sarah?' she whispers. She doesn't know if it's the shock of hearing her own voice or Mel approaching, but the woman drops down onto her chair again. She stares into space, not focused on anything or anyone in particular. Her face is blank, her skin pale and, if it wasn't for the shallow rise and fall of her chest, she would otherwise appear dead.

'Miss Sarah,' Mel repeats, kneeling down on the floor beside her, 'what did you just say?'

Mel knows full well what she said, but more to the point, she wants to know *why* she said it.

'No?' Mel says. 'What do you mean? I'm so glad you spoke to us. It's good to hear your voice.' She wants to encourage her to say more but is concerned she'll make her clam up again. 'Would you like a drink of water?' Mel reaches over and pours from the jug on her table, handing her the glass. Miss Sarah takes it but just holds it in her lap with shaking hands, the water trembling inside.

Mel stands up again, looking over at the others. '*Please*, Miss Sarah, if there's something you want to say, then for God's sake just—'

'Don't,' comes another voice from behind her.

Mel swings round as Michael approaches her.

'Don't be impatient with her, Mel,' he says, a pained expression on his face. 'It's not her fault.'

'What are you on about, Micky? If she knows something, then she needs to tell me. Why else would she suddenly speak after years of silence?' She turns back to Miss Sarah. 'Do you know anything about Kate?' Mel asks, trying her hardest to keep calm. 'What did you mean by "no"?'

'No…' Miss Sarah manages to whisper again, staring at the book on the floor.

'Mel, stop,' Michael insists. 'This is all my fault. All my doing. Look…' He sighs. 'Sit down, will you? There's something I need to tell you.'

Michael briefly touches Miss Sarah's arm, as if to reassure her, though Mel has no idea about what or why he seems so protective of her.

'I just want to know that Kate is safe, but now everyone's gone weird and… and…' Mel's mind is all over the place.

'Mel, you're going to be angry with me,' Michael begins. 'Probably more angry than you've ever been, but I need to confess something. Let me apologise in advance, but…' He comes up close then, taking her aside and whispering quietly in her ear. 'I'd say there's every chance that Angus *is* your brother, so don't be hard on him either. It makes perfect sense now.'

'Well, not to me it doesn't!' Mel snaps back, her heart thundering as if it's about to burst from her chest.

'Do you remember the DNA test I bought you for Christmas?' Michael says as Mel goes to sit down again.

Mel crinkles her nose as she thinks. 'Um… yeah, what of it? I hate to tell you, Micky, but I chucked it out. I was in no mood for that then. Or ever.'

'No, you didn't,' Michael says, closing his eyes and taking a breath as he sits down next to Mel.

'What?' Mel is aware of Tom and Angus nearby, each of them silent.

'It didn't get thrown away. Before I went home from yours that night, I took it out of the bin. You'd already collected the saliva, remember?'

'Yes, I remember doing that, but I put the test tube in the rubbish when I was in the kitchen getting us more drinks.'

'I know. I happened to see you do it,' Michael says. 'So later, I fished it out and took it home and… and, well, I registered an account online and sent it off to the lab. I'd already paid for it, so thought I might as well. Whatever came back, if anything, I was going to let you decide what you wanted to do with the results.'

'Michael!' Mel says, astonished. 'You had absolutely no right to do that and—'

'I know, I *know*…' He holds his hands up both in defence and shame. 'I was out of order, I admit. When I got an email a few weeks later saying the results had come back, I decided not to look. It didn't seem right, given how determined you were *not* to find out about your past. By then, I was too ashamed to tell you what I'd done, so I thought I'd just let sleeping dogs lie.'

Mel sits there, taking it all in, aware of Miss Sarah sitting perfectly still at her table.

'And then…'

'And then *what*?' Mel whispers. Her hands are still shaking as she reaches for her phone, obsessively checking the volume again, making sure she hasn't missed any calls.

'And then I had an email alert about a message received on the account. From a potential family member.' Michael clears his throat and looks away again.

'What? Why the hell didn't you tell me? I mean… this is serious stuff to be meddling in, Micky. What were you *thinking*?' Mel half stands up, then sits down again, shaking her head.

'So I logged into the account I'd made and, apart from the unread message and dozens of possible connections for third, fourth and fifth cousins dotted all over the place… well, I saw that you had another, much *closer* connection listed.'

Mel stares at him, her eyes boring into his, scowling.

Michael takes another deep breath. 'At the top of the list of all these cousins was a parent and child connection. The science was all there, something about measuring the amount of DNA a person shares with another, I forget now. But the parent-child connection listed was someone who was one hundred per cent confirmed as your…' Michael closes his eyes briefly before taking Mel's hand. '…a hundred per cent confirmed as your mother,' he says, looking Mel directly in the eye.

'My *mother*?' she says.

Michael nods.

'Who?' Mel whispers.

Michael turns, looking at Miss Sarah.

'*What?* Mel croaks. 'What are you saying? That Miss Sarah is my… our… mother?' She looks over at Angus to see if this makes any sense to him. But he just sits there looking confused.

'It was Sarah who had messaged me via the DNA testing website,' Michael goes on. 'She… well, she naturally believed I was you when I replied to her. When she mentioned an inheritance that was due to you, I admit, I thought the same as you at first, that it must be some kind of scam, but then—'

'Michael Vincent Smith, I do *not* bloody believe you!' Mel stands, yanking her hands away from his, not realising he'd even taken hold of them. 'This is… well, this is fraud or something, I don't know. How *could* you?'

'It all just got out of hand,' Michael says, tears collecting in his eyes. 'I understood why you didn't want to know anything about your parents, and your mother especially, for abandoning you. But then I'd witnessed first-hand the life you'd had with Billy, and I couldn't let you go back to that. Like you, I knew he wouldn't be in prison for ever, and I've seen him worm his way back into your life before, Mel. I didn't trust him not to do that again. I couldn't let that happen to Katie, apart from anything.'

'No, no, *no*, this isn't happening,' Mel says. 'Who the hell am I able to trust any more if I can't trust you, Micky?'

'I'm sorry, darling,' Michael says earnestly. 'Please, forgive me. I truly meant no harm.'

Mel strides over to the bar, leaning against the freshly painted wood, wondering what all this means for her, for Katie. She glances at Miss Sarah, unable to absorb the news that this woman who refuses to speak is actually her *mother*. She looks far too young, for a start – barely a decade or more older than she is. She wants to study every inch of her, take her by the collar and shake her, force her to tell her everything, while at the same time hugging her and crying on her shoulder. Nothing makes sense.

'Angus?' Mel finally says. 'What do you know about this?'

Angus shakes his head. 'I mean… well, nothing. I'm as shocked as you are, obviously. And I want answers, too, of course.'

Mel notices his cheeks colour, his eyes flick away.

'In the interests of complete honesty, Mel, I did eventually confess to Miss Sarah who I was in our messages,' Michael continues. 'I told her that I was your friend and had bought the test as a gift. I explained why you didn't want anything to do with your birth mother and… well, she completely understood. If it wasn't for the inheritance, then I wouldn't have given out your address for the solicitor to contact you. She said she would make sure it was all completely anonymous.'

'Ohhh, I *see*,' Mel says, her voice incredulous. 'So that's why you were so damned keen for me to read the letter.' She shakes her head as the penny drops. 'So was it Miss Sarah who refused the inheritance? And her mother *did* leave her the estate?'

'Darling, I don't know any more than that. All I wanted was to secure a better life for you and Katie away from that... that monster. But now he's followed you down here anyway and, oh God, this is all such a mess.' Michael gets up and goes over to hug Mel. Surprisingly, and against her better judgement, she lets him.

'I'm sorry,' Michael whispers into her neck, squeezing her a little harder.

'But how is any of this going to help find Kate? That's all I care about right now,' Mel says, pulling away from him. She goes up to Miss Sarah again. 'Just tell me why you said "no"?' she says. 'If you really are my mother...' Mel hesitates, feeling giddy and unreal at the same time. 'If you really are, then Kate is your granddaughter and she could be in danger. I know that you've been talking to her, discussing her father. So if you've got something to say, if you know where she is, then for God's sake, *please* tell me.'

Mel drops to her knees, taking hold of Miss Sarah's hands. They feel cold and clammy, as though they've never touched another human being, or at least not for a very long time.

Miss Sarah looks directly down at Mel, something lighting up deep within her insipid eyes, as if they're taking on a colour of their own, like the life is coming back into them.

'Mum,' Mel says, almost choking on the word, 'if you truly care for me and your granddaughter, then please, tell me what you know.'

Miss Sarah swallows drily. Then she takes a sip of water. Her lips part and Mel hears her raspy breaths wheezing in and out of lungs that sound barely used.

'Man…' she says so quietly that Mel wonders if she even spoke. 'Man…' she says again.

'Man?' Mel repeats. 'Is that what you said?'

Miss Sarah nods, squeezing her hands as if to confirm that she's correct. Then she coughs, turning her head away slightly. 'Kate,' she whispers.

Behind her, Mel feels the collective tension, everyone desperate to know what she means, if it will help them find Kate.

'Do you mean Kate is with a man?' someone says from behind. Mel turns to see Angus hoping for an answer to his question.

Miss Sarah nods.

'Christ,' Mel says, grateful for Angus's intervention. 'What man, and where can we find him? Is it Billy?'

Miss Sarah coughs again, taking another sip of water.

'D-d… Don…' she says, tears filling her eyes, making them seem bluer than ever. She shudders.

'It's OK,' Mel says, 'you're doing fine. Tell us what you know, Miss Sarah… *Mum*.'

'Don… ald. Donald Bray,' she whispers, as though the words are made of lead.

Mel turns to the others, her eyes huge as she glances between the three men, her mouth hanging open. Her eyes land on Tom's, noticing his expression change to one of shock.

'Oh, Christ,' he says, his jaw clenching tight, a hand coming up to his brow. 'Bray lives out that way, down Combrook Lane. We need to find Kate. And *fast*.'

CHAPTER FORTY-SIX

Mel dials PC Gordon's mobile number. It takes a moment to connect but then goes to her voicemail service. Her heart sinks. 'Hi, yes, this is Mel Douglas from Moreton Inn. Can you call me back urgently, please? I may have a lead about Kate. Thanks.'

She paces about, clutching her phone, praying the constable gets in touch soon.

'Call 101 and get put through to the local police station,' Michael says. 'Don't wait for her to phone you back.'

'You're right,' Mel says, her voice wavering. She dials and waits to be connected to the nearby force, giving all the details to them yet again, including Donald Bray's name, to the officer on duty.

'He pulled up the original case file and is going to see what he can do,' she says after hanging up. 'Apparently they're short-staffed, but he says he'll try to get someone to look into this new information soon.' Mel shakes her head. 'What am I supposed to do meantime? I don't even know if anyone's actually out searching.'

Distraught, she leaves the others to discuss what the best plan is and heads out towards the toilets. But she stops in her tracks when she sees the back door open and Miss Sarah standing in the middle of the excavated site, staring down into the trench. She follows her out, wondering how she unlocked the door.

'I didn't see you leave the bar,' Mel says, approaching her. But then she already knows Miss Sarah has an uncanny knack of appearing and disappearing around the place like an apparition. 'Are you OK?'

Miss Sarah doesn't say a word. Rather, she just looks down into the concrete-lined hole, staring at the place where the anthropologists removed the remains. They'd dug another, bigger hole around it in order to check and sift through the surrounding soil, in case there were any other relevant artefacts. Or more bones, Mel had thought.

'So sad, isn't it?' Mel says. 'I wonder what happened?' She glances at Miss Sarah, whose eyes are dancing over the site, her mouth twitching and her shoulders tense as she stares into the hole. Mel spots a bunch of keys poking out from her cardigan pocket, unsurprised that she has a set if she's lived here so long. It makes her wonder if that's where the key to room seven has ended up.

'Maybe we should have just left it well alone,' she says. 'It would all have been buried again once the trench was backfilled. Let the poor little mite have some peace. It'll be in a lab now, being examined every which way, I suppose. I understand the police have to investigate, but—'

Miss Sarah lets out a noise – something between a sob and a growl.

'Are you OK?' Mel asks again, taking her hand.

Silence.

'It's pretty hard to take in all this stuff about mothers and daughters, right? Especially on top of everything else. I don't know much about this DNA website, but maybe there was a mix-up.' Though Mel knows the chances of a mistake by the DNA lab, as well as encountering Miss Sarah at the very place she's inherited, are extremely remote.

She sighs, feeling the warmth of the sun on her back as the pair of them stare down into the trench. It almost feels like a funeral, Mel thinks. Only without a body.

Suddenly, Miss Sarah drops to her knees and swings her legs over the edge of the hole. Her feet and hands scuff in the dirt as she lowers herself down into it. Before Mel can do or say anything, she's frantically tearing at the mud with her bare hands, clawing and scratching away at the side walls with her fingers. As she works, she lets out throaty little noises, her hair coming loose from its usual bun. Long, faded blonde strands of it fall around her face as she works.

'Miss Sarah, what are you *doing*?' Mel says, getting down on her knees. 'What are you looking for?'

Miss Sarah doesn't say a word, rather she sinks her hands into the soft earth on the inner side of the trench, to the left of where the anthropologists had excavated. Her hands move fast, more soil falling away as she works, her fingernails filled with dark crescents of mud. Then she spins around and tries another area, her breathing getting faster and the little moans getting more urgent. She swipes her hair out of the way, smearing muck on her face as the dirt mixes with the tears on her cheeks.

Mel climbs into the trench beside her, trying to catch her hands. 'Miss Sarah, stop. You'll hurt yourself. What are you doing?' She finally manages to take hold of her frail wrists – though they seem anything but frail as she forces herself away from Mel, tearing into another section of earth. 'Please, this is madness. Mum, stop!'

On hearing this, Miss Sarah slows, her hands leaning on the edge of the trench, her back hunched, her head hanging down. Her shoulders bounce up and down in time with her sobs. Mel pulls her into her arms.

'OK, it's OK,' she says, stroking her hair, which feels surprisingly soft. 'Let's get you back inside and I'll make you a cup of tea.'

Slowly, Miss Sarah looks up at Mel. She sniffs as she hauls herself out of the hole, brushing herself down as she follows Mel back inside.

*

'Tom has been telling me about this Donald Bray character, Mel,' Michael says, a concerned look on his face as she heads back into the bar with Miss Sarah. 'He sounds shady and dangerous. I don't like it.'

'Me neither,' Mel replies, agitated. 'I've had a couple of run-ins with him,' she says, remembering the newsagent, as well as last night, how he almost hit her when she was crossing the road. 'I swear he's got it in for me.' She lets out a little whimper, forcing herself not to fall apart.

'Bray is a nasty piece of work,' Tom says. 'But from what I know, he's a bit of a recluse these days,' he adds. 'He must be well into his seventies by now, but still fit with it. My dad had a few ugly encounters with him back in the day.'

'Recluse or not, I want to go up there, see if there's any sign of Kate. I can't just sit here and do nothing, especially if the police aren't on it yet.' Mel stands, zipping up her hoodie.

Miss Sarah is sitting in her usual window spot again, looking as though she's been in a fight, but she manages a small smile when Nikki brings her a pot of tea. When they came back inside, Mel had pulled a stern face to the others, shaking her head to warn them not to ask questions about the state of her.

'But I don't see what Billy has got to do with Bray,' Mel says impatiently, trying to work out some kind of link. 'Billy doesn't know this part of the country, as far as I'm aware, let alone any old men around here.'

'Maybe it's just coincidence, Mel,' Michael says. 'But I agree, and I think a scout around that area is worthwhile. I'm sure the police are out searching as best they can, but it doesn't look as if they've got the resources to treat this as urgently as we'd like.'

'Agreed,' Angus chips in. 'I'll help search too. It'll at least make us feel as though we're doing something.'

'I'll second that,' Tom says, standing up, the three of them gathering by the door.

'Let's get on with it then,' Mel says. 'Every second counts here.' She glances at Miss Sarah, the early-evening light spilling in through the window around her.

'Try not to worry,' Michael says quietly, coming up to Mel and grabbing her wrist as she's leaving. 'I'll stay here and hold the fort, in case the police come or Kate returns. And I'll keep an eye on her, too,' he whispers, tracking her eyes to where Miss Sarah sits.

'Thank you, Micky,' Mel says, squeezing his hand before dashing outside, following the others to Tom's pick-up truck.

CHAPTER FORTY-SEVEN

Mel sits in the passenger seat with Angus behind her in the back of the large truck. She buckles up as Tom pulls away, obsessively checking her phone has enough charge in it and that she's not missed any calls. 'Is it far?' she asks Tom as he pulls out of the car park, the wheels spinning on the loose tarmac.

'Not too far,' he replies, focusing on the road as he speeds down the hill. 'Combrook Lane joins the village on the other side of the bay. It heads inland for a mile or so before petering out at a field gate. It's a while since I've been down there.'

Mel acknowledges him with a nod, wishing he could drive faster but the road is narrow and winding.

'I'm not trying to scare you, Mel, but a lot of parents stop their kids playing down there because of Bray. Even when I was a boy, Dad wouldn't let me cycle out that way.'

'Oh God,' Mel croaks, not sure she wants to know any more.

'Like I said, Dad had a number of run-ins with him. Axes were well and truly ground,' Tom continues, his eyes fixed firmly ahead.

'Over Joyce?' Mel is aware that Angus is listening from the rear seat but he remains silent, not knowing about these people.

'Mum died when I was young and Dad was very protective of me after that. He never met anyone else, but the poor guy always had a thing for Joyce. Maybe he saw a softer side to her or something, I don't know,' Tom says, his hands tightening on the wheel as the truck lurches around a narrow bend at the bottom of the hill.

For a moment, he concentrates on the road, speeding too fast through the village. Mel grabs hold of the door handle to steady herself.

'When I went into the bar as a teenager, it was clear that Donald Bray had some kind of control over Joyce. He was always hanging around.'

'Control?' Mel asks, her eyes scanning around urgently in case she catches sight of Kate.

Tom shakes his head as if he doesn't want to say.

'If it's got something to do with Billy and Kate, then you have to tell me,' Mel says loudly, trying to be heard above the engine noise as Tom hammers through the gears, driving over the speed limit along the esplanade.

'Bray was violent and argumentative, especially to any men who so much as glanced at Joyce. Word was that he used to knock her about a bit—'

When Mel suddenly turns, gasping at him in horror, Tom falls silent for a moment.

'I never saw evidence of that, mind you. But Joyce never exactly seemed happy either. She could be as surly as the best of them.'

'Not everyone who's survived abuse is miserable, you know,' Mel says, staring out of the window again, her eyes darting everywhere.

'I know,' Tom says, touching her arm briefly. 'Bray liked to think he was Lord of the Manor. I once saw him hurl a tankard at a bloke just for chatting to Joyce. He was vile when he spoke to her, or anyone else for that matter.'

'Dear God, please don't let him have Kate,' Mel mutters under her breath and the sound of the straining engine as they head out of the village and up a steep hill, mirroring the one on the other side of the bay.

'So where does Miss Sarah fit into all of this?' she asks, wishing they could go even faster. 'The detective who came about the bones said that Joyce was her mother. Is that true?'

'Everyone used to speculate. But Miss Sarah never said a word, and no one ever dared ask Joyce. Lots of gossip, but no one really knew.' Tom steps on the brake as he swings the truck around a tight bend.

'Do you think Bray is Sarah's father?' Mel continues, shuddering at the thought of being related to him.

'Damn, missed the turning,' Tom says, swinging round to look behind, one arm lashed over the back of Mel's seat as he reverses back down the steep hill. The engine wheezes and grinds. 'There, look,' he says, putting the truck into first gear. 'Combrook Lane.'

Mel sees a small sign half concealed in the hedge as they turn down the single-track lane, leaving the village behind. 'Christ, I can't stand to think of Kate all the way out here last night,' she says, a sob tightening her throat.

'Right, keep your eyes peeled,' Tom says. A breeze comes into the cabin as Angus winds down his window to get a better view. 'We don't really know what we're looking for and, of course, she could be long gone from the area now if she's with her dad.'

'Agreed,' Mel says, leaning forward and peering out of the front window. She prays that Kate is with Billy. She doesn't like the sound of this Bray character one bit.

'You've got the campsite in there,' Tom says, pointing to a faded sign in a gateway showing a tent and toilet symbol. 'And further down there are a couple of farms.'

'Campsite!' Mel cries out. 'Oh my God, of *course*. Why didn't I think of that before? Quick, go back. Billy often camped in the back of whatever van or car he had at the time.' Mel doesn't mention that it was when he was either homeless or the court had banned him from coming near her. 'I bet that's where he's taken Kate.'

Tom reverses and turns into the basic-looking site. He bumps along the track as they head into the field, driving around the dozen or so camps that have been set up. There's one small motorhome and the rest seem to be two-man tents, apart from a couple of larger, family-sized ones pitched.

'No sign of his van,' Mel says, scanning around. 'Look, there's the office. Drive up and I'll ask the owner.'

When Tom pulls up alongside the small office building, attached to the side of an old farmhouse, Mel leaps out and dashes inside, frantically ringing the little bell on the counter. 'Hello?' she calls out. 'Anyone here?' A moment later, a woman, mid-fifties, saunters in from outside.

'Sorry, love. I was just hosing down the shower block. After a pitch?'

'No, no. I'm looking for someone, actually. He may have camped here. Billy Morgan. He drives an old red Transporter. Have you seen him?' Mel whips her phone from her pocket and shows the woman a picture. 'It's urgent.'

She takes a moment to look. ''Fraid not,' she says, pulling off her yellow rubber gloves. 'Not had anyone new in for three or four days now. And no one in a red van. Sorry, love.'

Mel rushes out and climbs back in Tom's truck. 'No luck,' she says, deflated. 'I was convinced I was on to something there. I can't think why Billy would be down here with Kate otherwise.'

'Unless it wasn't Billy she was seen with,' Angus chimes in, causing goosebumps to break out on Mel's arms.

Tom steers the truck down the track that narrows even further as it veers inland, driving as fast as he dares. 'There's the Grangers' farm on the right there,' he says, pointing to a long drive with a white farmhouse at the end of it. 'And a bit further on is another farm, though I can't recall who owns it now. At the end of the lane, there's a collection of old barns and an old cottage, if I recall rightly.'

'Bray's place?' Mel asks, glancing across at him.

Tom nods, focusing on the road that's now so narrow it has grass and weeds growing down the middle.

'Let's head straight there, then,' Mel says, feeling fear creeping up her throat. 'There's no time to waste.'

It's Angus who leaps out of the cab to open the rickety five-bar gate marking the end of the lane. Not locked, but not fully open either, he walks it back, holding it wide and pressing up against the brambly hedge as Tom drives through. He waits for Angus to get in before driving on again.

'Creepy,' Mel says, leaning forward and peering up at the canopy of trees that bear down overhead as they drive in. Nothing like the little grotto Tom made in the spinney the other night, she thinks. More like a sinister hawthorn-and-bramble tangled thicket with trees like gnarly fingers all around them.

'There are the barns over on the left,' Tom says, pointing to another gateway off the rough track. 'Falling down now, by the looks of it. And down here is where Bray's place is.' He steers round to the right, the land sloping downwards, still surrounded by trees and high hedges, making it dark and gloomy.

'Dear God, don't let Katie be anywhere around here,' Mel mutters, suppressing a sob as they pass what looks like an old pigsty, half of its rusty, corrugated tin roof having fallen in with ivy strangling the weathered bricks. Beyond that are old livestock pens, rotting bales of straw fallen from what would once have been a stack, and a heap of manure up against a weathered grey shed of some kind.

Tom follows the track around the corner beside the shed, and Mel sees what looks like another half falling-down farm building – a part-brick, part-timber structure with a corrugated tin roof. Two small, dark windows are set either side of a flaking, dark green painted door, and it's only the uneven chimney poking out from the low roof that makes it identifiable as a house.

'Bray's place,' Tom says in a dour voice, peering around as he cuts the engine and unclips his seat belt. 'I'll go and give it a recce.'

'I'm coming too,' Mel says, getting out of the truck, with Angus following as they head across the uneven cobbled and weedy yard. She hears the distant screech of seagulls beyond the thick trees, and the air is still and chilled – almost completely devoid of light because of the heavy canopy of trees around them.

'Did you hear that?' Mel whispers, catching up with Tom and grabbing the sleeve of his check shirt.

'Just a rooster,' he says in a low voice. 'Heard us coming probably,' he adds as they draw up to the dilapidated house.

'No wonder Bray is a miserable bugger living here,' Mel says, turning to check Angus is still with them. 'Do you think we should knock?'

'No,' Tom whispers, creeping up to one of the small, paned windows to the side of the door. Slowly, he edges closer, cupping his hands against the grimy glass and peering inside. 'Empty in here,' he says quietly.

Mel takes his lead and goes up to the window the other side of the door, also shielding her eyes with her hands as she stares in.

'*Christ…*' she half cries and half whispers, clamping a hand over her mouth as she quickly ducks down. She glares up at Tom, her eyes wide, her forehead crumpled into a frown. Forcing herself not to scream out, she slowly lowers her hand and frantically mouths *Billy* over and over, while jabbing her finger towards the window.

CHAPTER FORTY-EIGHT

Mel hardly dares move, her thighs burning from the strain of crouching down below the window. Tom has pressed himself flat against the wall, and Angus is down low beside Mel.

'Did you see Kate?' Tom whispers, barely audible.

'No,' Mel mouths back, wishing to God she had. She'd be in there by now if that was the case. 'Billy was… he was acting weird,' she tries to tell Tom but, judging by his expression, he can't quite hear her. 'He was on the floor.'

'Injured?' Tom whispers back.

Mel shakes her head. 'No. He was getting up, but slowly.'

Tom looks puzzled. 'We should go in. Kate must be in there somewhere.'

'He won't hurt her,' Mel says, her voice getting louder. 'But he *will* hurt us.' Mel covers her mouth briefly. 'He carries a knife, Tom.'

Tom gives a brief nod. 'No knocking,' he whispers. 'We surprise him. I'll distract him while you two go and find Kate. Get her out as quickly as possible.'

'Sshh,' Angus says, putting his finger over his lips as Tom's voice creeps louder.

Tom nods. 'The place isn't big,' he whispers. 'Two-up, two-down. Ready?'

Mel gives a nod, glancing at Angus. 'Thanks, bro,' she says, squeezing his arm. A second later, Tom is in front of the door slowly turning the handle. When it doesn't give, he takes a step back and raises his right leg, kicking hard at it with the sole of his foot. The old, panelled door judders and gives a little but doesn't open, so Tom launches his foot several more times, the thud of his boot and the splintering wood sending a pigeon clapping out of a nearby tree.

He grunts as he kicks for a fourth time, the door finally giving and slamming inwards, bouncing back off the wall. He grabs it, heading inside with Mel following. Her heart feels as though it's in her mouth, blood pounding through her ears.

'Oi…' comes a voice.

'Billy!' Mel cries out, feeling sickened to see him. 'Where the hell is Kate? What have you done with her?'

For a second, Billy is motionless – half stooping behind a grimy old armchair positioned beside a rusty stove, his arms out ready for action. His eyes have the same intense look in them as when he'd done a few lines of cocaine – his pupils huge, the whites bloodshot – his stare darting about as he sizes them up, figures out the situation.

'Shut up!' he hisses, his expression fearful. The only time Mel has seen him look scared.

'All right, mate,' Tom says. 'No need for that. Let's calm down and have a little chat, shall we?' He approaches Billy, towering over him, his strong arms raised in front of him for defence. But Billy remains frozen, standing behind the chair, looking between Tom, Mel and the other side of the room, a panicked look on his face.

Remembering what Tom said, Mel scans around the run-down room looking for Kate. It's dim inside but there's no sign of her in here, not even any of her belongings. And there's no sign of Angus either. He can't have followed them inside.

Aware of another room off to her left, Mel takes her chance while Billy is distracted and turns to go through the doorway, her body alight from adrenaline.

And then she screams – a scream so loud, so piercing and all-consuming, at first she doesn't even realise it's come from her.

'Ka-*aaate*!' she shrieks, clutching her temples as she sees her daughter.

Mel is aware of a scuffle going on between Tom and Billy behind her, the scrape of the chair being dragged across the room. But she can't take her eyes off Kate standing in the doorway, white as a sheet, her head tipped back with an arm wrapped tightly around her neck and the face of a grotesque and angry-looking man leering down from behind her – Donald Bray.

'Let her go!' she shrieks, launching herself closer. She feels something tug on her sweatshirt – Tom trying to grab her – but she pulls away. It's only when she sees the knife at Kate's throat that she skids to a stop, raising the palms of her hands as she backs off.

'Don't hurt her,' Mel pleads, forcing her legs not to buckle. 'I'll do anything you say, just don't hurt my daughter.' She catches Kate's eye then – a terrified stare as though the fear is being squeezed out of her by the monster's tight grip around her throat.

'Seems that Mummy's as much a fucking nuisance as this little darling, eh?' Bray says, the croak in his voice belying his bulky stature.

Mel feels sick at the sight of him touching her daughter.

Suddenly, Kate jerks forward as she's shoved from behind with a knee in her back.

'You ain't nearly as pretty as this little one, though,' he says to Mel, pushing his big, weathered face close to Kate's, nuzzling her pale neck.

Kate lets out a little whimper, her entire body trembling. 'Mum…' she bleats, choking back a sob.

'It's OK, love. Just do as he says,' Mel says, screwing up her eyes for a second.

Kate gives a few tight nods, her breath fast and shallow.

'Can't a man be left alone to enjoy what God's sent him?' Bray says, exposing a rack of yellowed teeth. His lower jaw and top lip are covered in a layer of patchy grey stubble. His head is mainly bald apart from white, greasy strands around his ears and his pate is waxy and liver-spotted. As he approaches, Mel catches the tang of a sickly, unwashed smell. And the stink of stale urine.

'Let her go,' Tom says, taking a few steps closer.

Bray tips his head back and laughs, tightening his grip around Kate's neck. She lets out another whimper, which turns into a cough.

'She can't breathe,' Mel says, desperate. 'Just let her go. She's done nothing to you.'

'That's where you're wrong,' Bray growls, shaking his head.

'You fucking arsehole,' Billy spits, dancing forward. Mel has never been so relieved to see Billy wielding his flick knife as he produces it seemingly from nowhere, snapping it open. He brandishes the six-inch pointed blade at Bray from across the room.

'If it's tit for tat you want,' Bray says, laughing, twitching the fishing knife over Kate's skin, 'then go right ahead. Silly girl needs teaching a lesson. And I was about to learn her something real nice.' He spits on the floor, a blob of yellow phlegm hitting Kate's Adidas trainer. 'Before I was interrupted by him.' Bray jabs a finger in Billy's direction.

He came to *save* Kate, not kidnap her, Mel thinks.

'And now you're disturbing me as well,' he growls, glaring at her and Tom.

'*Mummy…*' Kate whimpers. Mel tries to reassure her with a look, but she daren't say anything. If it wasn't for that knife, Mel would have hurled herself at Bray – bitten, kicked, scratched and punched him until Kate was free.

'Only person needs teaching a lesson is you, you fuckwit,' Billy says, raising his knife and lunging forward.

'Billy, no!' Mel cries, launching herself between Billy and Bray. 'Don't be so stupid,' she says, suddenly feeling a sharp pain in her arm as the knife catches her. She flinches and when she looks down, she sees a thin line of blood oozing from her skin, but she ignores it. It's not deep.

'If you let Kate go, Mr Bray, we'll leave you in peace as if none of this ever happened, OK?' Mel says, trying to reason with him.

Donald Bray is shaking his head and laughing before Mel has even finished speaking. 'Thing is, plenty already *has* happened. This little miss saw fit to make *my* business *her* business.' He tightens his grip, hoisting Kate up by her throat, forcing her to stand on tiptoe. Her hands come up to Bray's arm, trying to loosen it as her eyes bulge.

'What the hell are you talking about?' Tom says. 'She's an innocent kid. Just let her go.' Mel sees the whites of Tom's knuckles as he forces himself not to take a swing at Bray. But that blade is centimetres away from Kate's main artery. It'd be over in seconds.

'So she has to take her punishment, like her stupid grandmother had to.' Another laugh, ending with a phlegmy cough.

Mel's mind races. *Grandmother...* Does he mean Miss Sarah?

'She's told me all about your little family tree,' Bray says to Mel, smirking. '*Daughter* of mine...' He flashes Mel a yellow-stained grin, making her hold back a retch. *Dear God, don't let him be my father, Kate's grandfather*, she prays to herself.

'What... what are you talking about?' Mel says. It doesn't even sound like her voice any more.

Bray grimaces, enjoying the fear he's causing. He kisses Kate on the head – a slow, lingering nip with his crusty mouth, her hair getting caught in the moisture as he pulls away. He licks his lips.

'Yummy,' he says, a contented look on his face. 'Miss Sarah was a pretty little thing, too. Looked a lot like this one,' he continues, jolting Kate. 'But when they get old, fourteen, fifteen, they lose their sweetness.'

'You *bastard*...' Mel whispers, absorbing what he means.

'If Joyce hadn't turned so miserable, and done what I wanted, then I wouldn't have needed her daughter, would I?' he says, drool visible on his lips. 'Sarah, Sarah, *Sarah*...' he says, almost a dreamy

look in his saggy old eyes. 'Such a little miss. *My* little Miss Sarah.'
He sighs and laughs. 'She hated me calling her that.'

'You disgusting piece of low-life shit,' Mel hisses. 'Let Kate go
immediately, or I'm—'

'*Miss* Kate, you mean,' Bray says, tilting his head down to her
again. 'My little Miss Kate.'

'She's not yours, you fucking monster,' Billy spits, stepping
closer. Mel knows he and Tom could easily overpower Bray if it
wasn't for the knife at Kate's throat.

'Billy, steady,' Mel says, not taking her eyes off Kate, holding
up a hand in his direction to halt him. But then all eyes are on
her as her phone rings, the shrill ringtone cutting through the
tension. Instinctively, Mel whips her phone from her back pocket,
looking at the screen.

PC Gordon.

'Leave it!' Bray yells. 'Drop it or she gets it,' he snarls, twitching
the knife again.

Reluctantly, Mel puts her phone back in her pocket and, after
a few more rings, it silences. Then it beeps with a voicemail.

'The police are on their way,' Tom says, his voice calm and
reasonable. 'Either you let Kate go now and we explain this was
all just a misunderstanding, or you face arrest for kidnapping.'

'Or for *murder*,' Bray says, laughing, a demented look in his
eyes.

Kate whimpers, her little sobs joining together into one long
wail as the tears come. Her legs shift about and she tugs at the skirt
of her denim dress, a pained look on her face. 'Mu… Mu*mmy*…'
she cries.

Bray's face suddenly turns sour, shocked, as he looks down,
trying to work out what is happening, his arm changing position
around Kate's neck.

Mel tracks his stare, realising before he does.

'You disgusting brat,' he spits, seeing the puddle of wee pooling around his feet, the wetness soaking down his grimy trousers. He shoves Kate over towards the fireplace, still within his grip. 'Stop it now!'

But the spattering continues as Kate can't help herself. He shoves her again but she stumbles, causing Bray to turn his back as he lurches sideways, trying to grab her and rebalance himself.

It's then that Mel spots the iron poker propped against the side of the chimney breast. Without thinking or considering the consequences, she lunges for it, grabbing it with both hands. While Bray's back is still turned, him still cussing Kate for wetting herself, Mel raises it high in the air.

All she sees is the spotted, waxy dome of the old man's skull as she brings the poker down as hard as she can on the back of his head, grunting from the effort. Nothing else in the world exists in that moment, except inflicting as much pain and damage as she can. She knows she only has one chance.

There's a loud crack of bone.

Followed by silence. Everything frozen.

Bray wobbles, his arm slackening around Kate's neck.

His feet sidestep and stagger and his arms flail, looking for something to grab onto.

That's when Mel delivers another, even harder blow to Bray's head. Blood pours out, dribbling down his neck.

'You *bastard*,' she grunts, everything fuelled by adrenaline. As Bray topples, releasing Kate, Tom makes a move and grabs hold of her, pulling her to safety. He scoops her up in his arms and rushes outside, ducking his head to get under the old door frame.

The old man lies on the floor, his head close to the hearth, blood trickling from the blow to his head. And then Mel sees even more blood – a large pool of it – dark red and thick, spilling out from beneath his prone body.

'Shit,' she cries, realising what's happened as she clutches her head in shock.

'He's fucking gone and fallen on his own knife,' Billy says, a satisfied look on his face, roughly pushing the old man's torso with his foot. When he doesn't move, he bends down and feels for a pulse under his saggy jaw, his fingers delving in the grey bristle. He looks up at Mel and shrugs, shaking his head as he holds a finger under Bray's nose for a moment.

'Think he's dead,' he says, standing up.

'Oh God, oh God... *no*...'

'Stop,' Billy says, coming up to her and taking her in his arms. 'You saved Kate.'

For a moment, Mel tenses at Billy's touch, but then she allows herself to be comforted, pressed close to him, the pair of them glancing out of the window at their daughter being looked after by Tom as he leads her over to his pick-up truck.

'But... but I *killed* him,' she says, her voice spluttering through the tears. 'I... I didn't mean to... I... I—'

'No,' Billy says firmly, staring into her eyes. 'No, Mel, you did *not* kill him, OK?' He picks up the poker then, wiping the handle over and over on his T-shirt before putting his own hands all over it. He raises his eyebrows and gives her a stern look, checking she understands, just as they hear the sound of police sirens.

CHAPTER FORTY-NINE

Kate refuses to get out of the pick-up truck. She sits in the front, huddled up in Tom's fleece, shivering. Two police cars sit diagonally blocking the entrance to Bray's yard. When he'd got Kate outside to safety, it was Tom who'd called 999.

'We were on our way here to check things out anyway,' PC Gordon explains to the group. 'After the sighting of Kate last night, and then your later message about Donald Bray, well, he's been on our radar for a while. Then we got the emergency call-out.'

'He... he had her... Bray had Kate,' Mel explains, breathless and numb as she sits in the passenger seat squashed in with Kate, her arms wrapped tightly around her daughter. The pair of them are shaking, the pick-up's door wide open as PC Gordon assesses the situation. The other officers had gone straight inside the house after Tom had briefed them.

A male officer comes out of the house, ducking his head and with a grim look on his face.

'Is everyone accounted for?' he asks. 'We're going to need an ambulance, a doctor. Fatal stabbing inside,' he directs at PC Gordon.

She takes a breath and nods, stepping away to talk into her radio. With the flashing lights, the four or five uniformed police officers swarming around as well as what's just happened playing out in her mind, Mel feels light-headed from shock and adrenaline.

'Where's Angus?' someone says. She looks up. It's Tom – Tom, who pulled her daughter to safety. Tom, who risked his own life by coming with her today, sticking by her.

'I don't think he came inside the house,' Mel says, remembering how she looked for him. 'He was with us and then… then he wasn't.'

'I didn't see no one else,' Billy says, leaning on the side of the truck. 'I'd not long been here when you turned up. I was all set to pounce on the fucker but… well, I was disturbed, wasn't I?' He rolls his eyes.

'How did you even know where Kate *was*, Billy?' Mel asks. 'And what are you even *doing* in Halebury?' She has so many questions, she doesn't know where to start. 'I… I thought *you'd* kidnapped Kate. I thought you'd taken her from me.' Compared to the evil she's just witnessed in Bray, she's almost pleased that Billy is here.

'Long story, innit, Katie?' he says, winking at her. 'I got out the nick a few weeks back, and first thing I wanted to do was see my girl. So we got talking a couple of times. Outside her old school and the like. I knew you wouldn't approve, Mel, so I did it on the sly.' He shifts awkwardly from one foot to the other, almost looking remorseful. 'But no way was I going to take her from you. She needs her mum. Prison changes a man, like.' He looks away briefly.

Mel doesn't know what to say. She doubts very much Billy has changed.

'I didn't have much, but I gave her some money and a couple of treats. I was trying to make up for being a shit dad. I know it's not much. When you moved away, I couldn't stand not to see her any more, so I came down a few days ago to see how my girl was doing. Wasn't going to bother you, Mel,' he says. 'Hand on heart, that's the truth.'

'And the phone you gave her?' Mel says, her voice deadpan, knowing Billy is a master excuse-maker.

He shakes his head and sighs. 'All right, I shouldn't have nicked it for her,' he says. 'But I wanted to keep in touch, like. I tried to call you loads of times to ask permission, but when you didn't pick up, I got cold feet, figured you hated me. I knew you wouldn't allow her to contact me on her regular phone, so that's why I gave her another one. In case she ever needed me or got in trouble.'

'But you hardly ever replied to me, Dad,' Kate says, scowling at him.

'I'm sorry, sweetheart. I've been… I've been busy.'

Busy dealing drugs or stealing, no doubt, Mel thinks.

'And I also gave her the phone because…' Billy hesitates, glancing over his shoulder, checking the officers are still distracted. 'Cos I always wanted to know where she was.'

'*What?*' Mel says.

'I put a tracker on her phone. And a good job I did,' he adds. 'It showed me where you'd moved to, of course, but when she didn't answer my calls the last twenty-four hours, I got twitchy and checked her location. I didn't like the look of where she was, out in the middle of nowhere, so that's why I came here. I saw through the window that git had got her tied up.' Billy wipes his hands down his face, a sweat breaking out on his forehead as he fidgets. 'He looked a big bastard, so I broke in round the back to take him by surprise. And then you tipped up…' He glances at Mel and Tom in turn.

'It seems our girl is a bit of a vigilante.' He reaches into the van and chucks her under the chin. Kate looks up and gives a little smile at her dad. 'Before he got the knife on her, she was giving that old boy a right dressing down, from what I could hear. But don't bloody do it again, all right?' he adds, squeezing Kate's hand as he leans over Mel. 'Leave it to the pros, next time.'

Kate nods, looking down into her lap.

'What do you mean, vigilante? What are you talking about, Billy?'

But it's Kate who replies. 'Don't be cross, Mum. I wanted to help Sarah,' she says. 'She's suffered so much, it's terrible. She told me everything. She's been talking to me since we arrived. She's really nice. I'm the only person she's ever spoken to about it, and she said it's because I remind her of her when she was young. She begged me not to tell anyone.' Kate sniffs, rubbing her nose. 'And she hates being called *Miss* Sarah.'

Mel glances at Tom.

'When she was young, that horrid man in the house abused her and beat her up all the time. He did terrible things to her. She was only eight when it started. And when she was only a bit older than me, she had a baby from him. Then she had another and another, and...' Kate breaks down, choking back her sobs, determined to be brave. 'Her mother, Joyce, didn't care about her. Not like you care about me, Mum. Sarah said Joyce had turned hard and cold and didn't look after her properly. She said it was because her mum's boyfriend, Donald, liked Sarah more and that Joyce was jealous. It was all so messed up.'

'Oh, *love*,' Mel says. 'You shouldn't have had to bear all this alone. Why didn't you tell me?'

Kate stutters then, glancing between Billy and her mum. 'I promised Sarah I wouldn't tell anyone. And... and you'd been through too much already. I love you and I love Dad the same, but all you did was fight. It tore me apart inside. I know Dad did bad stuff he shouldn't have. I can't forgive him for that, but he's still my dad. When I heard about that man hurting Sarah, I didn't want him to get away with it. It was like I could... like I could punish Dad but without actually hurting him, if you see what I mean. I thought it would make me feel better, and Sarah too.'

Kate takes a moment to catch her breath. Mel glances at Billy – his head hanging low.

'Sarah told me who had hurt her, that he still lived nearby. And she told me how she was frightened every single day of her childhood, how everyone made fun of her cos she didn't speak, because she was… somehow different from the other kids.' Kate sniffs, takes a breath. 'And you know what? I knew exactly how she felt.' Her face crumples into a scowl.

'Oh, Kate…' Mel says, hardly able to stand to hear it.

'It was easy to find out who the man was. Everyone talks in this village. I spotted him a couple of times going into the village shop after I'd got off the school bus. He'd go in for his paper and tobacco, and one time I followed him around a bit. Chloe told me where he lived and I looked it up on the map. Last night, I figured I had my chance. I snuck out while you'd gone to see Tom with that cake and—'

Mel lets out a deep groan and hangs her head.

'Cake?' Tom says, bewildered.

'Long story,' Mel says, not wanting to interrupt Kate's flow. 'I came round to make it up to you, but I saw through your window that… that you had company.'

'Ahh, yes, I did. My sister, Lena, is over from Canada for a couple of weeks. She's staying with Dad but came round to mine last night. It was a big reunion. I've not seen her in nearly five years.'

'Your *sister*?' Mel says, wishing the ground would swallow her up. She clears her throat, patting Kate's arm. 'Carry on, love.'

'It took ages to walk all the way up here. And it was scary on my own, but I wanted to spy on him, maybe even catch him doing… doing some bad stuff and get photos. I was going to send them to Dad and get him to sort it, or I would call the police. Maybe I was going to let his tyres down or put something horrid in his letterbox. But…' Kate covers her face. 'But he must have seen me arrive because he suddenly came out and grabbed me. I tried to get away, but he was too strong and dragged me inside. He shoved me in a room and locked me in until today. All I had was water. I was so scared, Mum,' Kate cries, nestling into Mel's hug. 'I was stupid and upset, and I wish I hadn't done it. I wasn't thinking straight after… after I'd found the skel…' She trails off for a moment, collecting herself, her shallow breaths heaving in and out of her chest. 'I thought I was going to die, that I'd never see you or Dad again.'

Kate sobs for a while, with Mel exchanging glances with Tom and Billy as she cradles her daughter, stroking her head.

'I… I feel like I'm stuck in these two worlds, Mum,' Kate continues, blowing her nose. 'Your world and Dad's world, because I love you both the same. But I'm just so angry about everything! Angry like Sarah is angry. And when I found those bones… I knew it was Sarah's baby. She told me the first time she got pregnant she didn't even know what was happening to her. She… she always had to hide in her room to keep away from Donald, and one day she just gave birth, all alone. Her mother didn't know and, if she did, she didn't even care. But the baby died and so Sarah buried it secretly one night. It was where Chloe and I were digging, so I knew her story must be true.' Sobs tighten Kate's throat as she tries to get it all out.

'Sarah told me there was another baby a year later and she had to bury that one too, near the first one, and her mother caught her doing it. Then she had two more babies but they lived. Joyce was so cross with her that both times she took them away as soon as they were born. She just left them to be found. Can… can you even imagine that happening?'

Kate breaks down again, burying her face in Mel's shoulder, shaking her head from side to side.

'No, love… no, I can't,' Mel says, fighting back her own tears.

*

As Tom, Mel and Kate wait in the truck as instructed by the police, it feels as if time stands still. The air in the wooded yard hangs heavy with a foetid smell – a mix of animal dung and tractor diesel. Billy paces around outside, chain-smoking, as they wait.

Mel glances at him occasionally, wondering what is going on inside his head – now, and way back.

Things had been good once, she tells herself. It wasn't all bad. She pulls Kate closer, not regretting meeting Billy because otherwise she wouldn't have her daughter. But she'll *never* forgive him for what he did to her, and for what he put Kate through.

Fifteen minutes later, PC Gordon comes out of the old house, her expression dour. Mel and Tom get out of the truck, joining the officer and Billy.

'A detective and a forensics team are on the way up. You'll all have to make official statements, obviously, but I'd like a quick rundown of what happened,' she says, addressing all of them.

Mel opens her mouth, ready to explain everything – how she'd only intended to stun Donald Bray just long enough to grab Kate. Though she suspects the consequences will be pretty dire, even if her actions are deemed to be self-defence. The man is dead.

But Billy gets in first, giving Mel a sharp look.

'I hit the old git with the poker when his back was turned,' he says, matter-of-factly. 'Sharp blow to the back of the head. He'd got my girl, a knife at her throat, so what's a man supposed to do? I hit him again and then he let go of Kate, but he fell down. Stupid bugger landed on his own knife.' Billy shrugs and lights another cigarette.

Mel feels Tom's eyes on her as her cheeks burn scarlet. She looks back at Kate sitting in the truck, her knees drawn up under her chin as she rocks gently, a frown on her forehead.

She *needs* me, Mel thinks. She needs her mother...

'Yes, that's correct,' Mel says to PC Gordon, giving a sharp nod of her head. 'Billy was acting purely in self-defence, for all of us, as well as in Kate's best interests.'

'Agreed,' Tom says a moment later, clearing his throat. He shuffles from one foot to the other.

PC Gordon stares at them all for a moment, her eyes narrowing, only speaking when an ambulance trundles into the yard through the narrow gateway. 'Right,' she says, raising her eyebrows and taking a breath. 'Billy, I'd like you to come with us to the station to make a formal statement. Mel, after Kate's had a medical check, you can take her home if the crew say she's OK. Officers will be up first thing to take your statements. It goes without saying that it wouldn't be a good time to leave the area.'

'Of course,' Mel says, glancing at Billy. He smokes the last of his cigarette before dropping the butt and treading on it.

'Do you have a vehicle here, Mr…?' PC Gordon asks Billy.

'Last name's Morgan,' he says flatly, flashing a quick look at Kate in the truck. 'Yeah, my van's parked a little way up, by them old barns. Didn't want to announce myself.'

'If you give me the keys, I'll arrange for someone to pick it up.'

Billy fishes in his pocket for the keys and hands them over, giving Mel a look. She knows he rarely bothered with road tax or insurance, let alone an MOT. But she also knows that he'll very likely talk his way out of that, as well as the mess he's purpose-fully landed himself in to protect her. And, while he might have twenty-four hours or so at the station, he'll likely be swaggering out of custody some time tomorrow.

'Take care, Billy,' Mel says as PC Gordon leads him over to the police car.

He stops, giving her a nod, raising his hand to his brow almost in a salute. 'Look after my girl,' he replies. 'Tell her I'll see her soon.'

Mel nods and, as she watches him get in the car – hands shoved deep in his pockets, head ducking low – for once in her life she actually feels grateful to him for turning up like the bad penny she knows he is.

CHAPTER FIFTY

Tom drives steadily – mainly to reflect the sombre mood, though of course Mel is awash with relief that Kate is safe, even if she is badly shaken up. She holds her daughter tightly, never wanting to let go, as they sit side by side in the front of the pick-up, relieved the paramedics had given her the all-clear.

'I don't know how I'll ever be able to thank you, Tom,' Mel says, touching his arm as he grips the steering wheel. 'For going through that with me, for being there.'

He gives a lopsided smile, glancing sideways with one of *those* looks in his eyes.

'You could bring that cake round?'

'Ah,' Mel replies, clearing her throat. 'I may… well, it may have got eaten. But I'll happily make you another, though I'll make sure it's not curry-flavoured this time.'

'Curry-flavoured?'

'Don't even ask,' Mel replies. 'You can help me, Kate. You know what my baking's like.'

Kate gives a little nod, snuggling up closer to her mum. 'Why have they taken Dad away? Will he get put in prison again?'

'So he can tell them what happened, love,' Mel replies, giving Tom a quick look. 'I'm sure they'll let him go soon.'

'Did he hurt that man Donald?' she asks. 'Is he dead? I didn't see anything. It was all so quick and I was really frightened. I can't remember a single thing apart from having a knife at my throat one minute and then Tom grabbing me.'

Mel makes a sound in her throat – not quite denial or confirmation.

'Did Dad save me?' Kate asks.

'Yeah,' Mel says through a sigh. 'Yeah, he saved you, love.' She kisses Kate's cheek.

Tom touches the brakes lightly as they round a descending bend, heading back down into the village, but then he steps on the pedal harder when he sees someone walking on their side of the lane and a car coming the other way.

'That's Angus,' Mel says suddenly. 'Pull over.' Mel winds down her window. 'Angus! Angus… it's us.'

Angus swings round, a panicked look on his face, but then relief when he sees who it is.

'We wondered where you went,' she says, leaning out of the window. 'Hop in the back.'

Angus nods and gets in the rear door, belting up behind Mel. 'Thanks for stopping,' he says. 'I'm so relieved you found Kate.'

'Where did you go, mate?' Tom asks, flicking a glance in his rear-view mirror.

'I… well, I hid outside for a while… in case you needed backup,' Angus says nervously. 'Then I went… I went to get help. I thought it best.'

Tom gives him another look.

'Wouldn't it have been quicker to phone for help?' Mel says.

'My battery had run out,' Angus replies in a way that almost sounds like a question rather than a statement of fact. 'I thought one of us should stay outside, you know, to get the police if needed.'

'I'm surprised you didn't see them pass before,' Tom says.

'Oh, oh, yes. I did. A big relief.'

'You missed all the action,' Tom says, giving another glance in the mirror. Mel spots the smirk on his face and gives him a little poke in the thigh. 'It's OK, Angus. I don't blame you for legging it. It wasn't pretty,' he adds.

'Sorry,' he says meekly. 'I'm… I'm just glad Kate is OK.'

*

'Uncle Micky?' Kate says as they go into the bar area. She runs up to him, launching herself into his open arms.

'My little Katie-Matey,' he sings back, grateful that Mel texted him an update. 'Christ, you had us all going there, young lady. Whatever it was you did, don't do it again.'

'I won't, I promise,' she says into his neck. 'I feel stupid and scared and—'

'Kate…' comes a voice across the room – a soft yet warm voice, almost singing Kate's name. Everyone turns to the table in the window. Sarah is standing there, her arms outstretched. Kate walks over to her.

'Nana Sarah,' she says as the pair embrace, sharing a whisper so quiet no one else can hear.

'Mum?' Angus says cautiously after Kate has sat down, taking the glass of water Mel has poured for her. Mel makes a lemon drink for Sarah then goes round closing all the shutters, not wanting anyone outside to see inside now that it's dark. She goes to check the sign outside, but Nikki had left it set to closed earlier. Both she and Rose have gone home.

Sarah stares at Angus, sipping on her drink, giving Mel a little smile when she tastes the gin in it. She tips her head sideways and squints at Angus, sizing him up. 'So you're Angus,' she says. Her voice sounds almost sweet, yet with an undertone of authority. As though she knows exactly what she's saying, is sure of every syllable, but has just been waiting for the right moment to say it.

Mel stops halfway across the room, balancing a tray of glasses and a bottle of Scotch for everyone. She catches Michael's eye, who beckons her to follow him out of the room with a flick of his head.

'I am indeed,' Angus replies. 'I'm Mel's brother. Which also makes me your son,' he adds, a coy, unassuming tone to his voice as he sits down beside Sarah.

'I see,' she says, hardly able to take her eyes off him.

CHAPTER FIFTY-ONE

Mel puts the tray down and follows Michael out into the back hallway, switching on the light.

'You OK?' he says, lightly taking her forearms, sliding his hands down to hers.

Mel shakes her head. 'Barely,' she says. 'What a bloody day. I don't even know which way up I am. But thank *Christ* Kate is safe. I'd never have forgiven myself if—'

'Sshh,' Michael says, placing a finger over her lips. 'That's not allowed, OK?'

'OK,' she says, managing a small smile. 'But I'm never letting her out of my sight again,' she adds. 'You wouldn't even believe what happened.'

'Nor you with what's happened here,' Michael says. 'Sarah spilled her guts to me while you were out. By the way, don't call her *Miss*. Trust me, just don't do it.'

'I already know that,' Mel says. 'And I know why.' She shudders. 'Did she tell you about Bray? The babies? Her past?'

Michael nods. 'Fucking tragic, all of it.'

'You realise that Angus and I are the ones who got taken by Joyce and abandoned? Him dumped on the police station door-step, and me put on a train like left luggage.'

Michael nods, glances at the floor.

'Tom says his dad remembers Joyce as a decent sort when she was younger. Walter, his dad, had a massive crush on her, apparently. She used to be vibrant and full of life, but Bray sucked it out of her over the years. Then he started in on her daughter.'

'Sadly, that all makes sense,' Michael says.

'How so?' Mel asks.

'First thing is that Sarah seems to trust me. Perhaps because I was the one who did the DNA test, rightly or wrongly,' he adds, holding up his palms in defence. 'And therefore I led her to you. But…'

'Go on,' Mel says.

'It figures why this Bray chap would latch onto Joyce. According to Sarah, she was worth a bob or two. Easy prey for someone like Bray, who'd got nothing going for him.'

Mel makes a face. 'Really?'

'Joyce had inherited a shedload. Her father owned a few factories in the north. This is going back some time now, and she got the lot when he died. She was only early twenties and had never had a good relationship with him, or a happy childhood. She lost her mother when she was a baby, so never had that role model. After her father passed away, she hotfooted it as far away from her home town as she could get.'

'Blimey,' Mel says, leaning back against the wall. 'That sounds tough.'

'Sarah said that Joyce started off in London, trying to make it as an actress and singer. It had been her childhood dream, but her father never allowed her to pursue it. Lawrence is a stage name, apparently, as she hated her family name. Though Sarah told me she never changed it officially. Then she fell in with the wrong crowd, lived a hedonistic, bohemian lifestyle. I mean, it was London in the Sixties, and she was loaded.'

'A stage name?' Mel says, realising that's why she couldn't find a record of Joyce's will. She imagines what life must have been like for her – a vulnerable young woman with a fragile childhood, gullible, naive, taken in by the wrong people, just wanting to be loved… Tears well in her eyes.

'Then she got pregnant with Sarah and everything changed. The father was a one-night stand, and Joyce decided she was sick of being preyed upon by... well, by "hungry" men, as Sarah put it. She had a child to think of, so she left London and came down to Dorset for a quieter life, giving up on her dream of fame. And that's when she bought Moreton Inn. She can't have been more than twenty-five, twenty-six by this time. Sarah wasn't much more than a baby, but from what she told me, Joyce loved the laid-back seaside lifestyle. It suited her and they fitted in. For a while, things were good.'

'Sarah told you all this while we were gone?' Mel says, amazed at how much she'd opened up.

'I couldn't stop her,' he says. 'It was like she was just unloading all this stuff. Spewing it out. I happened to be the nearest – or rather, the *only* pair of ears. Like I said, she seems to trust me.'

Mel listens, riveted.

'So fast-forward a bit, and Joyce is loving her new life, bedding in to the community, building up her business. Sarah remembers plenty of suitors, mind. One man after another vying for her mother's attention. Joyce had money, a business, a home, don't forget. She was bound to attract people.'

'This is the complete opposite to how I'd imagined her.'

'Then one man in particular got his teeth stuck right in and wouldn't let go,' Michael says. 'Enter Donald Bray.'

Mel shakes her head. 'Round and round it goes,' she says, looking upwards in an attempt to stop herself from crying. History repeating itself over and over and over.

Michael puts a hand on her shoulder. 'When Joyce died...' he makes a pained face, 'Sarah said... well, she said that her mother had a stroke. To say that the pair of them didn't exactly get on by this point would be a massive understatement. Because of her trauma, Sarah hasn't spoken a word since she was fifteen. Joyce had become a husk of the woman she once was, all because of Bray.

Bray was only interested in getting his hands on her money. He'd invested decades of his life in this, don't forget.'

'But surely Sarah was the sole beneficiary in Joyce's will? Why did Bray think he'd have a chance of getting his hands on it?'

'You're right. Sarah did inherit the lot, much to Bray's disgust. But she didn't want it. By this point, Sarah despised her mother and to her, it was dirty money. Joyce had turned a blind eye to the abuse all those years, knowing about it but not doing anything to help. Her idea of cleaning up the mess was to take away Sarah's babies. She showed no sympathy and never once tried to get rid of Bray from their lives. Sarah said he was a fixture – a dark presence hanging over them. In their own ways, Sarah and Joyce had both given up.'

'Bloody hell,' Mel says, trying to absorb everything.

'So that's why, when Joyce died, Sarah didn't want any of her money. She told me it was at the wake here, after her mother's funeral, when she overheard a couple of guests discussing DNA tests and how you could find out your ancestry, who your family is. She thought it was worth a shot, in case either of her two children had done it and would be a match. She ordered herself a kit online. She knew the basics of using a computer and had Joyce's old laptop. She wanted to pass the inheritance on.'

'So if you hadn't bought me the DNA test kit as a gift, and sent it off without me knowing, then none of this would have happened?'

'Nope,' Michael says.

'Did Angus do the DNA test too?'

'Apparently not,' Michael says. 'Sarah told me... well, she told me he wasn't so easy to trace. Joyce had apparently left him outside a police station, and he was adopted a few months later. There was a paper trail, but it took a long time. Sarah hired a private investigator through her solicitor in Exeter to track him down. She did it all by email, sending them the money to find him. And when she did...'

'What?'

'When the private investigator made contact with Angus on Sarah's behalf, Angus told him he didn't want anything to do with his mother. Like you, he was torn up about his past.'

'But that's not what he told me.' She remembers how Angus had told her he wanted to find his mother, that he felt he was getting close. Little did he know just *how* close, she thinks.

'Really?' Michael says, his eyes wide. 'How… odd. Maybe I got some details wrong. Look, it's… it's a sensitive subject for both of them, so I suggest we let them deal with it and not mention anything. Sarah was very distressed telling me.'

'I agree,' Mel says. 'Did she say why she wanted to remain anonymous when she did finally make contact?'

'She did. Simply because she had no idea how either of you would take it, and I'd already told her via the DNA website that you weren't keen on meeting your birth family, that you'd always felt abandoned. Her default assumption was that you'd both be angry, and you can't deny that's true. She wanted to test the waters first. She said it was a terrifying thing for her to do – like acknowledging her past, accepting what had happened.'

'Oh, poor Sarah,' Mel says. 'I'm not angry at all now I know the whole story, the reasons why. It's a tragic tale, and I can't begin to imagine what Sarah suffered. She was so… *alone*.'

'All she wanted was to know that you and your brother were OK – financially, at the very least. She split the value of the estate equally between you, but for some reason she decided that you were best placed to run the hotel. I didn't press her on this.'

Mel thinks for a moment, shaking her head. 'I don't understand. Angus confided in me that his inheritance… well, that it was only a couple of thousand. That's a far cry from being equal to a hotel and three hundred-odd grand in the bank, right?'

Michael pauses, frowning. 'Indeed. That's odd too. And it's something you should discuss with Angus further, perhaps. The poor guy must feel… a bit miffed. But enough is enough for tonight.' He gives Mel a tight squeeze. 'C'mon, let's get back in there.'

Mel agrees and takes Michael's hand when he holds it out, leading her back through into the restaurant area. She stops a moment, looking around, feeling dizzy from exhaustion and relief. Tom is sitting on a stool, talking to Angus over a couple of pints, while Kate is sitting at Sarah's table, subdued but happily showing her photos on her phone.

'Kids bounce back,' Michael whispers in Mel's ear as she looks at Kate with a concerned expression. 'But only when they've got mums like you,' he adds, squeezing her hand.

Mel gives a little nod and smiles, taking a deep breath and following Michael as he leads her over to Tom, gesturing for her to sit down beside him. As he goes off to get her a drink, saying he'll phone out for a few pizzas to be delivered, Mel looks around her again, seeing a flash of Moreton Inn as it was the first time she and Kate walked in several months ago – that old-fashioned, uncared-for place that sent her heart into overdrive wondering how on earth she was going to cope.

It's so different now, she thinks, feeling proud of what she's achieved. There's a long way to go with the renovations, she knows that, but the best building work is the new life she and Kate are constructing – with the unexpected bonus of what feels an awful lot like… like *family*, she thinks, taking the drink Michael hands her.

'Penny for them?' Tom says quietly, leaning closer. Mel feels the warmth of his hand on her knee.

She gives him one of her sideways looks, along with a wry smile as she puts her drink down. Then she unzips her hoodie, pulling it open at the front.

'Nah,' she says, giving him a wink.

Tom can't help the loud laugh when he sees it, rocking back in his chair, giving her one of *those* looks in return as he lifts his fleece revealing his 'Yess' T-shirt beneath.

CHAPTER FIFTY-TWO

Five weeks later

Mel snaps photographs of the build. These last few weeks, she's been documenting progress, getting prints made of Moreton Inn's transformation, with her and Kate spending several evenings sticking them in an album and writing memories, notes, adding keepsakes.

'Our journey,' Mel had said. 'And it's just the start of it,' she'd added, swelling with pride at how Kate had been recovering from her ordeal. She knew it would be a long process, with some days better than others, but she was making progress. Her school had not only been accommodating if she'd needed time off but had also organised counselling for Kate, to help her work through the recent trauma as well as the deeper pain she'd harboured over the years, with sessions set to run through the summer holidays, too. And Mel was also considering a therapist for herself – coming to terms with Bray being her biological father wasn't going to be easily swept aside, even if he *was* dead. Though for now, she mostly managed to keep it from her mind by focusing on Kate.

'Oi, oi,' Nige says, wheeling a barrow of cement over to where Tom is laying the final course of bricks before the extension roof goes on. 'Smile, mate,' he shouts up the scaffolding, pointing at Mel.

Mel takes a photo of the pair of them, having decided not to confront Nige about what he'd scrawled on the wall in room ten. It was Tom who confessed to what had happened, that he'd caught Nige in the act when he should have been working. He'd gone looking for him – Nikki telling him she'd seen him go into one of the bedrooms. She'd thought it was for a maintenance job.

'As soon as I saw what he was doing, I wrestled the can of paint off him,' Tom had said. 'But the damage was done. I couldn't believe he'd do something so low. I tried to scrub it off the wall, but it wouldn't budge. I was hoping to source some more of the green paint to go over it before you saw, but it was going to take a while to arrive.'

'But why?' Mel had asked, confused. 'Why would Nige want to do such a thing?'

'He wasn't thinking straight at the time and he's remorseful now,' Tom had said. 'Though that doesn't excuse him.' He sighed. 'It's all about Rose. Well,' Tom had added, 'all about Rose and Nige.'

'What about them?' Mel was confused.

'You mean you've not noticed?'

'Noticed what?'

'The pair of them are mad for each other,' Tom had explained. 'Always have been. Despite what he did, Nige is a good bloke. But he's also Bray's nephew. And while he's in control of it most of the time, he's got a bit of a temper.'

Mel had thought back to a recent conversation with Rose: they were in the kitchen, planning new dishes for the menu.

'The difference between people like you and me,' Rose had said out of the blue, chewing on the end of her pencil, 'is luck.'

'Sorry?' Mel had replied, confused. She'd looked up from her calculations, trying to get her head around profit margins and menu prices.

'This place,' Rose had said, folding her arms, a sour expression on her face.

Mel had frowned, given a little shake of her head. 'I don't understand.'

'For instance, if Nige had inherited somewhere like this, then we'd be married by now, sorted for life. He's old-school. Wants to look after me,' she'd continued. 'Serves us right, I suppose,' she'd added in a mutter, getting up to put the kettle on. 'Me and Nige. We're well suited.'

Mel had gone back to her spreadsheet then, though what Rose had said made it hard to concentrate.

'So Nige and Rose are bitter that Bray didn't inherit Moreton Inn from Joyce?' Mel had gone on to ask Tom. It was all becoming clear.

'Exactly,' Tom had said. 'Nige is Bray's only living relative.'

'And then, in turn, it would have passed to them. But I stopped them getting what they wanted.' Mel had shaken her head.

'Correct again,' Tom had confirmed. 'To Rose, you represented everything she wanted but couldn't have. Deep down, she's not a bad person either.'

'From what I can tell, I think what upsets Rose the most is that Nige hasn't proposed to her yet,' Mel had said, remembering Rose's sad expression. 'Poor woman,' she added. 'I actually feel quite sorry for her.'

It was later that day that Mel had another chat with Rose. The restaurant had been busy, with most tables occupied, and Mel was helping in the kitchen.

'This smells delicious, Rose,' she'd commented about the soup as she served it into dishes for table eight. 'You've excelled yourself again.'

Rose had made a noise, turning away, almost as if she was embarrassed. It was as Mel had been garnishing the dishes, putting out the sourdough that Rose placed a hand on her arm.

'I'm sorry,' she said, eyes down.

Mel nodded at Nikki as she came to take the bowls out. Then she turned her attention back to Rose, aware they didn't have much time to stop and talk. 'Sorry?' she'd asked.

'For what I did. The glass in your soup.'

'Ah,' Mel said, suddenly understanding where this was going.

'It was Nige's idea. He… he said if we scared you off, made things difficult for you, then we might get the hotel.' Rose covered her face with her hands. 'And to me that meant marriage, security, everything I've never had.'

'Rose, you could have done more than scare me off. You could have killed me!' Mel had managed to hold back her anger, though only because they had a busy restaurant. 'And the dead mouse?' She began plating up the next order.

Rose gave a shameful nod. 'If we couldn't have Moreton, we didn't want anyone else to have it either.' She'd let out a pitiful sob.

After service was over, Mel had sat her down for a chat.

'I wasn't thinking straight,' Rose confessed. 'Please don't sack me. If you give me another chance, I promise I'll make it up to you. Nige is sorry too, I know he is, but he worries about money, about looking after me.'

And to Rose's surprise, Mel had said she understood, even giving her a pay rise.

'Just tell me one final thing,' Mel had asked. 'The cake I made for Tom… the curry powder…'

Rose gave the tiniest of nods.

Mel had rolled her eyes. 'I thought I was going mad,' she'd said with a laugh. 'But look, I do understand,' she added, giving her a hug, 'how it feels as though you've got nothing and nobody. That the whole world is conspiring against you.'

Rose had nodded, looking tearful, but relieved and grateful.

'And you know what?' Mel had added. 'You could always propose to Nige yourself.'

Now, Tom turns round, grinning down at Mel from the scaffolding. 'Is it coffee time yet?' he calls back. 'And there's still been no sign of that curry cake you promised.' He gives her a wink.

Mel laughs. 'Will a packet of chocolate digestives do for now?' she asks, putting her phone away. 'And I promise, I haven't forgotten the cake.'

She heads off to the kitchen to make the team of builders hot drinks. Since the police gave her the go-ahead to commence works again, it's been full steam ahead.

With Sarah's statement to the police about the two stillborn babies, further excavations were carried out and the other remains located. Again, the bones were excavated and removed for analysis to corroborate Sarah's story, and the case was in the hands of the court for a verdict on the situation. DI Armitage's opinion was that the judge would be extremely sympathetic, given the circumstances, and lay the case to rest, but of course, legal procedure had to be adhered to.

And now that both babies' remains had been released and cremated, Sarah wanted to scatter the ashes into the sea from her favourite spot to sit as a child. 'It's where I went to escape Donald,' she'd confided in Mel. It also happened to be the place where Mel had binged on the champagne and cake that night after seeing Tom with his sister.

'Here you go, you lot,' Mel says, carrying the tray of mugs outside. She knows by heart who likes which drink, and how many sugars. 'This is yours, Nige,' she says, handing him his tea and then dishing out the others.

A couple of the guys light up cigarettes, one in particular reminding her of a young Billy – his bright eyes never still, his body wiry and lithe. He's even got the cap, she thinks, remembering how Billy would always wear his, even when inside.

'I had a call earlier,' Mel says to Tom, Billy still playing on her mind. He sits down beside her, playfully nudging her so she shifts across on the pile of bricks. 'From Billy.'

'And?' Tom says, knowing she was waiting for news.

'He's been cleared,' she says. 'Self-defence, no further action…
or something. I can't remember his exact words, but he's got off.
The investigation took its time.'

'They had to be thorough,' Tom replies.

Mel tenses as she remembers how they grilled her and Tom
about events, how they scoured the scene at Bray's house, confirm-
ing, among other things, that Billy's prints were on the poker. And
they'd brought in specially trained officers to talk to Kate, to gently
coax out her version of events. Even Chloe had had to make a
statement. And of course, Sarah revealed her story, leading up to
how Kate had taken it upon herself to get revenge on her behalf.

'But Billy was mainly asking about Kate.' Mel sips her tea. 'And
when he can see her.'

Tom gives a slow nod, looking at Mel. 'How do you feel about
that?'

'Oddly OK,' she replies. 'And Kate wants to see him. He's
actually agreed to go through the court to arrange contact. He's
resigned to it being supervised, to travelling down here twice a
month to see her. He told me he hopes that one day she'll be able
to stay in Birmingham with him for a couple of days here and
there. I could hardly believe it when he told me he'd got a job and
is renting a flat of his own.'

Tom nods, taking it all in. 'As long as Kate is happy and safe,'
he says. 'And you, of course,' he adds, leaning over and giving
her a kiss.

'You'll get the lads jeering if there's much more of that,' she
says, grinning, nudging his shoulder with hers.

*

'Mum?' Kate says later that afternoon in a way that tells Mel she's
got something on her mind. She's not long been home from school,
and Mel knows she saw her counsellor for another session today.

Mel looks up from her sewing machine, taking her foot off the pedal and holding still the fabric of the cushion cover she's making. Kate comes to sit down next to her, having grabbed a bottle of Coke and a bag of crisps from behind the bar.

'What's up, love?'

Kate pauses, staring at the ceiling in thought as she crunches. 'You know how keeping things inside isn't good?'

'Mmm, I do,' Mel replies, turning to face Kate.

'Well… there's something I have inside that isn't good.'

'Do you want to tell me?'

'You'll be cross, Mum, but my counsellor asked me today what I thought was best – keeping it inside and it sitting there for ever, making me sad, or telling you and you getting annoyed for a bit and then it's gone.'

'And what did you decide?'

Kate puts the crisps on the table and takes a breath. 'I decided that I should tell you it was me who put the money in your locker at The Cedars.'

'Ok-*aay*,' Mel says calmly, forcing herself not to react. 'I really appreciate you being honest, Kate.'

'It was Bob's idea. I was helping him tie his laces that time and we were just chatting. I told him that you were really worried about money and sometimes went without. He got the cash from his jacket pocket and gave it to me, telling me to put it in your locker, knowing you'd find it in there. You'd already given me the key so I could get some snacks out.'

'Oh, *darling*,' Mel says, seeing the pain on Kate's face. So she was wrong about Josette setting her up.

'Bob said he'd let Josette know what he'd done, in case it was against the rules. He didn't want you to get into trouble.'

No, Mel thinks. In that case, she *wasn't* wrong about Josette. The woman knew Bob had given her the money but had wanted her gone. The cash presented the ideal opportunity.

'Are you cross?' Kate asks, picking up the crisps again. 'When you lost your job, I… I felt like it was all my fault.'

Mel smiles. 'Not in the least cross,' she says, giving Kate a hug. 'It was a very kind thing that Bob did, and not your fault Dragon Boss had it in for me. Some people just make it their business not to like others in life, Kate. Remember, it says nothing bad about you, but everything rotten about them.'

'Amen,' Kate says, holding up her palm for Mel to high-five. 'Is it OK if I go to Chloe's house on Friday after school for a sleepover? It's the last day of term.'

'Fine by me,' she replies. 'On one condition,' she adds, sticking her hand into Kate's bag of crisps. 'No archaeological digs.'

*

'Are you OK?' Mel asks. She reaches across and squeezes Sarah's hand as they stand at the shore several days later, watching the gentle waves lap up the shingle. The tide is midway and on its way out, with enough slabs of rock exposed for the three of them to stand on and do what they came to do.

'Yes, I am,' Sarah replies, tipping her face upwards into the breeze. She closes her eyes for a moment, breathing in deeply. 'I'm fifty-four,' she says. 'And I am finally laying my babies to rest. The babies I had when I was only several years older than her.'

They both look over at Kate, who's out of earshot, stooped down and gathering fossils.

'I used to escape down here, you know. I'd sit for hours on those rocks with my nose stuck in a book. It was only the tide creeping up on me that forced me to move. It was an escape. No one ever missed me. I can't tell you the number of times I imagined running away, but in the end I always went back.'

'I understand that,' Mel says, grateful that Sarah has also agreed to therapy, to deal with the trauma behind each and every one of her self-inflicted scars. 'Kate,' Mel calls out, 'come over here.'

'It's time,' Sarah says, holding the urn in her hands. Her scarf billows around her neck, her loose blonde hair whipping around her face. 'I'm glad they're together,' she adds, tapping the lid before Kate draws up.

'Like me and Angus are together now, too,' Mel says, squeezing Sarah around the waist. 'I spoke to him last night on the phone. He sends his love.'

Sarah looks at Mel for a moment, as if she's about to say something, her mouth opening then closing. Kate bounces up, a fistful of shells and fossils to show them.

'Come on then,' Sarah says. 'Do you want to help me sprinkle the ashes out to sea?'

Kate nods, shoving the shells into her pocket and taking hold of Sarah's arm. She walks with her grandmother to the rocks, helping her step down to where they meet the sea. Mel joins them, standing the other side of her mother as Sarah prises the lid off the pot. She says a little prayer before gently tilting and shaking the urn.

The wind catches the ashes, carrying them in a swirl before they land on the water's surface, spreading out and dissolving in the waves as they get washed out on the retreating tide.

'Bye bye,' Kate whispers, echoing her grandmother.

'Bye,' Mel mouths too, fighting back the tears as she links arms with her mother. Three generations of women standing strong at the edge of their future.

CHAPTER FIFTY-THREE

'God, I remember this,' Sarah says, pulling another bundle of clothes from the wardrobe. 'Mum loved it. Used to wear it all the time.' She holds up an orange and cream blouse with a large pointed collar.

'So Seventies,' Mel says, stripping the old bed of its sheets. Joyce's room – room seven – hasn't been touched since she passed away, and Sarah says it's time for her things to go, for the room to be decorated and made ready for guests. It's been out of bounds for over a year, with Sarah keeping the key on her at all times. She'd not been able to face going inside.

'I reckon Kate would love a few of these things,' Mel adds. 'She adores vintage stuff.'

'Let's save some for her then,' Sarah says, eyeing the sheets as Mel bundles them up. There are several patches of dark, dried blood smeared on the striped flannel. 'He did that,' she suddenly says, pointing at the black sack Mel has stuffed them into, ready to be disposed of. Mel knows they're the sheets Joyce died in.

'Bray?' Mel asks. Sometimes Sarah wants to talk about him, sometimes not.

She nods. 'Mum had a stroke, as you know. But he didn't realise that I saw him laying into her with his fist, even after she'd just died.' Sarah shakes her head, sighing. 'He was mad as hell that he hadn't managed either to persuade her to write him into her will in time or marry him. Mum had some good sense, at least. He told the doctors he'd attempted to revive her, but she'd fallen on her face as he tried to get her out of bed. I knew different but I had no voice. Literally.' She adds: 'I learnt that things were easier when I didn't speak.'

It's as they're carting the last of the black sacks out to the car for the charity shop that Sarah stops Mel, a hand on her arm. 'I'd like to go and visit Angus,' she says. 'Something's happened that's not quite right and… and I need to make it right,' she adds with a small smile.

Mel tries to read her eyes and, for the most part, she can. She doesn't want to bring up the subject of money, ask why she inherited far more than Angus. But she's sure their mother had her reasons and perhaps now wants to settle the difference.

'I think that's a wonderful idea,' she says. 'He's been saying for ages he'd love you to come and stay. Between you and me, I think he gets lonely. He loves his job, but it's hard work for little money. I can vouch for that. I'm sure he'd love the company.'

'Yes,' Sarah says, 'that's exactly what I thought. It's time to put a few things right.'

*

'Micky!' Mel says loudly, answering his FaceTime call. As usual, she's covered in paint and dust, wearing her overalls and a headscarf, and she hasn't stopped grafting since Kate went off to school earlier. 'You're a sight for sore eyes,' she says, sitting down on the bare boards, leaning up against a wall.

'And you're just a sight,' he says, laughing. Mel sees he's in his shop, hears the lazy rhythm of jazz in the background.

'The presidential suite will be ready for you soon,' she jokes. 'When are you and whoever the latest guy is coming down to stay? I miss you so much.'

'It was Phil but, alas, Phil is no more,' he says with an overstated flourish. 'I'm back swiping, my darling. It's my destiny.'

'What happened to rekindling some of your past loves, like I suggested?' Mel smiles, knowing Michael will never change. 'Anyway, come alone, then Kate and I get you all to ourselves,' she says. 'But hurry, before I get booked up. Honestly, you wouldn't believe the response I've had to the little launch I did. We had a food-tasting evening with an eight-course menu and local craft beers. Half the village must have come in. Plus, I've had quite a few guests staying and some have already left glowing reviews. I've even had an enquiry about hosting a forti-eth birthday party. And that scumbag journalist came crawling back, can you believe, asking for rates for his wedding reception. I took delight in telling him I was booked up. Things are on the turnaround, Micky.'

'I'm so pleased for you,' he says, going on to ask about Kate, as well as Tom. Mel feels herself blushing.

She tells him how well Kate is doing, that she's flourishing at school. 'And Tom and I are just taking it slowly,' she confesses. 'But things are good. Plus I still owe him that cake.' She laughs, resting her head back against the wall.

'And what about Angus? Did you sort the… the money situ-ation with him?'

Mel lowers her voice. 'We spoke, yes. Honestly, the poor guy works all hours and is really strapped for cash. I know only too well what that job's like.' Mel sighs, wondering whether to tell Michael. She doesn't want to lie, so decides to keep it vague. 'Look, between you and me, Micky, I transferred him some cash. I wouldn't have been able to sleep otherwise.'

Michael sucks in a breath. 'You did?' As expected, he looks shocked. 'That's very kind, Mel. But how… how much?'

'It's not going to make much difference to me but it means the world to him. He's a bit of an oddball, but I like him. And he's my brother.' Mel still hasn't tired of dropping the words 'mother' and 'brother' into conversations.

'And it means Angus can get ahead in life a bit. He deserved a break,' she says, avoiding the question. She knows he'll be cross with her.

'Yes, yes, he does,' Michael says slowly, nodding his head. 'He certainly does deserve a break.'

'Anyway, the good news is that Sarah… *Mum*… knows there's this huge disparity, a kind of elephant in the room. She's gone off to stay with Angus for a day or two. She left just an hour ago. I think she's gone to make good and sort it out. Apparently, she still has a large amount left in trust from her grandfather, all taken care of before she was even born.'

'Sarah's gone to see Angus?' Michael says, looking surprised.

'I know, right? She's getting braver by the day. I got her a pay-as-you-go phone. I wanted to drive her, but she insisted on taking the train. Angus is picking her up from the station.'

Michael nods, a frown forming. 'Well, good for her. And good for you too, my darling. Everything sounds wonderful. I'm so proud of you.'

'It is, Micky, it really is. For once in my life I can truly say that I'm happy.'

CHAPTER FIFTY-FOUR

Tom switches over the vinyl on his turntable, replacing the Pink Floyd album with a Thin Lizzy LP, and sits back down next to Mel.

'I'll do a quick reading before your dad gets here then,' Mel says, shuffling her tarot deck. Tom looks intrigued, taking another slice of the home-made cake she'd brought round to share. 'And don't make that face,' she adds, laughing. 'I'm really into the cards. They've never let me down.'

'It's my cake appreciation face,' he replies through a laugh and a full mouth. 'Anyway, I like it that you're...'

'Strange?' Mel finishes for him, laying out some cards in a spread on the little table in front of them. She nudges him, giving him a look. 'And save some cake for your dad and his carer.'

'No, I was going to say quirky,' Tom says with a wink. 'So go on then, what does the future hold?'

Mel stares at the cards she's dealt and laid out on the coffee table, slowly shuffling the others. She frowns.

'Don't tell me... you're going to meet a tall and handsome man who you'll fall madly—'

'No,' Mel says quietly. 'No, they don't say that at all.' She shudders as a chill creeps up her spine. She shakes her head. 'Five of Pentacles, Three of Swords... The Tower, The Moon.'

Mel stares up at the ceiling, sighing.

'These are... these are potent cards together,' she says, shaking her head and staring, pondering the combination. 'With the tarot, you don't simply take each card at face value. A reading is the sum of its parts.'

'So what do they mean?'

'Poverty, heartbreak… betrayal. An impending and disastrous event with no way to stop it…' Mel points to each card, frowning, staring, trying to make sense of them. 'That's just the start.'

'And The Moon?' Tom asks.

Mel looks up at him. 'Secrets,' she whispers, jumping as the front door suddenly knocks. 'But I need to clarify with more cards,' she adds. 'The reading is incomplete.'

'I can't wait,' Tom says in a silly voice. 'I've a nice bottle of red we can open later, too. Might make it more palatable,' he jokes. 'And by the way, you look beautiful,' he adds, stopping before he goes to the door, giving her a kiss on the lips. 'I love that dress.'

'Thanks,' Mel smiles. 'It's new, and it's about time it had a proper outing.'

'*Dad*,' Tom says warmly as he opens the door, giving him a hug. 'And Shelley, thanks for bringing him down. Do both come in. You're looking well, old man.'

'If you say so, son,' Walter says, shuffling inside. 'Hip's been giving me trouble again.'

Mel watches as Walter gets his bearings, taking off his jacket with Shelley's assistance. He leans on his stick, shuffling across the room, wheezing his way over to an armchair. Tom helps lower him into it.

'Dad, this is Mel from up at the Inn. Do you remember her? You met a few weeks ago.'

'Hi, Walter,' Mel sings out as the old man looks up at her, as if he's only just realised she's there. 'How are you?'

Walter stares at her, his lower jaw quivering. His blue, almost frosted-looking eyes flick over her as he tries to focus. He licks his lips, as if he's about to speak but can't find the right words. He scratches his chin, slowly rubbing shaking fingers over his grey stubble.

'Well, I'll be darned. Is that you, Joyce?' he says, his face lighting up. 'I've been looking for you all this time.' He chuckles. 'How's that girl of yours? Terrible business,' he says. 'Just terrible what happened.' He shakes his head, clacking his lips together as he looks away, frowning.

'No, Dad, this is Melanie. The new owner of Moreton Inn. It's not Joyce.' Tom mouths *Sorry* at Mel, who shakes her head in return, smiling.

'Nice to meet you, Walter,' she says, bending down and holding out her hand. Walter takes it, gripping it firmly, clasping it within both of his. He pulls her closer, tugging her down. Mel gets down on her knees next to him.

'No need to be so formal, Joycie. It's me, Walt.' He brings her hand to his mouth, shaking as he draws it close, giving it a kiss.

'Dad, you're confused. This isn't Joyce,' Tom repeats, laughing kindly and rolling his eyes at Mel. 'Fancy a cuppa?'

'I'd rather have some of what you're having,' he laughs, spotting the champagne bottle.

'There's cake, too,' Mel says. 'For you both,' she adds, looking over at Shelley.

Soon, they're eating a slice, with Mel still sitting on the floor beside Walter.

'You've got cream round your mouth, Walt,' Shelley says, leaning over with a napkin. 'There you go.'

'Did you make this, Joycie?' Walter says, looking at Mel. 'It's delicious.'

Mel glances at Tom, wondering if it's just better to go along with it.

'Yes, I made it, Walter,' she replies. 'I'm glad you like it.'

'How's that girl of yours now, Joycie? Is she talking yet?' Walter shakes his head. 'Terrible goings-on.'

'My daughter is called Kate,' Mel says.

'Sarah. That's it. *Miss* Sarah,' he continues, ignoring Mel. 'Poor, poor lass. She had a little baby girl, didn't she? But you had to get rid of her, Joycie, do you remember? There'd have been none of those goings-on if you'd married me.'

'Dad…' Tom says, but Mel holds up a hand, mouthing *It's OK* at him.

'Walter, that baby is me. I'm Sarah's baby girl.' She doesn't expect Walter to take in what she's saying; he seems so resolutely fixed in the past. But she can't patronise him either. She never did that with any of the residents at The Cedars.

As expected, Walter doesn't seem to hear her. 'Delicious cake,' he says again, lifting the glass of champagne to his mouth and slurping some down. 'This is the life, eh?' He laughs – a phlegmy, choked-up laugh. And choked up with tears, too, Mel thinks, noticing his watery eyes.

'Sarah turned out another baby, mind.' Walter looks at Tom and Shelley in turn, shaking his head, as if what he's saying is for their benefit. 'A little boy. Do you remember him, Joycie? Terrible shame what happened. Terrible goings-on.'

Mel looks at him and smiles. 'Yes, that's Angus. He's my brother, Walter. He lives in Taunton.' She smiles, giving him a pat on the leg. 'He's all grown up like me now.'

'But that can't be,' Walter says, staring at her, looking puzzled. 'You told me the little mite didn't survive.'

'No, Walter, Angus is fine,' Mel says with a smile, though her mind is stirring. 'He works as a carer. He doesn't have a family but he likes riding his bike and he enjoys painting watercolours. He showed me photos. They're quite good, actually.'

'Watercolours?' Walter says in an incredulous voice. 'A bike? What are you talking about, Joycie?' He shakes his head, looking confused. 'That night I bumped into you in the Inn car park as I were coming out of the bar, you'd got your harassed face on. I remember that well enough. Told you if the wind changed, it'd stay that way, Joycie. I'd had a beer or two, but you were in a hurry and in no mood for larking about, I remember that much.' He chuckles to himself. '"Up to no good?" I asked you.'

Mel listens intently, realising that Walter is somewhere else in his mind completely – back in nineteen-eighty-something.

'Gripping onto a bundle for dear life, you were. Wouldn't even stop for a kiss or a cuddle.' Walter takes another bite of his cake, seeming to take for ever to chew and swallow. 'I walked you over to your car and that's when I heard the cry. A baby's cry coming from inside the bundle.' He laughs, his shoulders jumping up and down. 'I said, "You gone and had a babby, Joycie?" but you didn't find it funny. It were all wrapped up in a rough, grey blanket. I remember its tiny fist poking out.'

'Dad, I'm not sure—'

'But I saw you were troubled, Joycie. More troubled than I'd seen you. You confided in me that you had to save Sarah's shame yet again. And that's when you showed me the babby, telling me that you feared for it, that no one would ever want him, that he was very sick.'

'Why, Walter? Why wouldn't anyone want the baby?' Mel takes another sip of champagne, again mouthing *It's fine* at Tom.

'Because the babby had no eyes, Joycie. You must remember his face, the poor little mite. He had sealed-up slits where his eyes should have been and his lips were all deformed, too. Oh, my heart bled for him. You were worried he wouldn't survive the night. Next day I saw you in the shop and you told me the babby had died in your arms. You said you'd got scared and left him wrapped up outside the local hospital so he could have some kind of burial.'

Mel stands up, puts her plate down on the table.

'I… I don't understand, Walter,' she says. 'Sarah's second live baby is my brother, Angus. And he was adopted and… and… he's not blind. Not in the least. He's *fine*.' Mel drops down onto the sofa as she absorbs what Walter is saying. She recalls how Angus had told her he'd been found outside a police station in Taunton, not a hospital local to here. 'Christ,' she says, reaching for her bag, pulling out her phone as it sinks in. Her hands are shaking as she stares at Tom, knowing he's thinking the same, going by his expression. 'Are you *certain*, Walter? Are you sure the baby boy died that night?'

'Never been surer of anything in my life, Joycie.'

Mel looks at Tom again, her heart thundering in her chest, fear written all over her face. 'Then who the *hell* is Angus?' she whispers to Tom. 'Whoever he is, he's taken me for a total mug,' she says, a hand coming up over her mouth. 'And I sent Mum off to see him earlier.'

'Call her *now*,' Tom says urgently, his body tense beside her. 'You've got his address, right?'

Mel nods.

'We can be in Taunton in under an hour. I've only had one drink.' He gets up to fetch his keys and phone. 'And Kate is definitely staying at Chloe's tonight?'

'Yes, yes, she's going there straight after school,' Mel replies, her hands trembling as she dials Sarah's number. As she waits for the line to connect, she accidentally knocks the rest of the tarot deck off the arm of the sofa. The phone rings out, going to voicemail.

As she leaves a message, she bends down to gather up the cards, but freezes, unable to take her eyes off what she sees. 'Oh *no*,' she says, covering her mouth again. All the cards are lying face down apart from one – The Fool. She looks up at Tom. 'We need to hurry. We *really* need to hurry.'

And as she grabs her bag, quickly saying goodbye to Walter and rushing out to Tom's pick-up truck, she realises that the only fool has been her.

EPILOGUE

I haven't been on a train in years. Years and years and years. Melanie made sure I got on the right one, fretting and fussing around me, showing me how to use the mobile phone she bought me, checking it had enough charge. She offered to drive me, begged even, but I wanted to go alone.

The countryside speeds past the window like the days of my life. All blurred into strips of colour flashing past – one field, one house, one tree, one stream, one town merging into the next.

'Angus will be there to meet you,' Mel had said, waving me off. I wonder what name I would have chosen for her, had she not been taken away, still wet from birth as my mother prised her from me. I caught a flash of her matted hair, her scrunched-up face, her clenching fists before she was gone. And she looked at me. I remember that. She turned her head and looked directly at me, her dark eyes seeking me out. Her first and last glance of her mother. Fate unknown.

'Amelia, perhaps,' I whisper to myself, face tilted to the train window. The man sitting next to me gives me a peculiar look as I talk to myself. 'Or maybe Sally.' But that's what I've done all these years. Spoken when no one is there to hear. Conversations with myself. It was easier that way. Safer. I kept it all inside. Rotting. Waiting. Biding my time.

It was only when I saw young Kate, how she reminded me of *me*, that I wanted to talk again. *Needed* to talk. Seeing her as I *should* have been – vibrant and alive, curious and loved – it did something to me. Made me feel safe. And we look so alike. It was as though she'd brought me back from the dead. Brought me back to *me*. I smile, gazing out of the train window.

*

There he is, standing just the other side of the ticket barrier, a long umbrella in one hand and a set of keys in the other. Angus seems nervous, shifting from one foot to the other as he jangles his keys, waiting for me to scan my ticket.

'Hello, Angus,' I say as he gives me a hug. I know he's being gentle, as though he doesn't want to break me, upset me. What people don't know is that on the inside I'm made of steel, that my frail bones and slight body are only my exterior.

'Hello, Mum,' he says, as though the word is foreign to him – or at least using it on me is. 'How was your journey?' he asks, as though I've travelled across the Sahara.

'Pleasant,' I say, and follow him out of the station, him shielding us both with his big black umbrella. He opens the door of his car – a small, silver vehicle that takes a number of tries to get started. He's had it for ever, he tells me. As he drives, he chats about the weather, about a film he watched last night, about how busy he's been at work. I listen.

Then he tells me he's taking me out for a late lunch. He drives us into the town, parking in an underground car park. He's a gentleman and opens my door, asking if I like Italian. We eat, chat for a couple of hours, catch up, share stories. Just like a mother and long-lost son would do.

*

'Welcome to 48 Nightingale Leys,' he says, later that afternoon as he pulls up on the drive.

'Very nice,' I say, peering up at the neat Fifties semi-detached house.

He opens my door then goes up to the porch, putting his key in the lock. He stops, turns to me. 'I'm… I'm just a lodger here,' he says. 'I hope you don't mind. But you'll have your own room and privacy.' Angus looks pained, embarrassed, as he stares at his feet. 'Things aren't easy financially and—'

'Angus, you don't have to explain anything to me.' I place my hand on his arm. What he doesn't know is that I won't be staying long anyway. 'Now come on, I'm dying for a cup of tea.'

'This is pleasant,' I say, looking around the living room as I sip my tea. It's a lie. It isn't a pleasant room at all.

Angus holds out a plate. 'Biscuit?'

'Thank you,' I say, my hand hovering over a pink wafer before I take it. 'My favourite,' I tell him, fighting the urge to crush it.

'I'm glad you came, Mum,' Angus says, leaning forward on his elbows, hands clasped, one knee jiggling.

'Indeed,' I say. 'I'm sorry to hear things have been tough financially for you.' I clear my throat. 'Mel tells me that things didn't work out fairly.'

He bows his head. 'No, they didn't, I suppose but—'

I raise my hand. 'It's why I came, Angus.' I smile, beginning to enjoy myself.

'It is?' he says, his eyes lighting up. I can almost see him salivating.

I nod. 'Now, why don't you get some photographs out, show me some pictures of you growing up with your adopted family?' I smile, wanting to savour this moment. Treasure it.

'Photos?' Angus says. 'Gosh… let me think. There might be some in the loft, but my sister – my *adopted* sister – has most of them.' He clears his throat.

'Why don't you go and look, just in case?' I suggest. 'I'll have another biscuit.'

Angus gets up, hesitating, as I bite into another wafer, watching him as he leaves the room. It's time for people to stop taking things from me that don't belong to them.

A noise. A rattling, a key, a door opening. I listen, slowly putting down my teacup, straining my ears. Someone has come into the house – has dumped a bag down in the hallway, dropped their keys on a table.

Angus is still upstairs, rifling around for the photographs I know he won't find.

'Hello?' someone calls out.

No one replies.

'Angus?'

Then I hear footsteps on the stairs – *thud, thud, thud* – Angus quickly coming down, followed by low voices coming from another room. The sound gets more urgent, louder, as if they're arguing.

I get up. It's coming from the kitchen. I stand outside with my ear to the door, hand cupped around it.

What the hell are you doing here…? I told you she was coming. Let me deal with it.

Then the sound of a kiss.

You have to go before—

'Hello,' I say, pulling the door wide open. The kitchen is as sparse as the living room. A table with two chairs, a kettle and a toaster on the grey worktops. A greasy stove.

The pair of them stand there, embracing, their faces close – shocked expressions on each.

'Did you find any photographs?' I ask Angus, smiling.

'No… no, I didn't. Mum,' he replies, a concerned look on his face.

'Shame,' I say quietly. 'And shame on you. Shame on you *both*.' I glance at one, then the other, shaking my head. 'You think I didn't know what you were up to, Angus?'

'Really, it's not what it seems,' he replies. 'You're muddled, confused. Why don't you have another cup of tea, Mum?'

'I don't want tea,' I say, almost feeling bad for him. I'm about to tell him what I *do* want when the doorbell rings – the sound chiming down the hall.

Unexpected.

'Excuse me,' Angus says, squeezing past, his head down, relieved to be leaving the room.

'I'm not surprised to see you here,' I say, walking further into the kitchen.

'You don't know what you're talking about,' is the reply I get.

'Oh, I think I do,' I say, completely confident about that.

'We're in love, me and Angus.'

'So I see.'

And that's when I hear the commotion coming from the hallway.

'Where is she?' a man says sternly.

'Where's Mum?' another voice demands.

Melanie.

Then the sound of Angus trying to calm them down, get them to leave, but it doesn't work because suddenly my daughter and her friend, Tom, have stormed into the kitchen.

'Mum, oh God, Mum, are you OK?' She glares at Angus, slinging her arm around me protectively. Then her eyes flick across the room. '*Michael?*' she says, shocked. 'What the hell are *you* doing here?'

Michael says nothing. Just stands there, his arms dangling by his sides, the large cuffs of his green shirt half covering his hands.

'We only spoke this morning,' Mel says, confused. 'I thought you were at home…' She trails off as Angus goes up to Michael, pulling him close. She frowns. 'You... *you* two?' she says, trying to take it in. 'You're... together?'

'I can explain, Mel,' Michael says, flustered. 'Angus is an... an old friend. You encouraged me to look up old flames, didn't you?' He laughs nervously.

'*Explain?*' she whispers, frowning. 'You can explain why Angus is nothing but a common thief and a con man, for a start. He's no brother of mine, and I doubt very much he's a carer. I want my fifty grand back, you bastard.' She goes up to him, prodding him in the shoulder. '*Now!* Transfer it back immediately or I'll report you for fraud.'

'*Fifty* grand?' Michael yells, turning to Angus, his expression disbelieving. He pushes Angus away. 'You told me she gave you ten! That it was five thousand for each of us. Jesus Christ...' He shakes his head, giving Angus a kick in the leg.

'*Each?*' Mel almost screams. 'Michael, how fucking *could* you?' She covers her face briefly. 'I *trusted* you.'

'It was all Michael's idea,' Angus chips in, a concerned look on his face. 'He set the whole thing up.'

'I was trying to help, that was all, Mel,' Michael says desperately. 'All I ever wanted was for you to have the family you never had and... and, well, things have been tough for me, too, Mel. The shop's not doing well, and... well, I tried to win back online what I'd lost, but got more and more into debt. When Sarah mentioned a son, I didn't see any harm in contacting Angus. We were together at uni in Bristol, and I knew he still lived down this way. I thought you'd like a brother. We weren't after money, I swear.'

Mel squints at him. It's clear she doesn't believe a word he says. 'And you've been gambling again?' She shakes her head in disbelief.

'He's lying,' I tell Mel calmly. 'Michael's mistake was that he assumed my baby boy was still alive.' I hug her. It's not the way I wanted her to find out, but she's tough; she's seen worse. I'll help her through this.

'So there was no private investigator tracking down Angus?' Mel asks.

'No, love,' I tell her, placing a hand on her shoulder.

'But... but the letter from the solicitor? It was the same wording as mine.'

Michael sighs. 'Mel, this has all just been a misunderstanding, really, I—'

'Christ, I've been so *stupid*,' she says, choking back an angry sob. 'That was *my* letter, wasn't it? You must have scanned it on your phone and doctored it with Angus's details on a fake letterhead.' She shakes her head, pacing about.

I take my phone from my pocket. 'Transfer the money back to Melanie immediately, Angus, or I'm calling the police,' I demand.

It's blood money. *My* blood money, and I suffered for every penny of it.

'Just do it,' Michael hisses at Angus.

I watch as Angus fumbles with his phone, sweating as he does as he's told. Ten minutes later, when Mel checks her account after Angus has done a test amount first for security purposes, she finally confirms the full amount has been received.

Then I call the police anyway.

Waiting for them to arrive, Tom prevents the pair of them from leaving, blocking the door. He'd have no trouble taking them on if they put up a fight. I take Mel into the living room, sitting her down and pouring her a cup of tea. She looks pale, in shock, so I offer her a biscuit.

'Thanks, Mum,' she says quietly, taking the last pink wafer. She stares out of the window nervously, watching out for the police.

'They were Joyce's favourite biscuit too,' I tell her.

She always kept a packet by her bed, to have with her morning tea. They fell onto the floor when I held the pillow over her face, got trampled under my feet as I used all my strength to squeeze the last breath out of her. For a while, she put up a fight, but it wasn't long before the thrashing stopped. At the time, I had no idea she'd had a stroke just minutes before, didn't realise that she'd probably have died anyway.

When I heard *his* footsteps coming, I hid behind the curtain, terrified of what I'd just done. I peeked out, witnessing the rage burst out of Donald as he discovered Joyce had died, leaving him with nothing. That's when he took to her face with his fist.

After he'd gone, I crept out from behind the curtains. I stood for a while, watching my mother, knowing she'd never be able to steal anything from me ever again.

Then slowly, not taking my eyes off her, I bent down and pulled a broken pink wafer biscuit from the packet. I bit into it and it tasted good.

A LETTER FROM SAMANTHA

Dear Reader,

Thank you so much for reading *Single Mother* – I do hope you enjoyed it as much as I loved writing it! I'm already busy working on my next novel – another twisty psychological thriller – so if you'd like to be kept up to date about my latest releases, then please do take a few seconds to sign up to receive all the news about my books.

www.bookouture.com/samantha-hayes

When my dad bought me a DNA testing kit for my birthday, I was so excited to find out about my ancestry and perhaps even get to make contact with relatives I'd never met. My dad loves nothing more than poring over the family tree, and he's gone back many generations, discovering that we have lots of connections in Scotland. So I happily sent off my DNA sample and, a few weeks later, my email pinged with the results. As an author, you can imagine that I was already exploding with so many 'What if…' scenarios that the results might throw up.

While my own ancestry was as I'd expected, revealing lots of distant cousins all around the world, I'd not been able to resist hitting up Google and finding out about people who'd received rather unexpected news after they'd sent off that little vial of DNA. Secret affairs had been uncovered, twins separated at birth had been reunited, and people were shocked to find out they'd been adopted, to name but a few of the surprise stories I found.

Privacy issues surrounding the information collected were tight, but what intrigued me more was, what if the DNA sample fell into the wrong hands *before* it even got sent off? And that's where the idea at the core of the story came into play – Michael retrieving Mel's DNA sample from the rubbish bin and sending it off to the lab without her knowledge. Initially, of course, his intentions were honest, but his money troubles drove him to be less than scrupulous once he made contact with Sarah.

As for the setting of the book, with the theme of families and relatives so central, all of that fell into place. I didn't want Mel to simply inherit cash – that would have been too easy. Rather, I wanted her whole life to be turned upside down, to drop her into a threatening and strange new world that, of course, initially seemed like a dream come true.

It so happened that my grandparents once owned a small hotel many years ago and, while it wasn't on the South Coast, the inspiration for Moreton Inn came from their slightly 'quirky' establishment. I even made the name very loosely similar! My grandparents loved this old hotel and, as a young child, I have my own memories of running around the endless corridors (and probably getting in the way!).

One regular customer, in particular, has stuck in my mind all these years and, while he was a man rather than a woman, he inspired the character behind Sarah. I have no idea of his name, but I do remember an almost ghostly character being at the hotel and appearing in places I didn't expect – and I don't recall him saying a word, ever! If he wasn't wandering around, he was sitting in the bar with a pint and, truth is, he scared me. But he gave me the idea behind Sarah's silence and what it might mean.

Of course, it wouldn't be a psychological thriller without real and present threats for the main character. Which is why, as a feisty, hard-working single mum determined to protect her daughter, Mel had to face her biggest fear yet – her past. Speaking out and escaping abuse is tough enough, but often the hardest escape to make is from the fear that follows. What if it happens again? What if I'm not strong enough to protect those I love most? Combine this with the 'nothing is quite as it seems' that I just love in psychological thrillers, and I had poor Mel spinning in circles from threats both new and old.

So that's just a little snapshot of how *Single Mother* came about and, if you enjoyed meeting Mel and my other characters, it would mean so much if you could leave a brief online review. I really appreciate reading the feedback, and it's a great way for other readers to choose their next book.

And if you're on social media, then do feel free to join me on Facebook, Twitter or Instagram, or pay a visit to my website where you'll find details of all my other books and a little bit about me.

Meantime, keep well and I'm looking forward to sharing my next book with you.

Sam x

samanthahayesauthor

@samhayes

@samanthahayes.author

www.samanthahayes.co.uk

ACKNOWLEDGEMENTS

Every time I write a book, I feel so lucky to be working with such a special and talented team. Massive thanks as ever to my amazing editor Jessie Botterill for everything you do with your ~~red pen~~ magic wand! The whole team at Bookouture is a joy to work with, so have some huge heartfelt thanks from me! Big thanks to Sarah Hardy, Kim Nash and Noelle Holten for shouting out to the world about my books, as well as Janette Currie for copy-editing, Jenny Page for proofing, and Lauren Finger for bringing everything together so seamlessly. Equally as big thanks go to my agent Oli Munson, and the whole gang at A.M. Heath.

A special mention and thank you to all the bloggers and reviewers who are so dedicated to reading, taking the time to share their thoughts and spread the word about my thrillers before and after they've been published. I appreciate it all – the tags on Instagram and Twitter, the blog posts and tours, the messages and kind words of support.

And as ever, thanks to you, my readers, for spending a few hours with my characters. There'd be no point doing it without you, and I hope to see you again between the pages of my next book very soon.

Last, but not least, much love to my dear family, Ben, Polly and Lucy, Avril and Paul, Graham and Marina, and Joe – one of whom is always having their ear bent about a plot twist, whether it's in a book or real life!

Sam xx

Made in the USA
Las Vegas, NV
19 August 2021

28463333R00184